Shadowlight

MIKE JEFFERIES was born in Kent but spent his early years in Australia. He attended the Goldsmiths School of Arts and then taught art in schools and in prisons. A keen rider, he was selected in 1980 to ride for Britain in the Belgian Three Day Event. He now lives in Norfolk with his wife and three step-children, working full time as an author and illustrator.

Shadowlight is the sequel to *The Road to Underfall* and *Palace of Kings* in Mike Jefferies' trilogy *Loremasters of Elundium*. *Glitterspike Hall*, the first volume of a new series, *The Heirs to Gnarlsmyre*, is also available in Fontana Paperbacks. Its sequel is *Hall of Whispers*.

D0522743

by Mike Jefferies

MIKE JEFFERIES

Shadowlight

Fontana
An Imprint of HarperCollinsPublishers

To Paul – who first gave me the reins
and set my foot in the stirrup. Would
that you were with me now to hear the
Warhorses shout against the shadowlight, for you were brave and feared
nothing in the dark.

A FONTANA ORIGINAL

First issued in 1988 by Fontana,
an imprint of HarperCollins Publishers,
77–85 Fulham Palace Road,
Hammersmith, London W6 8JB.

9 8 7 6 5 4 3

Copyright © 1988 Mike Jefferies

The Author asserts the moral right to be
identified as the author of this work

A CIP catalogue record for this book
is available from the British Library

Printed and bound in Great Britain by
HarperCollins Book Manufacturing, Glasgow

Shadowlight

Doubts crowded in the darkness, whispered fears spread through the warriors in the battle crescent as all eyes waited on King Holbian.

'What if Thanehand fails to destroy the Nightmare, Krulshards? What then will become of the sunlight of Elundium?'

The battle crescent trembled and swayed, stirred by each man's fears of what the new daylight would bring. A hand gently touched the King's elbow, making him start in the darkness, setting the steelsilver battlecoat he wore jingling with sweet musical whispers of the daylight yet to dawn.

'It is time, my Lord,' Breakmaster called quietly, lifting his hand and pointing out beyond the darkened Causeway Field to where a streak of cold grey light edged the dark bulk of Mantern's Mountain.

'The grey hours are upon us, Lord, and the battle crescent stands as you commanded; every warrior is in his place.'

Slowly King Holbian turned towards the horseman. 'The city folk?' he asked, gripping Breakmaster's arm in his brittle fingers. 'Will they be safe if the Nightbeasts come?'

Breakmaster nodded, sweeping his rein-hand out towards dark shapes huddling behind the battle crescent. 'I have placed the Nighthorses before them, my Lord, they will protect the city folk whatever the new daylight brings.'

King Holbian laughed, releasing Breakmaster's arm. 'They are the new Elundium, Breakmaster, they are here to witness our last great moments and welcome a new king to rule in my place!'

'But, Lord,' cried the horseman, 'you have an age of daylights yet.'

King Holbian sighed, putting his finger on Breakmaster's lips. 'I am old beyond counting, frail and brittled with age; help me now to see out my last daylight for we stand in the shadow of the Palace of Kings.'

Waiting for Old Legends

As the King spoke he unbuckled a small silver buckler at his throat and removed the steelsilver battlecoat from his shoulders. Carefully he placed it in the horseman's arms. 'When this daylight is at an end and I am laid to rest in my father's house, then this precious battlecoat shall be yours.'

For a moment the King paused, looking out beyond the towering walls of Underfall across the darkened Causeway Field. Smiling he turned back to Breakmaster. 'With it I give you Beacon Light, the Queen of Horses, for you were there at her breaking and made her proud and brave to serve me during these last desperate daylights. Go! Go now and spread the battlecoat across her back.'

Breakmaster fell to his knees, the battlecoat clutched in his outstretched hands. 'Lord,' he cried, tears coursing down his cheeks, 'I asked for nothing but to love you, and to serve you all my days against the Nightbeasts. There was no ambition for such a treasure, such a beautiful gift.'

King Holbian smiled, putting his ancient hand on the horseman's shoulder. 'I know it,' he whispered, 'and without your love and loyalty I would have perished long ago in the ruins of the Granite City beneath the Nightbeasts' shadows. The gift is given and cannot be taken back. Go now and prepare Beacon Light for me. Let me come to her this last time proud, and sure of my purpose. Go, true friend, go.'

Breakmaster rose, blinking away his tears, and stepped backwards into the shadows.

'Use it well,' called out the King. 'When Elundium is safe once more, ride out into the morning sunlight and listen to the sweet music in the battlecoat's weave and remember how we stood side by side and laughed at the Nightbeasts' shadows. Remember then our greatest moments.'

'But, Lord,' ventured the horseman, gathering his courage and stepping back to the King, 'Nevian, the Master of Magic, counselled me to put the coat about your shoulders to keep you warm and safe on our dark flight from the ruins of the Granite City. Surely you should keep it close about your shoulders?'

King Holbian laughed, a soft light glowing in his eyes. 'Our flight from the Nightbeasts is over, Breakmaster. If Thanehand fails against the Nightmare, Krulshards, it will be here upon the Causeway Field that the last moments of sunlight will shine in all Elundium – here beneath the walls of Underfall. For this was foretold long ago in my youth and not even the power of magic or music in the steelsilver can stop what must unfold.'

Breakmaster nodded dumbly and retreated into the shadows to prepare Beacon Light for the daylight yet to dawn.

'Be proud,' shouted the King as Breakmaster hurried away, 'for we kept the light and the people of Elundium safe through the darkest hours.'

Angishand, Thane's mother, moved quickly through the dense huddle of city folk, urging them to keep close to the battle crescent, yet all the while her eyes were drawn towards the dark bulk of Mantern's Mountain looming against the starry skies.

'Keep safe, my child,' she whispered over and over again, shivering and twisting the hem of her shawl tightly between her fingers as she remembered Thane's last night in the Granite City. They had wanted his death then and had shouted for it through all the levels of the city but now . . . She laughed nervously, catching the noise in her throat, stifling it back into silence. Nobody had realized then that the fate of Elundium would rest so heavily on his shoulders, even the King had sent him beneath a blanket of darkness to perish at World's End.

Angis sighed and turned her head, listening to the dark whispers rising from the assembled warriors, and heard Thane's name as the chill dawn breezes strengthened. Angis shivered again, pulling her shawl tight and heard far away the first blackbird herald the new morning, and saw the feathered edge of the blood-red sun breasting World's End.

Beacon Light stood waiting in the centre of the battle crescent, her neck arched beneath the steelsilver coat. It rippled in the grey dawn breezes, shimmering with the colours of watered silk. King Holbian smiled to see her so proud, battle dresssed as the great Warhorses of yesterlight. 'It will be us the Nightmare strikes at first,' he whispered, moving to her side and gently stroking her velvet-soft muzzle.

'Silver against black we will fight for the sunlight! Good against evil we will fight to save Elundium!'

Beacon Light neighed and struck at the dew-wet grass with her hoof, tossing her head in the half light. King Holbian laughed, setting his foot in the stirrups, and with Breakmaster's help he climbed stiffly up into the saddle. Turning, he looked at the sheer walls of Underfall, casting his gaze across the rows of galleries that seemed to stare back at him, black empty eyes edged with twisted metal spokes climbing up into the morning light. On the highest gallery the great Lamp of World's End paled against the growing strength of the new day.

'I will come to you, Palace of Kings, when the Nightmare is dead!' he shouted before turning to the assembled battle crescent.

For long moments he sat watching his warriors. Then slowly he stood up in the stirrups, his hand on the hilt of his sword. 'Warriors!' he cried, sweeping the sword aloft. 'Who will stand with me against the Nightmare, Krulshards? Who will stand with me if Thanehand fails?'

The battle crescent shifted as corn touched by a summer wind as each warrior took a step forward.

'Lead us to the Gates of Night!' shouted Errant, spurring Dawnlight, first stallion of the Nighthorses, out of the crescent and galloping to the King's side.

'Lead us! Lead us!' chanted Grey Goose, Captain Archer at the far end of the crescent, rattling his quiver of new-forged arrows as he urged the Archers to step forward.

King Holbian hesitated, drawing Beacon Light's reins tight in his hand. 'Our place is here as the legends foretold, upon the Causeway Field. We dare not climb towards the Gates of Night.'

Errant shaded his eyes against the new morning's light and looked up at the heather meadows where the sunlight reflected from a forest of fast-moving spear blades and broad Marching swords. 'Others have gone before us, my Lord. Look! They are spread out across the mountainside in a mighty battle crescent. Nightbeasts run before them shadowing the morning in their haste to retreat towards the Gates of Night.'

'Tombel leads them!' shouted Breakmaster, shadowing his eyes. 'Look, he carries the emblem of the owl in blue and gold.'

'Tombel!' cried the King, riding on a few paces and scanning the steep mountainside.

'Yes, my Lord,' answered Errant, riding Dawnrise forward to stand beside the King. 'He marshalled all the warriors with the tattoo mark into a mighty battle crescent and led them out into the wild grasslands beyond the ruins of the Granite City to hunt the Nightbeasts. Clearly he has swept across all Elundium on their heels driving them back to their foul beginnings.'

King Holbian gripped Errant's arm, his eyebrows drawn into a worried frown. 'Tombel may be on their heels but he cannot outrun them; they will escape into the City of Night and strengthen the Nightmare against Thanehand. He will be lost in their darkness.'

Errant twisted in the saddle, sweeping his hand in the direction of the Nighthorses. 'Pledge me, Lord, to ride to Tombel's aid. Let me follow him with the Nighthorses of Underfall. We could strengthen his warriors before the sun has touched the Causeway Field.'

King Holbian shivered with indecision, rubbing at the cracks age had spread across his face. Quickly he looked from left to right at the dark shapes of his warriors in the battle crescent. 'If you take the Nighthorses it will weaken us and strip the city folk of their protection.'

'But, Lord,' urged Errant, 'the Nighthorses were gathered from the dark side of the morning to fight in all the wild places on this mountain. They are fleet of foot and could outrun the Nightbeasts and seal the Gates of Night against them.'

'The smell of battle is in their nostrils, my Lord,' cried a strong deep voice from the first rank of Marchers.

'Thunderstone!' called out the King, bending in the saddle to search along the crescent.

Thunderstone laughed and stepped forward quickly, the horsetail sword resting easily across his shoulder. 'The smell of Nightbeasts makes them fretful on the bridle.'

'Would you send them, Keeper of World's End? Would you break my battle crescent?'

Thunderstone knelt, offering up the hilt of the horsetail sword, saying, 'Lord, the Nighthorses of Underfall will not fail you. They are battle ready to run the Nightbeasts to ruin.'

'Time runs before us, great Lord,' interrupted Errant, pointing with his sword at the retreating Nightbeasts.

King Holbian looked quickly from the foul black shadows to the rising sun, his knuckles tightening against the reins. 'It is decided! I pledge you, Errant, Captain of Gallopers, to seal the Gates of Night and bring victory to all Elundium!'

'The pounding of hoofbeats will be music to our ears,'

shouted Breakmaster above the rising clamour as the Nighthorses surged forwards, rearing and plunging in excitement.

'No!' thundered a voice from the eaves of Mantern's Forest where it bordered the dark side of the Causeway Field.

The Nighthorses skidded to a halt, milling in confusion at the flickers of white light that flashed and sparkled across their path. Beacon Light neighed and reared up, making the King snatch at the bridle to keep his balance.

'Who dares to challenge the last Granite King?' he cried, pirouetting Beacon Light and spurring his way angrily into the shadows beneath the trees. 'Who dares to halt the King's battle crescent?'

The voice laughed with a strong deep sound that rang clear in the half light and as it fell silent a tiny point of light began to grow, soft light that shone with all the colours of the rainbow.

'Who else, Lord, but I, Nevian, the Master of Magic, the Keeper of the Sunlight, would dare to challenge the greatest King who ever ruled in all Elundium?'

'Nevian?' whispered the King uncertainly, easing Beacon Light into a walk beneath the trees.

Soft laughter mingled with the rainbow light as Nevian stepped forwards and put his hand upon Beacon Light's bridle. 'I have stilled you, Lord, to watch old legends come to life.'

'But . . .' cried the King, pointing up into the new morning's sunlight. 'Nightbeasts are in the heather meadows retreating towards the Gates of Night. If they pass into the darkness all will be lost.'

Nevian slowly shook his head, and while he led the King back into the centre of the battle crescent he told him quietly, 'Thanehand must face the Nightmare alone if he is to be worthy of the Kingship of Elundium.'

'But I am the King! I can help him!' cried Holbian, trying to pull away from the magician. 'Let the Nighthorses gallop on to the high plateau and seal the Gates of Night while I gallop to Thane's side. Let me go!'

Nevian only shook his head again more firmly, holding on to Beacon Light's bridle, digging his heels into the short springy turf. 'Darkness is your weakness, Lord. Remember the bondbreaking. You dared not enter the City of Night. No, it is here you must wait.'

King Holbian, his face black with anger, tried to force a passage but Beacon Light would not pass the billowing folds of the rainbow cloak. 'All Elundium will be plunged into darkness if Thanehand fails!' he cried.

But Nevian only smiled, his eyes softening as he searched the ranks of Marchers for Thunderstone. Turning back to the King he answered quietly, 'Do not try and foretell the future, my Lord. We stand here on the threshold of a new age, the age of Men, and I in all my wisdom think that they will grow beyond the greatness of the Granite Kings.'

Nevian paused a moment, lifting his hand to summon Thunderstone. 'Thanehand is not alone, my Lord. He has a guide in the darkness who will show him the way into the City of Night.'

'Who?' hissed the King, leaning forwards in the saddle, his anger forgotten. 'There is none born in all Elundium who could walk in that foul darkness.'

Nevian laughed, throwing back the rainbow cloak. 'There is much that fills Elundium, my Lord, beneath the surface or beyond our sight. Much that we pass by without a second thought. Willow Leaf, the Tunnel slave, was born into the Nightmare's darkness yet he has returned to the place of his torment to guide Thane through the blackest night so that we might keep the sunlight.'

'Willow Leaf? A Tunnel slave?' whispered the King, his old eyes growing round with astonishment.

Nevian nodded impatiently, one eye on the strengthening daylight. 'All will unfold before you, my Lord, if you are in your appointed place.'

Without waiting for the King to answer Nevian turned to Thunderstone and placed his hand on the hilt of the horsetail sword saying, 'Long long ago I foretold the moment when we would gather on the Causeway Field to greet the new king. Do you, the Keeper of Underfall, the last Lampmaster of Elundium, remember my words?'

Thunderstone frowned, casting his mind back across the suns to another dawn beneath the walls of Underfall. He shivered, remembering the proud death of Equion and touched the silver strands of the horsetail before he slowly answered the magician. 'You foretold that the new king would set his standard on the Causeway Field and that it would drive the shadows back.'

Nevian nodded, tightening his grip on the hilt of the sword. 'The standard of the new king is here, Lampmaster. You have touched it and held it close to your heart, but as yet it cannot be set before us for it has no staff or banner pole to rest upon.'

'I have touched the standard of the new king?' Thunderstone cried, stepping back a pace.

Nevian laughed, keeping his grip on the sword. 'A truly royal standard, fashioned from the rag ends of the great banners that hung in the Granite Towers, woven by the mother of Kings in the shadows of the great wall that ringed the Granite City. Yes, Thunderstone, you have touched it and you have carried it beneath your cloak until yesterlight; then as the darkness fell the Battle Owls, Mulcade and Rockspray, stooped and took it from you.'

Thunderstone pulled his cloak aside and stared down at his faded leather jerkin. 'But that was Thane's summer scarf. Esteron returned with it bound across his wounds. I was keeping it safe for Thane's return, I did not know!'

Nevian drew closer to the Keeper of World's End. 'There was no safer place in all Elundium for such a treasure than the fastness of Underfall, nor so fearless a Captain to guard it.'

Thunderstone paled and began to stutter but Nevian stilled him, a finger on his lips. 'Take the horsetail sword a dozen paces beyond the King and drive it point-deep into the Causeway Field. Let it stand there proudly marking out the daylight hours and if Thane defeats the Nightmare let it be the banner pole of the new Elundium!'

'But what if Thanehand fails? What if the Nightmare comes down from the City of Night?' Thunderstone whispered, reluctant to move forwards. 'My hands will then be empty!'

Nevian smiled, sweeping his eyes across the warriors of the battle crescent. 'If Thanehand fails it will be the King the Nightmare strikes at first and then, in that moment of terror as they clash, light against darkness, good against evil, jump forward and take back your sword.'

Thunderstone carefully unsheathed the sword, walked twelve paces out into the empty field and drove it, double-handed, point-deep into the springy turf. With steady hands he stilled the quivering blade, kissed the hilt and returned to the Master of Magic.

'Go to your place in the battle crescent,' whispered Nevian, 'and remember that what often seems the easiest tasks to others are in truth the hardest ones to perform.'

Thunderstone bowed his head, tears in his eyes. 'Not since you first placed that horsetail sword in my hands has it ever left my side.'

'Yet now it serves an even greater purpose than keeping back the darkness,' answered Nevian gently. 'For now it heralds the new Elundium!'

Thunderstone nodded and took his place before the warriors of World's End, but his eyes were blurred with tears.

Breakmaster had taken the King a few paces into the Causeway Field and was pointing to something that flashed in the sunlight above the dark summit of Mantern's Mountain. 'What magic is that?' called out the King, seeing the glitter of sunlight on bright metal above the summit.

Nevian frowned, moving back to the King's side. 'It is a King's blade, my Lord, hot-forged by Durandel, the Master Armourer, for Thanehand to use against the Nightmare, Krulshards, but . . .' Nevian hesitated, watching Eagle Owl hover for a moment, the sword held in his talons, before he stooped down towards a billow of dust that erupted near the summit of the mountain. 'But with all my magic the sword has arrived too late, for Thane has already passed into the darkness!'

'Then everything is lost; there will be no new king on the Causeway Field. Darkness will swallow the daylight!' cried King Holbian, turning back towards the crescent.

'No! No!' shouted Nevian, catching at the King's sleeve and pointing at the steep slopes above the high plateau. 'Look at the Warhorses!'

King Holbian followed the Magician's hand and saw rank after rank of proud warhorses massing on the black hole that had appeared where the dust cloud had billowed up.

'There are Border Runners among the Warhorses!' cried Breakmaster.

'And savage Battle Owls!' called out Errant.

'Thanehand is not alone!' shouted Nevian.

'Nor will the darkness take us,' answered the King, spurring Beacon Light back into the centre of the restless battle crescent. 'Hold still!' he shouted, standing up in the stirrups. 'Thanehand has broken into the City of Night. Chant his name aloud and the daylight will yet be ours! Chant his name. CHANT HIS NAME!'

Shadow-black clouds poured out of the torn summit of the mountain; darkness began swallowing up the new daylight as it spread across the Causeway Field. The ground trembled and shook. Night had filled the morning sky yet it could not drown out the warriors' chants, and the clash of their arms rumbled and thundered through the crescent, lifting men's hearts as it echoed across the steep mountain slopes.

'Hold still!' shouted the King against the black winds

shrieking about him. 'Keep your places,' he cried above the shrill music of the steelsilver coat. Before them, bending against the wind, stood the Keeper's sword, the silver strands of horsetail twisting and turning in the darkness as they waited, shouting for the new Elundium.

'The storms are lessening, my Lord,' called out Nevian, as he moved to stand beside the horsetail sword. 'Now is the testing hour.'

'Hold still!' shouted the King. 'Keep good order in the battle crescent.'

'I feel no end to it, Lord,' cried Breakmaster moving closer to the King. 'No end to the black torment and it must be long past the noonday hour.'

'Noon or not I curse this darkness,' hissed the shivering King, for without the sunlight or the steelsilver coat about his shoulders he was freezing, turning back into brittle stone, and the spider-fine cracks on his hands and face that the stonemason had repaired were opening a little wider each time he moved.

Out of the Darkness

Thane looked up from where he knelt beside Elionbel in the high chamber of the City of Night. He watched Krulshards' malice billowing out to spread shadows in the early sunshine before it sank back slowly into limp folds of black despair about the Nightmare's headless shoulders.

Rising to his feet, Thane pulled at the hilt of the sword he had driven through Krulshards' rotten heart, but it was stuck fast, pinning the body to the tall column of black marble that rose up towards the ruined chamber roof, now open to the sky.

Wiping at the smears of Nightmare blood he turned to Elionbel, knelt and put his arms about her. 'It is over,' he whispered, laughing and crying, as he helped her to her feet. 'Krulshards is dead. The Nightmare that blackened Elundium is gone forever. We are free of his darkness. Look at the sunshine, look at the Warhorses, the Battle Owls and the brave Border Runners, we have won the sunlight. Look!'

Elionbel struggled, twisting in his arms. 'No! No!' she cried against the sudden silence that had filled the high chamber of the City of Night. 'We will never be truly free of him! This is only the beginning of the real Nightmare darkness that will cover all Elundium.'

Thane laughed. The relief at holding Elionbel safely in his arms and the death of the Nightmare, Krulshards, bubbled through his veins making him lightheaded with the joy of victory. Easing his grip on Elionbel's arm he pointed down at

Krulshards' severed head where it lay face-down in the dust. With his foot he pushed away the tangle of dead locks hanging lifelessly from its skinless, bony crown. 'Krulshards is destroyed. Look around you, the Nightbeasts are dead or dying without his life force. They are nothing now but heaps of rotting flesh. My final dagger slash that cut his foul head from his shoulders has freed Elundium from his everlasting darkness!'

Elionbel shook her head fiercely, breaking free from his embrace. 'No!' she cried, again running to where her mother lay a few paces beyond the tall column of rock. Kneeling, she unclasped the cold stiff fingers from the hilt of Kerzolde's dagger where it protruded from Martbel's chest and wept as she whispered, 'The bastard child that Krulshards tore from your body has gone, gone from beneath the malice. I fear that Kerzolde or the other Nightbeast took it in the height of the battle and I know that nothing will be safe until I find it and destroy it. Thane has not ended Krulshards' darkness and I dare not tell him. I pledged to keep the Nightmare's foul rape a secret and I will, Mother,' she sobbed, slipping Kerzolde's blood-sticky dagger beneath her cloak. 'None will ever know of the terrible thing you suffered on the high wall of the Granite City. I will find the bastard child that the Nightmare named Kruel and I will kill it with Kerzolde's black blade.'

Bending forward with tears in her eyes Elionbel tore the Nightmare's withered life thread away from her mother's throat and threw it forcefully down into the dust. Then footsteps sounded across the chamber: figures were emerging through the shafts of sunlight and voices were calling her name. 'Elionbel, you are safe, let us help you carry your mother back into the sunlight.'

Elionbel hesitated, looking everywhere at once. 'Who?' she whispered, biting her lip and turning towards Thane, the blindness of her tragedy clearing from her eyes as she looked about her at the Battle Owls, the Border Runners and the proud Warhorses.

Thane smiled and quietly motioned to Eventine, Kyot and little Willow Leaf to come forward. 'Without the great bows of Clatterford and Stumble Hill the Nightmare's life thread would have strangled you to death. It was Eventine and Kyot's steady hands and careful Archers' eyes that severed Krulshards' life thread.'

'But we were blind in the darkness even with the glass-tipped arrows of Clatterford before Willow Leaf broke through the roof and brought sunlight into the City of Night,' laughed Kyot, putting his arm around Willow's shoulders.

'And without the sunlight and a clear sky Eagle Owl could not have delivered the sword into my hand and ...' Thane fell silent, his voice trailing away as he looked down on Martbel's lifeless body. Somehow it was not the moment for battle talk.

Elionbel smiled through her tears and reached out to take Eventine's hands. 'It all happened so quickly; one moment the pain of black despair and then running footsteps, brilliant flashes of white light, shafts of summer – thank you, thank you,' she whispered as new tears welled up.

Esteron left the ranks of Warhorses, picking his way across the littered chamber floor, and brushed his muzzle against Thane's shoulder, snorting a greeting. Thane looked up into Esteron's gentle eyes and stroked his neck, running his hand along the horse's shoulder to touch the place where the Nightbeast spear had torn into his flank, putting an end to their headlong rush across Elundium on the Nightmare's heels. Snow-white hair had grown in a broad band where the spear had entered, as white as the nightflowers which had blossomed in the darkest night outside the Wayhouse, the Hut of Thorns, on the road to Notley Marsh.

'Oh, Esteron,' he whispered, caressing his velvet muzzle. 'Each daylight I dared to hope you had reached the Healer of Underfall, but it was only on the lawns of Clatterford that I learned from Kyot you were safe.' Esteron whinnied and arched his neck, striking the chamber floor with a foreleg. 'I sent Rockspray to find you and tell you that the Nightmare had taken Elionbel and her mother into the City of Night.' Thane paused and looked up into the broken roof, searching the ledges and perches of ragged rock, looking for Mulcade and Rockspray. 'I know they brought you here,' he whispered, turning back to Esteron, 'I saw them stooping down through the broken roof with my summer scarf stretched taut between them. The picture of the sun embroidered with Elion's needlepoint was ablaze with the morning light. It drove the shadows out of this terrible place, but they are nowhere to be seen now.'

Willow laughed and touched Thane's sleeve. 'At the moment when you thrust the sword through the malice and struck the solid column of rock they rose up and vanished as quickly as they had come.'

Grannog, the Lord of Dogs, who had led the Border Runners into the City of Night, snarled at the ruined malice that hung about Krulshards' shoulders in black folds of despair and leapt past the tall column of rock, snarling and snapping at the dead locks of Krulshards' hair spread across the chamber floor, trying to catch them in his teeth and pull the severed head into the sunlight.

Thane watched Grannog for a moment and shivered with horror knowing he must take the head out into Elundium to prove that Krulshards was truly dead.

'We must return to the daylight,' Willow called anxiously, watching the sun move across the blue vault of the sky above the broken roof.

'Will you carry Martbel?' Thane whispered to Esteron. 'Will you ease Elion's burden upon your back on our long walk into the sunlight?'

Esteron snorted and whinnied and slowly knelt at Elion's side. 'Twice you have come to me,' she whispered, burying her tears in his mane. 'Once you brought rescue in the morning light and saved me from the Nightbeasts in

21

Hawthorn Hollow and now your great strength will carry Mother out of the darkness. Oh, Esteron . . .'

'We must hurry,' urged Willow, 'the shadows are lengthening in this foul place!'

Elionbel nodded and knelt beside her mother, binding up the torn remnants of her cloak tightly about her lifeless body. Stepping back she watched numbly as Kyot and Willow carefully laid Martbel across Esteron's back.

Thane stood with his feet astride the Nightmare's head, gathering his courage. 'All Elundium shall see your death,' he shouted, bending and grabbing at the tangled strands of hair, winding them around his fingers. Straightening his back he pulled, straining every muscle and slowly the Nightmare's head began to move, lolling from side to side, spilling a trail of black glistening saliva from its lips in ragged patterns in the dust.

Kyot sighed and fell into step with Eventine, locking his bow arm through hers. All around them the Warhorses and the Border Runners crowded for the archway. 'There seems little joy in Krulshards' death,' he whispered.

Eventine took his hand, intertwining her fingers with his. 'Our victory is overshadowed by Martbel's death. I fear there is something in this darkness we have missed or overlooked in this moment of victory. Something has gone unsaid that only Elionbel knows about.'

Kyot nodded, sadly remembering how he had found his father savagely mutilated by Krulshards in the tower on Stumble Hill and how it had filled his mind with dark thoughts. 'You will help Elionbel through her tragedy, I know it,' he answered, ducking his head beneath the low black arch.

'*Shush*!' hissed Eventine, halting abruptly and letting the last of the Warhorses pass them. 'I hear a noise on the far side of the chamber. Something moves in the darkness – listen!'

Kyot turned his head from left to right, straining his ears

for the slightest sound. Eventine reached back into her quiver and took the last glass–tipped arrow. 'There! Over there! Do you hear it?' Eventine hissed, releasing the arrow in a brilliant flash of morning sunlight against the farthest wall and in the moment while the light blazed they saw a low black hole, barely big enough for a man to crawl into. Far away, fast-running footsteps and the dry rattle of a Nightbeast's armour echoed, growing fainter as it fled down into the depths of night, muffling into nothing as the arrow's light died away.

Kyot laughed and turned to follow the Warhorses. 'That Nightbeast will not get far without Krulshards' life force. Leave him to die and rot in this foul place. Leave him to the darkness.'

Kerzolde had taken the baby, Kruel, as his master Krulshards had told him and they had escaped, following the dark tunnel which sloped steeply away from the high chamber. Kerzolde paused, his head twisted to one side, listening. 'Curse you, Thanehand, Galloperspawn!' he spat. 'Curse you! Curse you!' Running footsteps echoed in the tunnel behind him, drawing closer. Kerzolde pushed his precious bundle deeper into the folds of his scaly battle jerkin, unhooked a long curved blade from his belt and crouched, ready, waiting.

Kerhunge, his brother beast, had followed, tumbling and stumbling down the steep tunnel. 'Kerzolde! Kerzolde!' he hissed, stopping abruptly and stepping hastily away from his brother's slashing blade.

'Our Master is dead,' he cried, clutching wildly at the long curved blade. 'I escaped as the foul Galloperspawn stepped on his shadow.'

Kerzolde hesitated, lowering the blade. 'Krulshards is the Master of Darkness, the true Nightmare, nothing can harm him here in the dark for he has no shadow. He will destroy the Galloperspawn!'

'No!' gasped Kerhunge, turning his savage head fearfully towards the high chamber. 'The chamber is broken. Sunlight cast a long shadow from our Master's feet and those Archers who came with the Galloperspawn cut through his life thread with arrow blades that exploded in foul flashes of bright white light. The Elionbel is free. In the heart of the battle I hid myself. I could do nothing. I saw our master stabbed to death by the foul Galloperspawn.'

Kerzolde trembled, turning his head in fear. 'Krulshards is dead!' he whispered. He reached a shaking claw into the folds of his jerkin to lift out the baby, Kruel.

'It is the end of our darkness!' cried out Kerhunge, falling to his knees in the choking cloud of dust that billowed up all around them.

'No!' shouted Kerzolde, thrusting the baby against the darkness. 'There must be new Nightbeasts spawning in the lower chambers. New Nightshards to fill and spread the darkness. New Nightmares that can swallow up the light and bring ruin to all Elundium!'

Kerzolde touched the baby, licking at his wrinkled forehead and stroking his slender fingers as he laid the small but perfectly formed baby on the tunnel floor. Kruel opened his pale eyes and cried just once, staring up towards the high chamber.

'Master, Master, Lord of Darkness, you are the new Master of Darkness, the new Nightmare!' Kerzolde whispered, as gathering up the baby he slowly turned his back on the chamber of Krulshards' death and took a step towards the lower levels of the City of Night.

'Come,' he hissed, 'we must do as our Master pledged us and take the baby far away from the warriors of Elundium and keep him safe until he is strong enough to bring back the darkness.'

Kerhunge nodded and made to follow, spreading his gnarled scaly hands on the tunnel floor, but he could not rise; his elbows bent, pulling him towards the ground. 'Kerzolde,' he gasped, crawling forwards, 'my life force is ebbing away. I cannot follow you.'

Kerzolde snarled impatiently, snatching at his brother's iron collar. 'Quick! Be quick before the Galloperspawn treads on our heels.'

Kerhunge sank lower, his breath dry and rattling in his throat. Kerzolde pushed and pulled, desperately trying to shake new life into his brother. The baby, disturbed by the violent movements of the jerkin awoke, and turning his head against Kerzolde's soft unarmoured skin, he bit savagely with his sharp pointed teeth, cutting into the Nightbeast's flesh. Kerzolde screamed, shaking the baby's needle sharp teeth out of his chest. Kruel, struggling for a handhold, thrust his long tiny fingers through an opening in the jerkin and scratched his fingernails across the coarse prickly skin of Kerhunge's cheek, leaving fine blood trails where his hand had touched the Nightbeast's face.

Kerhunge twitched, his hands trembling violently, black flecks of spittle dribbling down his chin. He felt his strength returning. 'Master!' he gurgled, stumbling up on to his knees and catching the baby's hand in his own. 'Master, Master!' he whispered over and over again, bringing the tiny hand to his mouth to lick and kiss it with his ragged purple tongue.

Kerzolde crouched against the tunnel wall sitting heavily on his haunches, staring from the baby to his brother beast. Slowly, almost gingerly, he in turn placed his broken claw against Kruel's hand and felt the delicate slender fingers close around it, gripping at the smooth brittle horn.

'The Master's seed is the new power,' Kerhunge whispered in awe. 'He has given us new life.'

Kerzolde nodded, carefully pushing the baby's arm back into the folds of his jerkin. 'He has more power than Krulshards, I can feel it, but we must find him dark meats and carrion flesh before he eats me back to the bone. Come, follow.'

'Who showed you this road?' asked Kerhunge breathlessly as he ran on Kerzolde's heels, following him through low twists and turns, always descending, spiralling downwards.

'Our Master did,' Kerzolde replied without looking back. 'He showed me the path, marking it with black footprints, but nowhere will be safe here in the City of Night, not even this secret way now that the cursed Thanehand has entered our darkness. We must escape out into Elundium, into the wild places where the warriors will not find us.'

'How can we escape from the warriors?' cried Kerhunge, gasping for breath.

'This path leads down through the lower chambers where new beasts are spawned. We will gather the beasts into a dense shadow circle and force a way out of Underfall straight through the foul Palace of Kings, destroying and killing, sweetening the bitter taste of our Master's death.'

'Kill the Galloperspawn!' Kerhunge answered in a snarl as the lower darkness swallowed them up, blanketing their harsh footsteps.

Kerhunge slowed to a walk, turning his head from left to right. 'There is death in the air. Can you smell it?' he asked, taking another careful step forwards.

Kerzolde half-turned, impatiently, sniffing at the heavy silence and stumbled, catching his clawed foot on an unseen dark shape spread across the Tunnel floor. Cursing he dropped the long curved blade and threw out both arms to keep the baby safe.

'Nightbeasts!' Kerhunge cried, dropping on to his knees beside Kerzolde and turning over the lifeless bulky shape. In silence they both stared down into the blank empty face that had as yet never tasted human flesh nor filled the shadows of Elundium with nameless terrors.

'The new beasts are all dead!' whispered Kerzolde, sniffing the thick dark air in the narrow tunnel.

Kerhunge wrinkled his nose and smelt the black shapeless lumps of carrion flesh, half-formed hands and legs, claws and heads that rose up hideously, blocking the road. 'They are all dead!' he cried, pushing his way through the piles of rank, wasted meat. 'Who will make the shadow circle now?' he cried, turning sharply on Kerzolde. 'Who will keep us safe from the warriors?'

Kerzolde slowly rose to his feet, and hesitantly reached inside his jerkin. 'I will touch them with the baby, he will bring new life into the beasts. Kruel will do it!'

Kerhunge nodded in agreement and squatting near Kerzolde they lifted a new beast's lifeless arm, offering it to the sleeping baby. 'Bring the new beasts to life, Kruel,' Kerzolde whispered, shaking the infant awake and pressing its tiny fingers into the wet, half-formed flesh.

Kruel gurgled, a bubble of bright spittle glistening in the blackness. Smiling he clapped his hands before digging his fingers into the meat. Closing his hand he tore away a thin sticky strip and crammed it into his mouth.

Kerzolde shock his head. 'No!' he whispered, patiently placing Kruel's hand on another new beast's arm, but Kruel struggled, slapping at Kerzolde's broken claw. Gurgling, he licked at the splatters of congealed blood drying on his lips and pulled another strip of flesh away, greedily devouring it.

Kerhunge dropped the new beast's arm back on to the Tunnel floor and stared darkly at the mounds of flesh. 'It is beyond his power to give them life.'

Kerzolde turned away, pushing the baby back inside his jerkin, and began cutting long strips of flesh to hang from his belt. 'If Kruel cannot bring them back to life at least they can feed him on the long journey ahead,' he muttered.

'Journey!' sneered Kerhunge. 'We are trapped here, defenceless without a shadow circle. The City of Night is ringed by foul warriors; Gallopers and Marchers gloat at every entrance, we will never escape!'

Kerzolde laughed with a harsh sound that fled quickly amongst the dead beasts and began feeling his way towards a low black hole at the far end of the Tunnel. 'With or without the shadow circle we must journey beyond the edges of Elundium into the Shadowlands where the Master's seed will be safe.'

'Shadowlands! Journeys!' mocked Kerhunge. 'The City of Night is ringed – ringed, I tell you – with fierce warriors.'

'Follow or stay,' answered Kerzolde, crawling down through the hole, 'and the cursed Thanehand will search every dark hole in this city for us, but I know of the way that leads up through the tombs beneath Underfall. It is a treacherous and difficult road but it will take us into the Shadowlands.'

Kerhunge moved to follow but then hesitated. 'There will be warriors in the Palace of Kings.'

Kerzolde turned, biting impatiently at his brother's fingers. 'Underfall will be empty, the warriors are on the Causeway Field or spread far across the slopes of this dark mountain. They will not think to look over their shoulders for us, but we must hurry now to snatch the chance of escape.'

Kerhunge nodded and followed on Kerzolde's heels, sucking at his raw knuckles as the narrow tunnel took them spiralling downwards into blackest night.

Kyot and Eventine quickly caught up with Thane as he laboured to pull the Nightmare's head towards the light. Kyot stumbled, tripping over the dead locks of Krulshards' hair and the head turned, the eyes staring directly in his own. 'No!' he cried, letting his spark fall to the ground and covering his eyes with both hands. 'I cannot look into Krulshards' face. Those eyes are staring, boring a hole straight through me.' Shuddering, he turned away, whispering and muttering as he sought a place to hide.

Eventine laughed softly as she bent and scooped up the spark. 'He is dead, Kyot, and can harm you no more. Those blind eyes are mirrors that reflect your doubts and weaknesses; look into them now and show all the strength and power of the Keeper of the Wayhouse Tower on Stumble Hill. Let the blind eyes see the careful Archer's eyes and know the measure of his defeat.'

Slowly Kyot turned his head, swallowed at the lump that

seemed to fill his throat and held Krulshards' dead-eyed gaze. Thane strode forwards, twisting the dead locks of hair more firmly in his hands and the head rolled over in the dust to stare at the black Tunnel walls that passed on either side. Kyot shuddered and took back his spark, knowing that even in death the Nightmare still held a power he could barely master.

The dark road Willow had chosen was easy to follow and took them down to a narrow crack in the sheer side of Mantern's Mountain less than twenty paces beyond the ruined Gates of Night. All about them sounded the echo of hoofbeats and the noise of swift running feet as the Border Runners emerged on to the high plateau.

'None can stop us now,' shouted Thane against the weakening darkness, for with every stride he took towards the widening crack of sunlight the severed head he carried became lighter in his hands and easier to carry.

Thane blinked his eyes against the brightness and stepped out through the narrow doorcrack. Laughing, he swung Krulshards' severed head in a wide shadowy arch shouting at the top of his voice, 'All Elundium is free from your darkness now!'

Far away upon the steep slopes of the mountain a stag roared, and Eventine laughed, running out into the sunlight and pointing up across the black storm rills that ribbed the sheer cliffs above them. 'Tanglecrown, the Lord of Stags has seen us and he will find a safe path across the mountain and bring Stumble and Sprint down to us.'

Kyot smiled and nodded, turning towards the plateau's edge. 'Sprint and Stumble are the bravest relay horses in all Elundium and they will follow any path Tanglecrown can find. I will go ahead to meet them.'

Elionbel shivered beneath her cloak and brought Esteron to a halt with a touch of her hand. She asked him to kneel while she eased her mother's stiff cold body down on to the ground. 'Mother,' she whispered in horror, looking down at the torn and bloody skirts clinging to the wasted husk that had once been Martbel. The bright daylight showed all too clearly how Martbel had suffered to give birth to Krulshards' bastard.

Quickly she cast her cloak across the body and half-rose to her feet. Thane had turned towards her, Eventine and Willow were but a pace away and beyond the plateau's edge she could hear the tramp of marching feet. Biting her knuckles she sought desperately to hide her mother's shame; she had to, she was pledged to it. Thane moved closer and as he did so he trod on a brittle, weather-bleached branch that lay hidden in the ragged purple heather and snapped it with a sharp sound. Elionbel stared at the broken branch and saw how she could hide her mother's body. 'Fire will hide her for ever,' she whispered to herself, searching with quick eyes for other weathered sticks or kindling wood. Standing up she ran to Thane and begged him to help her, saying, 'Mother will not be safe or free from Krulshards' shadow, not until we have thrown her ashes to the four winds. Help me to build a funeral pyre. Please help me!'

Thane frowned, shaking his head. 'But it is not the custom. We should carry Martbel's body down into the fortress of Underfall, she will be safe there, laid within a ring of sharp Marcher longspears, and I will guard her until each warrior has looked upon the tragedy of her death and paid a homage to the greatest warrior woman in Elundium.'

'No, no, we cannot. I promised Mother,' Elion cried biting at the lies that spilled so easily from her lips.

'But your father, Tombel, is sealing the lower skirts of this mountain, leading the battle crescent up towards the night plateau. He will be with us before the sun reaches the noonday hour, surely we should wait until . . .'

'No, he must not see her like this, it would break his heart. No, no, I cannot wait, I must burn Mother's body before the sun turns our shadows. She pledged me to it with her dying words, she feared that it would kill Father to see her so. Please, please help me!'

Elion looked away unable to hold Thane's gaze and, stooping, she began hurriedly to collect kindling wood.

Thane moved to stop her, untangling Krulshards' dead locks of hair from his fingers and letting the head fall to the ground. 'No,' he began to say when Kyot's shout stopped him and made him run to the plateau's edge.

'There is a thick black fog below, over the Causeway Field and it's rising. Listen, you can just hear the tramp of marching feet from somewhere below. Perhaps the fog is all Krulshards' stored-up darkness that poured out of the summit of the mountain when Willow broke into the high chamber.'

'The sound of marching feet must be Tombel's battle crescent. Remember, we saw the Marchers in a great ring around the base of this mountain before we entered the City of Night,' Thane answered, staring at the fog.

Torn in two and unable to decide what to do Thane stared down into the swirling blackness, wishing he had Mulcade's sharp eyes to penetrate the gloom. Should he build a funeral pyre or place sharp spears into the ground around Martbel's body? Turning, he watched Elionbel gathering the kindling wood and saw her despair. She was right, her father was proud, it would break his heart to see how Martbel had suffered.

'Kyot, come quickly,' he called, his mind made up. 'We must help Elionbel build a funeral pyre before the marchers reach the high plateau.'

'This fog will cover everything!' Kyot cried, gathering bundles of kindling wood and weathered sticks as he retreated across the plateau close on Thane's heels. Esteron snorted in alarm and drew the Warhorses into a tight crescent on either side of the rapidly growing pyre, for he could smell black tallow in the ghost tails of fog sweeping across the plateau. The Border Runners heard the panic in Kyot's voice and fanned out across the plateau, quickly gathering all the sticks Thane needed to finish building the pyre.

Thane thanked Grannog, rubbing his hands through the thick sable coat as he knelt beside the Lord of Dogs and asked him to guard the pyre until Martbel's ashes had been scattered to the four winds. Grannog growled, his hackles rising razor-sharp along his back, and led the Border Runners into a tight circle around the funeral pyre, facing outwards towards the plateau's edge where feather tails of black fog were creeping towards them. Thane and Kyot lifted up Martbel's body into the centre of the pyre and secured it between the uppermost twigs. Taking out his spark Thane turned and took Elionbel's hand to draw her close to him. 'Forgive me for doubting you,' he whispered as he lit the spark. 'But I ran too slow to rescue Martbel.'

Elionbel shivered and looked at the black fog that was spilling towards them. 'No!' she answered fiercely, snatching the spark. 'You did not fail. Mother's death began on the high walls of the Granite City. Even with wings on your heels you could not have changed or overcome her tragedy. The darkness survives because – because . . .' Elionbel choked on the truth, her mother's last words shouting in her head: *Hide my shame. Let no one know of the bastard, Kruel.*

Elionbel swallowed and opened her mouth to speak as dark shapes breasted the plateau's edge. Stoops of owls rose hooting and shrieking into the air. The Border Runners snarled and leapt forwards and the Warhorses closed their crescent around the funeral pyre. Thane grabbed at the spark and threw it blazing into the base of the pyre and the bright greedy flames leapt from branch to branch

'We will stand, battle ready, and sing Martbel's praises until there is nothing left but her ashes,' cried Thane, turning towards Elionbel and reaching inside his cloak for the tiny silver finger bowl that she had sent to him as a token of her love. 'The tragedy of this moment lies heavily on my shoulders for it started less than twenty paces from where we stand when Kerzolde stole your finger bowl; he snatched it from my belt as we fought between the Gates of Night. But I found

32

the bowl, tarnished and spoilt amidst the ruins of your home at Woodsedge and I knew that Krulshards had taken you.'

'He came in revenge,' Elion sobbed, blinking away the tears as the pyre burned. She took the bowl and traced the love legend with her little finger, then she shook her head and looked up into Thane's eyes. 'He knew my name and came in black terror to Woodsedge, but Mother would not lie before us now if she had not tried to take my place. It was not only your doing, Thane.'

Thane closed his hands around Elion's so that the cup was between them. 'Do you wish that I had never lifted the finger cup in ignorance to my lips at the honour feast in your father's house?' he asked her in despair.

Elion looked steadily into his eyes, remembering clearly their first moments, seeing again the shadowy hawthorn hollow in the depths of the black forest, boiling with foul Nightbeast shapes all screaming for her death. He had come then, unasked and unexpected, a raw young warrior with a picture of the sun on his arm, bringing hope with each glittering sweep of his sword as he crossed the hollow. 'No,' she whispered, shaking her head to scatter the memory. 'Fate drew us together and wove our lives into one; through sunshine and shadow it cannot be otherwise, nor will I ever wish it so!'

'But the finger bowl!' Thane cried, numb to Kyot's hand tugging at his sleeve, trying to draw his attention to the plateau's edge. 'If only I had not taken it into battle before the Gates of Night, your mother would be with us now.'

'If I had not engraved it with our names entwined and given it to Errant to deliver into your hands ...' Elion whispered, looking at the flames greedily devouring her mother's body. 'Mother was warrior born,' she shouted above the noise of the roaring flames, 'she knew I had engraved the cup and never once spoke against it. She chose to stand against the Nightmare so let us sing her honours out loud and mix them with the hot sparks that climb up into the morning sky.'

Eventine knelt and plucked some sprigs of ragged purple heather and threw them one after another into the roaring flames. 'With each flower that is devoured by the fire we will sing the lay of Martbel, warrior wife and loving mother, who gave all she could to keep the darkness back.'

'She gave me comfort from the cold,' Thane began to chant when Kyot finally managed to gain his attention.

'Thane, Thane,' he cried, 'Tombel's marchers are approaching through the fog, look!'

Thane turned and stared at the plateau's edge. 'Tombel!' he cried, seeing a forest of Marcher longspears casting dense sun shadows across the purple heather. Before them in the heather Grannog crouched, his lips curled in a silent snarl, while the owls hovered overhead.

'Tombel!' he whispered again, gripping Elion's arm and turning her towards the plateau. 'Look, it is your father's battle crescent.'

Elionbel bit her knuckles and sighed with relief. 'I have kept your secret, Mother,' she whispered, taking a step away from the pyre and towards the advancing warriors.

'Once more, great Marcher Captain, we meet before the Gates of Night,' Thane called as Tombel strode towards them.

The Border Runners silently parted to let him pass, Esteron neighed and the ranks of Warhorses cantered out across the plateau to reveal the fiercely burning funeral pyre. Tombel strode forwards, the black mist glistening in tiny shadowlights on the standard of the owl in blue and gold that he proudly held before him. 'We come through the blackest night to win the sunlight. We ran without rest to destroy Krulshards!' he cried.

'You come too late,' answered Thane quietly, pointing at the severed head.

Tombel stopped, mid-stride, his Marching swords frozen

in his hands, his mouth falling silently open as he stared at the severed head. 'By all the sunlight!' he gasped.

'Father, oh, Father!' Elionbel cried, rushing forwards and throwing herself into her father's arms.

Tombel let the standard of the owl sway and topple to the ground as he gathered Elion up into his arms. 'Child, we have searched across Elundium,' he choked, tears of joy filling his old eyes. 'We ran without hope and fought without rest on the Nightbeasts' heels.'

Elionbel pressed her face into the coarse weave of her father's battlecloak and wept, letting her grief and the terror of the darkness drain away. 'Thane followed us into the City of Night,' she sobbed. 'He rescued us from the Nightmare.'

'Us!' whispered Tombel, the muscles in his arms tightening as his heart began pounding wildly. 'Us?' he cried again, pushing Elion away. 'Where is your mother? Where is Martbel?'

Thane moved quickly to where Krulshards' head lay in the heather and lifted it up by its tangled hair. 'Lord,' he said through trembling lips, 'I came too late to rescue Martbel. Kerzolde stabbed her to death while I fought with Krulshards. Forgive me, Lord, I could not save her.'

Slowly Tombel searched the plateau, looking blindly past Thane, forgetful of his victory until his eyes rested on the fiercely burning funeral pyre. 'Martbel!' he shouted, taking a huge step towards the roaring fire. 'Love of all my yesterlights,' he cried, frantically pulling at the fire-charred sticks at the base of the pyre. 'You must not leave me here alone. Where in all Elundium will I ever find that soft smile and gentle touch?'

'Father, she died a warrior's death and pledged me to burn her body before the new sun set. She was in terror of the dark.'

'I dared to hope that both of you lived,' answered Tombel, his voice broken with despair. 'Throughout each dark moment of those desperate daylights on the Nightbeasts' heels I called out your names. Why even as that black fog spread across the Causeway Field and shadowed the sun we heard a great cry that shook the mountain's roots, and the Nightbeasts we had run down to the very Gates of Night crumpled and fell into nothing, dying before our swords and spears could spill one drop of their foul blood. Great changes were in the air and we ran as we had never done before, hand in hand lest we lose our way in the blackness, tight-lipped to save each breath on the last uphill slopes of this dark place, only to arrive too late. Oh why did you put fire to Martbel's body and take her for ever from my sight? Were my Marchers not worthy enough to set a ring of long spears about her against the darkness?'

'If we had known . . .' said Eventine gently, taking Tombel's hand.

'But we were less than half a league below this place when you lit the spark, surely you heard the jingle of our armour, or the tramp of marching feet?' cried Tombel, anger boiling up in his heart.

Elionbel bent her head, new tears welling up as she strove to hide her mother's shame. 'If I had heard your footsteps . . .' she sobbed, taking a step towards her father.

'My footsteps!' he shouted turning on her angrily. 'You rushed a spark without a second's thought and we have run without rest clear across all Elundium!'

'Would you have me go against Mother's pledge?' Elionbel answered quickly, catching her breath as she fought to hide the truth. 'Once as the Nightmare dragged us into a dank forest we cried out for your help, Father, but you were deaf to us, our cries were muffled by the tramp of marching feet.'

'When the grey swan flew overhead?' interrupted Tombel.

'Yes,' nodded Elionbel sadly, looking up into the bright morning sky and blinking away her tears. 'Alone and beautiful she came, beating the bleak morning mist beneath her darkening wingspan, crying out in a haunting voice. I think she was telling us Thane would follow and rescue us no matter how black the road became. Again and again she swooped low over our heads as the Nightmare, Krulshards, ran us beneath the eaves of Mantern's Forest. The swan drove Krulshards to a rage with her sweet music and he feared her presence would tell you where we were hidden. He hurled a black barbed spear he kept hidden beneath his malice and it pierced her breast, driving her away across the winter grasslands.'

'The grey swan of doom,' whispered Tombel, turning towards Elionbel. 'We heard it, daughter, and saw it swooping low across the grasslands and I thought it was an omen, a sign that sent us far on the wrong path.'

'No,' said Thane, quietly, 'the grey swans led me tirelessly across Elundium on Krulshards' heels and paid dearly with their voices for finding Elionbel. Blame them not, my Lord, for without their help Elion would also be dead.'

'And they led us to you, Thane, when you were lost in the marsh,' added Kyot, smiling.

'And they showed us the doorcrack into the City of Night,' murmured Eventine, shading her eyes as she picked out two lines of dark shapes rising up from beyond the steep summit of Mantern's Mountain towards the distant sun.

Thane followed Eventine's gaze and for a moment watched the swans. 'All Elundium shall be yours to fly within and any stretch of water that you choose shall be named Swanwater in payment for leading me to Elionbel. I promise that the new king shall grant this,' he cried, and as if in answer one swan left the line and turned and swooped low across their heads, the morning sunlight shining brilliant white upon her breast.

'Thank you, Ousious,' Thane shouted, intertwining his fingers with Elion's and lifting their hands above his head in salute. 'You kept your promise and through the greatest danger brought me to the one I love. I will never forget your sweet voice.'

Tombel sighed softly, lifting his eyes from the pyre. He turned to Thane as the grey swans dipped out of sight below the plateau's rim. 'You really did it, Thane. You trod where no other warrior in Elundium dared, you have ended the darkness, you have destroyed the Nightmare, Krulshards.'

Thane laughed nervously pushing Krulshards' severed head forwards with the tip of his boot and sweeping his hand back towards the gathered company. 'His death belongs to all of us. Fate drew us together, I could not have done it alone.'

Tombel looked from one to another, his sad face slowly creasing with joy and laughter. 'No more darkness! No more Nightbeasts! Just look how the sun sparkles – ' He hesitated, gripping Thane's arm. 'If only King Holbian could have seen this moment . . . if only he could have shared this triumph.'

'Lord, there was a King on the Causeway Field,' interrupted Willow, 'I saw him as I left the eaves of Mantern's Forest. He looked old and brittle sitting astride a proud chestnut horse; he wore a cloak that glittered with the shine of steelsilver and all about him were gathered a great company in ragged dirty clothes.'

'King Holbian!' shouted Thane, turning towards the wreath tails of black fog that boiled along the plateau's edge. 'It is the King's battle crescent that waits on the Causeway Field.'

'We must go to him, our greatest Granite King,' cried Tombel, 'for he has returned from the dead leading all the city folk that vanished in the siege-lock on the Granite City. Willow, show us where he awaits.'

Thane bent down and wound his fingers into Krulshards' dead locks of hair, lifted the severed head and sprang up on to Esteron's back. 'Come,' he shouted, 'let us descend to the Causeway Field and kneel before King Holbian.'

Elionbel hesitated beside the pyre twisting purple heather between her fingertips. 'None will know, Mother,' she whispered before turning towards the plateau's edge. Eventine paused beside the cooling pyre and stared down at the rag ends of cloak and skirt that had not been consumed by the fire. 'There is something here, something hidden that has the smell of disaster,' she whispered, touching the smooth oiled wood of her bow. Behind her a stag roared and hooves scattered loose shale as Tanglecrown led Sprint and Stumble down to the plateau. Turning, Eventine laughed and waved a greeting, the secrets of the fire forgotten.

The Last of the Granite Kings

As the black storms boiled out of the broken summit of Mantern's Mountain King Holbian hunched his back against the wind, seeking what shelter he could from his borrowed cloak. 'Light would be a rare treasure,' he whispered, closing his fingers around a spark and thinking back to the lights in Candlebane Hall.

Dimly, the beginnings of an idea formed on the edge of his mind, and smiling, he straightened up in the saddle. 'Even false daylight would be better than this gloom, let the mirror of Candlebane Hall shine out here across the Causeway Field.'

Casting the cloak aside he called Breakmaster and Errant to his side. 'We shall have light in this black, forgotten place. Ride with all haste against the wind; ride along each sweep of the crescent and tell the Marchers, Gallopers and Archers, even tell the city folk, to light each and every spark and candle brought out of the Granite City. Let them blaze bright in this darkness, let them show the Nightmare the power of the people of Elundium!'

Laughing, the King spurred Beacon Light until he stood beside the Master of Magic. 'I am still the King of all Elundium, and I say that we shall have the light of Candlebane Hall even here in this dismal place!'

'Hush,' whispered Nevian, holding up his hand, 'for there is much beyond the Causeway Field I do not understand.

Listen, I hear the roar of flames, the tramp of marching feet, and the pounding of hooves.'

'Enough of what lies beyond our sight,' interrupted the King. 'Turn your head and listen to the crackle of a thousand sparks. Look towards the crescent.'

'Sparks!' cried the magician spinning round. 'Beware, Lord. You act dangerously in making false daylight for if it is the Nightmare just beyond our sight he will swallow up your feeble light. This darkness that tests your courage is nothing but a lifetime of Krulshards' hatred of the light boiling out of the City of Night. Hold your courage steady. Soon the darkness will pass, but you must order your warriors to hide their lights.'

'No!' cried the King. 'This is not the time for caution, this is the moment for risk. The last great moments of the Granite Kings are here and they shall end in a blaze of light.'

'But the smoke from the candles' tallow wicks and the sulphur fumes of the sparks will lay heavily across the Causeway Field. When this rush of dark wind falls away to nothing, it will lay as a black fog that hides the sunlight.'

'This wind will not change and my warriors will not hide their lights,' shouted the King, crackling his own spark into life as he pirouetted Beacon Light back towards the crescent but even before he had reined him to a halt he felt the wind against his face dropping and saw too late the wisdom in Nevian's words, for a clear blue sky had begun to break through Krulshards' dark storms only to recede and fade away as the candle fog spread above their heads.

Behind him the magician laughed harshly. 'It is still the place of Kings to make our fate. Perhaps your haste will yet bring old legends to life.'

'How so?' shouted the King, twisting his head but Nevian's answer was muffled in the black tallow fumes and fell away to nothing.

'Curse! Curse my haste!' muttered the King, throwing his spark angrily on to the ground as he watched the furthest ends of the battle crescent dim and fade into the deepening gloom. All around him warriors choked and coughed while the city folk shifted this way and that on the edge of panic as the thickening fog settled over them.

Breakmaster ran breathlessly to the King's stirrup, leading his pony, Mulberry, on a tight bridle. 'Lord, the storms have turned against us, I could barely feel my way back along the front rank of the battle crescent.'

Bending stiffly forwards in the saddle King Holbian gripped the horseman's hand. 'You must go back,' he said. 'Go and snuff out every flame that has been lit, for I have brought this darkness through my haste for light. Go, hurry before we choke to death in these foul fumes.'

Breakmaster saw panic in the King's eyes and felt it through his brittle grip. Breaking free he turned without a word and vanished into the still fog. The King heard his voice crying out faintly to extinguish the lights as he moved along the crescent.

Nevian took a step backwards away from the horsetail sword and lifted his head to stare up into the gloom, his eyebrows creasing into a frown. Something was passing overhead through the heavy fog, he felt the draught of its passage and watched the fog begin to swirl and twist itself into whirlpools and eddies. Shrill cries and hoots floated down across the crescent while the ground beneath their feet trembled and shook with the noise of marching feet.

'The last moments of Elundium have come!' shouted the King despatching Errant to draw both curves of the crescent so tight that the warriors, though blinded by the fog, touched shoulder to shoulder and the Nighthorses pressed flank to flank behind a glittering sweep of spearblades.

'The Nightmare is upon us!' cried Breakmaster. 'I have seen his shape through the black fog!'

Thunderstone heard the horseman's cry and sprang forward to retrieve the horsetail sword but Nevian stilled him with a hand upon his arm, bidding him to wait and see what Fate had brought on to the Causeway Field.

Tiethorm felt panic as he waited in the centre of the strike of Archers at the far end of the crescent. 'We are useless here; we should move with the tide of battle, sweeping where the danger is the greatest.'

'No, no! We should surround the King,' urged Grey Goose, first Archer of the Granite City. 'That is where the Nightmare will strike.'

'But careful Archer eyes are always set at each end of the crescent to see all before two armies clash, surely that is our pledge?' interrupted a doubtful voice from within the strike.

'Move to the centre of the crescent,' hissed Grey Goose, his mind made up. 'If this black fog clears we will see nothing but the grim doors of Underfall, surround the King and keep him safe. Let us be first to face the Nightmare!'

Without another word the Archers bent double and raced along the broad sweep of the crescent, a hand's span beneath the other warriors' spearblades. 'Who called you?' shouted the King, his face dark with anger. 'Who gave you leave to break the crescent?'

'Lord,' cried Grey Goose, falling on to one knee, 'just as we were together on the black road beneath Elundium, let us stand with you now and be first against the Nightmare.'

King Holbian's face softened as he remembered their escape from the ruined city. 'Be easy, brave Archers, and return quickly to your places. Your sharp eyes are needed at each end of the crescent.'

'But, Lord . . .' Grey Goose began to plead when the King hushed him into silence. The fog was thinning, sending ghost tail shadows fleeing across the Causeway Field, everywhere around them the rattle of armour and the jangle of battle harness sounded. Dark shapes were looming through the lessening gloom.

Nevian laughed and spread his arms, shaking out the folds of the rainbow cloak as a great Bird of War stooped to his

43

shoulder and folded his wings. 'Behold!' the magician cried, pointing up past the bulky shape of Eagle Owl at the other two owls, stooping fast towards the hilt of the horsetail sword, a bright banner stretched between their talons. 'Behold the standard of the new King descends on to the Causeway Field to drive back the shadows.'

'Old legends have come true. It is just as you foretold!' cried the King, rubbing his eyes against the sparkling light that reflected from the folds of Thane's summer scarf where it rested, draped across the hilt of the sword.

'You have helped Fate to make it so, even the tallow fog from your candles spread this false darkness,' whispered the magician, taking the King's hand and pointing beyond the sword to where the Causeway Field was filling with warriors, Warhorses and Border Runners who passed through the steep pine forest on the lower slopes of the mountain and hurried towards them. Before them rode a small company of horsemen. And at last the sun broke through.

Thunderstone laughed and wept with joy as his ancient eyes picked out Thane on Esteron. Turning, he ran to the King's stirrup. 'Look, my Lord, the boy you sent to grow strong in the fortress of Underfall: Thanehand who carried our hopes into the darkness – he has returned.'

'He carries a dark shadow in his right hand, my Lord,' added Breakmaster, moving close to the King.

Holbian shaded his eyes against the afternoon light then spurred Beacon Light forwards to meet Thane. Thane hesitated as the King rode towards him. Everywhere he looked was a sea of faces silently watching him. King Holbian laughed and reined Beacon Light to a halt. 'Long long ago beneath the walls of Underfall Nevian foretold that I would greet you gladly here upon the Causeway Field. I doubted it then and in the thrust of youth even strove to make it otherwise, jealously guarding my crown, but now I see the wisdom of Nevian's words and greet you with joy,

Thanehand, for you are indeed worthy of the Kingship of Elundium.'

'No, Lord!' Thane cried in dismay, jumping lightly to the ground and holding up the severed head. 'I love you, my King, and sought nothing but to serve you. I bring you Krulshards' head. The darkness is over and the Nightbeasts are dead. Now you can rule in easier times, my Lord.'

King Holbian's gaze swept across the Causeway Field then he looked down at Thane. 'No, Thane, I am beyond my time and strove only for this moment. Fate called you out and has fashioned you into a king and all Elundium has been gathered here to see you crowned.'

'No, Lord,' whispered Thane again, shrinking backwards, 'I could not be a king.'

King Holbian laughed and with the help of Thunderstone and Breakmaster he dismounted stiffly from Beacon Light's saddle. 'Already you have brought old legends to life and driven the shadows back and done more than I ever dared by entering the City of Night and killing Krulshards, but now time runs before us and leaves us little time for debate. Come and kneel before me and take the crown for when this sun reaches evening time and vanishes beyond World's End I shall turn back into brittle stone and Elundium will be Kingless. Come, kneel quickly for Fate has tested you and found you worthy of my place.'

Thane made to take another backward step as terror took his heart but Nevian stopped him with firm hands. 'Hold still! All Elundium is watching!'

'But I am only a Candleman's son,' Thane gasped in horror, as Nevian forced him down on to his knees. Shakily the King was reaching up for the steelsilver crown that rested on his head.

'Worthy or not,' hissed Nevian, 'many have paid a high price and laboured hard that you might kneel before Holbian. Remember Silverwing, the Battle Owl, and brave Amarch, your grandfather's Warhorse, stabbed to death before the

Gates of Night. Why, even Archerorm and your own father, Ironhand, came forward when Fate called them. Now kneel and be worthy of them!'

Thane bowed his head, a large tear gathering in the corner of his eye as he remembered the blind Battle Owl and the beautiful Warhorse. 'All for me,' he whispered.

'They saw beyond your humble beginnings, Thane, to the man who would walk in the darkness and one day destroy the Nightmare. Theirs were the first whispers of your name for the Kingship of Elundium: they believed in you and helped you through blackest night. Now take the crown.'

Blushing deep scarlet Thane looked up at the King. 'I am ready, Lord,' he stuttered hesitantly, 'but I do not know what a king should say or do, and I have no skill for ruling or government.'

King Holbian smiled, holding the glittering crown aloft. 'Fate has tempered you through pain and hardship and given you the courage to walk in the dark where only Kings may tread, that is claim enough. The rest of Kingship will come easily if you are careful with those who walk at your side. Breakmaster and Errant are both pledged to serve you as faithfully as they served me. Elionbel will be a brave queen, loyal and true through the blackest hours and no King could wish for better friends than Kyotorm, the new Keeper of the tower on Stumble Hill and Eventine, the beautiful Lady of Clatterford.'

'You know of Elionbel and my race across Elundium on Krulshards' heels?' exclaimed Thane, half-rising.

Holbian laughed. 'All Elundium knows of it, Thane, and loves you all the more for it, but the daylight runs before me and there is much to do before I turn to stone.'

Thane reached up and carefully eased the heavy steel crown into place upon his head. Rising slowly to his feet he stumbled as he tried to keep his balance and would have fallen, but Nevian's strong hands steadied him. Everywhere across the Causeway Field the shout for his Kingship filled the air. Again and again the ground trembled and shook to the clash of spear butts on shields and then as one and without a signal the warriors, Marchers, Archers and city folk knelt and offered up their bright sword hilts and polished spear shafts in salute as the shadows began to lengthen.

King Holbian spread his hands and silence fell once more. Slowly he unsheathed his sword and turned its hilt towards Thane. 'With this, my sword, I commend to you the people of Elundium. Be their shepherd and guard them well, the weak and the strong, the young with the old, that they may all walk at peace in the sunshine.'

Thane closed his left hand around the hilt of the sword and took it gently from the King's fingers. Moving to stand beside the horsetail sword he drove the King's blade point-deep into the turf. Turning to face the multitude of waiting faces he lifted Krulshards' severed head with both hands high above his head and then without pause he brought it firmly down on to the sword's hilt, impaling the broken windpipe on the bright metal. Black blood splashed across the blade, the skinless jaw snapped open and it seemed a single dead howl of rage fled, echoing low across the bleak shoulders of Mantern's Mountain.

'The Nightmare is dead and gone. Long shine the sunlight in all Elundium!' shouted Thane. Lifting up the summer scarf, he held it with both hands and stretched it taut then turned towards King Holbian. 'Beneath my banner, great King, I shall honour every word and pledge and do your bidding throughout Elundium.'

King Holbian took the summer scarf from Thane's hands and brought it to his lips. 'I bless this, the new banner of Elundium,' he cried, sweeping it in a glittering arc of light above his head. 'For it will shine brighter than the owl in blue and gold and bring a better light into this shadowy world.'

'No, my Lord,' Thane said quietly as he took back the scarf, 'the standard of the owl shall always hang beside the picture of the sun and each daylight they will together watch over the people of Elundium.'

King Holbian smiled as he took Thane's hand and spoke softly. 'The beginnings of this moment were at our first meeting in that secret room high in the towers of Granite. Even then as you sat at my feet, a frightened child fleeing from the Chancellors, I saw it. Yet I dared not utter one word for Nevian had foretold that Fate would push you out into a raw and dangerous world; he said that it would be your making.' Laughing quietly the King touched Thane's summer scarf again, letting his brittle fingers pass over the silky threads. 'Who would have guessed how many royal banners would have to pale and age in the Towers of Granite to make the new standard of Elundium.'

'But, Lord, this picture of the sun was only a forgotten scarf I took from my mother's pocket on the night of my flight from the Granite City.'

King Holbian laughed again, gripping Thane's arm. 'That, Thane, is the power of Fate, for it moves all the little things, pulling them this way and that to serve its purpose. But enough of idle chatter, the sun is drawing the shadows long and you must help me to find my resting place in the Palace of Kings; in the vaults beneath the fortress of Underfall.'

Thane knelt and took the King's brittle, chilling hand into his own and brought it to his lips, answering in a quiet voice, 'Lord of all that is dear to me, there are no vaults beneath the fortress of Underfall, there is nothing but the bleak bones of Mantern's Mountain that muffle the footsteps of the warriors who guard it.'

King Holbian thought quickly, searching in every corner of his mind. He shivered, remembering the dark narrow flight of steps he had once found an age of suns ago. Beckoning Breakmaster and Errant to give him courage in his last journey he turned towards the sheer walls of Underfall where they rose black against the setting sun and shouted in a loud voice, 'Now is the moment when I must descend into the darkness and dwell forever beyond the light.'

'It was foretold, Lord,' whispered Nevian as he cast the rainbow cloak across Holbian's shoulders to warm him and helped him towards the great doors.

'Time has run out from me,' Holbian sighed in a voice full of regret. 'That is the curse of the darkness for it measures time, heralding each daylight and marking its beginning and its end, pulling each hour of beautiful light into an endless stream of yesterlights. One more moment, I beg you, Nevian. Let me pause and look once more across the broad sweep of the Causeway Field, let me see the people of Elundium, the proud Warhorses and the Battle Owls; let me look on all that I strove for.'

'Just for one moment,' Nevian said, helping Holbian to turn. As he stood with a hand on Breakmaster and Errant, Eagle Owl, the Lord of the Owls, stooped on to his shoulder and Equestrius, the Lord of Horses, with Thoron on his back, broke from the eaves of Mantern's Forest to gallop hard across the Causeway Field, leading a great crescent of Warhorses towards Underfall.

'Lord of Lords,' Thoron cried, 'we have ridden hard through all the wild places to be with you on the Causeway Field but as this sun turned towards evening we feared we had come too late.'

Holbian smiled as he clasped Thoron's hand. 'It makes my tired heart shout with joy to see you again for you have brought hope with the morning and chased away my fears at night. Walk with me, Thoronhand and help me to find my place in the darkness.'

As Thoron knelt to kiss Holbian's hand Equestrius neighed, calling out the Warhorse challenge, and knelt beside Thoron in homage to the King. Far and wide across the Causeway Field proud crescents of Warhorses answered and knelt for King Holbian.

'All is forgiven, Lord,' whispered Nevian, taking the King's hand and placing it on Equestrius' shoulder. 'The bond-breaking is over, Krulshards is dead and you can rest secure that Elundium will flourish in Thanehand's care.'

King Holbian sighed, the cares of Kingship falling from his shoulders. He lifted his hand and caressed Eagle Owl's smooth shiny talons. 'Be with me as I enter the darkness for now there is nothing to fear.'

Kerzolde knelt before the narrow crack that led into the tombs beneath Underfall and shivered, afraid of what might wait ahead. He hesitated. Without the Nightmare's malice to hide behind, he feared the light and knew nothing but half-truths and whispers of what lay beyond Elundium. 'Shadow-lands and darklights,' he muttered, as Kerhunge pushed impatiently against his shoulder, eager to be far away from the foul warriors that ringed the City of Night.

'Get back and wait your turn,' Kerzolde spat, moving forwards and wriggling through the narrow crack Krulshards had found and used as a secret entrance into the vaults. Kruel had slept soundly during their flight down through the darkness, growing a little stronger on the dark meats from the spawning banks but he was awake now, fretful and hungry, clawing and biting into Kerzolde's coarse, hairy chest. Cursing, Kerzolde tore a thin sliver of flesh from the strips hanging from his belt and pushed it with his one good claw through the opening in his battle jerkin. The baby quietened as it devoured the meat and Kerzolde stood rock-still, staring at the frozen kings.

Kerhunge scrambled through the narrow crack. He sneered at the rows of petrified stone kings that stood before him and, raising his rusty spear blade, he lunged forwards. 'Leave them,' snarled Kerzolde, pulling at Kerhunge's scaly armour. 'This is not the time to seek revenge.'

Kerhunge lowered his spear blade and muttered under his breath, then he fell behind Kerzolde. 'Master would have broken every foul stone king into a thousand pieces if he had been with us.'

'Quiet!' hissed Kerzolde, turning sharply and jamming his broken claw into Kerhunge's dribbling mouth. 'We are beneath the fortress of Underfall; guards patrol each courtyard, owls hover sharp-eyed in every doorway. Quiet!'

'How will we escape?' gasped Kerhunge, pulling back from his brother's stifling claw.

Kerzolde tilted his head on one side and listened, his clawed foot on the first broken step that led up into the innermost courtyard of Underfall. 'This place is empty. All those foul warriors must be on the mountainside. Only one, no two, guard this place,' he hissed, opening and holding up his one good claw and pointing to the steps. 'They are moving towards us, crossing the cobbles beyond the first low archway that leads into the outer courtyards.'

Kerhunge wet his spearblade, licking at the barbed cutting edge with his ragged purple tongue. 'Revenge!' he whispered, nimbly climbing the steps to crouch in the shadows of the low arch on the far side of the courtyard.

Kerzolde sniffed the air and laughed. A black tallow-filled fog was drifting in curling ghost tails across the cobblestones, spinning through the low archway to darken the inner courtyard. Escape would be easy now. Once they were beyond the outer doors they would melt away, disappear to find the Shadowlands.

The crunch of armoured boots drew closer, cutting short Kerzolde's thought of escape. He crouched down, frozen on the stone-choked steps, his broken claw drawn across the baby. Kruel moved within the jerkin and struggled against the claw. As he opened his mouth to cry out, Kerzolde tore at the strips of Nightbeast flesh hanging from his belt, scattering broad drops of black blood across the steps, and crammed a sliver of the meat into the baby's mouth. The guards paused beneath the low archway, staring into the deepening blackness.

'What was that?' hissed the nearest guard.

'Nothing,' answered the other, pulling his cloak more tightly about his shoulders. 'Nothing but the bones of Mantern's Mountain groaning in the dark.'

'We should search each shadow,' muttered the first guard, taking a reluctant step into the blackened courtyard.

'But nothing has entered the Great Doors or passed by us in the outer courtyards,' replied the other guard, turning away. 'Come on, come away from this dismal place.'

Kerhunge licked his lips letting a dribble of spittle trickle, forgotten, down his chin. He was greedy to kill yet he waited until the nearest guard was turning, stepping back under the archway, afraid to search the courtyard on his own. Kerhunge lunged silently, rising out of the shadows. Twice his long scaly arms rose and fell as his black spearblade cut through the unsuspecting warriors' cloaks, shattering their backbones in one quick stroke. Gurgling with delight he bent down and turned each helpless guard on to his back then slowly slit their throats with a curved skinning knife.

'No time,' hissed Kerzolde, crossing the courtyard and roughly pushing Kerhunge away from the dead guards as he knelt to drink their warm sticky blood. 'We must use this black mist to escape. Quickly, follow me.'

Reaching the great door they halted and looked out. Black fog boiled across the Causeway Field, muffled shouts and the jangle of battle armour sounded everywhere. Kerzolde looked to left and right, undecided. He knelt, put his ear to the ground and listened, then, rising in panic, he stared up past the sheer walls of Underfall, putting a protective claw over the baby.

'Warriors are descending from the Gates of Night. Owls fill the air and I can hear that foul Granite King we had siege-locked in the Granite City. He is before us with marching warriors on the Causeway Field.'

'Which way?' snarled Kerhunge, clawing at his brother's arm. 'Which way now?'

The fog was moving, swirling as it thinned above them. Stoops of Battle Owls filled the clearing sky. Kerzolde crouched as if to hide and saw the moment of their escape slipping away. Hesitate one second longer and they would be seen. Kruel struggled beneath the broken claw and cried out. Kerzolde leapt to his feet, but which way could they escape? Everywhere before them was full of warriors. As he had feared, the Causeway Field was closed against them. The ground beneath their feet trembled to the beat of Warhorse hooves. To the left and the right, shapes – warrior shapes – were closing in. Turning back towards the sheer walls Kerzolde searched, stumbled and almost fell into the deep slime-filled drainage dyke that skirted the walls.

'Where are you?' hissed Kerhunge spinning round, setting his spear against the drifting mist. 'Where have you gone?' he snarled.

'Jump down into the dyke, there is no other way to escape,' called Kerzolde from somewhere near Kerhunge's feet.

Kerhunge looked down into the murky shadows. Behind him armoured boots were crunching on the gravel of the Causeway Road, Border Runners barked and the sharp jingle of battle harness drew closer.

'Curse all foul warriors,' hissed Kerhunge, scrambling down into the deep dyke that ran along the base of the sheer granite walls, taking the fortress's waste beyond the shoulders of Mantern's Mountain into a dark culvert surrounded by broken boulders and mounds of rubbish. Kerhunge descended in a shower of loose stones and sank with a dull splash up to his waist in stinking black slime.

'Hush!' hissed Kerzolde, drawing the top of his jerkin tight to keep Kruel safe as he gathered clawfuls of the slime and rubbed it over his hairy face. 'This black mud and the shadows from the overhanging galleries will hide us from the sharp-eyed owls, it is our only way of escape.'

'The smell of this place will hide us even from the keen

noses of the Border Runners,' grunted Kerhunge lowering himself until just his head appeared above the mire.

'Cover everything,' whispered Kerzolde.

Kerhunge snarled with disgust and slapped handfuls of the black slime over his head, plastering his tangle of lank hair to the prickly skin of his neck.

'Everything!' insisted Kerzolde in a hushed whisper. Above them horsemen cantered along the lip of the dyke, their shadows skimming over the black slime.

Kerhunge scooped up two handfuls of the waste and buried his face in it. Spitting the foul taste of it out of his mouth he looked up at Kerzolde. 'Which way now?' he whispered.

Kerzolde turned and pointed along the curve of the dyke, through a rough–hewn tunnel that passed beneath the Causeway Road, to a black hole half-hidden in a wilderness of broken stones. Rank marsh grasses and black-flagged bulrushes grew on either side of the gaping culvert and all around it, trapped in a swampy gully, stagnant pools of water caught the afternoon sunlight.

'That is the only road we can take to escape from these warriors,' whispered Kerzolde, wading carefully through the slime, keeping in the blackest shadows and hardly causing a ripple to spread across the surface. Kerhunge sank as low as he could until his chin touched the black mire and followed.

'Kerzolde,' he hissed, shrinking back against the steep wall of the dyke as huge Border Runners came to the edge, sniffing and growling at the black mud. 'Help me,' he whispered fiercely.

Kerzolde, turned, a sneer of hatred on his lips. 'Nothing, not even the Border Runners could scent you in this foul ditch. Keep well away from them and follow me.'

Kerhunge crept forwards with one eye on the savage dogs. They could sense something was in the ditch and kept pace with it, their hackles raised razor-sharp along their backs, but when Kerhunge emerged from the tunnel that ran beneath the Causeway Road the dogs had turned away to join the great company of horsemen and Marchers descending through the dissolving fog from the high plateau.

The dyke widened, suddenly shallowing, forcing Kerzolde and Kerhunge on to their knees to remain hidden from any eyes that might look their way. Ten crawling paces and they were in amongst the bulrushes. Kerzolde grunted in relief, stood up and wiped the slime from his face. Turning, he stared hatefully out across the Causeway Field while carefully lifting the baby into the sunlight.

'Curse you, Thanehand, Galloperspawn!' he spat, catching sight of Thane in the centre of the crescent of warriors. Thane was standing before the Granite King, lifting Krulshards' severed head, a black shadow in the afternoon sunlight, and showing it to the crescent. The old King was holding a crown above Thane's head.

'Curse you, Nightstealer,' spat Kerzolde holding the baby up so he could see who had destroyed his father.

Kruel blinked and peered out through the bulrushes. He clapped his hands together, a snarl of anger on his lips as the sunlight caught his face. Kerzolde stared at the baby and cried out in surprise.

'Owls!' cried Kerhunge, cutting short his brother's shout and grabbing at his arm as a dark shadow wheeled across the sun and turned towards them. Stumbling and splashing through the stinking swamp the two Nightbeasts ducked out of sight into the darkness of the culvert a moment before the owls stooped low over the dyke.

'Look!' hissed Kerzolde breathlessly, holding up the baby against the light at the entrance to the culvert. 'Kruel is shadowless!'

Kerhunge gasped in wonder and reached out to touch the baby, seeing that he left no trace or mark to show his passage through the sunlight. Kerzolde laughed with delight, hiding the baby safely in his jerkin. 'Yes, and we have saved him from the warriors. Mark my words, brotherbeast, he will grow from this daylight to be more powerful than his father, and take all Elundium as his own.'

Kerhunge nodded in agreement and was about to turn away from the sunlight and wade forwards, following the sound of running water that echoed somewhere ahead in the darkness of the culvert when he saw movement in the reeds. He crept a pace nearer to the entrance and peered out. Kerzolde followed. Ahead of them, two figures, clasped together, slowly rose out of the bulrushes, turned and stared out across the Causeway Field. One of the figures cursed loudly. 'Two warriors!' Kerhunge snarled, drawing his blood-smeared blade.

'No!' hissed Kerzolde pulling him back into the darkness. Hearing a voice, the two figures ducked down again into the reeds. 'They are not warriors. One of them is dressed in Chancellor's rags and he holds a dagger against the other's throat. And the Chancellor cursed the Granite King. He hates him as much as we do. Leave them to the warriors or the Border Runners to find; we must follow the water and escape to the Shadowlands.'

Silverpurse, the Chancellor's son, waited until the sounds from the culvert had died away before he rose, forcing Pinchface, the Loremaster, to his feet on the point of his dagger. He watched King Holbian advance across the Causeway Field. 'You will pay with your life for murdering my father!' Silverpurse spat between clenched teeth. 'When I have gathered strength I will take your crown and slit your throat,' he hissed at the fading figure of the King then he prodded the helpless Loremaster out of the reeds into the rough broken scrubland that stretched towards the shadows of Mantern's Forest.

Eagle Owl hooted softly and spread his wings as King Holbian, unaware of his enemies' escape turned and passed between the great wooden doors to take the first steps into the shadows of Underfall. Thunderstone hurried before him, lighting torches to show the way into the inner courtyards. Behind him Thunderstone could hear footsteps and easy laughter mixing with the jingle of battle armour as the King followed, gathering together the last threads of Fate that had drawn all Elundium on to the Causeway Field to be at the crowning of the new King. Thunderstone reached up to spark a guttering torch then cried out as the new light flooded across the cobbles before him, showing two twisted bodies lying across the entrance to the innermost courtyard. 'Beware, my Lord, there is black murder in Underfall!'

'Murder?' cried Nevian, leaving the King's side and moving quickly to where Thunderstone stood over the twisted bodies. Noting the terror frozen into their dead eyes, Nevian straightened, staring searchingly into the low arches and flights of stone steps that led up into the darkness shrouding the lower galleries. 'It is more than murder,' he whispered. 'Something terrible has survived the Nightmare's death to walk in this fortress.'

Nevian turned and the bright colours of the rainbow cloak shone in the half light. He called to Kyot and Eventine and bade them take a strike of Archers and search throughout the fortress. 'Search every gallery and walkway, leave no stone unturned,' he urged them in whispers.

Kyot and Eventine nodded, turned noiselessly to climb the lower stairways and vanished into the gloom.

Nevian, his forehead creased into a thousand wrinkles, drew Thane aside. 'There is no time to spare, the shadows are lengthening, we must rest the King in the tombs below this fortress before he turns to stone. We must hurry and find the entrance to the vaults, I know it is somewhere in this blackened courtyard.'

'Willow has sharp eyes in the dark for he was born in the City of Night. He could find the entrance faster than anyone else,' Thane suggested, then Mulcade hooted softly, pressing his talons through the weave of his cloak and making him laugh. 'The owls will search with him for they have the sharpest eyes in all Elundium.'

'Willow,' Nevian called out, 'your King has great need of you to find him a way beneath the ground.'

Willow broke through the press of warriors surrounding the King and entered the darkened courtyard, stepping past the dead warriors. Slowly he searched, his large round eyes probing every shadow, his shell-shaped ears listening to every sound. Pace by pace he crossed the courtyard until he stood beneath the sheer, rough-hewn wall of Mantern's Mountain. Kneeling, he touched the cobbles, feeling for the first step. 'Here, Lord,' he cried to Nevian as he found the hole cut into the bones of Mantern's Mountain long before the first Granite King had been laid to rest.

Armed with flickering torches Breakmaster, Errant and Thunderstone brought the weakening King to the edge of the first step. Below them a once-broad flight of stairs had been squeezed and pushed together by the shifting mountain to erupt into a tangle of broken stone choke. Nevian took the brightest torch and bade the King wait while he picked a way down. Bending left and right he stooped to push the stone choke aside and gradually descended to the bottom of the steps. He turned and held the torch aloft to examine the way. 'This must have been the path Krulshards used to enter Elundium to take Elionbel prisoner,' he whispered, looking down at the blackened footprints etched and burnt into the broken stone. Moving the torch a little to the left he frowned, seeing new marks on the stone, faint claw scrapings and tiny splatters of drying blood. He drew a shallow breath and touched the spots of blood, tasting the wet fingertip with his tongue. 'Nightbeast blood!' he hissed, wrapping the rainbow cloak tightly about his shoulders. Rising, he hurried into the vaults, driving the shadows before him as the bright torchlight found and entered every corner.

'Nevian,' a faint voice called urgently from the stair head, 'the King can hardly stand, his body is growing cold and brittle.'

Nevian turned and quickly strode between the rows of petrified Granite Kings, remembering each one he had taken from the living rock to set against the Nightmare, Krulshards. Old and weary they looked, battered and defiled by the Nightmare's black hatred. Nevian smiled wearily, seeing all the damage that Krulshards had wrought as he fled from the City of Night through the tombs beneath the fortress of Underfall, yet these stone Kings had stood proudly against the wear of time, forever frozen in the dark, their brittle swords and spears raised to strike a foe they could not defeat. Sighing, Nevian turned towards the ruined stairway, blind to the dancing shadows his torchlight threw behind him across the low rough-vaulted ceiling as the frozen stone Kings seemed to jump and sway in the moving light.

Nevian had found what he sought, the final resting place for King Holbian: a finely carved stone throne set before all the other tombs, etched with pure silver and surmounted by two sculpted owls, their wings spread out to protect their King, their talons open, ready to strike. It was the most beautiful stone carving Nevian had ever seen and inscribed around the base of the throne in flowing letters ran the words, *This is the seat for the greatest Granite King that ever walked in all Elundium, for he truly knew his weakness and strove to overcome it.*

'Easy, my Lord,' whispered Breakmaster, gripping at the rough stone wall for balance with his free hand as he helped King Holbian down the steps. Thunderstone supported the King's other arm while Errant carefully lifted each of his armoured boots and placed them step by step on the slow descent. Willow helped Nevian to clear a path through the stone choke and Tombel and Thane went before them to light the vaults with bright torches but Elionbel hesitated at the brink of the stairway, afraid to enter darkness again.

'Elionbel, where are you, Queen of Queens?' Holbian cried out as Breakmaster and Thunderstone eased him into the seat of the throne. 'Come to me, my child,' he called with his last strength. Elionbel swallowed, trying to gather her courage as a frail hand touched her sleeve, making her jump and spin round.

Angishand had followed in King Holbian's footsteps to the very brink of the stairwell. She smiled in the flickering light and took Elionbel's hand. 'Be not afraid,' she whispered. Bending, she rummaged in the meagre bundle of possessions she had brought with her on the flight from the Granite City and pulled out a sparkling twist of thread. 'It will shine in the dark,' she whispered, numbly weaving the thread between Elionbel's fingers and turning her towards the steps.

'Come with me,' Elionbel asked, holding tightly on to Angis' hand. 'Be with me in the dark.'

Angis smiled and descended the first step. 'I will be with you, Elionbel, until your courage returns,' she whispered. Elion felt safe beside Thane's mother and keeping pace with her she entered the black vaults beneath the fortress of Underfall. She shivered in the damp airless atmosphere and hurried to reach the throne to kneel before King Holbian and put her hand into his brittle fingers.

Holbian smiled and opened his eyes. 'So little time,' he mumbled, looking at the throng of anxious faces that surrounded him. Beckoning to Thane he called him forwards. 'As you shall rule so shall Elionbel be at your side, for she will be the mother of Kings. Guard her well, Thanehand.'

Thane took Elion's hand and brought it to his lips. 'Our love was strong enough to destroy Krulshards, my Lord, and it will flourish tenfold in the sunshine.'

For a second, a shadow crossed Elionbel's face. Nevian frowned, his sharp eyes seeing her pain. Something was out of place. Turning his eyes inwards he searched the future and caught a glimpse of the days to come, dark days when the sun would hide beneath a web of shadowlights, a time of terror when the darkness showed as starkly as black winter trees etched against the sun. Leaning forwards, he touched her arm and searched her face but she blinked. The moment had passed, his vision had faded and the shadow had gone.

'Lord,' Thane began, blind to what Nevian had seen, when a loud clatter beyond the outer edge of the half-circle made him pause, all heads turned. Willow Leaf, forgetful of where he stood had wandered amongst the stone Kings, gazing in wonder at the vaulted roof, marvelling at the skill of the mason when he accidentally dropped his stone–searcher on to the rubble-strewn floor.

King Holbian smiled. 'So this is the young man I have heard whispers of. Come here, Willow Leaf, for that is the name Nevian told me you carried.'

Willow, blushing and red-faced, took a step forwards, stopped and pointed back at the blank wall he had been standing against. 'Lord, you fear the blackness of this place and yet I was born in the darkness of the City of Night and can see much others would miss. There is a secret window, Lord, rough-hewn into the face of this room, let me work a few moments with my stone–searcher and you will have light here beneath the ground.'

'Light?' the King asked, gripping the arms of the throne and pulling himself forwards. 'Light, here in the tomb of the Palace of Kings?'

'Yes, Lord,' answered Willow, quickly retrieving the stone-searcher and using it as a lever on the hidden fault he had seen in the wall. Deeper and deeper the sharp steel point sank into the narrow crack. Willow twisted and turned the grey metal shaft until suddenly the fine stone dust billowed up in a cold draught of air. The wall had moved, the slabs of stone grated against each other as they separated. Blood-red light flooded in, paling the torchlight. Daylight was at an end, the dying sun rested for a moment at World's End, saluting the last Granite King. King Holbian could rest now.

Squaring his shoulders, he called out as loudly as he could so that everyone gathered around him could hear, 'Share your fears with the ones you love and never forget that I in all my foolishness and pride strove to hide my fear of the dark and almost lost this beautiful land to the Nightmare, Krulshards.'

'Lord, do not leave us!' shouted a dozen voices as King Holbian sank back wearily into the throne. Nevian felt the King's cooling forehead and lifted his hands for quiet. Breakmaster and Errant broke through the press and knelt at the King's feet, tears of sorrow coursing down their cheeks.

'Greatest Captains,' Holbian whispered, 'promise me, promise . . . that you will serve your new King as faithfully as you have served me.'

Elionbel felt herself jostled aside, the King's words echoing in her head as the press of warriors tried to touch the dying King. She saw the truth in what he had said and knew that she must tell him about her mother's bastard, Kruel, the Nightmare's child. 'I cannot hide it, Mother, no matter what shame it brings upon us,' she whispered, slowly lifting her head to stumble out the truth but at the moment she opened her mouth a great shout of despair and sorrow filled the chamber, drowning her voice.

'Lord! Lord!' she cried, forcing her way through the warriors until only Breakmaster, Errant and Thunderstone were before her, blocking her path. 'Hear me, Lord,' she cried, pulling at Errant's shoulder, trying to force a passage. She squeezed past him and fell awkwardly at the King's feet but it was too late, his eyes had crystallized and his ears had become stone. His brittle fingers were tightening onto the two stone Border Runners carved on the armrests of the throne.

'Promise me . . .' grated the King's last stone whisper as Breakmaster fell weeping beside Elionbel.

'Lord, to the letter it shall be as you bade me, I shall guard the new King,' she answered between sobs.

Strong hands pulled Elion to her feet and shook her. 'He cannot hear you, he has turned to stone,' shouted Thane against the rising death chant.

Elion looked desperately from the stone King, past Nevian whose rainbow cloak was fading in the moment of the King's death, to Thane, but her lips were trembling, her resolve weakening. She shook her head and tried to form the words to tell him of the bastard. 'What?' he shouted, bending his head against the noise.

Elion's gaze swept back across the press of warriors towards the King and caught a glimpse of her father, Tombel, kneeling beside Breakmaster. Quickly she swallowed her words; she could not shame him, not before his King or the three great captains. He had suffered so much losing Martbel and both her brothers, Arbel and Rubel, to the Nightmare. In despair she turned away, feeling trapped and alone within her secret.

Eventine and Kyot arrived breathless at the doorway of the vaults at the moment of the rising death chant. They looked across and saw the despair on Elionbel's face, but try as they might they could not force a passage through the warriors to get to her.

Nevian stood in silence at King Holbian's side, feeling his own magic melting out through his fingertips, watching the rainbow cloak fade and lose its colours, knowing that with the death of the last Granite King his time in Elundium was drawing to an end. Thunderstone and Tombel wept unashamedly at the King's feet while Errant and Breakmaster gathered their courage and took the first step to fulfil their pledges. Rising, they turned and unsheathed their swords and knelt before Thane, offering up the polished hilts.

Thane just managed to touch both swords before he was lifted and carried bodily out of the tomb, hoisted up on strong Archers' shoulders. Beside him Elionbel was also carried aloft and he reached across, taking her hand.

'You are my Queen!' he shouted as they were swept up

and out of the gloomy vaults into the courtyard. 'The Queen of all Elundium!' he called after her as her hand slipped out of his, the moving crowds of warriors forcing them apart as they poured out into the Causeway Road. 'We will meet by starlight on the Causeway Field, beside the Nightmare's severed head.'

Elionbel waved her hand and she was gone, carried from room to room through the great fortress of Underfall, the shout for her Queenship going before her. Thane rode shoulder-high on the backs of the Archers of Underfall down on to the Causeway Field and bravely acknowledged the shouts of Kingship that greeted him. As the evening wore on he was carried far beyond his friends of Underfall and the archers of Stumble Hill amongst other Marchers, Gallopers and Archers who Tombel and Errant had gathered from the far corners of Elundium to form the great battle crescents that had chased the Nightbeasts far across Elundium. Here the shout for his Kingship fell away, muffled to a whisper, for they knew nothing of him but battle rumours telling of a boy born to Candlebane Hall who rode upon a wild Warhorse. They had heard how Battle Owls perched on his shoulders and savage Border Runners ran at his heels. Magic was woven into his name and they feared that this had forced their dying King to push him forwards to take his place.

Thane sensed their anger and mistrust and quickly jumped to the ground, stilling those who had carried him with a whisper, telling them to retreat back into the fortress of Underfall.

'But these warriors mutter against you,' answered Tiethorm, first Archer of Underfall, reaching back into his quiver for a steel-tipped arrow.

'No!' hissed Thane, putting his hand on Tiethorm's arm. 'I will not shed the blood of any man in Elundium. I pledged King Holbian to shepherd all the people. Withdraw quietly, melt back into the shadows and let me settle these black whispers.'

Tiethorm reluctantly slid the arrow back into the quiver and took a step backwards but angry murmurs rose all around them as the grim-faced warriors from the battle crescents made to follow. 'What now?' cried Tiethorm, raising his empty bow in a gesture of defiance.

Thane put his hand on the Archer's bow-arm and stepped between him and the advancing warriors. 'Fall back,' he whispered to the men of Underfall, 'give me space to settle their fears.'

Silently Tiethorm retreated three paces and each Archer knelt on his command, reaching back into his quiver, fingers lightly touching the feathered flights of new-forged arrows. 'We are ready, Lord. If one hair upon your head is hurt we will build a wall of dead warriors.'

'No!' laughed Thane, stretching out his empty hands and walking towards the warriors of the battle crescents. 'Only fools and ignorant men would lift a hand against me on this, the night of Holbian's death, for he pledged all Elundium to follow me and whoever loved him would never defy their King.'

The warriors shuffled to a halt, unsure of the half-starved youth who stood before them. 'Unsure or not,' called a distant Marcher Captain from amongst the dark mass of warriors, 'I have not yet called you King and you are but a handful of Archers against our battle crescent. You are a long way from the safety of the walls of Underfall. It would take only a moment's killing and we could choose a King from our own.'

Thane laughed and shook his head looking beyond the broad sweep of warriors that stood before him and pointed into the darkness beneath the eaves of Mantern's Forest where a thousand amber eyes looked on. 'We are not alone, warriors, nor so easily silenced. Think twice before you act foolishly.'

'Border Runners!' cried a frightened voice.

'And Warhorses!' cried another.

The dark mass of warriors hesitated and drew together. The ground trembled and shook to the thunder of hooves as Equestrius and Esteron, sensing the danger Thane had walked into, swept across the Causeway Field leading the Warhorses and the Nighthorses of Underfall, surrounded by packs of savage Border Runners. They silently filled the ground behind Thane and his Archers. Thane stood quite still and waited until the galloping horses had come to a halt and snarling Border Runners had crouched on either side of him before he spoke, addressing the tightly packed press of warriors in a clear firm voice. 'Tonight I ask nothing of you except that you keep the peace in honour of the greatest Granite King, but tomorrow in the light of the new sun I will stand before you again and then, with all Elundium watching, you will make your choice of the new King of Elundium.'

Turning quickly and giving whispered thanks to the Border Runners and the Warhorses, Thane sprang lightly onto Esteron's back and led the Archers back acoss the Causeway Field towards the sheer shadow-black walls of Underfall.

Darkness had long come, turning the night sky deep indigo before Thane finally reached the place where he had pressed King Holbian's sword point-deep into the turf. Dismounting wearily, he called out Elionbel's name and waited beside the Nightmare's severed head until she came, gathering her cloak against the chill night air from the nearest camp fire.

'Kingship will not be easy,' he whispered in a worried voice, taking her in his arms and turning her so that they looked out at the twinkling camp fires spread far across the Causeway Field. 'There are many who doubt me,' he sighed, watching the ribbons of dancing sparks rise up to mingle with the stars, 'and tomorrow by the light of the new sun I must gather all the courage I can find and stand before the people of Elundium to let them choose me as their King.'

'There can be no other; the King chose you!' Elionbel answered. 'How could you doubt?'

Thane sighed and wearily shook his head. 'By tomorrow's light you will see.'

'Well, I shall be beside you,' Elionbel said fiercely, 'for we are love-matched and nothing will ever part us again.'

Thane smiled, feeling safe at last. He was tired of Kings and Nightmares and just wanted to sleep here beneath the stars beside the one he loved. Sighing, he cast his ragged cloak aside and drew her into the soft bed of rugs that had been prepared for them, feeling the warmth of her body next to his. He let his mind drift back across all that had happened since they reached the Causeway Field. Frowning, he half-rose suddenly and shook her arm. 'What troubled you as the King died? What were you trying to tell me?'

Elionbel stirred at his touch, waking from a dream in which her mother's anguished voice echoed, pleading with her to hide her shame. 'What?' she asked, shaking the sleep out of her eyes and sitting up next to Thane.

'You were trying to tell me something in the vaults,' he replied.

Elionbel looked away, shivered in the cold night air and shook her head. The moment of telling had passed, she could not betray her mother's pledge, her courage had failed her. 'It was nothing,' she whispered, snuggling back under the cloak, 'it was nothing but shadows in the light.'

Pledging the New King

The grey hours had streaked the sky with light. Dawn was
breaking across the Causeway Field and the first blackbird
waited beneath the eaves of Mantern's Forest to sing to the
new sun. Esteron lowered his head and nudged Thane's
shoulder, gently pushing him awake. Thane yawned,
stretched and sat up, shivering in the chill dawn winds and
reached for his cloak. He looked down at Elionbel and
smiled. Yesterlight had not been a dream, she was safe and
at his side. Turning, Thane saw the crown had turned to
stone during the night where it lay beside him in the wet
grass. He reached towards it and touched the jewels of
morning, sending the ice-cold beads of water skidding across
the polished granite surface.

'Who will call me King today?' he whispered, gazing out
across the countless forms of the sleeping warriors spread
around him on the Causeway Field. He remembered how
they had looked at him fearfully and remained tight-lipped
when the dying King had called out his name. He knew that
this crown of polished stone rubbed smooth with another's
hands was little with which to claim a kingdom.

Searching further across the Causeway Field Thane caught
his breath as his eyes picked out the NIghtmare's severed
head spiked firmly on to the hilt of King Holbian's sword,
the tangle of matted dead locks streaming out like black
shadows in the morning breeze. 'That trophy would be claim
to any kingdom,' he whispered, rising to his feet. 'But in truth

it belongs to King Holbian and I will claim nothing through the Nightmare's head or King Holbian's sword or crown. Come, Esteron, we must place the stone crown on the King's head and put Krulshards' remains at his feet. Will you help me?'

Esteron snorted and knelt for Thane to mount. Mulcade hooted softly from somewhere above in the brightening sky and stooped on to the crown, hooking his talons around the polished rim. Spreading his wings he beat the air and helped Thane to lift the heavy crown. Mounted, and with the crown balanced in his lap, Thane smiled at the owl and then bent low to take the Nightmare's head and the King's sword, letting Esteron silently find them a way through the sleeping warriors.

In the shadow of the great doors of Underfall he came upon Stumble and Sprint grazing beside Tanglecrown and waved them a greeting, calling softly in case he woke Kyot or Eventine who slept nearby in the centre of a large strike of Archers.

Kyot stirred, woken by the clatter of hooves, and jumped to his feet as Esteron passed between the great doors. He snatched up the Bow of Orm and a quiver of steel-tipped arrows and ran after him through the outer courtyards. 'You cannot abandon me!' he cried breathlessly, his voice echoing in the emptiness of the inner courtyard as he caught up with Thane. 'We are as brothers, even if you are now a king!'

Thane turned awkwardly in the saddle at the sound of Kyot's voice, doing his best to keep his balance on Esteron's back as he descended between the piles of stone choke that littered the steps leading down into the darkened vaults. 'We shall always be as brothers, Kyot. Never, never think that I would abandon you or put Kingship between us. I am setting things right before the new sun rises and giving back the crown of the last great Granite King to its rightful owner and returning the trophy of darkness that I took for him from the City of Night.'

'But the crown is yours!' exclaimed Kyot. 'I know the legends say only Kings can walk in the darkness and I saw King Holbian place the crown upon your head. And the Nightmare's severed head proves your right beyond any argument. No man would dare to challenge you!'

Thane laughed, cutting short Kyot's rush of words. 'Legends, dear friend, are not a claim. Fate helped me and armed me to achieve what seemed impossible. Now come with me and see a little why I cannot take as my own King Holbian's crown or anything else that was his by right.'

'But he took your pledge,' answered Kyot. 'How could you break your word so easily? Are you afraid of Kingship?'

Thane laughed again. 'Of all men in Elundium you should know I would not break my pledge, especially to the King. Now follow.' And he spurred Esteron forwards between the rows of petrified Kings.

Kyot shook his head uncomprehendingly and leapt to the bottom of the steps in a dozen large strides, where he lit his spark against the darkness. He hurried forwards halting only when he stood before King Holbian's stone throne. Kneeling, he kissed the King's cold granite knuckles then rose and moved back a pace.

'Why do you only kneel before King Holbian?' asked Thane, dismounting and lowering the crown on to the ground. 'Surely you should kneel before all the Kings who fill these vaults?'

Kyot frowned and turned to point at the shapes crowded beneath the rough-vaulted roof. 'These are only statues. King Holbian was real. He was my King, I knelt before him yesterlight on the Causeway Field and called your name for King when he commanded it. He will always be my . . .'

Thane nodded and finished Kyot's sentence for him. 'He will always be your King. Do you see now how I cannot take his place so simply?'

Turning away from the throne Thane walked to the window Willow had opened in the sheer wall of Underfall and looked out at the sleeping warriors below. Beckoning to Kyot he pointed across the still, dawn-dark Causeway Field. 'How many of them would do as you did if they came to these vaults? Remember King Holbian was their King. Tell me truthfully how many of them do you think will still shout my name in the light of the new sun without King Holbian to prompt them?'

'Lord,' cried Kyot kneeling beside the window, 'I meant no disrespect. I shall be ever faithful. I . . .'

Thane smiled and put his finger to Kyot's lips, silencing him, and pulled him to his feet. 'I do not doubt you. Remember we are as brothers. But for the thousands gathered on the Causeway Field it is a very different matter. To them I am little more than a name, a ragged youth pulled up by a dying King who saw too much in legends, jumped at shadows and lived on rumours.'

'But the warriors of Underfall, and my strikes of Archers from Stumble Hill, you have led them into battle, they know that you are Kingworthy.'

'Some will call my name, yes, but the guardians of Underfall are forgotten warriors, condemned men sent in chains to end their days defending the light here at World's End, their voices would be little but a whisper against yesterlight's shouts.'

'My Archers!' cried Kyot. 'They are proud men who love you and would follow you anywhere. They will call for you to be King.'

Thane took Kyot's hand and shook his head sadly. 'They may shout for me, Kyot, but they see magic mixed with everything I do. The Border Runners brought me to the tower on Stumble Hill, the Warhorses and the Battle Owls flocked to my standard and even the picture of the sun I took from my mother at the moment of our parting shines with a strange light that many will fear.'

'But the Nightmare's head, surely that will settle any

argument?' insisted Kyot, looking down at the hideous trophy where it rested against King Holbian's armoured boot.

'Now that he is dead there will be many who will say luck and circumstance gave me the power to cut off Krulshards' head. No, I will not have the people of Elundium call my name with doubt in their hearts. I will go before them with empty hands as the sun breaks free of World's End, then they can truly choose.'

'But the crown is yours! Even if you leave the sword and the Nightmare's head here in the vaults, at least take the crown.'

Thane smiled and shook his head. 'Everything will change, Kyot, for we stand on the threshold of a new beginning. Look, the rim of the sun has breasted World's End, the new Elundium has begun.'

'Everything will change?' asked Kyot, the colour draining from his face as he caught a glimpse of the daunting tasks that stretched before Thane.

'Yes, and leaving the crown in the old Elundium is only the first step,' answered Thane. 'I am trying to begin the new Elundium properly as King Holbian would wish it.'

'You will have me beside you, you will not be alone,' whispered Kyot.

Thane bent forwards, his hands upon the high rim of the crown. 'To have such a friend as you – I need not fear the future.'

'We will face it together,' laughed Kyot, reaching for the other side of the crown. Mulcade and Rockspray hooted and stooped from their shoulders, hooking their sharp talons on the smooth, polished rim.

'Together we will give King Holbian all that is rightly his,' cried Thane as they slowly lifted the heavy crown above the King's head.

The new sun had broken free of the shadows and the first shafts of sunlight were moving across the vault towards King Holbian's throne. 'Now!' called Thane, letting the crown slip from his fingers on to the King's head. It slid lopsided and awkwardly across the flowing locks of stone hair before grinding to a halt above his forehead. Thane bent and with both hands brought the stone sword up across King Holbian's thighs, pressing the hilt against his rigid hand. The sun, moving through the first station of the day, now streamed in all its glory on to the throne. Thane felt the hot rays on his back and watched, spellbound, as the old King's hair softened, the crown gently slipping into place.

'My Lord, I love you,' whispered Thane, tears streaming down his face. The King's fingers slowly opened and let the hilt of the sword slip into his hand. His leg moved, the armoured boot lifted off the base of the throne and allowed Thane to push the Nightmare's head beneath it. The shaft of sunlight moved as the sun travelled on, the flowing locks of hair stiffened beneath the crown, the fingers tightened on the hilt of the sword and the boot crunched heavily into Krulshards' head, trapping him forever in the age of the Granite Kings.

Thane knew now that he had truly served his King and smiled with relief as he stepped away from the throne. As he turned towards the window a soft voice from far away seemed to whisper from the last Granite King, 'Now all Elundium shall be yours, Thanehand!'

Thane and Kyot quickly left the tombs and hurried out. They stood for a moment between the great doors of Underfall and looked out across the Causeway Field. Everywhere cooking fires made the early morning air hazy. Gallopers cantered easily through the dew wet grass calling the warriors and the city folk into wakefulness but beyond the furthest dykes, hard against the eaves of Mantern's Forest, the great battle crescents that had doubted Thane's claim to Kingship were forming grim, menacing lines that swept as far as the eye could see. 'That is where my courage will be tested,' Thane whispered, pointing out across the Causeway Field. 'There is the shadow of mistrust that I must dispel to become a king.'

'Well, at least you will not be alone,' answered Kyot. 'Look, Nevian is upon the Causeway Road, and with him is your grandfather, Thoron, upon the great Warhorse Equestrius. Elionbel and her father are with him and Errant and Breakmaster follow a pace behind. Thunderstone and Eventine are walking with them.' Kyot paused, shading his eyes against the early sunlight before he laughed, pointing at a wide crescent of Warhorses and Border Runners massing on the high pastures above the pine forest on the shoulder of Marten's Mountain.

Esteron snorted and pawed the ground, striking sparks between the great doors. Thane smiled and ran his fingers through the horse's mane. The Warhorses would not come to him today, they were gathering beyond the Causeway Field to watch him take the Kingship if he could. Sprint and Stumble lifted their heads and neighed fiercely, cantering to Thane's side as if knowing that he was about to face great danger. 'Easy, easy,' Thane whispered, reaching down and taking Stumble's reins while Kyot put his foot into Sprint's stirrup and jumped quickly on to his back, nocking a new-forged arrow on to his bow string.

Nevian arrived before them, a dozen frowns creasing his forehead, and held up his hands in dismay. 'Black rumours are everywhere and half-truths grow as thick as summer weeds. Tell me, what has become of the first day of the new Elundium and why are you waiting here, Thanehand? Why are you not riding amongst your people, treading on gossip before it begins? Where is your touch of Kingship or did I labour all those suns to watch you let it idly slip away? And where is the crown and the Nightmare's head? They would still any rumours.'

Thane laughed and grasped the magician's hands. 'I have used the wisdom you taught me and I have given them back to King Holbian,' he answered. 'That was the first step of

Kingship, for they belong to the age of the Granite Kings. Now I will ride out amongst the people and see who will have me for their King.'

'Given back the crown and the head? Letting the people choose? I have toiled for nothing!' cried Nevian, throwing his hands up in despair. 'I thought you worthy of King Holbian's crown.'

Thane held the magician's gnarled fingers and looked long and searchingly into his eyes. 'If I am to rule Elundium, surely I must be myself, a man made of flesh and blood.'

Nevian smiled as he held Thane's gaze and nodded slowly, shaking out the folds of the rainbow cloak. 'You have grown, Thane. There is wisdom in your words, Kingly wisdom.'

'Your cloak!' gasped Thane, holding up his wrist where the fine rainbow threads still shone with bright colours. 'It looks duller than the thread you used to mend my wrist.'

Nevian sighed and nodded. 'You are growing in strength to rule Elundium, but my time was with the Granite Kings, my magic seemed to melt away from my fingertips as King Holbian died, draining the colour from the cloak.' Nevian paused, frowning. 'Yet for some reason a little colour remains in the folds but I know not how or for what purpose the power remains.'

'Thane,' Kyot whispered urgently. 'The battle crescents that would not shout your name are creeping towards us across the Causeway Field.'

Thane looked up and fear passed as a shadow across his eyes; his hands tightened on Nevian's arm. 'Come with me,' he urged. 'Be with me as they test my courage.'

Nevian smiled, then laughed, and turned towards the Causeway Field. 'Lead on, great King, and we shall follow.'

Thane clung to Nevian's hand for a moment longer, bringing the gnarled, almost bird-like fingers to his lips. 'I will not fail you, Lord,' he cried before leading Stumble to stand before Elionbel. Stumble snorted and arched his neck as Elionbel took the reins. 'Treat him well,' Thane whispered, 'for there is greatness beneath this horse's common coat. He is as swift as a Warhorse and as tireless as a Border Runner with a heart full of courage that will keep you safe wherever you ride. Elionbel, Queen of Elundium, I give you Stumble the orphaned relay horse from Stumble Hill and no better gift could any Queen wish for.'

Stumble neighed and struck sparks on the cobblestones with his worn shoes, then stood perfectly still for Elionbel to mount. She thanked Thane, her love shining brighter than the sun between them. Eventine laughed and sprang lightly on to Tanglecrown's back. She rode the Lord of Stags to Elionbel saying, 'Now we shall be sisters, Elionbel, for we are both mounted on the finest steeds that ever galloped across Elundium.'

Thoron had stood a little apart, his hand on Equestrius' bridle, a deep frown of concern on his ancient face as he watched the battle crescents forming. 'They were tattoo-pledged to serve only King Holbian, that is why they cannot take Thane as their King,' he said at length, reaching up to caress Eagle Owl's talons as they pressed into the thick weave of his cloak where it hung from his shoulder.

'What?' exclaimed Nevian, spinning round at the sound of Thoron's voice.

Thoron smiled and bared his arm. 'Your mark bound us all to King Holbian. Look, it has not faded or dimmed with his passing but still burns as brightly as the day you traced it upon my arm.'

'My magic!' cried Nevian throwing up his hands in despair. 'That is where the rumours and black whispers begin amongst the ones I pledged to guard King Holbian after the bondbreaking.'

'Strong magic, my Lord,' answered Tombel. 'It bound the bearers of the tattoo mark across the length and breadth of Elundium to love their King. Without it we would have lost faith and fallen into shadows long ago.'

Nevian laughed harshly and paced backwards and forwards

between the great doors. 'I cannot undo magic. What I have created must remain, I am not strong enough now that the Nightmare is dead.'

'Yet *we* love Thanehand,' cried Thunderstone. 'Why have we not turned against his claim to the Kingship?'

Nevian frowned and stared at Thane. 'Why indeed?' he whispered, shaking out the folds of his faded rainbow cloak. Mulcade hooted and spread his wings, making as if to stoop from Thane's shoulder.

'Perhaps,' called Eventine, 'perhaps we love him because we know him. Because we have seen the makings of his claim to the Kingship.'

Thunderstone nodded slowly. 'Yes. Time and again he rallied men's hearts and taught them to walk proudly in the half light of World's End. I loved King Holbian, yet I will gladly offer the hilt of the horsetail sword to Thane.'

Thane smiled and took the sword hilt. 'Rise, Thunderstone, Keeper of Underfall, and last Lampmaster of the Granite Kings, rise and be a part of the new Elundium that begins today.'

Tombel knelt beside Thunderstone and offered up the hilt of his broad Marching sword saying, 'I have seen you grow from humble Candleman into a great warrior who ran alone across all Elundium to rescue my fair Elionbel. You are more than Kingworthy, my Lord.'

Thane put his hands on Tombel's shoulders and pulled him to his feet. 'You were my teacher and drew out of me the best I have to offer. Be with me now, greatest Marcher Captain, be with me in this, my most testing hour.'

Errant and Breakmaster slowly knelt and began unsheathing their swords but Thane stopped them, a hand on each of their arms. 'Help me as you did King Holbian, freely and without a pledge, for I would not take your love for him, not until the time for mourning is past.'

Breakmaster rose with tears in his eyes and gripped Thane's hand. 'The birth of the greatness was there, Lord, on that first night when we met in the shadows of the Granite City as you fled from the Chancellors.'

Thane smiled and turned Breakmaster towards the advancing crescent. 'You would be the greatest horseman in all Elundium if you could hide me now from those whose hearts are yet against me.'

'We led those battle crescents,' Tombel and Errant cried. 'Let us speak to them and brighten their hearts towards you.'

'No!' answered Thane firmly. 'Each man and woman must make their own choice, but you may gladly stand beside me, showing who you would have for King.'

'What of the city folk, my Lord?' asked Grey Goose. He had stood on the edge of the debate watching the people of the Granite City move this way and that as the rumours of Thane's right to be King spread across the Causeway Field.

'Go before me, Archer,' Thane urged, 'and tell them they will be free to choose. No man will raise a hand against them, the warriors of Underfall and the Archers of Stumble Hill will see to that. Now let us ride down on to the Causeway Field and see who will have me for their King.'

Shout after shout echoed against the walls of Underfall. Swordblades clashed on to shields and a forest of spearshafts trembled the ground as the warriors of Underfall and the Archers of Stumble Hill proclaimed Thane King, and each warrior knelt and touched Thane's hand to pledge their loyalty to him. Nevian moved to Thane's side and urged him to stay close to those who had been faithful. 'You will be safer,' he counselled. 'The centre of the battle crescents who are against you is less than half a league from us.'

Thane looked up across the heads of the warriors waiting to touch his hand and saw the dark, threatening lines of the crescents drawing closer. Heads turned and followed his gaze and an uneasy silence spread from those around him in receding ripples as far as the walls of Underfall. City folk and warriors alike edged backwards leaving the trampled turf bare and empty between Thane and the grim faces. Thane laughed, snatched up his standard of the sun and spurred Esteron into the clear ground before the battle crescent. The warriors stood, unsure and sullen, in brooding silence. Nevian called to Thoron, Errant and Tombel to follow him and hurried after Thane, the faded rainbow cloak billowing out in the afternoon breeze.

Kyot spurred Sprint on to the clear ground and tightened the new-forged arrow he had already nocked onto his bow. Tanglecrown crouched then sprang high above the mass of warriors, his crystal-tipped antlers catching the sunlight. Eventine laughed as they landed beside Kyot and she nocked an arrow onto her own bow. 'We are spine-matched, my loved one, and ready to die for our King,' she whispered proudly.

Elionbel collected Stumble's reins and rode him forward across the bare turf to stand beside Thane. 'I love you,' she whispered quickly and touched his hand.

Mulcade and Rockspray stooped from a clear sun–bright sky on to Thane's shoulders and spread their wings ready to attack. Two savage Border Runners broke cover from beneath the eaves of Mantern's Forest and ran snarling and growling to crouch, one on either side of Esteron; their yellow fangs bared against the silent warriors.

'Now you must choose your King!' Thane cried in a loud voice, lifting the summer scarf in a sweeping arc above his head.

'Choose now!' cried Nevian. 'Choose as King Holbian pledged you and remember my tattoo mark bound you only to serve the last Granite King. The one who takes his place does not test your love for King Holbian.'

Dark murmurs whispered along the sweep of the crescent and here and there a warrior stepped forward hesitantly and knelt before Thane to offer up his sword or his spear.

'Come forward!' shouted Thoron, pirouetting Equestrius and cantering the length of the battle crescent, baring his arm to show his tattoo mark of the owl in blue and gold. 'I too carry Nevian's mark and loved King Holbian, but he is dead and turned to brittle stone. Choose as I did and honour your dead King's wishes.'

Tombel strode forwards and stood before the hesitating warriors, his two great Marching swords turned hilt towards them. 'I also carry the tattoo mark and loved my King enough to lay my life at his feet. Two Marcher sons and a loving wife are a high price to win the daylight and yet I will honour King Holbian's choice: I take Thanehand as my new King and will serve him all my days.'

'We loved our King!' shouted a man called Ustant from the battle crescent. 'And we marched for him and many of us died beneath the Nightbeasts' shadows to win this sunlight. We drove the shadows back without the help of Warhorses and savage Border Runners; we found our way, fumbling through the darkness without the sharp-eyed owls to guide us, only to arrive too late upon the Causeway Field and discover a ragged youth has thrust himself forward to take the King's place!

'Magic must have forced the King to choose Thanehand!' Ustant continued, urging the other warriors to stand firm with him. 'King Holbian lived on signs and legends, he was always looking for the one who would follow him.'

'We want a King free from legends and magic,' shouted the warrior standing next to Ustant in the front rank. 'We want someone we can trust, someone who doesn't meddle in magic or has owls on his shoulders, someone who does not ride a fierce Warhorse nobody else dare touch. We want someone who doesn't have savage dogs running at his heels.'

'Magic!' thundered Nevian, throwing back the flowing folds of his rainbow cloak. 'Magic has kept you safe through the darkest suns of King Holbian's reign! How dare you shout against magic!'

Thane frowned and touched Nevian's arm, whispering to him, 'There is more than a tattoo mark and the love of an aged stone King. These warriors fear the very fabric of what

80

has kept them safe and that fear has blackened their hearts and made them blind. Let me go to them and show them I have no magic.'

Nevian shook his head sadly. 'It is too dangerous,' he answered. But Thane dismounted. 'They will not believe you, their blindness is too complete.'

Thane smiled and stepped forwards, deaf to Nevian's voice. The two Border Runners kept pace with him, pressed one against each leg. 'Warriors, I come to you unarmed and without one word of magic to take your pledges. It was only Fate that guided me and pulled each thread leading to the Nightmare's death.'

'If that is the truth,' cried Ustant, interrupting Thane, 'send those Battle Owls up from your shoulders, break your pact with the Warhorses and despatch those Border Runners that crouch beside you. Then, perhaps, we may choose you as our King.'

'No!' shouted Thane, seeing a little of Nevian's anger and feeling his own begin to rise as he faced so much blind ignorance. 'I will not send my friends away nor will I break faith with those that kept Elundium safe, for they came without asking and they did not count the cost as they fought to rid Elundium of Krulshards. They have the right to share this sunlight without suspicion or fear casting a shadow where they tread.'

Black whispers ran the length of the battle crescent and it wavered, rippling with doubt. 'But we dare not touch the Warhorses or the Border Runners,' cried a voice. 'And the Battle Owls are savage birds of war with razor-sharp talons that could rip out our eyes if we went near them.'

Nevian laughed and strode fowards. 'The bonds were broken an age ago because King Holbian raised his sword in anger against me but now he is dead and the bonds are renewed again. Surely you saw Equestrius, the Lord of Horses, kneel before the King moments before we passed into the fortress of Underfall? Surely you saw Eagle Owl stoop on to his aged shoulder? Come and touch Esteron or Equestrius, or place your hands on the owls' talons, find the truth in my words.'

'Come forward!' urged Thane, running his fingers through the soft sable coats of the Border Runners that sat beside him. 'Come forward without your fears and touch the two dogs that helped Kyot find me in the grasslands. Come, and be a part of the new Elundium.'

But the battle crescent remained still, watching the high meadows where the Warhorses began to move.

'Come forward!' cried Nevian, using the rainbow cloak as a bright banner and driving it into the centre of the crescent. 'Now is the moment. Or remain forever chained by your blind fear, in the last daylight of the Granite Kings. Come forward or stand forever frozen, watching beside the Greenways' edge until you have lost your fear and can clearly see and share all the beauty of Elundium. Pledge yourselves now to Thanehand or wait beside the Greenways' edge until he summons you one by one to serve him! For he is the rightful King of all Elundium, chosen by the last Granite King.'

The crescent swayed and trembled, twisting backwards and forwards, breaking into a thousand pieces. The warriors were milling in confusion, some touched the Border Runners and knelt to kiss Thane's hand and called him King, but the greater mass would not come near Esteron or the unblinking owls. They could not overcome their fear and retreated, running away beneath the shadows of the eaves of Mantern's Forest. Halting, they turned, drawn together by Ustant, and lowered their spears cursing magic and the name of Thanehand. Kyot spurred Sprint forwards, putting himself between them and Thane, calling to his archers to come and defend their new King.

'THANEHAND!' rose a deafening shout as the warriors of Underfall, Stumble Hill and all those who had spoken their pledge surged forwards after them but Nevian ran quickly to Kyot's side and put a hand on his bow string, easing the arrow towards the ground.

'There will be no bloodshed,' he cried, halting the surge of warriors with one sweep of the rainbow cloak, bidding them to lower their forest of spearblades. Beyond the broad sweep of warriors hoofbeats thundered across the Causeway Field. The Warhorses had descended through steep pine forests to fan out in a fast-moving crescent on the Causeway Field; Border Runners crowded amongst them, growling and snarling, the light of battle in their eyes.

Striding into the path of the galloping horses, Nevian raised his arms and commanded them to be still. 'They are cursed enough. Let them vanish forever from our sight.'

Turning, Nevian looked into the shadows beneath Mantern's eaves and called out, 'This is your last chance, pledge-takers. Come and kneel before your King or be cursed always to stand, summer and winter, beside the Greenways' edge.'

'We spit on your magic curses!' snarled Ustant from the shadows of the forest. 'Your rainbow cloak has faded and with it your powers, Master of Magic. It is not you who holds our fear but Thanehand and the Warhorses. We will retreat and choose a King of our own, and wait our chance to take all Elundium from the throne-stealer.'

Behind Nevian the Warhorses roared a challenge and surged forward. The sky darkened beneath the beating wings of the grey swans of doom. Kyot's Archers bent their bows and the spearmen stretched to throw but the undergrowth shook and rustled and the shadows were suddenly empty, the pledge–breakers had fled, vanishing between the close-tangled trees.

Nevian sighed and let his hands fall to his side. Turning, he walked slowly to where Thane stood. 'They were beyond my help. Their hearts were darkened with fear, but they cannot harm you or the beginnings of the new Elundium. I have spun a magic spell that will hold them upon the Greenways' edge,' he said quietly.

Thane frowned. 'But you said your magic had faded with the passing of King Holbian. Surely they will gather beyond our sight and choose a King of their own?'

Nevian laughed, the colours of the rainbow cloak dissolving in the late afternoon sunlight. 'Keep faith, my King, and watch the Greenways' edge and see who waits to serve you if troubled daylights darken the sun . . .'

'Nevian!' Thane shouted, reaching out to touch the vanishing cloak, but the shadow of the grey swans of doom passed slowly overhead and made him look up. He waved to Ogion, Lord of Swans, and smiled to see his Queen, Ousious, alone, white and beautiful in the sunlight. 'Choose a place,' he shouted, forgetting the magician for a moment. 'Any stretch of water in all Elundium and it shall be yours to name as the new Swanwater. It is given by the new King in payment for showing the Nightmare's path.'

Kruel Vanishes

Kerzolde forced a passage through the fast-flowing water, hooking his one good claw into the low moss-covered rocks that filled the darkness just above his head. 'Curse Thanehand, the Galloperspawn!' he muttered again and again, trying to keep his chin above the black waters threatening to suck him under.

Kruel had climbed out of the battle jerkin up on to his shoulders and rode high above the raging waters laughing and pulling roughly at Kerzolde's ears, his tiny curved toes splashing with delight. Somewhere ahead the culvert bent sharply, muffling Kerhunge's warning shouts. Kerzolde slowed. The roof of the culvert had become smooth; there was nowhere to take a clawhold; the floor dipped and sloped steeply away. He slipped, his clawed feet skidding on smooth boulders; the current caught him, twisting him away from the wall. Kruel's laughter turned into a scream of panic, his legs tightening around Kerzolde's throat, his sharp nails gouging into the Nightbeast's bristly cheeks as they sank beneath the water.

'Kerhunge!' Kerzolde screamed as the water flooded into his mouth and rose, bubbling, over his head.

Kerhunge heard the baby's scream and ran back along a narrow ledge he had found just before the culvert disappeared into a steep weir. He had shouted a warning to Kerzolde and hurried on to explore a narrow crack that opened towards distant daylight. 'Kerzolde!' he snarled, kneeling on the ledge and searching, stretching down into the black fast-moving waters, sweeping his curved skinning hook backwards and forwards across the wide channel until he felt it catch and tug at Kerzolde's iron collar. Leaning back he pulled with both hairy hands on the handle of the hook, and bit by bit he hauled his brotherbeast out of the boiling waters on to the narrow ledge.

'Fool of a beast!' he snapped, holding the baby upside down to shake the water out of it. 'I shouted back a warning to tell you of the weir and how to climb out on to the ledge.'

Kerzolde coughed and spat out mouthfuls of water. He knelt on all fours and shook the water out of his scaly armour. 'Kruel,' he gasped with his first breath. 'Where is the baby?'

Kerhunge quickly brought the wet bundle to his face, rubbed his cheek lovingly against it and thrust it back into Kerzolde's claws. 'Master would strip back your armoured hide and expose your raw flesh to the sunlight for being so careless,' he snarled, dribbling bright spittle over the baby's head.

Grunting with relief, Kerzolde took Kruel back and slipped him inside his wet jerkin then turned towards the distant hint of daylight that shone through the jumble of rocks. 'Lead us forwards,' he muttered, pushing the baby deep into the folds of his jerkin, well out of harm's way. Frowning, he touched the baby again, prodding it gently, measuring it with both claws, feeling how much Kruel had grown since their escape from the City of Night. 'He has grown so quickly,' he whispered, knowing he would soon be big enough to walk.

'Quickly!' hissed Kerhunge from a place beside the narrow opening. Turning his hideous head he beckoned Kerzolde to the daylight crack. 'Look,' he hissed as his brotherbeast settled beside him. He was pointing across the barren boulder-strewn slope that spread below them to where a Marcher lay bound and chained in the centre of a circle of Nightbeasts. Tilting his head, Kerhunge listened to the shouts and curses that rose up from the struggling man.

Kerzolde watched for a moment, scratched his chin and spat at the ground. 'Those beasts are dead,' he whispered. 'All dead and trapped by their armour into the moment our Master died.'

'Dead? All dead?'

Kerzolde nodded slowly. 'Watch those black carrion crows that have just strutted into the circle.'

Kerhunge bent forwards and watched the biggest crow. It had reached the Marcher and stretched out its neck to peck at his legs. The man shouted and lashed out, sending the crow flapping lazily out of his reach. Turning its bright cruel eyes towards the Nightbeasts it searched their bulky shapes before spreading its wings and in a single bound alighted on a scaly Nightbeast shoulder. Cawing shrilly it sensed the putrid stench of death and pecked at the bristly face, loosening and plucking out a rotten eye. Noisily the rest of the flock of crows rose up in a cloud of black flapping wings and settled on the Nightbeasts, prodding and searching between their armoured hides, tearing out thin strips of rotting meat. As they settled to their feast, snapping and fighting over the tastiest morsels, one by one beneath the weight of the fighting crows the rotten corpses toppled and crashed to the ground.

Arbel the Marcher twisted in his chains and watched the crows feasting in horror. He only just managed to wriggle aside as the nearest Nightbeast fell beside him, scattering across the ground its grizzly trophies of half-chewed hands and skulls that had hung from its belt; a curved scythe and a rusty dagger fell less than a hand's span from his bound wrists. He twisted on to his back and drew up his knees to his chest and, with a shout of effort, he kicked out. He rolled over in a scatter of loose stones and his hand closed on the cold rusty blade of the dagger. Gasping for breath he turned his head and with his eyes narrowing he saw a Nightbeast descending from a dark crack in the rocks above. He knew the one-eyed beasts. He knew that hideous face belonged to the Nightbeast who had helped Krulshards steal his sister,

Elionbel and feasted on the servers' bodies at Woodsedge. With Kerzolde almost upon him, Arbel ground his teeth in helpless rage, gripped his dagger and tried to rise to his feet.

Kerzolde raised his own dagger high above his head and made a strike but Arbel was too quick for him, throwing himself sideways moments before the blade crashed harmlessly to the ground where he had been kneeling. Kerzolde screamed with rage and lifted the blade to strike again. Arbel watched him, his eyes narrowing into glittering slits. 'The darkness!' he cried, kicking furiously to get away from the Nightbeast. 'I want to serve the darkness!'

Kerzolde hesitated. Never before in all his master's dark stories had a Marcher, Archer or Galloper loved the darkness. Kruel stirred within his jerkin and cried out. 'The darkness!' Arbel repeated, snatching desperately at the Nightbeast's hesitation and staring at the moving bulge in Kerzolde's jerkin as he tried to get back on to his knees. 'Ever since your master's nightmesh entangled my feet on the lawns of Gildersleeves I have dreamt of the darkness.'

Kerzolde slowly lowered the blade. He did remember the two Marchers they had tried to catch and kill on the lawn of Gildersleeves but, kneeling beside Arbel, he pressed the blade roughly into the angle of his jaw. 'Why should I believe you, Marcher?' he hissed, drawing a bead of trickling blood on to the dirty blade. 'Why?'

Arbel choked against the rusty metal point. 'I stopped my brother, Rubel, following you. I stabbed him in the ruins of Woodsedge. I was following your master, not chasing him when these Nightbeasts captured me. They thought I was Thanehand and were bringing me to your master.'

Kerzolde sank back on his haunches and summoned Kerhunge from the daylight crack where he had been keeping watch. 'He wants to serve the darkness,' sneered Kerzolde. 'He wants to serve our master.'

Kerhunge laughed and eased a long black blade from his belt. 'Let the new Master choose. Bring out Kruel.'

88

'No!' snarled Kerzolde stepping backwards hastily and pressing his one good claw protectively across the opening of his jerkin.

'He must choose. He is our new master,' insisted Kerhunge in a hushed whisper. 'One scream or teardrop from the baby and we will kill the Marcher, but if he laughs or touches the Marcher we will let him live.'

Kerzolde thought for a moment, burying his head low between his shoulders. There was sense in Kerhunge's words. So far, each time they had shown the baby warriors, Gallopers or Marchers, he had screamed with rage, making the ground tremble. Yes, he would choose, then they could kill the Marcher at their leisure.

Lifting the baby carefully through the opening in his jerkin Kerzolde shook him awake and held him up. 'This is the darkness, this is the new Master of all Elundium,' he snarled, thrusting him into Arbel's face.

Arbel stared, open-mouthed, his hands tingling, the hairs on the nape of his neck rising and falling in gentle waves. He was so close to the pure blackness of night he could almost taste it. Sighing, he stretched his neck to touch the baby. Kruel awoke and stared back with unblinking blue eyes. Gurgling he clapped his tiny hands together and touched Arbel, scratching his sharp nails across his neck. Kerzolde hissed and jumped backwards, snatching the baby away from the Marcher. He had felt the baby change at the touch, swelling in his claws, growing stronger through the contact with Arbel.

Kerhunge snarled and leapt at the Marcher's throat. 'No! No!' cried Kerzolde pushing his brotherbeast roughly aside. 'Only Kruel has the power of life and death. You cannot kill the Marcher yet.'

Pulling hard on Kerhunge's armoured sleeve Kerzolde drew him away from the Marcher and secretly pointed at the baby. 'Look at the likeness between them,' he whispered.

'That is why I hesitate to kill. There is a bond between them. I can smell it.'

'The Marcherwoman!' Kerhunge hissed. 'Did she spawn them both?'

'Perhaps.' Kerzolde shrugged his shoulders, setting his armoured hide rattling. 'Perhaps, but until we know for sure we must keep him alive.'

'Show me the darkness again. Show me the baby,' shouted Arbel, trying to move nearer and rattling the chains that bound his wrists, making both Nightbeasts turn towards him.

'Here,' hissed Kerzolde, holding up the baby. 'How would you, a Marcher, serve Kruel? Where would your place be in his new darkness that will smother all Elundium?'

Together the two Nightbeasts closed on Arbel and squatted down just beyond his reach, staring at him in brooding silence. Krulshards would have let them kill him but now they had to wait and watch his every movement until Kruel gave them a sign. Kruel wriggled free of Kerzolde's claws and sat on the ground between them tearing absently at the strips of rotten flesh hanging from Kerzolde's belt.

Arbel stared at the baby seeing what he thought were glimpses of his mother, or his sister, Elionbel. Shaking his head, he shivered. 'It cannot be possible,' he whispered, shutting his mind to the horror of what might have happened. Kruel had let the strips of meat fall forgotten to the ground; now he was staring, unblinking, into Arbel's eyes, searching and probing with a look sharper than a carrion crow's beak. Arbel gasped for breath, the surface images were gone, now he could see deep within those pale unblinking eyes, down, down into the bottomless blackness he yearned to serve and he saw that it was more powerful than the darkest night. He shivered with delight, wetting his lips with a greedy tongue as he struggled to rise.

'Come to me,' whispered a voice that echoed in his head. 'Come with me into the darkness and be a part of me.'

The chains seemed to slip together, link grating on link

allowing him to rise clumsily to his feet and stagger forwards. The baby was summoning him, drawing him with a will far stronger than his own.

Kerzolde watched Arbel get up and made to draw his blade to defend the baby but Kruel turned his pale eyes on the Nightbeast and stilled him. Gurgling, Kruel rose unsteadily to his feet, clapped his hands and tripped forwards on to his knees. Laughing, he crawled towards the Marcher.

Kerhunge snarled and sprang forwards, his hairy hands stretched out to snatch the baby away from Arbel but Kruel cried out, splitting pebbles with his voice and freezing Kerhunge mid-stride. Laughing and dribbling, he turned back and beckoned Arbel, pulling at the hem of his cloak until he toppled him down amongst the broken stones at his side.

'Master, Master,' Kerzolde whispered in terror as the baby prodded Arbel's face, pulling open his bottom lip and exploring his mouth, pushing his tiny slender fingers into the soft flesh of the Marcher's cheeks. Arbel choked and cried out as the baby forced his tongue far back into his throat. Smiling, Kruel bit savagely at the tip of his nose and then licked at the fine beads of blood oozing from the needle-sharp teeth marks. Kruel spat out the blood, growled with anger at the taste and pulled at the chains that bound Arbel's wrists. Then, giggling quietly the infant climbed upwards and sat astride Arbel's chest and closed his slender fingers around a single link of the chains. He sat quite still and squeezed the Nightbeast chain until the metal softened and became as wet as clay, dissolving at his touch.

'Stronger than his father, the Nightmare!' whispered Kerzolde watching in awe as Kruel destroyed each link of the chain. He played with Arbel's leg chains, absorbed by the patterns they made in the dust, before melting them into black, misshapen lumps of metal.

Arbel rubbed life back into his blackened wrists and massaged his numb ankles before lifting up the baby. 'I will love you as a brother,' he whispered, kissing Kruel's forehead, 'but I will serve you as the greatest power of darkness in all Elundium. So great and so powerful are you that you can defy the sunlight and stand without casting a shadow!'

Arbel looked at the Nightbeasts and laughed, his lips curling back in hatred as he reached for a discarded spear-shaft and slowly stood up. 'Now I hold power,' he sneered, tucking the baby into the crook of his arm and lowering the blade of the spear to touch Kerzolde's throat just above his iron collar.

'N–n–n–no!' cried the baby, wriggling frantically until his hands were on the shaft of the spear. The shaft grew hot and smelt of burning wood; the metal tip glowed and hissed where it touched Kerzolde's bristly hide.

'N–n–n–n–no!' shouted Kruel and the shaft burst into flames, dying into a thousand charcoal cinders that fell, crumbling, to the ground.

Arbel stepped back, blowing on his blistered fingers and quickly put the baby on the ground. Kruel looked up unblinking into Arbel's eyes. Laughing, he waved his hands. He drew the Marcher down to sit beside him and turned his head then summoned Kerzolde and Kerhunge, stretching out his tiny fingers to take their claws and hands.

'We are to be friends. Kruel commands it,' whispered Kerzolde, staring hatefully at the Marcher.

Arbel nodded and stared back without blinking, taking the baby's other hand. 'We are to serve Kruel together and keep him safe until he is strong enough to take all Elundium as his own.'

Kerhunge shrugged his shoulders and spat at the ground, hitting a poisonous weed worm as he nodded reluctantly. Being friends with a Marcher was beyond his understanding but he would wait: Kruel would change his mind and then he could kill the Marcher. Kruel saw the worm and cried out for it. Kerzolde reached down and hooked up the vicious, bright yellow, scaly weed worm and made to crush it with his one good claw to render it harmless for the infant to play with.

'*No!*' screamed Kruel, reaching out for the bright orange stiny. '*No!*' he cried again touching the worm. Once, twice the worm arched its back, twisting to strike, thrashing the needle sting at the baby's fingers, but gradually it grew still in his hands, the yellow colour deepening through shades of ochre into indigo until its scales hardened into brittle armour and shone blacker than the night, its sting turning dark violet and retreating into the poison sac, dripping with lethal venom. Gurgling with delight, Kruel placed the weed worm on Kerzolde's arm and watched it slowly climb between his armoured scales up towards his neck. Kruel clambered after it, laughing, and plucked it back, putting it on Arbel's arm.

'Erm, erm,' he chanted, prodding its shining black scales and making it arch its back and stab the needle sting towards Arbel's bare skin. Arbel sweated, his muscles tensing into knots. 'Erm, erm,' Arbel repeated, forcing himself to remain steady as the weed worm slowly crawled towards the darkness in the folds of his cloak. Kruel turned his head, the worm forgotten, and stared at the black carrion crows feasting on the Nightbeasts' carcasses.

Tilting his head he listened to them and watched their cruel sharp beaks tear at the rotten flesh. 'Caw, caw,' he called, shrilly imitating their voices and the biggest crow tore away a long sliver of flesh then alighted on his shoulder to press the dead flesh into Kruel's mouth.

Kerzolde laughed as he watched the baby chew on the meat. 'Armoured worms with deadly stings hidden in our pockets and black crows to set against the Battle Owls, what next will the Master's seed find to help him take Elundium as his own?'

'Everything he touches reflects the darkness,' whispered Arbel, carefully pushing Kruel into the opening at the top of Kerzolde's battle jerkin. The crow squawked and bit at

Kerzolde's claw before it settled on the Nightbeast's shoulder.

Arbel carefully shook Erm out of the dark folds of his cloak and grimly picked up the armoured worm. 'Kruel will want Erm close to him,' he laughed, slipping the worm inside Kerzolde's jerkin.

Kerzolde snarled and shuddered, waiting for the needle sting to strike and he cursed Arbel, but all he felt were Erm's tiny claws scuttling across his chest towards the place where Kruel had settled to sleep.

'We must find the Shadowlands you whispered of in the City of Night,' Kerhunge hissed. 'You said they were some-where we would be safe from the sharp-eyed owls and foul warriors.'

Kerzolde nodded, turned and searched the dark horizon. 'They are out there!' he said, pointing with a sweep of his one good claw. 'Out beyond the shoulders of Mantern's Mountain, and you shall smell the shifting shadows over there where the air is dark and heavy!'

The fortress of Underfall and Thane's crowning lay many daylights behind them as Thane reined Esteron to a halt and shook the dust of the long journey from his shoulders while he gazed in wonder at the Granite City. Elionbel halted Stumble beside him and gasped as her eyes swept over the sheer granite walls, each one seeming to rest balanced upon the one below as the inner circles rose up to meet the eaves of Candlebane Hall, still shadowed beneath its steep, weather–bleached roof.

'It was worth a dozen daylights of hard riding ahead of the people to see the new City. Nevian spoke of Willow's promise to rebuild the Granite City out of the Nightbeast rubble but look at it, a wonder of all Elundium!' Thane whispered standing in his stirrups and leaning forward for a better view.

Behind them hoofbeats sounded on the Greenway and Willow brought Starlight to a halt in a cloud of dust. Her sides were sweat-streaked and her nostrils were wide as she laboured for breath. 'Lord!' Willow cried, jumping lightly to the ground and running to Thane's stirrup. 'I have ridden hard to keep pace with you but Starlight is no match for Esteron and Stumble!'

Thane laughed, dismounted and helped Elion to the ground. 'I wanted to see the city, Willow. I wanted to see what you had done with those piles of rubble left like tidal wreckage by the Nightbeast siege.'

'Well, my Lord?' answered Willow, nervously blinking his large round eyes. 'Our skill with picks and shovels was learned beneath the Nightbeasts' lash, I fear we had no knowledge of the daylight or how to raise a city above the ground.'

Elionbel took Willow's hand and pointed at the tall Tower, the gentle sloping roofs and soft angles of the pink stone houses. 'The colours and the shapes are beautiful,' she whispered, 'but I thought that granite was grey.'

'We used the powdered stone and mixed it with coloured mortar to mirror the sunlight at dawn,' ventured Willow. 'It echoes all the glory of the sunshine,' he continued, not quite sure whether Thane liked what he saw.

Thane laughed easily and put his arm around Willow's shoulder. 'It is a wonder beyond words. But how many windows are there in the Great Wall?'

'Windows? There are no windows, my Lord; there are a thousand walkways that lead out into the sunshine. Each wall is a hollow colonnade with inner courtyards full of soft shadows and places to rest.'

'How could you defend such a place?' Elionbel asked, a shadow of worry crossing her face.

'Defend?' laughed Thane. 'Who would we need to defend it against? The Nightmare is dead and the warriors who would not have me as their King have vanished just as Nevian foretold. Elundium is free of all foul Nightbeasts' shadows. Come, let us ride to the Great Gates.'

'Lord,' Willow hesitated, 'my people are still in the City. Let me ride on before you and lead them out.'

Thane frowned. 'I promised your people could stay wherever they wished in all Elundium. If your people want to stay in the Granite City then it shall be theirs, but—' Thane paused, remembering the long column of city folk slowly following along the Greenway in their hoofprints '—but I would ask that your people delay their choice until all the city folk who survived the Nightbeast siege and the long secret road of escape have returned to the places they once called their own within the City.'

Willow blushed and knelt. 'Lord, we had such joy just being free beneath the sunshine and gazing at the canopy of bright stars filling the night sky overhead that none of my people have claimed a single dwelling within the City. It was a great blessing to give our labour as we chose and rest whenever we wished upon the broad walkways that crown the high walls of each circle of the City.'

Thane laughed and pulled Willow to his feet. 'I see hard daylights of labour and little time taken for rest. Come, Willow Leaf, Master mason, and lead us to the threshold of your triumph for you have truly built a city fit for Kings.'

Elionbel remounted Stumble but for a moment she held him on the bridle while she looked back along the dusty Greenway towards Woodsedge. Sadly she shook her head, it was less than two daylights behind them yet she still saw clearly the shattered timbers of the ruined doorway and the Nightmare's footprints burned into the threshold stone. 'I could not enter,' she whispered to herself, 'I did not have the courage to disturb old memories.'

Thane had entered the ruined Wayhouse and knelt beside her father, comforting him for the lonely times ahead. 'Come with us,' he had urged, 'and share in the new Eludium.' But Tombel had shaken his head, begging Thane to let him dwell in the ruins of Woodsedge. Turning his head towards the broken stairway he had insisted that he could hear Martbel's footsteps and wished to remain there with her.

Thane shivered and had taken Tombel's hand, remembering her last shout as the one-eyed Nightbeast had plunged his dagger into her. 'She will be with you always,' he had answered, 'here or in the Granite City. Everywhere you call her name, she will be there. Come to us soon and rejoice in our wedding ties.'

Tombel had looked up, smiling gently. 'I will dwell here in Martbel's memory until the warriors and city folk who follow us on the Greenway crowd the broken doors of Woodsedge, then with my grief put aside I shall march before them to the gates of the City.'

Thane had smiled and risen to his feet. 'My grandfather, Thoron, will stay with you for he will bring you comfort. We will wait for both of you to reach the gates of the Granite City before we announce the day of the wedding.'

Tombel had smiled through his grief and accompanied Thane out of the Wayhouse, walking with him as far as the Greenways' edge. 'I will come to you soon, daughter,' he had whispered, gathering her in his arms, and together they had wept, sharing their grief.

Elionbel had looked across her father's shoulder through the broken doorway and had seen the shadow of happier daylights. 'I cannot enter, Father,' she whispered, 'but when time has grown a skin across the wounds and I can stand in the stone-flagged hall without seeing Krulshards' face in every shadow then I shall once more be able to call Woodsedge my home.'

He had nodded, blinking at the flood of tears coursing down his cheeks and Thoron took his arm, turning him slowly back towards the ruined door. 'I will bring Tombel to the gates of the Granite City and we will laugh again in happier times,' he called as the empty shell of Woodsedge had swallowed them up.

Elionbel sighed, shook her head to scatter the memories of

97

their parting and turned Stumble to follow Thane. Mulcade hooted and stooped to her shoulder, pressing his talons gently into the soft blue weave of her cloak. Smiling, she lifted her hand and ruffled the owl's chest feathers. 'You are a great comfort,' she whispered, urging Stumble into a canter to keep pace with Esteron.

'Wonder of wonders!' Thane laughed, bringing Esteron to a halt and dismounting before the new gates of the City. Reaching out he touched the smooth pink walls, marvelling at their soft, almost transparent surface. Behind him a great shout of surprise mingled with the hoofbeats that thundered on the Greenway and he turned, hands on hips, and waited.

'It looks a little different from the last time you saw it,' he laughed, striding forwards to greet Breakmaster, Errant and the rest of the company who had ridden with him from the crowning on the Causeway Field.

'Lord, we could not believe it, we thought magic was in the air – the colours, the . . .' Breakmaster dismounted, his voice falling into a whisper as he stared open-mouthed at the new city. He reached out a gnarled and leathery hand to touch the iron studwork lacing the new gates in bold patterns. 'Willow!' he cried, spinning round. 'This was a pile of splintered wood and stone choke that lay beneath a fog of granite dust. You have worked a wonder.'

Willow laughed and spread his hands nervously. 'Nevian, the Master of Magic, walked with me through the ruins. He told me the history of each place that we passed.'

'But it is so different,' gasped Grey Goose, stepping carefully through the shadows of the gates and staring at the archways and the colonnades running along the base of the great wall. Where once mean and narrow houses had crowded together he now saw broad windows that looked out across neat, cobbled streets. 'There is more space, and it is so beautiful,' he added, shouldering his bow.

Willow smiled. 'Nevian only talked of what had been, he told us nothing of how the City had looked before the

Nightbeast siege. He counselled us to rejoice in our freedom from the darkness and let our hearts dictate how the City should grow.'

'It reflects your love of the sunlight,' laughed Thane. 'All those arched windows almost seem to turn as petals on a flower to follow the path of the sun as it travels towards World's End. And you have a fountain beside the gate, how did you work that wonder?'

Willow looked towards the plume of sparkling ice-cold water that bubbled into a narrow ornamental stone trough. 'It rises beside Candlebane Hall, my Lord,' he answered, 'amongst the rubble of the fallen granite Tower.'

'The Armoury!' cried Breakmaster. 'It must be the underground river we dammed to escape along the secret road. The Master mason said it would flood and fill the tunnel behind us.'

Willow shook his head. 'We knew not where it came from but we rejoiced to have such pure water and brought it by spiralling channels down through each level of the city, feeding it into a dozen fountains before it reached the shadow of the great gate. I thought that weary travellers could drink from the wayside cup to mark the end of their journey, or perhaps before setting out . . .'

Willow's voice trailed away. A long dustcloud wound back along the Greenway marking the column of city folk and warriors. His people were hurrying out through the gates, kneeling silently for a moment before Thane to lay their masonry tools on the Greenways' edge and then crowding along the edges of the deep dykes that lay in the shadow at the base of the outer wall. Thane took the wayside cup and dipped it into the fountain. Turning, he lifted the cup steadily in his hand.

'My friends,' he called in a strong voice, 'before you stands the new Granite City. Let every traveller, old or young, drink from the wayside cup before they pass through the gates. Let it be our custom, our sign of peace and friendship to begin or end the Greenway Road with the wayside cup.'

Thane lifted the cup to his lips and began to drink. Elionbel took the silver finger bowl that had been her love token to Thane from beneath her cloak and dipped it into the fountain. Although battered and defiled by Krulshards' skinless hands it still shone, catching the reflections of the sunlight and showed clearly her name engraved with Thane's along the rim. 'Look!' she whispered, touching Thane's arm. 'Each one of those who rode with us has a finger bowl attached to their belts. They are all raising them to salute us!'

Breakmaster laughed and drew a small wooden finger bowl from beneath his cloak which he dipped into the fountain. 'The story of how you sent Thane the finger bowl as a token of your love has gone from camp fire to camp fire spreading faster than the flames that devoured the kindling wood. The love between you has touched everybody's hearts. Grown men weep when they tell how Thane crossed Elundium all alone to resue you, Elionbel, from the City of Night; of how when all seemed lost and he lay weak and helpless in the marsh upon a mat of reeds he held up the tiny finger bowl and Rockspray, the great Battle Owl, took it in his talons and delivered it into Kyot's hands, who came to rescue you. '

Thane smiled, a faraway look misting his eyes, and linked his arm through Elionbel's. 'Much gets forgotten in the telling, Breakmaster,' he answered. 'What of Stumble's great race on the Nightmare's heels, what of Ogion and Ousious, the grey swans of doom, who sacrificed their sweet voices that I might rescue Elionbel?'

'Many threads were pulled, Lord. A few are forgotten and still the story takes a whole night to tell and the grey hours are touching the sky before the part where Willow Leaf breaks into the high chamber, bringing daylight into the City of Night.'

Thane laughed and placed the wayside cup beside the fountain before lightly springing up into Esteron's saddle.

Cantering forwards he pirouetted between the gates, casting sparks across the cobbles. 'Lest we forget from this daylight forwards I name this the Stumble Gate in honour of the bravest relay horse in all Elundium who carried me tirelessly on the Nightmare's heels to rescue Elionbel!' he shouted.

Stumble neighed furiously, arched his neck and struck bright sparks with his hooves before kneeling for Elionbel to mount. 'I will never forget,' she whispered, leaning forwards to caress his neck then urging him to follow Thane up the broad cobbled way to Candlebane Hall and the one remaining Tower of Granite. Behind her the shouts of the company gradually faded into silence until all she could hear in the empty city was Stumble's measured hoofbeats as they entered the highest level and halted before the wall hiding Candle-bane Hall.

Thane had dismounted, and waited at the beginning of the long ramp Willow had raised that wound its way up towards the top of the wall. 'Come with me, Elionbel, my Queen,' he laughed, holding out his hand to her.

Elionbel laughed, jumped to the ground, gathered her skirts and cloak hems into a bunch and chased after Thane, catching her hand in his. Side by side they breasted the last step and stood on top of the wall. 'I have been here before,' she whispered, the colour draining from her face as she remembered. She shook her head and blinked back her tears then turned to look out across the sparkling new City. 'I told him we would defeat him,' she hissed through brittle, clenched lips. 'I told him he could not destroy the beauty of Elundium.'

'Who?' asked Thane, shading his eyes and following her gaze across the bright sun-washed roofs that spread out below them.

'Krulshards!' she hissed, her eyes glittering with hatred.

Turning her, he held her close, pressing his lips softly against hers. 'Rejoice, my love,' he whispered. 'Rejoice to stand here again, for you can trample on the place where he thought he had conquered the daylight and cast a sun-shadow across these stones to swallow up his burned black marks.'

Shakily, Elionbel nodded and moved to the exact spot where Krulshards had defiled her mother. Boiling with anger she lifted her foot and stamped on the blackened stones. She spread her cloak to pass a shadow across the top of the wall and, turning, she stared hard at the stones then caught her breath as she watched them turn pure white in the sunlight.

'You see, he is destroyed and gone forever,' Thane whispered, putting his arm around her shoulder and leading her across the wall towards the slender clear spanned stone bridge that curved across the water to meet the broad stone steps leading to Candlebane Hall.

'Wonders of Elundium!' he cried, his foot on the narrow bridge. 'Willow told us the water for the fountain rose from the rubble of the fallen Tower but, look, the inner circle of the city has become a deep lake. At least twenty of the steps that once followed the wall down to the cobblestones below are now under water. Candlebane Hall is an island that rises sheer in the clear water.'

'The swans!' Elion gasped, squeezing his hand. 'Look, they are nesting amongst the flowers and bulrushes that Willow must have planted amongst the boulders of the fallen Tower.'

'Swanwater. This shall be the new Swanwater,' cried Thane, running down a shallow flight of steps, his ironshod boots echoing as he followed the inner curve of the granite wall. Kneeling on the bottom step he stared into the cold deep water before he reached out his hand towards the swans amongst the fallen rubble. 'You have truly blessed this city by making it your home and I promise you will have my protection for as long as I live,' called out Thane.

Ogion and Ousious turned their heads at Thane's voice, entered the water and swam silently to where he knelt. 'It is yours forever,' Elion whispered, running her hand across

102

Ousious' pure white chest feathers. She felt for the Nightmare's wound but it had completely healed. The swans bent their necks, hissing softly and brushed their bright orange beaks against Thane and Elionbel. Turning, they swam out into the lake and took to the air, beating the clear water into a sparkling silver spray beneath their wings.

'Yours forever!' shouted Thane, sweeping the summer scarf above his head to catch all the beauty of the summer sunlight. 'Yours forever!'

Shadowlands

Pushing the baby deep within his jerkin Kerzolde led Kerhunge and Arbel away from the ring of Nightbeast carcasses, following the scent of dark winds into the Shadowlands. They vanished amongst the streaky ghost tails of mist that boiled out to engulf them from the shifting fog banks lying across their path. Soon they were lost, stumbling blindly between the stunted wind-bent tangletrees or falling headlong in a rattle of armour into deep rock-choked hollows. Arbel stopped the two Nightbeasts, drawing them down into a hollow and shouting to them above the roaring winds that no one would ever find them in this desolate place; they would be safe here from the warriors and the sharp-eyed owls.

Cursing and snarling, the Nightbeasts had nodded in agreement before seeking the most sheltered side of the hollow to fashion a rough shelter from the jumble of broken boulders and wind-cracked rocks scattered all about them.

Kruel had grown quickly, stretching taller with each shadowy daylight and feeding greedily on the dark carrion meats Arbel or the Nightbeasts scavenged from beyond their hollow. He had become strong-boned yet graceful, quick-witted and inquisitive, searching everything, turning over every stone and pebble, looking in every secret place. Now he knelt beside their rough shelter with his eyes fixed unblinking on a dark crack. 'Come to me,' he whispered, letting the words fall almost noiselessly in the dry barren air of the

Shadowlands. Before him sharp claws dug beneath the ground, two bright eyes blinked in the darkness of the crack.

'Come to me,' he whispered again, lowering his slender fingers into the darkness. Smiling, he felt the sleek body of the shadow rat shrink away from his touch. With a shout of triumph he hooked his fingers behind the rat's two sharp cutting teeth and pulled it clear of its nest. It shrieked as he swung it above his head, flinging it high into the air, and laughing as he caught it by the tail. 'You are mine!' he shrieked, biting it savagely behind the ear, sinking his teeth deep into the rat's flesh.

'No! No!' shouted Arbel leaping to his feet. 'Do not kill it, make it serve you, Kruel. Make it a part of the darkness.'

Kruel hesitated, his piercing eyes narrowing as he dangled the rat by its tail. 'Part of my darkness?' he repeated, sitting back on his haunches and stroking the rat's grey fur.

Arbel nodded and leant forwards. 'Kerzolde, Kerhunge and I are not enough to take Elundium. To claim all Krulshards' darkness you must control armies of men to set against the warriors, and armies of birds and beasts to set against the Warhorses and the Battle Owls.'

Kruel sank his head on to his chest and drew dark patterns in the dust with the terrified rat, remembering all the one-eyed Nightbeast had taught him of his father, Krulshards, and the darkness that Thanehand, the Galloperspawn, had taken from him. 'Darkness!' he muttered, lifting up the rat. 'How can I spread the darkness with creatures like this?'

Arbel smiled and lifted Kruel up on to his knee. 'When you are full-grown we will sweep across Elundium bringing darkness and despair wherever we go.'

Kerzolde grunted and nodded his hideous head. 'We will strip the skin from Thanehand while he is alive and make our new Master a beautiful suit of armour.'

'We will feed on his bones,' snarled Kerhunge, from where he searched amongst the rocks for food. 'If we have any teeth left to chew with after living on these rotten grubs.'

Kerzolde spat on the ground and threw a dry, gnawed bone at his brother then cursed him into silence. 'You have much power, Kruel,' he spluttered, turning back and dribbling on the boy's head. 'Power to defy the sunlight and stand shadowless against it. Power to spread your darkness through whatever you touch.'

'Make the rat a part of your darkness,' urged Arbel. 'Just like the weed worm.'

Kruel laughed and brought the frightened rat to his lips, kissing and licking at the wound on his neck. 'You shall be mine,' he whispered, watching the sleek grey fur darken and grow brittle beneath his touch into a mass of needle spines that rattled as it trembled in his hands. Putting the black shadow rat down upon the ground he pushed it firmly with his foot, sending it scuttling towards his hole.

'Fetch me more darkness,' he commanded, standing and digging in the pocket of the rough breeches Arbel had fashioned for him to wear. Crying with delight he pulled out the weed worm and set it on the ground beside the rat. 'Fetch me darkness,' he commanded again, touching the arched sting with his toe and pushing the black-armoured worm away from the rocky hollow they used as a refuge from the biting dark winds sweeping across the Shadowlands.

Arbel smiled and rubbed his hands together. He had watched Kruel growing stronger, seeming to squeeze whole suns of time out of each daylight and he knew that they would soon take the road back into Elundium. Catching these small animals and vermin was only a beginning. Bending, he stared hopefully at the black crack in the rocks, expecting a horde of black rats to appear but nothing happened. Sighing, he rose to his feet, wrapped his cloak tightly above his shoulders and went out to search for food.

Kruel followed Arbel with his eyes then frowned and climbed up into Kerzolde's arms. He curled into a ball and settled down to sleep. 'Is Arbel my brother?' he whispered.

'Only I tasted it in his blood when we first met and I feel it each time we touch.'

Kerzolde hesitated. He had kept the blood tie between Arbel and the boy a secret, afraid of the power they may hold between them. 'Master,' he answered slowly, wiping his one good claw across his mouth. 'The Marcher Arbel came upon me in the Wayhouse of Woodsedge, he drove me out from feasting on your mother's servers. He may have ties for they both came from the same Wayhouse.'

Kruel scratched at Kerzolde's armoured hide, digging beneath the scales. 'It is time for the truth,' he whispered, looking up and holding the Nightbeast's gaze.

Kerzolde grunted and tried to shrink away from the piercing eyes. He could feel them probing, stripping back his secrets, looking deep into his rotten black heart. 'Master,' he whispered again, growing giddy with the lies that waited to tumble off his ragged purple tongue.

'I know the truth,' whispered the boy, closing his eyes and letting the Nightbeast escape from his pitiless stare. He had looked deeper than ever before, stretching his dark powers that nudged and whispered at him, peeling back every moment of Kerzolde's life from the time of his spawning deep within the City of Night. Frowning, he shook Kerzolde. 'Look at me!' he shouted, feeling anger course through his small body. Digging his fingernails savagely between the Nightbeast's armoured scales he felt his muscles tighten. 'I want the truth about Elundium. The truth about my father, Krulshards, not the tangle of dark images and half-lies you have fed me on.'

Kerzolde tried to cower backwards but Kruel held on to him, seeming to grow, to swell with the power. 'Master, I only tell you truths as I see them,' he cried, catching his breath as he watched the pale skin on the boy's forehead begin to stretch and tighten, the fire-red veins on his temples blackening beneath the surface.

Kruel hesitated, looking from his hands to his arms, letting

Kerzolde go. Something was happening, something ... He reached up and touched his forehead, feeling the racing pulse on his temples. A voice was calling him, a voice from somewhere inside. His head shouted, telling him, urging him to grow. Frowning he ran his fingers across the smooth, taut skin towards a spot that burned with a black fire beneath his golden curls. 'Krulshards!' he cried. 'Father, Father!'

As his fingers found the place, a ridge of brittle skin, he sighed with relief then pressed his nails into it and the hot fire faded a little. His fingers felt warm and blood-wet. Laughing, he dug them deeper and split the skin, releasing the tightness in his head and sending the voice inside to a whisper. Breathing deeply he drew his blood-sticky fingernails down his forehead and along the bridge of his nose.

'Master Kruel!' Kerzolde cried, reaching out in real terror as the boy threw back his head, pulled at the loose ends of skin and peeled them down across his eye lids. Looking down he picked at the raw bundles of sinews and pushed them up under his cheekbones then shook his head violently, releasing a tangle of black locks that had lain hidden from the moment of his birth beneath the skin on the top of his head.

'Kruel!' whispered the Nightbeasts in awe. 'Beneath the surface you are very like your father.'

Kruel stared at Kerzolde for a moment, blinking the blood out of his eyes. 'No, I am more, much more!'

'But you are in his image,' answered Kerzolde, making to touch the boy's skinless arm with his one good claw.

'No! Do not touch!' shouted Kruel, jumping to the ground and struggling to pull the loose skin off his shoulders. Biting at his fingertips he released each finger in turn then he bent double and trod on his empty hands to wriggle free his arms. Stretching and flexing the raw grey muscles in his shoulders he stretched up and cried out as the cold wind bit into his exposed nerves. 'No!' he screamed again as Kerzolde spread his arms to protect him from the bitter cold. 'Do not touch me,' he snarled, crouching down and curling his naked lips.

Without a pause he wrenched at the hanging folds of skin, splitting them across his chest and tearing them down over the slight bulge of his belly, forcing the wet, bloody tailends of skin over his thighs, pulling it away from his knees and calves until he stood, shivering and raw, naked and glistening, a mass of sinews and muscle.

Staring at Kerzolde he began to laugh. White teeth and pale eyes mocked as he bent and gathered up the heap of blood-sticky skin. 'I am both man and Nightmare. I am both darkness and light. The voice in my head shows me the power and tells me the truth.'

'Does Krulshards speak to you?' asked the Nightbeast, creeping forwards on his knees.

Kruel smiled, his blood-wet lips drawn back into a sneer. 'My father is dead. I am the only power of darkness.'

'What does the voice tell you that I have not already taught you? I know the truth, I was there at Krulshards' side.'

'Truth?' snarled the boy, retreating into the deepest part of the shelter and squatting on the ground. 'You see the truth through a dark curtain and it distorts and twists everything, turning the warriors of Elundium into giants and giving their Battle Owls the wings of eagles. I have looked into you and seen your truth.'

'But, but . . .' stuttered Kerzolde, stumbling forwards, 'I hide nothing.'

'Nothing?' sneered the boy bringing the first handful of skin to his mouth and devouring it greedily. 'I saw more than Arbel, I saw two Marchers and a blonde girl in your heart, Kerzolde. Who are they?'

Kerzolde paled, the bristly hair on the nape of his blunt neck rising in waves of fear. 'The Elionbel! She tried to stab you moments after your birth. She cursed you and swore to destroy you.'

Kruel laughed, cramming his mouth full of skin. 'She is but a weak woman, nothing,' he mumbled, pushing the loose ends of skin between his teeth.

'No, Master, she is blood-tied to you,' whispered Kerzolde, 'just as much as the Marcher, Arbel, and that may give her power. I was only holding the truth until you were stronger.'

Kruel frowned, the grey flesh wrinkling across his forehead. He had felt a bond with the Marcher but what of the Elionbel? In her he saw only hate, raw hate, and not one moment of love or worship.

'I will eat her,' he laughed, finishing the last mouthful of skin as he looked down at his fingernails and toenails that lay in the palm of his hand. 'When all Elundium is mine and she stands before me bound in chains, then in the first moment of real darkness I shall eat her!'

'Yes! Yes!' Kerzolde agreed and crept nervously forwards until he knelt a pace away from Kruel. 'Master, you have grown taller and a new skin is forming, stronger and darker than the birth skin you have just climbed out of.'

Kruel pushed his finger– and toenails into place then stood up. He stretched and flexed his fingers, touching the drying skin. 'It hides my purpose,' he laughed, reaching for the breeches that lay on the ground beside him. Shivering, he turned his head and looked down at his upper arm where he found a large, irregular patch of raw flesh that ran from his shoulder to his elbow and where the new skin did not meet. Carefully he picked at the edges trying to pull them together.

'You have grown, Master, and the new skin does not quite cover but we can hide your arm beneath a cloak or a jerkin. The Marcher will sew or find you one.'

Kruel shook his head angrily and cursed the skin, spitting at the ground. 'What will happen next time I grow? What does this new skin cover?'

A shout of delight filled the hollow making both Kruel and Kerzolde jump and look over the ruin of broken boulders. Arbel ran towards them with something cupped in his hands. 'Kruel! Kruel!' he shouted, descending into the hollow and opening his hands to reveal a baby shadow rat with a brittle black coat. In speechless astonishment he looked at the new-

110

grown boy. 'Kruel!' he cried dropping the rat and reaching out to touch the tangle of dead locks that spilled across his forehead and created a strange contrast with the piercing pale blue eyes.

Kruel smiled and caught Arbel's wrist. 'There is blood between us! You are a part of me!'

Arbel froze. 'Brothers? We are brothers?'

'Yes, yes!' laughed Kruel. 'The Marcherwoman, Martbel, spawned us both. I drew the truth of it from deep inside Kerzolde, he was there in the City of Night at the moment of my birth.'

'Brothers,' repeated Arbel. Now he knew that what he had pretended could not have happened was the truth. He knew that the Marcherwoman Kerzolde had whispered of was his mother. He shuddered and began to turn away, remembering Martbel from the sunshine daylights of Woodsedge but Kruel tightened his grip on Arbel's wrist and pulled him back, holding his gaze and seeing a glimpse of the agony he was suffering.

'She spawned us both!' he hissed. 'You in the daylight and me in the darkness. We were not the Masters of yesterday but together we hold the power to make tomorrow.'

Arbel blinked at a tear, the first he had shed since Krulshards had cast the nightmesh about his ankles, and put his arms around Kruel's shoulders. 'I love the darkness but there is a part of Elundium I cannot escape from.'

Kruel laughed, bent and snatched up the baby black rat by its tail. 'The memory will fade as we grow in power. All the daylight will be swallowed up. Look how the light weakens around the body of this rat.'

Arbel sang quietly to himself as he honed the rusty spearblade he had salvaged from the circle of dead Nightbeasts into a glittering razor-sharp edge. Kerhunge rolled over in the bottom of the hollow, muttering and cursing in his sleep. Suddenly he cried out and jumped to his feet, clawing

111

frantically at something attached to the soft skin beneath his arm.

'Erm!' laughed Kruel seeing what had startled the Night-beast. Quickly he crossed the hollow and carefully pulled the weed worm's needle-sharp sting out of Kerhunge's arm, whispering and stroking the shiny black worm with its armoured scales as he slipped it back into his pocket.

'Master,' cried Kerhunge, staring at his hands, 'look!'

Arbel and Kerzolde crossed the hollow and stared down at Kerhunge. Kruel took one of the Nightbeast's coarse hairy hands and slowly turned it over, following the black shadow spreading along Kerhunge's fingers. He laughed and looked up into the Nightbeast's face. 'Erm carries my darkness,' he cried, watching Kerhunge's skin change through deep indigo into deepest shadow, then gradually the colour lightened until Kerhunge had almost returned to his normal rancid colouring.

Kruel leered, the seeds of an idea forming in his mind. Bending down he whistled, calling in a high-pitched shriek until the centre of the hollow was seething with sleek black shadow rats making a brittle rattle as they moved. Stretching his hand out he caught one of the rats by the tail and held it out to Arbel. 'They carry my darkness, brother. Let it bite you to see if it fills a Marcher with my shadows.'

'No, No!' cried Arbel, hastily stepping backwards and throwing his arms out in alarm.

Kruel took a step towards him, dangling the rat by his fingertips. 'You must obey me,' he sneered, holding Arbel still with his eyes.

The rats in the centre of the hollow had turned towards Arbel, following Kruel's voice, their red eyes staring, their brittle spines quivering. Slowly he bared his arm, unable to resist, but his jaw was locked in a grim line of terror as he watched Kruel bring the rat to him. Its nostrils twitched and it sniffed at the hairs that had risen along Arbel's arm. It scratched at his skin with its sharp cold claws then bit savagely at him, sinking two long curved teeth into the flesh of his arm. Arbel screamed, the holding spell broken, and lashed out at the rat, sending it flying out across the hollow.

Crouching, he pinched the wound between two fingers to stop the flow of blood and stared hatefully at Kruel. Kruel stared back without a moment's remorse, watching Arbel's skin carefully, searching for the shadows. 'There is the darkness,' he whispered with joy, pointing with a sharp fingernail at the blood–stained skin around the wound.

Arbel tried to cry out. His fingers were tingling with cold black shadow, the darkness was travelling through his veins, showing as starkly as winter trees etched against a pale, rain-washed sky. The blood rushed and bubbled through his head, pounding in his ears. Kruel was laughing, holding him, growing, smothering him with warm darkness. He tried to move, to follow Kruel's dancing steps but his legs were too heavy. He tried to touch, but his hand was too numb. He tried to shout but his mouth fell open in dry silence. He was now a part of the darkness, the total blackness of deepest night, lost and blind to the weak sunlight that shone across the Shadowlands. Somewhere in the darkness he could hear the whispers of Kruel's breath and the groan of stones splitting into a thousand grains of sand. A hand was shaking him, pulling him out of the darkness. Kruel was laughing, slapping his face, each handprint getting sharper and more painful.

'Brother! Brother, wake up!' Kruel cried, dancing with delight, pulling at Arbel's hand.

Arbel shook his head and stumbled forwards. His feet were still numb and it felt as if he was walking on his ankles. 'What happened?' he gasped, flinching with pain as the weave of his cloak brushed against the ratbite on his forearm.

'My darkness was in you,' cried Kruel. 'One tiny bite and you were full of shadows. Blackness billowed around you. Look at your skin–the darkness lingers.'

Arbel held up his hands and stared at the dark mass of

113

veins that pulsed just beneath the skin. The numbness was receding to a tingling in his fingertips, the skin colour of his hand lightened, but the tangle of veins still showed winterblack. Turning to Kruel, he shook his head. 'I already love and worship you, brother, it was no test of your power for me to feel the wonder of darkness. It was just a cruel trick, forcing me to take that ratbite.'

Kruel laughed and took Arbel's arm, licking at the swollen, angry wound, soothing it with his tongue. 'Test or not, the shadow rats do more than just carry the darkness in the colour of their coats, they will give it to each warrior they bite. Come, brother, it is time to leave the Shadowlands and try a little darkness on Elundium.'

'Master, you are not strong enough,' cried Kerzolde. 'Wait until you are fully grown then we will take all Elundium as our own.'

'Fool!' snarled Kruel, pushing the Nightbeast aside. 'We will creep in secret, a shadow rat or two in attendance and see how much darkness they can make.'

'But you have nothing to set against the standard of Thanehand the Galloperspawn,' cried Kerzolde as he was roughly pushed aside, 'and there are only three of us to defend you!'

'Standard!' hissed Kruel, closing his hand around Kerzolde's iron collar and pulling him to his feet. 'What is this standard the Galloperspawn carries?'

'A foul picture of the sun, Master, it shines with white fire and burned blindness into our eyes as we fought to defend your father, Krulshards,' cried Kerzolde.

'A hideous standard,' spat Kerhunge, 'that drew the warriors of Elundium wherever it flew above the battle field; thicker than hungry maggots on a fresh carcass they flocked about his bright rag.'

'Side by side with the foul emblem of the owl in blue and gold,' muttered Arbel from where he stood on the high rim of the hollow with his back to the shifting fog banks as he looked out towards the distant peaks marking the edge of the Shadowlands and the beginnings of Elundium. 'Together they hold so much power.'

Kruel frowned and picked at the raw flesh on his upper arm, trying in vain to draw both edges of his new skin together. 'We must have our own standard to set against the picture of the sun. Something so powerful it will swallow the light.'

'As black as Krulshards' malice,' whispered Kerzolde, beginning the steep climb out of the hollow.

'My father's cloak!' cried Kruel, pulling Kerzolde back into the hollow. 'That would have the power to swallow daylight. But where is it?'

Kerzolde paled and shrank away.

'Where?' shouted Kruel, forcing the Nightbeast to look into his eyes. 'Where is it?' he whispered, searching back into Kerzolde, seeing through his eyes their perilous escape, the dark culvert boiling with angry water, the high doors of Underfall and the frozen Kings beneath the ground.

'Where?' he hissed, searching and finding the narrow crack and squeezing into the beautiful darkness of the City of Night. Laughing, he took Kerzolde's hands and through him followed the winding roads that spiralled upwards through the empty silence until he reached the high chamber and shuddered to see the broken roof, the heaps of Nightbeast dead. Everywhere the noise of battle shouted at him, forcing him to jump backwards. He cried out as Battle Owls stooped, savage Border Runners snarled and War Horses reared and plunged. Above his head the bright banner of the sun was carried by two owls before him in the centre of the chamber. Thanehand laughed and gloated and shouted something as he drove a glittering sword double-handed into towering black shadows. 'Father!' Kruel cried as he watched Krulshards' last moment in the bright spark-light that danced and burnt along the blade as it pierced his father's heart. 'Father,' he whispered again as the sword sheared through his backbone and fused in a blinding flash of light with the column of rock. Weakly he let Kerzolde go, for now he knew where to look for the malice.

'We must enter the City of Night. Come, Kerzolde, lead us back into the darkness.'

'The gates are sealed against us, Master. There is no way into the City of Night.'

'You lie! You lie, you black-scaled beast, there is a way through the tomb of frozen Kings. I saw it clearly in your heart.'

'Master, we would never be able to creep past all those foul warriors who guard the fortress of Underfall. It was pure luck we escaped by that secret road.'

Kruel laughed and whistled to the shadow rats. 'The Palace of Kings shall be mine,' he shouted, scrambling up over the hollow's rim. 'Mine! Mine! Mine! It will be the first part of Elundium to become a part of the darkness, my darkness!'

A Night to Remember

Thane eased himself against the back of the Honour Chair
and let the noise and laughter that filled the Great Hall pass
over his head, to vanish in the hanging flags and battle
emblems covering the walls. Smiling, he watched the servers
clear a space before each guest and place there a finely
hammered silver cup bound by a broken chain. Quickly the
hall fell silent and all eyes turned expectantly towards the
King. Thane nodded to the Master Server and tall pitchers
of sparkling water drawn from the fountain beside the
Stumble Gate were taken from table to table until each tiny
finger bowl had been filled to the brim.

'We will wait,' commanded Thane, turning his eyes
towards the doors and tilting his head to one side as he
listened.

Breakmaster caught Thane's eye and barely nodded, showing that he was ready for the moment when the doors would
swing open. Elionbel frowned and fidgeted with the lace ends
of her sleeves. 'Whom do we await?' she asked in a whisper,
leaning close to Thane.

But he only smiled and answered, 'Listen and watch the
door.'

Far away the sound of tramping feet and hoofbeats echoed
in the lower circles of the City. Mulcade hooted and stooped
from the Kingpost beam above the fireplace to perch battle-
ready on Thane's shoulder. Footsteps echoed beside the
hoofbeats on the broad winding stairs. Warriors, Marchers,

Archers, all made to rise but Thane bade them to stay with the palm of his hand. Standing, he lifted his finger bowl and cried a greeting as the tall doors were flung open.

'Welcome to Tombel, the greatest Marcher Captain in all Elundium who has triumphed over the shadows of despair and to Thoron, the great Galloper. Together they lead the people of Elundium back into their city.'

'Welcome!' shouted the guests, rising as one.

Elionbel dropped her cup, rose to her feet and ran to her father, throwing her arms about his ancient shoulders. 'Father, oh, Father,' she cried, weeping with joy.

Thane looked past them, a gentle smile softening his face. 'Grandfather,' he said, quietly offering Thoron the finger bowl, 'all Elundium welcomes you into the city, for you brought hope in the morning and chased away our fears at night. Without your quiet courage all would have been lost.'

Thoron smiled, drank from the cup and shook his head. 'No, Thane,' he laughed, giving the cup back and lifting his hand to stroke Equestrius' muzzle, 'it was the courage of the Warhorses, the Border Runners and the Battle Owls; without them we could have been lost in the shadows.'

Thane laughed and ran his hand through Equestrius' mane, holding Thoron's eye for he knew the truth in his grandfather's words. Thoron smiled and taking back the finger bowl in his gnarled fingers, he turned, raising it towards the Lord of Horses. 'I drink to an old friend who came without being asked and did not count the cost that we might be rid of the darkness.'

'Equestrius, Equestrius! Lord of Horses!' shouted the feasters stamping their feet and calling for their cups to be refilled.

Thane lifted his hands and waited for silence. 'In forty daylights Elundium will have a Queen, for now that Tombel has come to the city Elionbel and I can be wedded in Candlebane Hall. Breakmaster, send messengers throughout the land, the day is named, the hour is called.'

'Lord,' cried Errant, King Holbian's messenger, rising to his feet, 'let me ride to Stumble Hill and Underfall to fetch Kyot and Thunderstone.'

Thane smiled and strode across the hall to grip Errant's hand. 'Go quickly with wings on your horse's heels and tell Kyot to bring Eventine and her father, Fairday, and every Archer and glassmaker who can be spared.'

Errant laughed and sprang lightly over the table. 'Lord, as Dawnrise is the first stallion of Underfall none shall pass him on the road. It shall be done,' he cried, running towards the doors.

'Wait!' called Thane, frowning. 'As you ride, spread the word and find Willow Leaf and all his people. They must attend as our honoured guests.'

Errant turned and held out his hands. 'Lord, they could be anywhere in all Elundium!'

Thane shook his head. 'No, look for beauty. Wherever the Greenway has been gardened there you will find them, for they travel to see all the marvels of the sunlight and I know they could not resist putting things right, trimming the Greenways' edge or pruning the trees. They should be easy to find.'

Errant bowed, turned towards the doors and quickly departed. Elionbel came to Thane's side and took his hand. 'Forty daylights!' she whispered, smiling with delight. 'I thought the worries of the Kingship had driven the wedding from your mind.'

Thane laughed, and linked his arm through hers. 'Everything has been secretly arranged from the moment we first entered the city but I had promised your father I would not name the day until he had finished his mourning for Martbel and brought the city folk to the gates of the City.'

At the mention of her mother a shadow passed across Elionbel's eyes and her hand tighted on his arm. Thane stopped and drew her close to him. 'What is it?' he whispered, putting his arm protectively around her shoulders.

119

'Nothing, just a shadow,' she whispered, shaking her head.

'Shadows, always shadows,' he answered, an edge of worry in his voice, before beckoning Tombel and his grandfather to the empty seats on each side of the Honour Chair.

Elionbel took a deep breath and forced the vision of Martbel, her mother, from her mind. Turning to Thane again she cried in a brighter voice, 'Forty daylights! That is not enough time to make a wedding gown!'

Thane laughed and put his lips to her ear and whispered, 'My mother, Angis, has been using all her needle skill in the highest room in the Granite Tower. Go to her, my love, and see what wonders have grown beneath her fingertips. Go now!'

Elionbel laughed, kissed his cheek then gathered up her skirts and cloak hems, called her servers and maids and ran gaily from the feasting hall. Thane watched her go and smiled to himself, happy to see her joyful again. Sighing, he turned to Thoron. 'Kingship is easy,' he said in a quiet voice, 'yet the smoothness of it troubles me. Both King Holbian and Nevian in their wisdom counselled me on the perils of ruling Elundium so I fear I have missed something, or that just beyond the horizon black clouds are building up to destroy this blissful sunlight.'

Thoron laughed and sat back in his chair. 'Elundium is at peace, Thane. Everywhere the daylight flourishes, the Greenways are neat and well trimmed back to the forest edge. People travel as they have not done for an age and everywhere laughter and easy talk fills the air. There are no black clouds, only word of a new King who makes and mends and sets right an age of wrongdoing.'

Thane frowned and shook his head. 'You speak so lightly, Grandfather, but what of the warriors that would not take me as their King? Is there any rumour of them? Surely they have not just vanished.'

Thoron moved closer to Thane, drawing his forehead into a thousand wrinkles. 'Rumour has it that they passed through

120

Mantern's Forest travelling only the wild roads that none but the desperate would use. Since then they have completely disappeared.'

Breakmaster coughed and lightly touched Thane's arm. 'Lord!' he whispered, drawing closer. 'Word came in today that warriors were seen just after the crowning in the grasslands beyond Meremire Forest, but none left the forest to cross the Greenways towards Stumble Hill.'

'Where have they gone?' muttered Thane, staring blankly at the laughing faces flanking him on either side of the hall. 'Where could they have gone? Surely they could not survive without food in the forest.'

'Word will come,' answered Thoron. 'You can lay ten Granite Kings or the hem of Nevian's cloak on it that if they are anywhere in Elundium you will soon know about it.'

'And nothing has changed?' pressed Thane. 'Nothing?'

Thoron laughed and shook his head. 'Nothing; well nothing except some gnarled old trees growing along the Greenways' edge.'

'Trees?' questioned Thane, leaning forwards. 'What trees?'

'Oaks. Hoary lichen-tangled old twists of timber that look ready for the axe,' answered Tombel.

'No. Hornbeam or cedar,' insisted Thoron. 'But the strange thing is that they seemed to have appeared where the rebellious warriors were last seen. I am sure I've ridden past them a thousand times before without really noticing them.'

Thane laughed, pushing his finger bowl aside. 'No, surely not even Nevian could have used magic to turn the warriors into trees! But are they only old trees?' Frowning, he fell silent and reached forwards to pick up his finger bowl, absently turning it between his thumb and first finger while he waited for an answer.

'Old?' repeated Thoron at length. 'Yes they were mostly old windblown trees but . . .' Thoron hesitated thinking back and remembering how much like warriors they had looked standing so still, so silent.

'They shall be cleared away,' interrupted Tombel. 'They cast dark shadows across the Greenways and keep out the light.'

'No!' burst in Thoron, turning to his aged friend. 'There is something about them. The way they stand, high-arching the road with their whispering boughs as if they are guarding or waiting. Perhaps they do have something to do with the warriors: remember, Nevian did curse them.'

Thane lifted his hand and waved them both into silence. 'How do they stand?' he asked, turning to his grandfather.

Thoron thought for a moment before spreading his gnarled fingers on the table's edge. 'They stand like this, in silent rows, with their roots buried in the Greenways' edge, each one touching the close-mown turf as if they were about to step over the road.'

'Do they stand on both sides?' questioned Thane.

'No!' laughed Tombel. 'They only stole our sunlight towards Underfall and World's End. On the other side the Greenways are clear for leagues beyond the drainage dykes.'

'Did they stand in the dykes?' asked Thane.

'No, they are as I told you,' Thoron replied, 'a single line, their roots touching the Greenways' edge.'

Thane frowned and sat back in the Honour Chair, deep in thought. He could not remember a single tree along the road that answered to the description his grandfather had just given him.

'A company of axe men could clear them in a dozen daylights, my Lord,' called out Tombel, breaking into Thane's thoughts.

'No!' he answered, leaning forwards forcefully. 'Against your peril set an axe or blade on any living tree along the Greenways' edge. Leave them be until we know more about them, but keep a careful watch and bring me news of their flowering or any movement that they might make.'

Somewhere near the Great Doors in the deepest shadow a

light began to move. Thane turned his head to watch and let the finger bowl fall forgotten from his fingers.

Laughter whispered, dodging between the silent feasters until it reached his chair. 'The warriors are cursed to stand beside the Greenways' edge,' a voice rippled out.

'Nevian?' Thane cried out, half-rising, but the light weakened, the voice melted and dissolved through all the colours of the rainbow back into darkness and the shadows were still once more. 'Nevian!' he called again, taking a step towards the doors.

Thoron rose and moved to Thane's elbow. 'If that were the Master of Magic, my Lord, I think he was rejoicing in your judgement to leave the trees where they stand.'

Thane smiled and reddened. 'Perhaps,' he whispered, turning and clapping his hands, calling for the feasting to be finished and the entertainments to begin.

Clowns tumbled through the doorway at Thane's command, bowing and vaulting their way across the polished stone floor. Pipers and lutists solemnly followed, each one bowing as they passed their King. Thane clapped his hands again. 'Begin,' he commanded and the clowns leapt into the air somersaulting in bright circles behind the noise and bustle of the entertainment. Thane quickly ducked out of sight through a low doorway and hurried away, sighing with relief. He left the Tower of Granite and walked alone beneath a star-filled sky down through the quiet city towards Stumble Gate. Hoofbeats on the cobbles sounded behind him and he spun round, hand on the dagger in his belt.

Thoron laughed as he caught up with Thane. He dismounted from Equestrius and fell into step with his grandson. 'Kingship is not quite as you said, is it, Thane?'

Thane smiled and took Thoron's hand. 'There is a side of it that terrifies me, Grandfather,' he answered. 'The bowing and the kneeling, the waiting on each word, each nod or blink of the eye. Sometimes I wish I had Mulcade's gift of flight or Esteron's tireless speed so that I might be far away from the endless feasting and noise, the banging on drums and the shouts. Sometimes I feel that it is me dancing through the hoop not the entertainers.'

Thoron stopped and turned Thane to face him. 'You were chosen, Thane. You cannot run away from your fate.'

'Yes, yes! I know that,' answered Thane impatiently. 'But I feel so alone. Everyone is so anxious to please, to say exactly what I want to hear.'

'But you have Elionbel, surely she . . .'

Thane shook his head and began to turn away. 'There is a shadow in her heart, Grandfather. I often see it in unguarded moments and because of it she tries harder than most to please me.'

'A shadow?' questioned Thoron in a troubled voice. 'Elundium is free of shadows; even Tombel has healed the wounds of losing his warrior wife. What troubles Elionbel? Is it Martbel's death?'

Thane shurgged his shoulders. 'I feel that it goes deeper than Martbel's death. Some other terrible thing must have happened between the Nightmare taking Elionbel and her mother from the Wayhouse of Woodsedge and my rescuing Elion from the City of Night. That much I am sure of, but what it is that could affect her so I dare not guess at.'

Thoron muttered something under his breath and once more fell into step with Thane. 'Where do you walk to seek comfort in the dark?' he asked as they passed out through the lower levels of the city beneath the Stumble Gate.

Thane called out to the guards who sat in the watching niches on each side of the gate, commanding them to let them past. He pointed out into the dark countryside. 'Out there, Grandfather, I feel safe. Amongst the nightsounds beneath a bright canopy of stars, I can hear the truth whispered in the hedgerow and no one courts me, eager to do my pleasure. Listen, Esteron is close at hand, I can hear his hoofbeats on the night wind.'

'There are Battle Owls and Border Runners near us,' whispered Thoron.

Thane smiled and looked at his grandfather in the darkness, remembering he was the greatest Errant rider Elundium had ever known.

Equestrius stiffened, his ears pricked and he snorted a quiet greeting to Esteron who trotted out of the darkness and halted before Thane. Thoron touched Thane's arm and silently pointed to two Border Runners that walked at Esteron's heels. Thane knelt and rubbed his hands through the Border Runners' thick sable coats. He laughed and pulled their ears playfully. 'They are near me always, ever since they helped Kyot find me in the grasslands.'

'Do they come into the city?' asked Thoron.

'No. They will not pass the Stumble Gate. I think then it would mark the end of their freedom,' Thane replied sadly as he climbed slowly to his feet.

Thoron took Thane's hand. 'You are my King, Thane, and within the circle of the City I must bow before you and treat you as others do but here in the darkness you will always be Thanehand, my grandson, whom once I lifted up to sit on Amarch's saddle while I called down the Battle Owls to perch upon your shoulders. Here in the darkness we shall be as before and share our shadows while we pass the night-time hours in secret glades by hidden pools. Come, ride with me until the grey hours.'

'Grandfather!' Thane cried, feeling his eyes grow wet with tears. 'How I yearned as a boy to ride beside you. How I dreamt of being tall enough to touch your stirrup.'

Thoron laughed and pointed into the darkness where he could faintly hear Errant's receding hoofbeats and said, 'Every man in Elundium is now poised to do your bidding.'

Errant pushed Dawnrise into a faster trot and moved out on to the crown of the road away from the gnarled old trees that nearly shadowed the Greenways' edge. He felt uneasy and turned up his cloak collar against unseen eyes, yet he knew he rode alone. Nothing moved in the bleak flat landscape that stretched to the horizon, nothing except the leagues of tall grass bent in whispering waves before the summer wind.

'We could reach Stumble Hill before night falls,' he urged, running his gloved hand across Dawnrise's shoulder, feeling the hard sheets of muscle ripple beneath the horse's skin as he surged forwards in larger strides to match the lengthening shadows. Looking up, Errant shivered and tried to close his ears to the whispering boughs that arched the road just above his head; their noise seemed to follow him even when the wind had fallen away to nothing and the sparse leathery leaves hung limp in the still air.

'Man or beast, step forwards!' he had often shouted with a hand on his sword, but nothing moved and sweet silence lasted but a second before the whispering began again. Sometimes Errant thought he saw eyes watching him, staring, blinking, following their every hoofbeat, but if he turned quickly in the saddle they were gone and the twisted trunks showed only deep age-worn bark furrows, scarred and weather-cracked beneath the hanging creepers.

The ground began to rise, the gnarled trees thinned until they stood in small uneven clumps clinging on to the edge of the road, their knobbly roots buried in the short springy turf. Errant laughed and spurred Dawnrise into a canter as they passed the last lichen-covered oak and galloped into the late evening sunlight. Before him he saw the Tower of Stumble Hill, its dark spire rising against the setting sun. Twisting in the saddle he looked back across his shoulder at the black line of ancient trees and sighed with relief: there was magic between their trunks, he had felt it and smelt it and he was glad to be on the open road again. Looking ahead, he could see movement beside the doors of Stumble Hill. There were strikes of Archers forming on either side of the road and he felt safe once more. 'I bring news from Granite City,' he cried, cantering through the strikes of bowmen who thronged the road. 'I bring news of King Thane's wedding ties to the Lady Elionbel.'

Reining Dawnrise to a halt, Errant quickly dismounted and picked up a stone jar of cedar oil. 'Bless my journey,' he whispered, tipping a little of the amber oil on to the ceremonial bow set inside the empty grave niche beside the doors of Stumble Hill.

Rising, Errant turned towards the doors. 'Kyot, Kyot,' he cried, a little impatiently, 'I bring you news, glad news of the King's wedding ties.'

'Good news at last,' shouted a voice from amongst the Archers. 'But it would have been better news if the King had ridden out himself to rid us of these trees.'

Errant tightened his hand on the reins and took a step closer to the stirrup. 'Where is Kyot?' he demanded. 'Where is the Keeper of Stumble Hill? He would not be afraid of a copse of trees or take the King's name in vain!'

The Archers mumbled and whispered together until one eventually stepped forwards. 'Kyot does fear the trees, messenger. He fears them enough to go fast riding with Eventine and a strike of Archers to fetch Eventine's father, Fairday of Clatterford, into the safety of Stumble Hill.'

'Gone?' questioned Errant, wiping the dust from his eyes. 'Running from a line of trees that mark the Greenways' edge?'

'Yes, messenger. They cast strange shadows and every daylight there are more of them,' cried the Archers.

Errant laughed, a dry mirthless sound and pointed into the gathering darkness. 'You would fear your own shadow, Archer, if you had the courage to look at it. I have ridden beneath those trees from where they first bury their roots in the Greenways' edge, five leagues from the gates of the Granite City to within sight of these doors. Yes, there is something about them – perhaps magic is woven into their branches and twisted trunks, but there is nothing to fear.

127

Why, need even forced me to sleep beneath their whispering boughs and they did me no harm!'

'Magic?' called anxious voices amongst the strikes of Archers.

'Yes, magic,' answered Errant turning to stare out across the darkening grasslands. 'But I doubt if it is there to hurt you.'

Errant's strength of purpose seemed to ease the tense atmosphere in the courtyard. One Archer laughed, another put down his bow and then a third called out, 'Let us drink a toast to King Thane and the Lady Elionbel.'

'And call for Errant, the messenger, to forgive our fears,' shouted another who recognized Errant.

Errant eased his grip on the reins, and took the offered cup and drank with the Archers but the joy of the moment was shortlived and less than an arrowblade deep. Everywhere he looked the Archers fidgeted, grim-faced, their eyes always turned towards the darkness beyond the Great Doors. A server came to take Dawnrise into the stables, but Errant hesitated and kept his hand upon the bridle.

'Come, Errant,' laughed an Archer, 'surely you would rather sleep the night hours here beneath our roof?'

Errant slowly nodded and handed over the reins. 'The trees made my blood freeze and the hairs tingle on the nape of my neck but for all their whispering and watching they did me no harm. However, I do fear your tenseness and the dull glint of new-forged arrows nocked ready on the strings.'

The Archer laughed and moved closer to Errant. 'Two daylights ago someone foolishly loosed an arrow into one of the first trees to appear on Stumble Hill – it screamed. It shook with rage, red sap poured from the wound. From that moment the trees that now stretch to the horizon began to crowd the road all about us. We stand battle-ready lest they attack.'

'Did you draw the arrow from the tree?' Errant cried.

'No, messenger,' answered the Archer. 'We feared to go close to it lest it snatched us up and tore us apart.'

Errant cursed under his breath and took a flickering tar-dipped torch from a bracket on the tower wall. 'Show me this tree, brave Archer, if you fear the King's wrath more than the wooden branches for I was told as I left the Granite City how he has pledged us all on pain of death to leave the trees unharmed and not to raise an axe or a blade to them.'

Fear spread among the Archers as Errant waited between the doors. 'Who will show me?' he asked. 'Who will show me the fool's arrow that I may put right your wrong?'

'I will,' answered a young Archer, stepping quickly forward and taking the flaming torch from Errant's hand.

The trees groaned and rustled in the darkness, the thick canopy of branches overhead swayed in the torchlight without a breath of wind. Errant shivered and kept close to the young Archer, keeping his own fears well hidden beneath his cloak.

'Here, messenger,' whispered the boy giving the torch back to Errant and pointing up to a thick trail of sticky red sap dried into the wrinkles and folds of the twisted bark.

Errant held the torch aloft and stared at the blackened arrowshaft where it protruded from an ugly wound in the trunk of the tree. Gathering his courage, he unsheathed his long cutting knife. 'I stand before you in the King's name,' he shouted. 'I bring you his word that none will harm you with axe or blade.'

The branches above his head began to sway violently, the leathery leaves rustled and whispering ran from trunk to trunk. 'I come,' he shouted again, 'to put right your hurts and pull the foolish Archer's arrow blade. I come in peace.'

Turning towards the ring of anxious Archers who had followed him, their faces showing fear in the torchlight, he asked for the Healer of Stumble Hill to step forwards. 'Have oiled cottons ready,' he commanded, handing the torch to the nearest Archer and beckoning two others to the base of the tree. He made them kneel to form a human step so that he could reach the arrowshaft.

The dense rows of trees became silent, nothing moved in the still night air. Pausing to gather his courage Errant laid his head against the trunk. The bark felt warm upon his cheek, almost like an acient skin that gently throbbed as if a pulse beat deep down inside. Errant shuddered and quickly drew away. Gripping the arrowshaft he pushed in the point of his dagger beside the barbed spines of the arrow's blade and forced the blade into the bark. Fresh hot sap bubbled up, spilling across his hand. The tree groaned and twisted away from him, the branches whipped above his head. Gritting his teeth he pulled and pulled until, with a shout of triumph, he toppled backwards from his precarious perch and fell to the ground, the sap-spoiled arrowhead gleaming dully in his hand.

'Oiled cottons, Healer,' he cried, throwing away the arrow. He snatched a handful of the cool oil-soaked pads from the Healer's sack and packed them into the tree's wound. The trunk shook and trembled, the branches writhed and danced in the torchlight and the whispering amongst the leaves ran far along the Greenways' edge into the darkness.

'In the King's name, stand in peace,' shouted Errant, resheathing his dagger and turning towards the doors of Stumble Hill. A branch reached down out of the darkness and touched his shoulder, turning him gently, drawing him back to stand before the scarred trunk. The whispering grew silent; it was as if a thousand eyes were watching, looking, remembering him.

'Stand in peace,' Errant half-whispered again before his courage finally failed and he fled, his cloak tails billowing behind him as he entered the safety of Stumble Hill. Breathing deeply, he smiled, slowed his pace and crossed the cobbled courtyard towards the glowing lamplight of the Archers' eating halls. Behind him the doors were closing and the night-time bell rang out clear across the silent Greenway.

* * *

Dawnrise stood, ready-saddled, as the last of the grey hours strengthened into a new morning. The sun burned with bright fire beyond World's End and the first blackbird of morning waited in the hedgerow to sing to the dawn. 'I will ride on to Underfall,' Errant said, speaking with new resolve as the light filled the courtyard and the doors of Stumble Hill swung open slowly. 'To bring word of the wedding tie and accompany Thunderstone into Granite City while you Archers must cast lots or split stalks of straw with new-forged arrowblades to choose who will go and who will stay. But, mark my words, King Thane wants every man who can be spared to be inside the Granite City by the fortieth daylight.'

'What of the trees?' shouted a dozen Archers as Errant gathered the reins and sprang up lightly into the saddle.

'The trees?' he laughed, pirouetting Dawnrise, casting bright sparks across the cobbles. 'Perhaps they have come to guard the Greenways' edge but touch them not and gather with all haste before your King.'

'But . . .' shouted the young Archer who had held the torch for him the night before.

'No more buts,' laughed Errant, spurring his horse through the doors and vanishing in a thunder of hoofbeats beneath the ancient trees. A flash of bright light from his sword hilt, a waving hand, and he was gone, galloping the Greenway leagues to Underfall.

Upon the Greenways' Edge

Sighing with delight, Willow rested his long curved scythe upon the Greenways' edge. He pressed his fingers into the warm new-mown grass. Breathing deeply he shut his eyes and let the scent of the grasses fill his head then he rolled over, laughed and threw up handfuls of the crisp wet cuttings and watched them scatter in the summer wind. 'We are free! Free to wander in such beauty,' he cried to the other Tunnellers spread behind him along the Greenway.

Oakapple smiled and straightened her back. Then she reached for a basket of forest fruits and sweet oven cakes she had brought for their noonday rest and sat down beside Willow. 'It is wonderful to be in the daylight, Willow, but sometimes the sheer size of it all terrifies me. The rolling hills and league upon league of empty grassland that lie beneath this limitless sky, it all seems so vast; it must stretch beyond for ever. It is all so different from the darkness of the City of Night: there I could reach out and touch both walls or the roof above my head with both my hands.'

Willow frowned and brushed his fingers on the coarse weave of his breeches. 'How can you fear it?' he cried. 'How can you fear a life without Nightbeasts? A life in this beautiful light, this is what we whispered about in the darkness and strove to win.'

'Yes, yes,' Oakapple answered, her voice full of confusion. 'Of course I love the light, Willow, but sometimes it makes me seem so small and vulnerable, a mere speck in this huge landscape with nowhere to hide.'

Willow's face softened as he took Oakapple's hand in his own. 'Sometimes at night as I lie watching the stars I feel there is a great space all around us, the empty silence that reaches up to touch the stars is all about me and yet, as small as it makes me feel, I rejoice to be able to see it, to smell it, to feel it.'

Oakapple nodded, tightening her fingers in Willow's hand and rested her head upon his shoulder as he continued, 'To travel freely in all Elundium was a great gift from King Thane, for through our wanderings we shall see everything that the Elders painted with words in the darkness and one daylight, I know, we will find the place that Krulshards stole us from. I know in my heart that somewhere in the Elders' stories there was a picture of our home.'

Willow fell silent and stared out across the sun-bleached grassland. Frowning, he shaded his eyes against the glare and rose to his feet. 'Hush!' he whispered. 'There are groups of Warriors in the grasslands. Marchers spread in rough order as far as I can see.'

'Warriors?' queried Oakapple, quickly gathering up the food she had set out for their rest. 'Surely the great battle crescents were all disbanded at King Thane's crowning?'

Willow nodded gravely, gathering Starlight's reins as he crouched down and signalled to the other Tunnellers to follow him. 'Rumour tells that only those who refused to pledge or take Thane as the rightful King of Elundium roam battle ready through the forest and wildlands near Mantern's Mountain. I did not think they would dare to come this near to the Granite City.'

'Perhaps they travel in secret, well clear of the Greenways,' whispered Oakapple moving closer to Willow.

'Well, whoever they are let us move out of sight until they have passed by. Take cover in those tangle tree thickets beyond the far side of the road. Quickly, run!'

With less sound than the wind whispering through the tall grass the Tunnellers fled across the Greenways and disappeared under the low, armoured, spiked branches of the tangle trees. The tramp of marching feet grew louder, the rattle of battle harness, mingling with shouts and curses, seemed to be almost on top of them. Willow drew the small splinter of steel that served him as a dagger and crouched, ready. His hands were damp with sweat; the short breaths rasped in his throat.

'We will stand and fight. I will send Starlight to Thane to warn him of these warriors. We will fight to bring her time.'

Willow turned and passed the message to the Tunnellers standing beside him. 'Use your scythes and hoes as weapons. Remember we will be defending Thane who gave us the freedom of the Greenways.'

Closer and closer drew the Warriors. They were now almost at the Greenways' edge, trampling the long grasses beneath their armoured boots. Willow rose and began to strip off Starlight's saddle and bridle but Oakapple tugged at his sleeve. 'Listen,' she hissed, 'there is fear in their voices, they are trying to turn away from the Greenway.'

'Put your ear to the ground and listen; it sounds as if the earth is being torn apart,' urged Willow.

Oakapple knelt and pressed her ear to the bare earth, shuddered and quickly pulled away. 'I can hear burrowing and digging in the ground,' she whispered. 'And voices in the distance – some must have escaped.'

When all was quiet again Willow slowly led Starlight out from beneath the dense thicket of tangle trees.

Oakapple ducked down and made to follow Willow through the narrow gap, only to bump into him and Starlight. Looking up she cried out in terror and covered her eyes. Before them in one neat row ancient oaks, elms and cedar trees stood statue-still, rooted on the Greenways' edge. Lichen and ivy creepers hung in chaotic loops from their twisted, weathered boughs while overhead, shading the road, leathery leaves spun in the summer wind, whispering as they rubbed together.

'In all Elundium . . . this is the greatest magic that I have ever seen,' gasped Willow taking a slow step forwards.

'It must be bad magic, trees did not grow like this in the Elder's tales,' called out one of the Tunnellers emerging from the thicket of tangle trees.

Willow thought for a moment, laughed and resheathed his dagger. 'Is everything we cannot explain called magic? Perhaps all trees grow from grim-faced warriors, perhaps they carry the seedlings within them and only start to grow once they reach the places they are meant to stand. Just because this wasn't in the Elder's tales doesn't mean it isn't the way of things in Elundium.

'Who amongst us has seen a tree grow since we entered the daylight?' he asked turning to the others.

'I think these trees are in some way tied up with the Magician's curses on the warriors who would not have Thane as their King. In the Elder's tales he built each tree, leaf and branch, with the tiny point of light he kept hidden from the Nightbeasts,' answered Oakapple fearfully. 'I always thought trees grew like that, spreading out from their centre.'

Willow laughed and again nodded his head. 'If these are magic trees grown from the rebellious warriors then we need not fear them for the Magician said that they were to wait and grow wise beside the Greenways' edge until Thane called for them.'

Slowly, one by one, the remaining Tunnellers emerged from their hiding places and nodded in agreement, whispering to each other about the wonders of Elundium.

'Walk amongst them,' called Willow, 'and listen to their whisperings, for they may tell us much of the land we wander in.'

'What of the Warriors who fled back into the grasslands?' called an anxious voice. 'Might they return and attack us?' They resolved to move warily.

Willow chose a dozen of the strongest Tunnellers and crept carefully between the trees. 'Feel their trunks,' he called quietly, 'they are still soft and warm from their rapid growth. This one even throbs as if it has a heart.'

'This one moves at my touch. Look, it trembles and sways,' laughed a Tunneller as he prodded at a tree trunk twenty paces from where Willow was standing.

'Treat them carefully,' Willow cried in dismay. 'Their roots are only moments old and still tender to the touch. Treat them with great care.'

Moving off the Greenway Willow slipped between two close-grown trunks into the grassland and beyond. Kneeling, he examined the trampled ground and saw everywhere broken or bruised stalks of grass, but amongst the trampling he saw discarded swords and spears, cloaks and crude sacks of meal, all thrown in ragged disorder just beyond the furthest leaf span of the new trees. Moving through the warriors' litter he searched for signs of their path, footprints that would show him which way they had travelled but they were too muddled for him to follow. Quickly he called the other Tunnellers back on to the Greenway and gathered them into a circle.

'It would seem that the warriors who did not touch the Greenways' edge are gone,' he announced. 'Vanishing, I should think, by the same way that they came.'

'How can you be sure?' asked Oakapple, peering through the trees.

'I cannot, but I am sure that if they are cursed with Nevian's magic then they will soon cross the Greenway and turn into trees. You cannot travel in Elundium without meeting a road.'

Willow's voice trailed into silence as he stared up at the branches that high-arched the road. For all his bold talk of magic trees he wasn't at all sure how much he could really trust them. There was something different about these trees. The way they whispered and seemed to watch, perhaps they would reach down and kill his people, perhaps . . . He laughed to dispel the fear forming in his mind. 'Let us treat these beautiful trees with great care and garden the Greenways' edge between their knobbly roots, and make this road fit for the King to use,' he called, stepping boldly forwards.

Oakapple sighed with relief and followed the rest of the Tunnellers between the trees. She secretly welcomed the swathes of shadow that crisscrossed the road with the patterns of black lace, for it gave her pale skin a chance to rest from the burning sun. Snipping and clipping she moved happily forwards, singing softly of the beautiful daylight that spread out across the empty grasslands on either side of the Greenway.

Willow paused beside her and followed her gaze. 'One daylight,' he whispered, 'we will find the place the Nightmare stole us from. I know it.'

Oakapple smiled at him, her eyes filling with pride. 'The Elder planted the seeds of daylight in all of us, but in you, Willow, they took root and grew strong enough to make you fight for our freedom. If there is a place for us you will find it.'

Willow laughed and put his arm around her shoulders, pointing across the vast landscape to faint crystal-tipped peaks painted along the horizon's rim. 'Do you see those mountains?' he asked.

Oakapple crinkled her eyes, shading them against the sun and slowly nodded. 'Yes, but they are as faint brush strokes washed against the skyline. They shimmer in the heat haze, appearing then disappearing.'

'Well, if you cast your mind back into the darkness, Oakapple, right back to those tight whispering circles we formed at the Elder's feet you will see it just as clearly as I do. The cascading waterfalls, the steep pine-clad slopes shrouded in morning mist, the still pools of crystal water reflecting a thousand flower-covered hills. It was all there in the pictures he painted, so clear, so strong that I can almost smell the nectar and hear the wind amongst the pines. But sometimes, like those distant mountains, the picture shimmers and disappears.'

Oakapple sighed sadly and leaned against him. 'The Elder was lost in the darkness, lost until Nevian found him and showed him all the wonders of the daylight. He cannot have known where the Nightmare stole us from.'

Willow turned on her, angrily pulling away. 'The magician must have shown him. How else would I know about the place I am searching for? Where else would the half-shown glimpses so lovingly woven into the Elder's pictures have come from?'

Oakapple bit her lip and wished she had not voiced her doubts. Above her head the new leathery leaves began to rustle, sending urgent whispers backwards and forwards along the Greenways' edge. Willow looked up at the noise, looked up into the canopy of moving branches and smiled, his anger forgotten. 'They know,' he laughed. 'I can hear it in their voices. They have seen the place of our beginnings.'

He listened for a while. 'The trees talk of stone-broken ruins on a steep hillside and tumbling bracken banks along the water's edge.' Willow ran between the trees and stared out at the distant mountains. 'If the trees could move they would lead us. Listen.' He paused a moment. 'They talk now of World's End and the sheer walls of Underfall.'

Oakapple frowned. All she could hear was the wind whispering through the leaves, there were no voices or places in the rustling. But then Willow had always been a little different, he had heard voices in the City of Night. Starlight and the great black Warhorse had talked to him in the darkness and it had led to their winning the daylight.

She nodded her head in reluctant agreement. 'Yes, yes!' she murmured. 'The trees will tell us which road to take. Perhaps we should follow their voices and garden the Greenway towards Underfall.'

A Fast Ride to Clatterford

Eventine stretched, yawned and opened her eyes to the faint glow of dawn spreading across the grasslands. Shivering, she rose, gathered her cloak about her shoulders and knelt beside Kyot. 'The grey hours are upon us,' she whispered, gently shaking his shoulder. 'It is time to ride on towards Clatterford.'

Kyot mumbled, pulling his cloak collar up over his chin then he slowly opened his eyes. 'Eventine,' he whispered, smiling and reaching out for her hand, 'each morning you shine more beautiful than the sun. Each . . .'

Eventine smiled and put her finger on his lips silencing him. 'It is time,' she insisted, leaning forwards to pluck the arrows he had placed in the cold earth beside his saddle as an arrowstand. 'We must ride on to Clatterford.'

Kyot sat up and looked out of their temporary resting place, past the silent sleeping Archers huddled in their blankets, out across the endless grasslands to where he knew the sky still held on to the indigo colours of the night. 'Morning will not yet have come to Clatterford,' he answered, stretching his arms. 'The peacocks will still be asleep.'

Eventine frowned impatiently and stood up. 'If we leave now and gallop tirelessly with the new sun we could reach my father's house before night falls.'

Kyot smiled and swept his hand across the sleeping Archers. 'What of the Archers? They cannot keep pace with

139

Sprint and Tanglecrown, we would leave them leagues behind.'

'Rockspray could watch over them,' she replied. 'He is a sharp-eyed bird of war and . . .'

Kyot shook his head. 'No, the Archers of Stumble Hill have run themselves into shadows with your haste, we will not leave them now that we are less than one daylight from Clatterford. Why, early yesterlight we saw groups of grim Marchers by the horizon's edge and only warriors not pledged to the King travel as they did, armed and battle ready.'

'But they scattered when they saw our Archer strike. Surely . . .'

Kyot laughed harshly. 'And today, seeing only two of us, fools galloping through the grasslands, they would attack. No, they may have fled only to gather more warriors against us; we must travel together.'

Eventine walked out past the waking Archers and called to Tanglecrown. Turning back, she glared at Kyot with glittering eyes. 'It is not the Marchers nor the wandering Nightbeasts that I fear, but each daylight hour we waste could put my father in greater danger. I was for fast riding, just the two of us, to reach my father's house before those ancient trees invaded Clatterford. What if they already surround the Crystal Hall?'

Kyot frowned and bent to collect his saddle. Now he understood Eventine's impatience with every slow start and break to rest. Perhaps he had been wrong to insist on a strike of Archers accompanying them to Clatterford. Rockspray hooted and stooped down through the chill morning air, breaking into his thoughts as he settled on Kyot's shoulder.

'Well, great Bird of War,' he whispered, lifting a hand to stroke the owl's soft chest feathers. 'What would you have me do, leave the safety of the Archers to your sharp eyes and gallop on to Clatterford, or stay here marshalling the men of Stumble Hill and moving forwards with caution?'

Rockspray held Kyot's gaze for a moment, blinked once

and rose, hooting, into the strengthening sunlight. He flew in a wide circle around their makeshift resting place as if he were searching the tall grasses.

'There, you see it!' Evantine cried. 'Even Rockspray agrees we should ride on to Clatterford. Look he is casting all about us for danger – he will watch over the Archers. Now, will you ride with me to Clatterford?'

Kyot laughed, the burden of choice lifted from his shoulders and he snatched up the Bow of Orm. 'Archers!' he cried, shouting the strike awake as he placed his saddle upon Sprint's back. 'Follow our tracks through the long grass to Clatterford. Travel battle ready with new-forged arrows nocked on to your bows and keep a sharp ear cocked for Rockspray's warning, for he will watch over your road.'

Eventine sighed with relief, tightened her girths and quickly mounted. 'We will meet again at Clatterford,' she shouted, pirouetting Tanglecrown and cantering out into the beginnings of the new morning.

Sprint snatched at the bridle and leapt forwards, neighing fiercely as he followed the Lord of Stags. Kyot looked back once and lifted his hand to wave to the assembled Archers before the tall grasses swallowed him up. Drawing level with Tanglecrown, Kyot reached across and took Eventine's hand. 'We will ride without rest,' he shouted above the thunder of their hooves, 'and race the sun to Clatterford.'

Eventine smiled and shouted something back but it was lost, tugged away from them in the roaring winds as they surged forwards.

'Trees!' laughed Fairday. 'Ancient trees that spring up at a moment's notice along the Greenways' edge? Never, never in all the legends, all the lore ... Look to the ford, to the boundaries of Clatterford, there is nothing out of place. Ask me about Nightbeasts and roving bands of warriors, armed and battle ready, but trees ...'

'Yes, Father, trees!' Eventine cried, loosing the girths on

141

Tanglecrown's lathered sides. 'We rode without rest, we feared you might be under siege.'

'We?' queried Fairday, climbing to the highest crystal step of the house of Clatterford and peering out across the ford into the last shades of daylight.

'Kyot is a league behind me. He had to dismount and run at Sprint's stirrup. Sprint was stumbling with weariness and would have fallen.'

Fairday frowned and took his daughter's hands. 'Fear indeed must have driven you to ride this hard across the wild grasslands. Tell me . . .'

Fast running hoofbeats sounded beyond the tall yew hedge that bordered the forge, the peacocks rustled their feathers and cried out to the rising moon. Kyot splashed through the ford and ran exhausted on to the lawn. Sprint snorted and halted beside him, his heaving sides showing white-frothed with sweat in the moonlight. 'There are no trees!' Kyot cried between laboured breaths. 'Clatterford is safe.'

Eventine ran to him, loosing the cloak clasp at his throat, taking his bow and heavily loaded quiver. 'Yes,' she answered with relief, putting her hand on the reins and stripping off Sprint's bridle.

Fairday laughed, embracing them both and called for fresh lamps in the Crystal Hall as he led them in out of the chill evening air. 'Rest, shake the dust from your cloaks, eat now and be refreshed and then by tomorrowlight we will talk more of wild warriors and magic trees.'

The daylights at Clatterford seemed to blend one into another but each evening time saw Kyot and Eventine walking the lawns and telling tales of Elundium across the silent carpet of grass.

Then one night, as they watched the last rays of the sun disappear, hoofbeats sounded beyond the ford. Fairday came out of the house, calling out the Archers, clapping his hands for his Candlemen to bring more light on to the lawns. Kyot took up his bow and quickly nocked an arrow on to the string.

'Who dares to enter Clatterford without my leave?' cried Fairday, stepping on to the lawns and spreading his sky-washed cloak to shield Eventine and Kyot. 'Stay still,' he commanded Kyot, motioning him back behind the cloak. 'I am the Master of Clatterford and it is my place to defend the house and all who are in it.'

The hoofbeats sounded closer, battle harness jingled in the falling darkness and a strong voice laughed beyond the ford. 'What welcome is this between old friends!'

Fairday let the cloak hem fall to the ground and took a step towards the ford. 'Thunderstone!' he cried as two figures emerged from the shadows and cantered in a white surge of spray through the ford.

Thunderstone laughed again and reined his horse to a halt then dismounted beside the crystalmaker of Clatterford. 'And Errant the messenger is with me. Well met. Well met beyond an age of suns and daylights!' he shouted, embracing Fairday, lifting him clear of the lawn and spinning him round.

Fairday laughed, gripping Thunderstone's arms as he regained his balance on the ground. He searched the aged wrinkled face before him. 'You wear well, last Lampmaster of Elundium,' he whispered, 'for one who has striven to keep the light in a world of shadows.'

Thunderstone laughed. 'Age falls from me with each daylight. The new King makes me young again for he lifted my burden and gave my old bones a rest from chasing Nightbeasts. Errant, Errant, come forward and meet the Master of the glass arrowblades that destroyed the Nightmare.'

'Lord!' Errant whispered, stepping into the light and bending his knee. The Glassmaker shook his head and pulled Errant to his feet. 'Kings are for kneeling to, Errant. I did no more than you to rid Elundium of the Nightmare and probably risked less forging glass arrowheads here in the safety of Clatterford while you galloped through great danger to raise a mighty army along the Greenways' edge.'

Errant raised his eyebrows. 'You have heard of all that passed at Underfall?'

'Little passes the sharpness of an Archer's eye,' replied Fairday, linking his arms with those of Eventine and Kyot and bringing them into the ring of bright torchlight. 'These two are my ears and eyes and tell me much that troubles my mind.'

'All Elundium be praised!' Thunderstone cried, taking Eventine's hand and kissing it gently.

'I have fretted with each daylight since I left the Tower of Stumble Hill that I might miss you on the road,' laughed Errant, gripping Kyot's arm. 'I have been searching for you with news, glad tidings of King Thane's wedding ties, but we must put wings on the horses' feet if we are to reach the Granite City by the fortieth daylight. The Archers of Stumble Hill told me of your journey to rescue Fairday from the ancient trees that suddenly appeared beside your Wayhouse.'

Kyot shivered, hunching his shoulders against the darkness. 'There is a magic, something dark and ominous about those trees.'

'Come, it is rare to have so many guests in this far-flung corner of Elundium. Eat with us and be refreshed,' broke in Fairday, clapping his hands for the servers to throw open the doors. 'There are no magic trees at Clatterford. Come sit at my table and tell me more of the Nightmare's death, and the crowning of Thanehand. Let nothing be left out in the telling, forget these magic trees!'

'You knew, long before, he would be King,' Kyot remembered, suddenly turning in astonishment as Fairday led the way into the Crystal Hall.

The Glassmaker laughed. 'It was there, my child. Kingship shone brighter than the fire in my forge. Fate was merely tempering him on a hard anvil. Did I not say to Eventine that she must find two travellers worn to rags and that all Elundium would fade if she passed them by?'

'But . . . but he and I were as brothers and yet I first saw

144

his destiny only in those last moments as he destroyed the Nightmare.'

Fairday stopped, turned and took Kyot's hand. 'Perhaps Fate needed your blindness to grow the bond of love between you. How would you have served him had you known that he would be King? Could you then have shared the danger, or shared the same shadow, or drunk from the same bowl?'

Kyot looked away, remembering how he had knelt after the crowning, offering up his bow and quiver and calling Thane 'my Lord', and 'great King', and how it had angered Thane. And how their love had grown thin and stretched by the time they had reached the Tower on Stumble Hill and Thane had been quick to agree to his staying as the new Keeper of the Wayhouse Tower. But in that last moment as they had stood together between the great wooden doors, Thane had wept and called him brother and begged him to come soon to Granite City. Kyot blinked and shook his head, scattering the memory and seeing clearly the truth in Fairday's words.

'One daylight,' Fairday whispered, releasing Kyot's hand, 'Thane may once again need that bond you forged upon the road to Underfall, and you, daughter, you might yet be his bowmaiden for there is still an unsung song in the Bows of Orm and Clatterford.'

Thunderstone and Errant nodded in agreement with Fairday's foresight and took their places at the long table, glittering with fluted cups and shell-shaped bowls. They placed their hands around his delicate crystal finger bowls set out before them and brought them to their lips. 'To our Great King!' they cried together.

Fairday laughed and reached for his tall stemmed glass. 'Surely you should honour the King with a proper cup and not with the finger bowls?'

Thunderstone smiled and touched the Crystalmaker's arm. 'I thought all Elundium knew of the story of the finger bowl, of how Elionbel sent hers as a love token with Errant into the

145

shadows of World's End for Thane to keep close to his heart and how in the darkness of despair it bound them together.'

'And shone ever bright in the marsh mud,' interrupted Eventine, sipping from her finger bowl. 'Without its glittering silver light we would have passed Thane by.'

'It is a sign, a symbol of everyone's love of Thane and Elionbel,' added Thunderstone, pushing back the fold of his blue cloak and lifting up a tiny silver bowl hanging from his belt by a fine silver chain.

Fairday laughed and leaned forwards. 'There seems to be much that my sharp-eyed Archers have forgotten to tell a simple glassblower. To the King and the fair Lady Elionbel!' he cried, lifting his finger bowl to his lips and sipping at the sweet scented water. 'Now tell me all that has come to pass since Thane left this house on his dark road to Kingship.'

New morning's light had touched the roof of Clatterford before the story of Thane's triumph over the Nightmare was fully told, and the peacocks had heralded the new sun with haunting cries before Fairday rose from his chair.

'Trees!' he muttered, pacing the eating hall. 'Trees that spring up along the Greenways' edge. They sound strange indeed.'

'King Thane would not have us harm them,' Errant answered. 'At least not until we know more about them.'

'That is the advice of a wise King,' Thunderstone interrupted. 'Much as I fear there is dark magic in these trees, I am more troubled by the bands of warriors that would not pledge themselves to Thane. They are seen everywhere yet they vanish again in the blink of an eye.'

'Yes! Yes!' called Fairday turning to Thunderstone. 'All along the borders of Clatterford I have seen them but they flee if I challenge them, scattering as chaff in a strong wind.'

Errant nodded. 'On the road through Meremire I saw them amongst the ancient trees, almost upon the Greenway, but as I looked back they had gone and more of those strange trees were crowding in their places on the road.'

'Their whispering chills my heart!' Eventine said, shivering and pulling her cloak more tightly about her shoulders.

'Well,' called out Errant striding to the doors and throwing them open to let in the new daylight. 'If these unpledged warriors keep vanishing, the sooner we are rid of them the faster will be our road, for now we must ride with the wind or miss the King's wedding ties.'

'You will come with us, Father?' Eventine cried, turning to him.

Fairday laughed. 'My King calls me, child, he summons everyone to be in Granite City by the fortieth daylight.'

The Darkness Enters the Palace of Kings

Prodded on by Kruel's impatience, Kerzolde muttered and cursed to himself, and led them back through the swirling mists and barren broken countryside into the echoing culvert that drained the sewers of Underfall.

'Beneath that fortress lies the tombs of the Kings,' he hissed, pointing with his broken claw.

Kruel shook himself dry and climbed up the steep slope of the dyke that lay in the shadows of the fortress of Underfall. Grimacing, he picked at the raw flesh on his upper arm and waited for the night to fall. 'Where are the warriors?' he hissed into Kerzolde's ear. 'Where are those guardians of the bright Lamp that shines across the Causeway Field?'

Arbel coughed and shivered below them in the wet slime at the bottom of the dyke.

'Quiet!' snarled Kerhunge, clamping his clawed hand across the Marcher's mouth and pushing him deeper into the mire. 'The cursed warriors will hear you!'

Arbel struggled, reaching for his dagger: now he would kill the ugly Nightbeast, now was the moment.

'Stop!' hissed Kruel, freezing them both with his voice as he watched the huge doors slowly begin to close, rumbling and bumping their way across the cobbles. Somewhere far away in the tangled undergrowth of Mantern's Forest a dog barked, while just beyond the sheer granite-grey walls of Underfall, ancient trees whispered and rustled on the Greenways' edge.

Darkness had fallen, the last shades of evening faded beneath a bright canopy of stars. 'Follow me now!' whispered Kruel slipping over the edge of the dyke and moving noiselessly through the shadows to the base of the wall. He spread his slender fingers and touched the cold granite, feeling the smoothness rubbed there by a thousand Nightbeast claws. 'I hear you,' he whispered, smiling in the darkness. 'I hear your screams and see your beautiful shadows but I will take this place for you without one shout.'

'What, Master?' hissed Kerzolde, running to Kruel's side and leaving a trail of foul-smelling slime from the lip of the dyke into the shadows of the wall. Kerhunge and Arbel followed quickly, pushing and snarling at each other.

'Quiet! Quiet!' snapped Kruel, pulling them both roughly against the cold granite. 'Stay still and watch for the warriors while I release the shadow rats.'

Arbel turned and crouched down on the close-cropped turf to stare out across the Causeway Field. 'Look!' he whispered, touching Kruel's arm and pointing with a dirty finger. 'There is something moving between those old twisted trees.'

Kruel turned and stared through the darkness, searching each leaf and branch, following the distorted bark patterns across the ruined thunder-shaken trunks. 'Branches move in the wind, nothing more!' snapped Kruel impatiently.

'But there is no wind,' answered Arbel in a hushed whisper.

Kruel shrugged his shoulders. 'We have nothing to fear from these trees, let them watch the beginnings of my power.'

Turning back to the wall, Kruel dangled two shadow rats by their tails against the cold granite. 'Find a way,' he whispered, stroking their brittle black fur. 'Find a crack or hole and creep into the fortress of Underfall. Bite the Gateman with my darkness, whisper in his ear to open the gates.'

Kruel placed the rats on the sheer wall and pushed them up towards the lowest gallery that showed in blackest shadows against the star-filled sky above their heads. Squeaking and scratching, the rats ran backwards and forwards searching for a clawhold on the smoothness of the granite.

'They cannot scale the wall, Master,' hissed Kerzolde. 'It is too smooth and as slippery as crystal.'

Kruel spat at the ground and raked his finger nails across the granite, gouging deep plough lines in the hard grey stone.

'Master!' Kerhunge hissed in wonder, touching the deep grooves in the wall. 'You could pull this fortress apart with your bare hands!'

Kruel laughed quietly and reached up, cutting more finger grooves, hand over hand his arms stretched grotesquely in the starlight, reaching far beyond their normal span until his fingertips touched rough granite.

Something was watching between the trees, Arbel could sense it and it made his flesh crawl. Turning to Kruel, he gasped to see his arms stretching flat against the wall, disappearing into the shadows above.

'There is always a way,' whispered Kruel, trembling with effort. 'Kerhunge's way would shout our purpose clear across Elundium, but who will notice a few scratches on the wall?' Laughing, he drew down his arms, put the rats back on the wall and pushed their sharp black claws into the first groove.

'I will seach the trees,' whispered Arbel, drawing a dagger. 'I am sure that something is watching us.'

'There was not a single tree standing beside the Greenway when we escaped into the Shadowlands,' hissed Kerzolde.

'Take care,' whispered Kruel, his pale eyes flushed blood-red in the starlight. 'Creep in secret.'

Arbel quietly crossed the dyke and crept on all fours into the shadows of the ancient trees. He rose slowly, dagger gripped ready and took one step. He stopped, frozen in fear. The trees had crowded together, their trunks less than a hand's span apart, their branches writhing overhead and snaking down towards him. Everywhere whispers ran through the night, bark creaked and age-bent boughs groaned, leathery leaves rustled and reached out to touch his face. 'Cursed trees!' he snarled, slashing at the nearest trunk, cutting deeply into the bark. The tree shook, a muffled groaning split the night silence. Lichen-covered branches struck out, knocking the dagger out of Arbel's hand. Turning him and tumbling him out across the Causeway Road they threw him roughly on to the Causeway Field.

'Quiet!' hissed Kruel, his voice stopping Arbel from renewing his attack on the trees, calling him back into the shadows of the sheer granite wall.

'There is magic in those trees,' cursed Arbel, rubbing at his bruises as he leaned against the wall.

'Leave the trees,' snapped Kruel, 'they are nothing but ancient stands of timber. You can burn them to the ground when all Elundium is under my darkness. Now, watch the the doors and wait for the shadow rats to do their work.'

Willow had followed the voices of the trees, taking his people back into the shadows of Underfall, now he slowly let the breath out of his lungs and dared to look again. Shaking with fear and wretched with despair, he lifted his head above the gnarled roots of the ancient trees and watched the black rats search along the casements and disappear into the lowest galleries. 'The Nightmare's darkness is not destroyed,' he whispered to Oakapple. 'That boy is a part of Krulshards. Look at his eyes: they shine blood-red, the dead locks of hair and skinless flesh on his upper arm speak of the Nightmare, but there is something about him – the face, the shape of the jaw. And that huge Marcher that attacked the trees. There is something about him that I recognize.'

'The one-clawed beast is Kerzolde,' whispered Oakapple trembling. 'I would know that Nightbeast anywhere.'

'Kerzolde with a Marcher and a young boy who has the look of Krulshards,' muttered Willow.

'Well, at least those trees defended us,' whispered the Tunneller crouching beside Willow.

Willow smiled and nodded, putting his finger to his lips and motioning to the others to keep silent and perfectly still. He reached out and touched the treetrunk Arbel had cut into and felt the hot bark trembling beneath his fingertips. A stifled cry from within the fortress of Underfall made them duck down out of sight behind the tree roots.

'What was that?' gasped Oakapple, clinging on to Willow's arm.

Slowly, he gathered his courage to look out again and saw that the great doors of Underfall were moving on their hinges, rocking backwards and forwards. The Nightmare boy was now standing before the doors with his hands on his hips as if waiting, with a gloat of victory spread across his face. Beside him the Marcher stood, sword drawn, while the Nightbeasts crouched in the doorposts' shadows ready to strike. The doors opened letting a crack of light spill across the Causeway. Two black rats scuttled out over the cobbles and ran up the boy's outstretched hands. Laughing cruelly, he crossed the patch of light and disappeared into the fortress of Underfall. The Marcher followed, beckoning to the Nightbeast to follow him. The doors rattled and swung shut, night silence once more descended on the empty Causeway.

Willow watched for long moments, searching every shadow carefully before he rose to his feet. 'Wait with Starlight,' he whispered to Oakapple. 'Wait while we search the Causeway Road before the Great Doors. I must find out who Kerzolde's companions were.'

'No!' hissed Oakapple. 'It is too dangerous. Stay with me. Stay . . .'

But his fingers untwined from hers and Willow had gone, to slip noiselessly between the trees, gathering Cedarbranch and another Tunneller to go with him.

'Not one sound,' he murmured to the others crossing the Causeway Road and putting his hands on the sheer granite walls, feeling for the marks the boy had made.

'Nightmare!' he whispered, letting the word hiss through

152

his teeth as his eyes widened. 'Something more powerful than Krulshards was here. Feel these grooves, they are still hot to the touch.'

'What could carve through granite as though it were as soft as rotten cheese?' asked Cedarbranch touching the hot grey stone fearfully.

'What indeed?' answered Willow, creeping on tiptoe into the centre of the Causeway. Pausing, he frowned and pushed his hand against the huge wooden doors of Underfall. They gave at his touch, creaking open across the cobbles. Willow shivered and stepped back a pace. He stared into the dark empty courtyards.

'Whole armies of Nightbeasts once washed against these doors and could not enter. Look how they smoothed and polished these tree-thick planks of wood, yet that boy entered effortlessly.'

'There was a cry from within the fortress,' whispered Cedarbranch, moving to Willow's side.

'Yes, it was the Gateman,' answered Willow in the slightest whisper, pointing to a black figure kneeling on the cobbles just inside the doors, its white eyes staring out blindly across the Causeway Field. 'No, do not touch him!' he hissed, grabbing both Tunnellers by their sleeves and pushing them roughly into the shadows beside the doors. 'Whatever has attacked the Gateman may take you too if you go too close to him.'

Cedarbranch shuddered. 'Those staring eyes and blackened bulging tongue!'

'He looks like a winter tree,' whispered the other Tunneller. 'All his blood lines are etched black beneath his skin.

'He is consumed by darkness, it races through his blood. Look! Look, he smiles and laughs, shutting his eyes,' whispered Cedarbranch.

Willow watched the kneeling figure for a moment then slowly drew his dagger blade and let the starlight flash on the bright metal, sending a beam of light across the Gateman's face. Bending, he scooped up a handful of loose granite chippings and cast them across the entrance. 'He is blind and deaf to us.'

Cedarbranch laughed nervously, moving back on to the Causeway to stare at the trembling figure. Willow grabbed the Tunneller's arm and again pulled him away. 'Stay clear of the Gateman, and watch the gates,' he hissed forcefully. 'I must follow those black Nighbeasts into the fortress of Underfall and find out their purpose. Wait here until the grey hours herald the new morning. If I have not returned by then take our people and find a place of safety, somewhere high and away from the shadows.'

'Willow, Willow,' both Tunnellers whispered hoarsely, but he was gone, moving noiselessly, running from shadow to shadow, his large round eyes opened wide against the darkness. At the entrance to the vaults he paused, feeling with his fingertips on the top of the first step. There were damp footprints and claw marks that stank of slime from the dyke. He shivered and wished he had a stoop of Battle Owls or savage Border Runners at his side. Willow carefully descended into the blackness. On each step he paused and turned his shell-shaped ears from left to right; ahead of him voices laughed and cursed. It sounded as if the intruders were searching for something. Willow crept fearfully, feeling his way amongst the petrified statues of the stone kings. Faint starlight showed through the window he had opened before King Holbian's stone throne. He could see the King's head and the two stone owls carved in his headrest stark-black against the night sky, and before him, the intruders.

'Granite Kings,' snarled Kerzolde, spitting in King Holbian's face and raising his mace to batter at the stone crown resting on his head.

Arbel laughed and struck at the King's hands, shattering his ancient fingers with one blow. The heavy stone sword twisted free of the King's broken fingers and fell, toppling,

154

against Arbel's arm, sheering through his armour and cutting him to the bone.

'Curse the daylight! Curse you, Granite King!' he shouted, dropping to his knees and struggling to strip the armour from his damaged arm.

Kruel laughed and knelt beside him. He pinched at the wound, sealing it in an ugly red weal. 'You are not yet strong enough, my brother, to do battle with Granite Kings, even dead ones. Stand back and watch me.'

Kruel reached out and took the mace from Kerzolde, wetting its brutal blunt end with his tongue. 'Watch!' he snarled. Looking down at King Holbian's feet, he raised the mace and began swinging it in a savage arc.

'Father,' he cried, suddenly seeing the Nightmare's head and letting the mace fly from his hands to smash against the far wall in a shower of granite splinters.

He fell on to his knees and looked at the smashed remains of Krulshards' head, the lank wisps of dead locks, the blind staring red eyes and shrivelled strips of rotten flesh. 'Father,' he whispered, hot tears spilling down his face.

Kerzolde knelt down beside him and hooked his one good claw behind the severed head, pulling it with all his strength, trying to free it from beneath the King's armoured boot.

'Enough! Leave it!' snarled Kruel. The hot tears had dried into blinding anger, the centre of his head burned and throbbed with pain. His skin was becoming taut; he was swelling, growing, just as he had done in the hollow. He reached with one of his fingernails into the ridge of skin on the top of his head and tore the skin apart. Eager to be rid of it he peeled and pulled, shaking his head from side to side. Willow gasped in terror and sank down to his knees amongst the shadows of the Granite Kings. Wide-eyed with horror he watched Kruel become blood-slippery in the starlight as he discarded his skin and shook out his new locks of hair, white-blond hair that shone with the crackle of hoar frost on bitter winter grass.

Kruel laughed, blind to his watcher, his eyes glowing with the fire of darkness as he squatted down before the Granite King. Greedily he began devouring the large handfuls of empty skin, eager to cover the raw sinews and bulging bunches of muscles hanging from his arms and legs. He had grown again and seemed to fill the tomb. A shadow rat fell from the pocket of his breeches and scuttled unnoticed across the rough granite floor into the shadows of the statues where Willow was hiding. Kruel was paling, the new skin was becoming firmer as it grew and thickened, drying across his flesh. Gingerly, he touched his face, feeling for loose ends of skin that would not meet. Arbel and the Nightbeasts crowded round him, searching with baited breath, watching.

'Perfect, perfect Kruel,' shouted Arbel. 'There is not a single blemish or mark upon your new skin. Nobody in all Elundium would know your origin.'

The shadow rat moved closer to Willow, sniffing at his foot, its brittle whiskers rattling in the darkness. Crouching back, it struck, its yellow teeth shearing through the coarse weave of his breeches into the soft flesh just above his ankle. Willow cried out, striking at the black rat with his dagger as it fled, escaping amongst the broken statues. Arbel half-rose at the cry. Kerhunge and Kerzolde snarled and leapt across the tomb, smashing at the stone statues as they closed on Willow.

Kruel laughed at them, and stretched out his hands. 'My rats have brought another warrior into the darkness. Leave him, let him see the real beauty of night. Bring me the mace that I might free my father's head from this cursed Granite King.'

Once, twice Kruel swung the brutal mace above his head, striking down savagely at King Holbian's ancient legs. Clouds of stone dust fogged the tomb, showers of shattered stone chips flew in every direction, the owls carved upon the headrest shrieked out, trying to free their talons from the stone to claw at the mace. The two stone Border Runners carved into the armrests of the throne snapped and snarled at Kruel's hands, breaking their brittle teeth on his strong fingers. King Holbian could not withstand such a battering and his stone crown burst into a thousand pieces as Krulshards' severed head rocked free from beneath his armoured boot.

'Father,' Kruel shouted, flinging aside the mace and gathering up the head. Gently he stroked the ragged wisps of dead locks and brushed out the sharp flakes of stone. 'I will take you back into the City of Night, back into the real darkness.'

Willow crouched, frozen, the blackness swallowing him, racing through his blood, thundering in his ears. His veins turned to indigo, his pale, almost translucent, skin was etched with a thousand shadowy lines. He could not move; his breath rattled and echoed far away in his throat; his fingers were tingling with numbness; the dagger trembled and shook in his hand as he watched, powerless to stop the destruction of the last Granite King. Nightmare visions filled his head; he was back in the City of Night, lost in the darkness, stumbling through the countless black chambers choked with the forgotten bones of his people. Nightbeasts tore at him, snapping his fingers in their brutal claws, lashing at his bare back with twelve-tailed iron whips. He saw the Elder's death and once again heard his last shout as he was crushed beneath clawed feet. He wept hot dry tears as the severed head broke free from King Holbian's foot and the Granite King crumbled into nothing. The darkness was fading, his fingers ached and burned, the joints were hideously bent and distorted where he had gripped the dagger. He tried to rise and toppled forwards, open-mouthed, on the rough granite floor.

Kruel sneered and looked for a moment at the small, still figure lying amongst the broken statues and turned towards the narrow crack leading into the City of Night that Kerzolde had just rediscovered at the far end of the tombs. 'That warrior isn't even tall enough to reach the bolts on the doors of Underfall,' he laughed to Arbel.

'Leave him here, perhaps he'll grow,' answered the Marcher, kicking Willow brutally in the side as he followed Kruel towards the secret way into the darkness.

Willow lay there helplessly, listening to the silence. His hearbeat had begun to slow; his fingers and toes were twitching and trembling as he tried to move them. Slowly he lifted his head and searched the tombs, watching each dark corner with fear. The grey hours had lightened the sky, morning was about to cast long shadows amongst the tombs of the Granite Kings. Willow struggled with all his might to get up from the stone floor, knowing that Cedarbranch would lead their people away with the new daylight and that he would never be able to find them.

Faint movement sounded in the courtyard above the tombs, iron-shod feet scraped on the stone stairway. Willow held his breath and fought to rise, the dagger shook in his twisted, blackened hands. The noises were closer now, someone was moving through the stone statues calling, whispering against the strengthening daylight. A large shadow crossed towards him. Now, now he must stand. 'By Nevian's sunlight . . .' he cried, using the last of his strength to stagger up on to his knees.

Screwing his eyes tightly shut against the pain that flooded through his body he lashed out, striking at empty air with his dagger. Cool hands gripped his wrist, stilling him. A soft, velvet muzzle brushed against his cheek and a gentle familiar voice sounded in his head.

'Oakapple?' he whispered, opening his eyes and trying to take a step forwards. 'Oakapple,' he cried again, toppling into her arms. 'The new Nightmare . . . the new . . .'

'Yes, yes,' she soothed, struggling to keep hold of him as he slumped against her. Starlight snorted and whinnied and knelt down beside her, taking Willows weight squarely across her back as he slipped from Oakapple's arms. Arching her proud neck she rose slowly and turned towards the entrance. Oakapple paused for a moment, the whites of her eyes showing clearly in the gloom of the vaults. Kneeling, she quickly gathered up the shattered pieces of King Holbian's crown and wrapped them in the tail of her cloak. She rose and fled, not daring to look back or pause for breath until she had reached the last stone step and felt the worn cobblestones beneath her feet.

'Run, run, find a place above the shadows,' sobbed Willow as the sunlight beyond the great doors of Underfall dissolved away his nightmare dreams and brought him roughly awake.

Slowly sitting up on Starlight's back, he stared down at the ring of frightened faces around him. 'Darkness,' he whispered, leaning forwards, 'real nightmare blackness that is worse than the City of Night. Worse than . . .'

Willow stopped, drawing breath into his aching lungs and saw that the Tunnellers' eyes were fixed, staring at his blackened and distorted hands where they rested on Starlight's mane.

'These are the marks of the darkness,' he cried, stretching out his gnarled fingers. 'The darkness that will creep into your bones, taking you, swallowing you up.'

'Darkness? What new darkness?' asked a dozen fearful voices in the circle of Tunnellers tightening around Starlight.

Willow leaned even further forwards and spoke in a hushed whisper. 'The Nightmare, Krulshards, spawned a son, a real Nightmare, more hideous and more powerful than you could ever dare to think of . . .' Willow paused, looking from eye to eye. 'You saw him standing beneath the walls of Underfall.'

'The Marcher who attacked the trees. Was that the new Nightmare?' asked Cedarbranch. 'He looked grim and battle ready.'

'No, no,' interrupted Willow. 'But there is a blood tie between them, I am sure. No, it is the boy who has Krulshards' power.'

'But he was only a boy,' called out one of the Tunnellers.

159

'He looked quite small and frail against those two Nightbeasts and the Marcher.'

Willow laughed, a dry sound without humour and turned towards the voice. 'You would not recognize him now. He grew in the tomb of Kings, splitting his skin quicker than a lizard, new locks of hair shimmering like winter frost. He ate the skin and it grew again, spreading across his body without a blemish, covering every rotten sinew and glistening piece of flesh.'

The Tunnellers in the circle had paled, their large round eyes wide-open with fear. With difficulty, Willow drew his leg up and on to Starlight's withers then pulled aside his breeches, showing them the ugly ratbite. 'That is how he will take you,' he cried, thrusting his tortured fingers into their faces. 'Black rats that carry a bite of darkness.'

The circle of Tunnellers moved in panic, stamping their feet, dancing on tiptoe. 'Rats, rats!' they cried, pushing and treading on each other in fear.

'Stop them,' whispered Willow to Oakapple. 'Make them stand still; they must listen.'

Oakapple shouted for order and made the Tunnellers spread in a broader circle beneath the ancient trees. Willow waited for the whispers of fear to settle and smiled to see that the ancient trees stood statue-still, each leathery leaf turned towards him.

'This new Nightmare is powerful enough to crumble granite beneath his fingertips. Powerful enough to enter the fortress of Underfall at the touch of his hand. He will take all Elundium if the black rats get into the Granite City . . .' Willow stopped, realizing the full horror of what he and all his people had done. Paling, he clutched at Starlight's mane.

'The City!' he cried. 'We have built a great wall of windows and vaulted archways. If the rats reach the city there are no doors to keep them out . . .'

The leaves above Willow's head rustled and rubbed

together, sending waves of soft murmurings far along the Greenways' edge.

'No! No!' Willow cried, looking up into the branches. 'There is no time to warn the King. We must build a new fortress, somewhere that is stronger than the Granite City, somewhere that the black rats cannot enter. It must be somewhere high above the shadows that Thane will see and know as a refuge against this new Nightmare. Yes, yes, it will be a castle rising sheer against the darkness. It will be a strong place to keep the daylight.'

The branches overhead whispered and sighed, stretching out across the Causeway Road, pointing with their leathery leaves into the wild lands beyond Mantern's Forest to a place of tall hills and narrow shaded valleys where all the Greenways that crossed Elundium had once met towards the great mound of sunbaked earth, the ancient meeting place of Kings that long ago had been named the Rising. Willow listened to the whispering leaves and slowly nodded his head. Quietly, he spread his hands and spoke again.

'The darkness did not take me as it took the Gatekeeper of Underfall. It has burned and twisted my fingers and has sunk me into nightmare dreams but it could not hold me and keep me. Perhaps for all of us born into the torment of night there is a little hope. If that is true we must hurry and build a safe place. Come quickly, follow me.'

Without another word the Tunnnellers left the Greenway and vanished between the close-grown tangle trees of Mantern's Forest. Willow slipped to the ground and carefully took Oakapple's hand between his crippled fingers. He whispered how much he loved her, knowing what courage it must have taken to come with only Starlight's help and rescue him from the tombs.

Oakapple smiled, her eyes softening. 'I love you, Willow. I love you enough to risk my life,' she answered.

Willow frowned, fearing to lose something precious that he had only just found. He looked out through the branches and sharp thorns of the tangle trees. 'We must prepare against this darkness or lose everything we love, even your foal,' he cried, turning to Starlight. 'If the new darkness touches him he will be lost for ever. You must go, gallop as never before to find him, then bring him and all the Warhorses that will follow you into the new fortress we will build.'

Starlight flattened her ears, showing the whites of her eyes and snorted in alarm. Willow urged her forwards. 'Go! Go!' he shouted as Starlight cantered away. 'Tell the owls and the Border Runners and bring all who will follow you into the Rising.'

Willow stopped and stared foolishly at Oakapple. 'The name, it was in the voices of the trees, they told me.'

Oakapple smiled and nursed his twisted fingers. 'Yes, and it will be a beautiful place that rises sheer in the sunlight. A tower of hope above a sea of darkness.'

'You heard it as well!' cried Willow. 'The voices in the trees telling us which way to go, naming the ancient crossroads.'

Oakapple smiled as she looked into Willow's pale haunted eyes and drew her cloak tightly around his shivering shoulders, pulling him close to her. 'It matters not, Willow, what we do not hear. You were the one who had the power to deliver us out of the darkness. I know you will keep us safe: you are our Elder now. That is why first the horses and now the trees talk to you and we, your people, will follow you to the ends of Elundium.'

Willow shrank into the cloak, his teeth chattering with fear. 'I dare not fail,' he whispered. 'I saw it there in the darkness as King Holbian shattered into a thousand pieces, the end of Elundium, the sun dimmed to a shadow, the darkness covering everything.'

Wedding Ties in Candlebane Hall

Thane hurried the length of Candlebane Hall to greet his friends. Eventine was led away to refresh herself after her journey but Thane kept Kyot by him.

'I'm glad you came,' Thane said, gripping Kyot's travel-stained sleeve and smiling everywhere at once to acknowledge the smiles and murmurs of the people who thronged the Candle Hall.

'We rode on the edge of the wind,' Kyot said as he stared around him and shivered. 'Kingship must be a difficult business; all these people, the noise, the crowds.'

'Difficult!' gasped Thane. 'That is not the half of it. If I frown the whole of Candlebane Hall will be thrown into shadow. But I must follow my fate.'

Kyot nodded, feeling his own face flushed with embarrassment at the half-caught whispering that followed their measured steps as they walked the length of the Candle Hall – whispers of the great battle with the Nightmare – and the soft touch of many hands as they passed through the throng. 'Forgive me, great warrior, I touch you for luck,' had met him at every turn.

'I need you, Kyot,' Thane whispered as they reached the far end of the hall and slowly turned towards the High Throne. 'I need a friend who will not treat me as a king, someone who will share my shadow and claim a full half of it.'

Kyot laughed and gripped Thane's arm. 'I would have

come sooner, leading the Archers of Stumble Hill, but we had ridden to Clatterford to guard Eventine's father from the trees and we missed Errant on the road. We have galloped with little rest to be here for the wedding ties. You know I would never desert you, Thane.'

Mulcade and Rockspray perched battle ready on Thane and Kyot's shoulders. Together they turned their unblinking eyes towards the doors of the Candle Hall and hooted softly. All eyes followed theirs and murmurs and whispers of excitement died away into silence. Kyot gasped and blinked.

Thane caught his breath and took a step. 'Elionbel,' he whispered, spreading his arms and gazing in wonder at her.

'Now is the moment,' Elionbel whispered to Tombel, her father, as she gathered her courage and stepped carefully across the threshold into the bright sunlight and slowly passed through her procession of guardians who had halted in the broad aisle. She proceeded into the cool polished shadows of Candlebane Hall past Fairday, the Master of Clatterford, Thunderstone, the Keeper of World's End, Duclos, the deaf swordsman, and a host of others whom Errant had gathered from the length and breadth of Elundium. She smiled nervously as she passed Errant, Grey Goose and Breakmaster who knelt, casting their cloaks of blue satin for her to walk across; past Angishand, Thane's mother, who had sewn her beautiful wedding gown and had caught into its seams a thousand daylights of happiness, to the place where Eventine stood, tired and dusty from a hard road, the great Bow of Clatterford still in her hand.

Squeezing her father's hand, she stopped beside Eventine and stretched out her other hand. 'Walk with us, Eventine, and put your hand that saved me from the darkness into mine, be with me now in this moment of joy.'

Eventine smiled and yet she saw the shadow of fear in Elionbel. She stepped into the broad aisle and motioned with her bow hand back towards the Candle doors. 'Let all of those who brought you from the darkness rejoice in this moment, let the wild and free walk with you to the high throne.'

Elionbel turned her head and looked back towards the Candle doors. 'Esteron! Equestrius!' she called, reaching out her hand. 'Stumble, brave Stumble,' she laughed as the little relay horse trotted out from between the Warhorses. Sprint neighed fiercely and cantered into the Candle Hall, the wind in the bow string attached to his saddle whispering a haunting tune of places far away across the endless grasslands.

Laughing with joy, Elionbel ran her hand across their powerful shoulders and touched the silver-threaded battle plaits so lovingly woven into their manes. 'When darkness held the road you came, so proud, so beautiful, so full of courage. Walk with me now and share this moment.'

Beyond the Candle doors late hoofbeats raced across the bridge that rose in one clear span above Swanwater. A stag roared, setting the candle flames dancing on their wicks.

'Tanglecrown!' Elionbel cried, waiting with laughter in her eyes until the Lord of Stags had passed between the doors and stood before her. Kneeling, Tanglecrown swept his huge stand of antlers in a glittering arc before holding them statue-still for Elionbel to place her hand between the razor tips on his soft forehead.

'Lead us forward, Lord of Stags, and light the shadows of Candlebane Hall,' she asked, turning back towards the throne.

Shadowy wings flapped between the Candle doors and fine droplets of water scattered across the threshold stone, sparkling with light. 'Ousious, Ogion!' Elion cried, beckoning to the grey swans and calling them forward. Kneeling between them she caressed their soft downy feathers and drew them close to her. 'Share your silent courage with me and walk with me to the wedding ties,' she whispered to them.

Ousious lifted her head and sang in silence of the winter-dark reeds and the love that had defeated the Nightmare then she gently brushed her bright orange beak on Elionbel's hand. Ogion proudly lifted his head and stared with glittering eyes at the waiting crowds thronging either side of the broad aisle, and took his place beside Elionbel.

'We are ready now, Father,' she whispered, smiling and she took her father's hand and moved forwards through the shafts of high vaulted sunlight that streamed down into Candlebane Hall.

'Look at the gown,' Thane whispered to Kyot as the procession drew closer. 'See how it holds the light.'

Kyot nodded, dry-mouthed. 'It watches us as Elion moves. There are countless peacocks' eyes needled into its weave.'

'Yes,' answered Thane, 'they catch the sunlight and glow fire-bright. Look at the colours.'

'Your mother must be the greatest needlewoman in all Elundium,' murmured Kyot. 'Look at the burning sun on the bodice and the cool starlight sewn into the hem, and the lace so delicate and spider-fine etched across the blue velvet. It tells the story of your triumph over the darkness. It is a wonder of Elundium.'

Thane laughed and stepped forward to take Elionbel's hand. 'My love,' he whispered, smiling as he led her up on to the dais at the foot of the High Throne. 'Though all the darkness stood between us we are here to be bound together through love, our lives to entwine for ever.'

Turning to face the sea of faces that spread across Candlebane Hall, he lifted his hands and cried out, 'Let the wedding ties begin.'

Soft laughter sounded in the shadows of the High Throne, gentle colours danced in the first shaft of sunlight shining through all the colours of the rainbow as Nevian, the Master of Magic, the Lord of Sunlight, stepped forward. Taking Thane and Elionbel's right hands, he joined them together and called in a loud voice: 'The light will be with those who love and cherish it, for they shall be blessed to shine in the darkness.'

'The light shall be with them always,' chanted every voice in the Candle Hall.

Nevian smiled and silenced the gathering with his piercing gaze. 'There are two others in this Candle Hall who shall be love-bound. This daylight two others may stand beside King Thane and Lady Elionbel and share these wedding ties, for without them and the sweet music they make in the darkness there would be no sunlight here in Candlebane Hall.'

Turning his head to the left, Nevian searched out Eventine and quietly called her forwards saying, 'Come, Lady of Clatterford, bowmaiden of Elundium.'

'Lord, I . . . I . . .' Eventine exclaimed, stepping backwards and clutching at her dusty, travel-stained cloak.

Breakmaster saw her confusion and hurried forwards, unbuckled her dirty cloak and spread the steelsilver battlecoat across her shoulders. 'None is more worthy, my beautiful Lady of Clatterford,' he whispered, 'for it is a gift of Kings that I have put about your shoulders and it shimmers with all the colours of a summer's day. Listen, and as you move larks' songs and meadow thrush will be with each graceful step you take.'

Nevian turned his head to the right and fixed Kyot with his eye, smiling with pride to see him now full-grown, a master of his own destiny. 'Come forward, Kyotorm, Keeper of Stumble Hill, first bowmaster of Elundium. Come to my left hand and let me tie your wedding knot, for your love has grown near to full flowering. Come, stand before me.'

Eventine and Kyot both blushed and made to kneel before Thane but he would have none of it and pulled them to their feet. 'These two are as brother and sister to me,' he said with joy, 'and in black times they shared my hardships and we walked hand in hand into the darkness. Gladly we will share these wedding ties. Come, Kyot and Eventine, give your hands to the Master of Magic; come while the full glory of the sunlight shines down on Candlebane Hall.'

Nevian laughed as he pulled two threads from the rainbow

cloak and held them up for all to see. He turned and wove the first around Thane and Elionbel's hands, and the second thread he wove around Kyot and Eventine's.

'Wedding ties are for a lifetime and through them will come the seeds of tomorrow,' he called.

'Out of the darkness, into the daylight,' chanted the gathering.

Nevian held up their rainbow-threaded hands and they shone with all the soft colours of a summer's day. Crying out, he challenged the Candle Hall: 'Is there any man, woman, Marcher or warrior born in all Elundium who would cut these threads?'

Silence spread across Candlebane Hall. Esteron snorted and pricked his ears as the Master of Magic continued with the wedding rites. 'Do you, Thanehand, King of all Elundium, take Elionbel, Marcher daughter of the Wayhouse of Woodsedge, to be love-bound with this rainbow thread to be your wife, to stand beside you in the sunlight, to share your shadow? Will you protect and honour her and take no others in her place?'

Thane smiled and looked steadily into Elionbel's eyes. 'While I live I swear to it all, for we are love-bound.'

Nevian nodded slightly and turned to Elionbel, his eyes softening. 'Do you, brave Elionbel, born of Marcher blood, do you take Thanehand, King of all Elundium to be love-bound with this rainbow thread to be your husband, to shelter in the same shadow and to share his triumphs and defeats, to take no others in his place?'

Elionbel lifted her eyes and searched the Candle Hall for her father. Briefly their eyes met and he nodded, clearly showing they had his blessing. Turning her head, she smiled at Thane. 'While I live I shall always love you and cherish each moment we are together in sunlight or darkness, in happiness and sorrow. You have this, my solemn vow.'

Thane brought her rainbow-threaded fingers to his lips

and kissed them tenderly. 'In sunlight, starlight or darkness we shall never part again, on this you have my solemn vow.'

Nevian smiled and lifted their interwoven fingers. 'That which has been woven together shall not be broken.'

Reaching beneath the rainbow cloak he brought forth a tiny set of silver scissors and cut the secret knot he had tied between their palms. Taking the loose ends, he tied them so that both retained on their middle finger of the right hand a single strand of thread, woven and interlaced into a shimmering ring. 'This thread shall be the sign, the binding mark of your love, let it shine everbright to the end of your days.'

'Everbright in the sunlight,' sighed the multitude with joy as Thane took Elionbel into his arms and kissed her.

Nevian laughed with delight and turned to Kyot and Eventine. He took their threaded fingers into his own and drew them to the edge of the dais, then began the wedding ties, chanting by rote, repeating each word and taking in exchange their solemn pledges.

Fairday laughed and smiled and wrung his hands both with joy and sorrow, the wet tears coursing down his cheeks, to gain such a son but to lose such a precious daughter. He leaned closer to listen to Eventine giving her vow.

'While I live I shall always love you and cherish each moment we are together, sharing one shadow in the sunlight, making sweet music with our bow strings, on this you have my solemn vow.'

Thoron gently touched Fairday's arm. 'She is a rare treasure,' he whispered, caught up in the moment and dabbing at his watering eyes.

'Yes, yes,' sobbed the Master Glassmaker, 'and the Crystal House of Clatterford will never be the same again. It will be quieter, more mellow in the sunlight without its fair lady Eventine.'

Nevian gave a great shout and cut the knot, rethreading the sparkling threads on each middle finger in turn. 'This shall be their sign, the binding marks in the tower on Stumble

Hill. Let no man be he base- or warrior-born put them apart for the thread shall shine everbright to the end of your days.'

'Everbright, everbright,' shouted the crowds, for they had taken the daughter of Clatterford to their hearts and now the ceremony was over they surged forwards towards the dais.

Tanglecrown knelt beside Sprint at their feet on the first step of the dais of the throne and Rockspray hovered above their heads casting a proud shadow in the shafts of sunlight.

'There shall be a feast,' shouted Thane, 'a wedding feast that will last a dozen daylights, the whole city shall eat and be merry and rejoice in these wedding ties for they mark the end of Krulshards' darkness and a new beginning in Elundium.'

Nevian laughed, shook out the rainbow cloak and linked his arms with the newly wedded then called out to Esteron and Equestrius, 'Lead us Lords of Horses to the feast of Kings.'

Nevian ate little and spoke less during the feasting, retreating into the folds of the rainbow cloak. He watched and listened to the easy talk and laughter that filled the night-time hours. Something was troubling him, nagging and gnawing at his bones, something was happening out beyond the city, he could sense it. He felt a dark shadow was threatening to cloud the sunlight, but what? His vision seemed muddled and yet his magic was growing stronger. New colours were weaving their way into his cloak and the half-thrown curse upon the rebellious warriors at Thane's crowning had held them still, full-branched as ancient trees upon the Greenways' edge. Turning slowly in his chair, he had secretly searched Elionbel's eyes and seen that the shadows haunting her in the Palace of Kings had grown, making her pale in the sunlight. Frowning, he touched Thane's arm and asked to meet him in the Candle Hall before the new sun rose.

Footsteps echoed across the empty polished floor as the grey hours lightened the sky and Thane, his coat tails billowing, hurried to meet the Master of Magic. 'What troubles you so that we should meet under cover of darkness?' he asked in a whisper as Nevian led him to the High Throne.

Nevian frowned and paced the polished floor. Finally he spoke. 'There is a darkness that gathers beyond my sight and there is a shadow in Elionbel.'

'She fights to hide a great fear,' answered Thane, letting his head sink into his hands. 'I have asked and begged her to share the burden that darkens her heart. Sometimes it seems to shrink almost to nothing and she laughs easily again but any mention of Krulshards or her mother and she is haunted again.'

'Does she speak of anything or plead a reason for her fear?' asked Nevian, drawing close.

'No, her lips tremble and her hands shake with terror but she will tell me nothing. I love Elionbel and treasure her more than my own life. What, oh what can I, the King of Elundium, do to take away this fear?'

'Be still, be still. Tell me, when did the shadow first darken her heart? Was it at the threshold of the Granite City or at the pledging on the Causeway Field?'

Thane shook his head, thinking back, remembering. 'It was before that, in the City of Night, at the moment of Krulshards' death. Yes, yes! I lifted her up to rejoice in the shafts of early sunlight Willow had brought into the darkness but she cried in terror, struggled out of my arms and searched the black malice that hung in shrouded folds about the Nightmare's shoulders. She shouted – yes, I remember what she cried – that this is only the beginning of the real darkness, and then she gathered up her mother's shrunken body into her arms and gently rocked her backwards and forwards, promising, pledging something to herself.'

Thane stopped and tilted his head to one side, listening to the criers calling through the lower circles of the city for the people to awake. 'Perhaps Willow saw something that I

171

missed,' continued Thane. 'Something that would cast such a shadow across Elion. Surely I would have to be blind.'

Nevian sighed and thought deeply. 'Sometimes, sometimes the looking makes us blind, or we snag our toes on stones we should surely see. The shadow was in Elionbel on the Causeway Field and through it I caught a glimpse of dark daylights but it was only a moment's vision that I thought was grief for her mother, Martbel. But now I see with the strengthening of my powers that it was more than that. Summon Willow and we will ask him what he saw in that first moment as sunlight flooded into the City of Night. Call him before the morning striker touches the daylight bell.'

'We cannot,' answered Thane helplessly. 'Willow and all his people have vanished. Errant took my summons through all Elundium searching far and wide to bring those who could come to the wedding ties, but the Tunnellers were nowhere to be found. Willow had asked leave of me to see the beauty of Elundium for the Tunnellers to wander as they pleased.'

Nevian muttered something and looked absently at the Candleman moving across Candlebane Hall, snuffing out each tall candle in turn. 'Willow is seeking his true home, to find and bury the roots of his people in the place Krulshards tore them from and I failed to set them on the right path!' he cried. 'In foolish haste I overlooked the ending of their homelessness.'

'I offered them all Elundium,' Thane whispered, 'but they would take nothing but the freedom to wander.'

Nevian laughed bitterly and stood up. 'They are too proud, Thane, to take what belongs to others. They will search until their feet bleed, lost from us, somewhere in the wildest stretches of Elundium.' He paused, spun around and gripped Thane's hand. 'Perhaps Fate has set them wandering for a purpose. Perhaps they needed to see in order to find.'

'They garden as they travel,' interrupted Thane. 'Everywhere, even amongst the roots of ancient trees where few would tread, they have trimmed the Greenways' edge and pruned the tangle trees, leaving neat bundles of branches, stacked ready for burning.'

Nevian laughed again, his face softening. 'The trees will not hurt you. No, they may yet be a blessing if the sunlight fails. We must watch and wait. Willow will send us news or come again to the Granite City when he has found what he seeks.'

Nevian began to tell him of the Rising and Willow. 'It stands a ruin now but once it was a great mound where all the Greenways of Elundium met. A meeting place of Kings that rose sheer above the landscape, beyond Underfall, beyond the endless grasslands, a place of waterfalls and wooded hills.'

'And Willow's people came from this Rising?' asked Thane, the question of the trees forgotten. 'Were they a people of Kings before Krulshards stole them?'

Nevian smiled and gathered the rainbow cloak into tight folds, muting its colours, hiding its brilliance. 'They were a people of tragedy,' he whispered. 'They were bound in chains by the first Granite Kings to raise the bones of Elundium into great cities, to make spires of sheer stone and places of beauty for others to wander in. They were even forced to cut the Greenways league by league across Elundium.'

'But the Rising?' pressed Thane. 'How was the Rising their home if they were prisoners?'

Nevian put his fingers on to Thane's lips and drew him out of the Hall into the bright sunlight. 'Willow's people were born into chains and passed from King to King. They knew nothing of freedom and merely bent their backs in numbing labour. Their last great task before the darkness came was to build the Rising, trampling the soft earth layer by layer until it rose above the shadows. It was the last place in all Elundium where they saw the daylight.'

Nevian shuddered, remembering the screams of pain, the weeping as the great mound rose. 'It is a place of beauty now, Thane, flower-decked and gentle in the sunlight, but thousands died and were trodden into the base of that pitiless mound, and thousands more of Willow's people were crushed and bound to wooden stakes and buried, standing in endless circles rising up towards the summit of the hill.'

'Why?' whispered Thane, his face whiter than the winter moon. 'Why such slaughter and why do you tell me of it?'

Nevian frowned. 'The Rising is a watchtower guarded by those thousands of sightless eyes in death. Willow's people watch for the enemies of the sunlight. I tell you because you must know of it, because as the new King of Elundium, Willow and his people belong to you and they can never be free until you release them on the summit of the Rising. Krulshards merely stole them moments after the first Granite King arose and he used them to spread his darkness through the City of Night.'

'They shall be free!' Thane cried angrily. 'I shall make them so!'

Nevian smiled and hushed Thane into silence. 'None know of this tragedy; none save you and I in all Elundium have talked of it. When I entered the darkness and found Willow's Elder and showed him all of the daylight I kept the tragedy of their earlier life a secret to give them hope that they might one day be free to see the sunlight.'

'But the Rising?' hissed Thane. 'Surely they would not want to return to that cursed place!'

'Oh yes, Thane, to stand in the place of their fathers. But remember they do not know what stands beneath the ground, how shoulder to shoulder their ancestors' blind eyes stare outwards, how Willow's forefathers guard the Rising, only a thin layer of soft earth keeping them from the sunlight. Yes, of all the places in all Elundium that is where they should receive their freedom and become the Masters of their own destiny. It would indeed be a just ending to their sufferings.'

Thane gripped Nevian's hand and knelt before him. 'Lord and Master of Magic, if I have any power in Elundium I shall truly make Willow's people free.'

Nevian nodded and pulled Thane to his feet. 'Beware, my King, it may take great tact to give something they already think they have. They are a proud people, tempered by timeless hardships, if they should find the Rising and discover what lies only finger-deep beneath the surface it may break their spirit, or burden them with hatred for the Granite Kings and all those who follow them.'

Thane thought for a moment and turned slowly towards the bridge that rose above Swanwater. 'I will send Errant to search for Willow. If any man can find him he will.'

Nevian quickly agreed. 'Despatch Errant in all haste but tell him nothing of what lies beneath the Rising.'

Thane nodded and turned towards the top of the high wall surrounding Candlebane Hall and Swanwater. 'You tell of the dark and hint at shadowlight that will hide the sun, but what in all Elundium can I do to stop it?'

Nevian stroked his chin and drew his eyebrows together. He slowly paced the high wall then, turning back to Thane, threw his hands in the air. 'It would be dangerous to panic the people and only fools fence openly with shadows they cannot touch. No, you must appear to be easy, even overconfident, you must seem to do nothing and yet secretly you must search everywhere for the beginnings of these half-formed shadows that trouble the sunlight. I counsel you to give every warrior his freedom, disband the battle crescents and send the warriors home. Thank the Warhorses and the Border Runners for their tireless help to win the sunlight and give them all Elundium to wander in, but bid each man, each warrior and every Warhorse, Border Runner and Battle Owl to be on their guard against new shadows that might threaten the daylight. Let the people of Elundium be your eyes and ears.'

'But if I break the battle crescents we will be defenceless,' cried Thane.

Nevian smiled and drew Thane to him. 'Warriors will watch the harder and guard you closer if they think you have sacrificed your safety for their freedom. But fear not to look out along the Greenway to where a line of ancient trees throws long morning shadows across the road. Do not forget that I have pledged them to do your bidding. Disband the battle crescent and spread your eyes and ears far across Elundium.'

'What of Elionbel? How shall I rid her of the shadow that touches her heart?' Thane asked as the rainbow cloak began to dissolve into the rays of early sunlight.

'Whatever haunts fair Elionbel she guards it with great secrecy,' answered Nevian, his voice growing fainter. 'I fear it is tied up with her nightmare journey across Elundium. There are scars etched deep by Krulshards' cruel hand that may never heal. I will speak with her and try to draw out her fears so that she will share her burden. I will go to her as the noonday bell strikes across the city.'

'I fear nothing, nothing!' Elionbel cried, her face flushed with anger, her hands white-knuckled and clenched at her sides.

Nevian spread his hands and tried to calm her. 'I am not guilty of anything,' she shouted, retreating away from the Master of Magic as if dreading his touch.

'Elionbel, Queen of all Elundium, I charge you with nothing, I only come to you to ease the shadow that haunts your heart. Talk to me of the Nightmare, share the horrors of that black time and use my strength to blunt your pain.'

Elionbel seemed to hesitate, to take a step forward. Her lips trembled, short breaths rasped in her throat. 'I cannot tell. The people would stone me, Thane will curse me,' she whispered, wringing her hands in despair. Raising her head she blinked back tears of despair crying, 'I am pledged to keep my own counsel in the sunlight.'

Nevian frowned, catching only half her whispered words and gently took her hands, touching the rainbow thread he had woven so carefully around her middle finger. 'Such loyalty is rare, Elionbel, but it has the power to destroy your

176

love for Thane. Tell me, child, who would ask you to carry such a burden of secrets?'

New tears were welling up, brimming in her eyes, as she remembered her mother's last nightmare moments. Shaking her head she turned slowly away. 'I cannot tell you. Mart . . . Moth . . .'

The words strangled in her throat, choking her back into silence, forcing her down on to her knees. The noise of that hideous high chamber in the City of Night thundered in her ears, a cruel face leered in the darkness, a child's face stared at her, mocking her without pity. 'I will kill it, Mother, then everyone will forgive me. I promise, I promise,' she whispered, gathering her courage and turning to the Master of Magic.

Taking a deep breath she faced him eye to eye. 'Martbel, my mother, suffered cruelly at the Nightmare's hand. He taunted her and beat her without mercy when he discovered that I was Elionbel, the one he had crossed Elundium to take. He mocked her for daring to deceive him – that, that is the secret I carry. Mother was warrior-born and proud and swore me to let no man or woman in Elundium know of her torment. She pledged me to burn her body lest my father should see the rags and bones he had worn her to for it would destroy him.'

Nevian took her hands and drew her gently into the folds of the rainbow cloak. 'Elionbel, First Lady of Elundium,' he whispered, blinking at wet eyes, 'you carry a great burden for your mother yet all Elundium would have knelt before Martbel and offered up their spears and shields to honour her battle against Krulshards. There was no dishonour in what she did.'

Elionbel shook her head, hardly daring to believe that Nevian had swallowed the thread-fine tissue of lies so easily. 'It is not easy to forget, as yet I cannot share it but . . . when the shouts of terror have dimmed in my heart, when I am sure that the scars of those black nights have shrivelled in the sunlight then I will go to Thane and share the burden.'

Nevian smiled softly and melted at her touch, fading into nothing as the sun rode behind heavy thunderclouds. Elionbel bit her lip, shivered and paced her room in the high tower. What if the bastard child had survived, where was it now? Was it somewhere out there in some dark corner of Elundium growing, gathering strength to swallow the daylight?

'No!' she hissed, clenching her fists. 'It perished in the clumsy one-eyed Nightbeast's claws. It shrivelled up and died! It . . .' Elionbel shook her head, pushing her dark thoughts away, trapped wretchedly in the silence of lies, not daring to hope that the child had perished. Sighing miserably, she prepared to descend, without appetite, to the table for the noonday meal.

'Elionbel must suffer alone, my Lord,' whispered Nevian, coming to Thane's side where he stood lost in thought beside the doors of Candlebane Hall.

Thane jumped, startled by the Master of Magic and turned sharply, his eyebrows drawn upwards.

'Yes,' continued Nevian, 'she has woven a web of lies and half-truths to keep some secret. There was a faint ring of truth in what she told me but much was tangle-tongued.'

'Why? Why would she need to lie? There is nothing she needs to hide from us!'

Nevian spread his hands. 'She guards a secret from those last moments in the darkness. Martbel is a part of it and pledged her to silence, that much showed as truth in her eyes.'

'Martbel!' cried Thane. 'She was too weak to pledge Elion to secrets. She was worn to less than a shadow, shrunken and feather-light through her sufferings at Krulshards' hand. Surely Elion does not wish to keep her mother's torment a secret from me? Has she forgotten that with Kyot and Eventine's help I brought them out of the darkness?'

'You must keep silent counsel and give her time,' Nevian insisted. 'Let nothing of this meeting pass your lips. Watch and guard Elionbel, keep her safe through the darker watches of each night. I will walk on the high plateau before the black marble Gates of Night and search for the truth of what shadows her heart.'

'Nevian! Nevian!' Thane cried, a thousand questions crowding in his throat. 'What if I . . .'

But the Master of Magic had gone in one bright sparkle of colour; the rainbow cloak had faded into nothing.

The Black Standard Leaves the City of Night

Kruel crouched on the edge of the high chamber, watching and listening, his eyes blinking in the sunlight. Behind them lay the secret spiralling road that had led them up through the City of Night, through beautiful darkness so thick he could almost taste it. Settling back on his haunches, Kruel searched the chamber and looked with careful eyes across the battle-littered floor, past the heaps of Nightbeast dead, past the broken spears, blades and rusty scythes to the sheer column of black rock that reached up a single broken finger, pointing into the shafts of sunlight which flooded down through the broken roof.

'Father! Father!' he whispered, half-rising and seeing for the first time the tall, headless figure pinned to the column of marble still wrapped in the shadowy folds of the black malice.

Gathering Krulshards' head in his hands Kruel rose and stepped into the chamber, he shrugged off Kerzolde's cautious claw, slipped through Arbel's restraining fingers and began to cross the chamber. 'Beware! The warriors of Underfall may have set guards,' hissed Kerzolde.

Kruel turned his head, a snarl of hatred twisting his lips, and whistled once: a high cutting note, that set the heaps of dead all around him trembling. Everywhere the floor seemed to move as waves of darkness crossed the shafts of sunlight, swallowing it up where it touched the ground.

A huge black crow shrieked and rose from Krulshards' shoulders, spiralling up through the broken roof. 'That is the guardian of my father's tomb!' cried Kruel, pointing a finger at the departing crow. 'And these,' he laughed, pointing at the shadow rats swarming across the floor, 'will bite any warrior we meet, trapping them into our darkness. Come, come and kneel before the Master of Darkness!'

Kruel hurried on, pushing his way through the heaps of dead and knelt before Krulshards. Lifting the hem of the malice he kissed the shadowy cloth and wept, casting the black folds of night over his head.

'I will avenge. I will avenge!' he sobbed. And then he rose slowly to his feet, his face set in lines of bitter hatred. Bending, he gathered up the severed head and after wetting the dry shrivelled ends of flesh with his tongue, he lifted the head and carefully set it back in place on his father's shoulders. The lank dead locks of hair hung limp in the sunlight. The eyes stared blindly forwards, the jaw fell silently open: bone-black fingers seemed to tremble where they gripped the hilt of the spark-scarred sword that held him, Krulshards, the Master of Nightmares, trapped forever in the City of Night.

'Father! Father!' Kruel shouted, trying to prise the bone-black fingers from the hilt of the sword, kissing the dry, cracked, skinless lips as he tried to breathe new life into his father, the Master of Nightmares.

'He is dead, dead,' whispered Arbel, falling to his knees beside Kruel; 'You cannot bring him back to life.'

'Dead!' echoed Kerzolde and Kerhunge, touching the hem of the malice.

'Dead!' shouted Kruel in blind anger, gripping the hilt of the sword with both hands. 'Thanehand will hang in this chamber. He will be dead! Dead, dead, dead! I will drive this same sword through his foul heart.'

Pulling with all his strength, Kruel tried to draw the sword out of the stone but his hands slipped on the bright metal, sending him reeling backwards across the chamber. Cursing he tried again and again. Arbel pulled with him; Kerzolde hooked his one good claw around the hilt. Kerhunge grunted, locking his hairy fingers on the sword but it remained stuck fast as Thane had plunged it in his moment of triumph through Krulshards' rotten heart, fused ever fast into the column of rock.

Shouting and cursing, Kruel strode through the chamber smashing everything in his path. 'Thanehand will die for this. Die! Do you hear me? He will die for this!' he screamed.

'When we are strong, Master, we will take all Elundium from him,' soothed Kerzolde trying to keep pace with him.

'Now!' shouted Kruel. 'Now! We cannot wait!'

Kruel turned, pushing Kerzolde aside, and pointed across the chamber. 'Look,' he hissed, 'we have black shadow rats and weed worms to spread the darkness. Everything I touch will become ours. Just as the gates of Underfall opened for us so will all Elundium fall. We shall take what is to be ours!'

Arbel laughed. 'I will follow you, Kruel, in the finest Nightbeast armour I can find in this chamber. I will be a Warrior of the Night!'

Kruel bent and loosed his dagger over a heap of Nightbeast dead. He cut off a limp Nightshard arm and pulled the smooth black armoured scales away from the rotting flesh. He threw it to Arbel. 'Here,' he shouted, hooking his fingers beneath the beast's iron collar and skinning the chest armour away, 'none will be able to defeat you in this. It is as smooth as water and harder than stone.'

Arbel laughed and threw aside his course woven shirt. He laid the Nightshard's armour across his chest. It itched and tickled and grew warm beneath his touch, rising and falling with each breath. 'It is a fine fit,' he laughed. 'It feels almost like a second skin. Look how smooth it is!'

Kerzolde sneered and touched the chest armour with his one good claw. 'Now you are almost one of us, Marcher. Now you have grown part of a Nightbeast's skin.'

'This is armour, not skin!' Arbel snapped, turning away from the Nightbeast and reaching for the face plates and helm that Kruel had stripped from its head and now held out to him.

'Take it off,' hissed Kerzolde, goading him. 'If it is only armour take it off.'

Arbel laughed and curled his fingers around the edge of the chest armour and tried to remove it. He frowned and pulled again, feeling with his finger tips along the sharp ridges and across the brittle scales. 'It has grown into my skin! It has grown into me!' he cried out, turning on Kruel.

Kruel smiled and thrust the face plates and helm at him. Kerzolde sneered, tapping him sharply on the brittle new skin. 'One of us!' he hissed. 'Take the helm and be one of us!'

Arbel hesitated, looking from Kruel to the hideous Night-beasts who crouched, leering at him.

'Be a real part of the darkness,' whispered Kerzolde, and Kerhunge, goading him. 'Wear it and look as beautiful as we do.'

Arbel ran his fingers over his face, feeling the high cheekbones and strong, well-set jaw. Shaking his head he began to back away. 'I cannot!' he cried. 'I am a man. I am a Marcher.'

Kruel laughed, stretched out his hand and gripped Arbel's arm. 'You are more than that, you are my brother with the blood of darkness flowing between us. Wear the Nightshard's armour and be my first Captain. Take the helm, take it and share my power.'

Slowly, his hands shaking, Arbel reached for and took the smooth, brittle face-armour and helm. The Nightbeasts had grown quiet, creeping back a pace out of his reach. Arbel watched them, fixing them with his eyes as he brought the helm down over his head, feeling the cheek plates touch his face. He felt the tingling and itching as the skin and armour grew together, the helm felt hot and heavy as it gripped his head, bowing him forwards. Laughter, screams and shouts of torment shouted and echoed in the helm somewhere deep

183

down in the heart of Mantern's Mountain. Far away he could hear the stones crack and the faint drip of water wearing away the rock. He felt ten leagues high and as strong as ten Granite Kings. Yet the sunlight grew harsh and hurt his eyes, soft shadows seemed to beckon him, Kerzolde tried to move, crying out as Arbel, the new Arbel, Captain of the Night-beasts, stilled him with a sudden blow, making him grovel on the chamber floor.

'My brother of darkness; Master of all that moves by night!' laughed Kruel, running his fingers over the sharp armoured spines that had rapidly grown along Arbel's arms.

Arbel slowly turned his head and tried to smile. 'Brother,' he shouted in terror, the sound echoing in the helm, the word grating in his throat, 'I am now both man and beast. Look at my hands, my legs – they are growing! Look, they are twisting out of shape.'

Kruel laughed. 'No, you will be strong and beautiful. Lay down in the shadow of the malice and let the strength of the Nightshard grow through you.'

Arbel fell to his knees, clutching his head in his hands and screamed. Blackness reached out, touching him everywhere, cold shadows of night swept across his body; he was falling, tumbling backwards, he could touch without feeling and feel without touching. Darkness was smothering his eyelids, swallowing him up. 'Kruel! Kruel!' he tried to call out through blackened brittle lips.

Kruel sat beside Arbel, huddled in brooding silence, hatred and anger boiled in his heart. He would destroy the foul Thanehand now he had seen how his father had suffered at the Galloperspawn's hands; he would take and destroy everything that belonged to him, the owls, the horses, the dogs. Darkness would take everything, everything he had seen in Kerzolde's simple mind. Rising, he stood before his father, Krulshards, and drew a long black dagger from within the malice. He gathered the folds of the black cloth in his other hand and cut it with two swift strokes, leaving only a ragged tatter covering the shoulders of the Nightmare pinned there by Thane's sword.

'Forgive me, Father,' he whispered, kneeling and kissing the fingers, gently caressing the loose folds of hanging flesh, 'but I need this cloak of shadows to spread your darkness across Elundium for it shall be my emblem, raised to cast a shadow over the sun and strike terror in Thanehand's heart!'

Arbel cried out and sat up carefully, turning his head from left to right. He clenched and unclenched his armoured fingers, touching the smooth scales of armour covering his arms. Rising slowly to his feet he looked down at Kerzolde and Kerhunge. 'Now I am more than you, Nightbeasts! Now I am your Captain!' he sneered, snapping a discarded spear-shaft that lay near his feet as if it were a stalk of straw.

Kruel laughed as he touched Arbel's arm. 'Brother,' he urged, thrusting a knuckle of polished armour before him. 'Look, look now at my Captain of Captains!'

Arbel took the polished metal and held it at arm's length; he gasped at what he saw. It was true, the armour had changed and grown while he slept, trapped in beautiful, black dreams; now it was smooth and black, reflecting dark shadowlights. It hugged each muscle, covering his body completely and rippling as he moved. Yet no matter how closely he looked or felt with his nails he could not find a single join or crack, even his eyelids were brittle armour.

He laughed, feeling his cheeks crackle as the armour stretched across them. Lifting his hands, he felt around the rim of the Nightshard's helm and ran his fingers through the fine spine-like hair that flowed across his shoulders. 'Beautiful!' he whispered, turning the knuckle of polished armour this way and that, touching and looking at the high cheekbones and the proud forehead now fused in smooth contours into the armour. 'Now I am a real warrior of the darkness. Now I am strong enough to destroy the sunlight.

Kruel laughed and tilted the crude mirror. 'You are naked darkness, brother. We must clothe you to enter Elundium.'

Arbel looked around the chamber, his eyes brightening. 'What better!' he shouted, stooping and picking up his marching belt with one hand while with the other he gathered a swarm of shadow rats. 'I will have a tunic of living darkness,' he laughed, threading the squealing rats, one by one, by their tails through the chain links of the belt. Bending again he gathered handfuls of the rats and wove their tails tightly together and flung them across his shoulders. Sharp claws skidded on the smooth armour and brittle spines rattled in rage but Arbel only laughed. 'Any warrior I embrace and draw within the cloak will be bitten into the darkness!'

Kruel laughed with delight, running his fingers through the cloak of shadow rats, letting their sharp claws cling briefly to him. 'You, brother, will strike terror into all you meet with your swarming shadows, while I, who have the power to deny the sun a shadow, will bring darkness across Elundium with this my father's malice. It will stand on every hilltop, spike and spire until there is nothing, nothing but black night. And then in final triumph, Thanehand, the foul Galloperspawn, will be hung here in this chamber to rot in my darkness!'

'Lead us onwards,' shouted Arbel, throwing the squealing cloak of shadow rats back across his armoured shoulders and turning towards the secret road that spiralled down through the heart of Mantern's Mountain, down into the tombs beneath the fortress of Underfall.

'No,' hissed Kruel, turning and looking up through the broken dome at the fading sunlight. 'My darkness is already creeping through the fortress of Underfall, there are shadow rats and weed worms in the tomb of the Granite Kings. We will begin the great darkness here on the summit of Mantern's Mountain. Come, it is time to trample the sunlight of Elundium into the shadows. It is time to reopen the Gates of Night.'

The Battle Crescents are Broken

Long summer days had drawn to an end; it was time for many partings. Thane sighed sadly and looked out of the Granite Tower across a changing landscape to where autumn leaves were already edged with the beginnings of white winter frost.

'Tomorrowlight you must return to Stumble Hill,' he murmured, turning to Kyot, 'before first winter snows block the Greenways.'

Kyot nodded silently and stared out across the maze of roofs that spread below them in ever-widening circles until they vanished in a haze of blue cooking smoke, fogging the shadows of the great wall. Frowning, Kyot looked beyond the City and for a moment stared at the neat rows of ancient trees: since the wedding ties they had seemed to draw closer to the Granite City. He turned and took a deep breath. 'You must call a Battle Council to discuss your safety before the City empties.'

'Battle Council!' laughed Thane. 'What need would that serve but to quicken warriors' hearts? No, no, there is no need for that, I am safe enough now that the Nightmare is dead. Tomorrowlight the last of the warriors will depart; you to Stumble Hill, Thunderstone to Underfall, and Fairday – ' Thane paused and smiled ' – perhaps the Maker of Glass arrowblades will travel with you, taking the Greenway to Stumble Hill.'

Kyot blushed and looked away. 'I love him dearly, Thane,

but the tower is a grim place of . . . of . . .'Kyot's voice trailed away as he searched for the words, looking for a way to explain how difficult it would be having Eventine's father, the Master of Clatterford, beneath his roof.

Thane laughed and gripped Kyot's arm. 'Yes, Kyot, Clatterford is a magical place, full of breathtaking beauty that will always outshine your Tower; but Stumble Hill is a jewel of Elundium, a rare treasure, that stands alone at the crossroads, worn smooth by the rub of Nightbeasts guarding the way to Underfall and keeping the Greenway open. See it for a moment through others' eyes, see the proud Archers ever watchful in the casement slips, listen to the sweet music in the armourers' hammers, for it was a place of war that kept us safe through the darkest nights.'

'If there was a beauty in our ever watchfulness, if it was a thing that you took pride in so much, then listen to me now. Call the Council, let those who love you prepare for the daylights ahead,' implored Kyot.

'No! No,' snapped Thane, remembering Nevian's words of counsel and knowing that he must keep his fear a secret from Kyot. 'I am the King and I say that there will be no Council nor a guard on the Granite City. We are at peace, do you hear me? There will be no Battle Council.'

Kyot paled and slowly knelt, his hand shaking as he held out the great Bow of Orm. 'Lord,' he said, 'there are rumours of a new darkness in the wild lands near Underfall, but you are my King and Master and are wise in all things. Forgive me, for I spoke from the heart as one who loves you and fears for your safety. I spoke as your . . .' Kyot hesitated, his voice trailing. He dared not say 'friend' or 'brother' from the tone of Thane's voice and the hard glitter in his eyes. Today was not a daylight for remembering a hard road shared together. Today he was a King who would not be crossed.

Thane touched the Bow of Orm, and signalled Kyot to rise, then dismissed him kindly, knowing that he was dangerously near to sharing his fears with his one true friend.

'Tomorrowlight,' he said softly, gripping Kyot's hand, 'we will drink from the Wayside Cup before you start on the long road home. Thunderstone shall be first for his is the longest road. Durondel, the armourer, Duclos and Morolda shall follow, leading out the warriors of the battle crescents that swept the Nightbeasts from Elundium. We will watch them together and remember our black road into the City of Night.'

'I shall worry each daylight for your safety,' Kyot whispered, his hand upon the door.

'Then be my watchman,' answered Thane, taking a pace after Kyot. 'Send me word if new shadows grow or if there are whispers of a new darkness to threaten the sunlight. Keep a keen edge on your arrowblades, watch each new . . .' Thane hesitated, he knew he had almost said too much but it was difficult being a king, keeping secrets, always watching, always walking alone even when the crowds pressed all around shouting your name, seeking your favours.

'Go quickly,' he whispered, sighing sadly, knowing that he must trust no one until he knew more of the shadows troubling Nevian and blackening Elionbel's heart. Pacing to the window, he watched Kyot leave the tower and run across the bridge spanning Swanwater, down into the bustling streets below.

'He may be King and the bravest man in all Elundium but I fear for him,' whispered Kyot, keeping pace with Thunderstone as they entered the breaking yards.

Thunderstone shook his head. 'There is nothing, nothing we can do, Kyot, if Thane will not call a Council nor a guard against the future. We must follow his will for we are all pledged to serve him.'

'He has disbanded the battle crescents,' Grey Goose muttered moving closer to Kyot. 'Warriors are to become farmers, servers, even Candlemen. He says that is the way forwards to a better Elundium.'

Kyot threw his hands up in despair. 'Who will guard the Greenways? Am I to put down my bow and harvest the grasslands?'

Eventine laughed softly and squeezed Kyot's hand. 'Do you remember that bowl of corn I left at your feet in the grasslands? Well, that is more than ready for harvest.'

Kyot frowned at her and almost answered harshly but the gentle laughter in her eyes stopped him.

'We will find a way to keep Thane safe,' she whispered. 'We will not sleep nor let the arrows grow blunt in the quiver. Each one of us will watch over him. Come, let us pledge ourselves to be Keepers of the King's safety. What say you to that?'

Silently they clasped hands, one above the other: Thunderstone, Kyot, Eventine, Grey Goose and Breakmaster. 'To the King!' whispered Fairday, casting his sky-washed cloak across his shoulder and placing his slender hand upon the others.

'The best of the Nighthorses shall stand ready saddled,' whispered Thunderstone, 'for I love my King more than life itself.'

'Archers in a strike shall crouch within the Tower on Stumble Hill,' whispered Kyot, 'for whether Thane wants it or not we are as brothers and I love him.'

'Tanglecrown will carry me fleet of foot,' whispered Eventine.

'I will watch over the King night and day,' whispered Breakmaster. 'Mulberry and Beaconlight shall be saddled ready, watch for them on the Greenway.'

'What of Tombel and Thoron? Surely they should be part of us?' asked Grey Goose, turning careful Archer's eyes towards the low shadows that flanked the courtyard.

'They dare not, for they are too close to Thane in blood,' answered a whisper from the shadows. 'And they could not keep secret what you pledge, for it goes against the King's wishes and whispers of treason.'

'Treason!' cried Thunderstone, his hand upon the horse-tail hilt of his sword. 'Come forwards and I will teach you, whoever you are, how to use the word treason, for I love my King.'

Nevian laughed and stepped quickly into the courtyard taking each one of them by the hand and drawing them into the shadows. 'Be seated,' he urged, pointing to a circle of stone benches, 'for there is much to say.'

'Why do you whisper of treason?' Breakmaster asked, spreading his hands. 'All we strive to do is keep our King from harm.'

'He has become blind to reason,' interrupted Kyot angrily, 'disbanding the battle crescents! Hasn't he heard the rumours of new shadows in the wild lands? Why he is turning us all into farmers or the like!'

Nevian smiled and pressed cool fingers on Kyot's lips. 'You, Kyotorm, must be especially patient for you are as a brother to Thane, bound close by shared hardships.'

'Brothers!' hissed Kyot. 'He will not have me speak as a brother, but forces me to bend in each argument. He wields his kingship until I bow and scrape as any other man, courting favours to dodge his temper!'

Nevian frowned. 'No! No, you speak now through the rawness of new hurt, but remember, Kyot, that Thane is a king, remember that for him true friends are hard to find and that one voice amongst the clamour for his favours is not easily heard.'

'I want nothing!' cried Kyot, jumping to his feet. 'Nothing but to see Thane safe.'

'Then you do want something and like every other man that seeks an audience you tried to bend his will to your advantage. You forget that Thane must stand by his judgements, right or wrong, if he is to govern Elundium and build a better world out of the ruins and ashes left by the Nightbeasts.'

191

'So by keeping my sword sharp I go against the King and dabble in treason?' muttered Thunderstone.

Nevian smiled and waited until the last Lampmaster had subsided into silence. 'You see too much in what Thane has ordered and you have twisted his words to suit your anger. He said nothing of reforging your weapons but sends each warrior back to his home. What would you do? Have every warrior sitting idly through each daylight here in the Granite City?' Nevian paused, his eyes sparkling with bright light as he held Thunderstone's gaze. 'But if in your wisdom and farsight you fear for the King you may, through careful watchfulness, hold the safety of all Elundium in your sword arms.'

'How so?' asked Fairday, leaning forwards to touch the hem of the rainbow cloak. 'There is secrecy in your words and half-veiled threats on the edge of your tongue.'

Nevian shivered and shrank back into the folds of the rainbow cloak, drawing it tightly about his shoulders as he searched the eyes of those gathered around him, debating how much he should tell them of his fears.

'I grow more cautious with each daylight for this cloak of bright colours should have faded with the passing of the last Granite King, my power used up, yet its colours grow in strength daylight by daylight. I cannot tell you what I fear but it is there on the edges of the wind and in each soft shadow. Elundium seems to hold its breath as if waiting for some black tragedy.'

'Does the King know of your fears?' asked Breakmaster. 'Surely if . . .'

Nevian nodded his head, hushing the horseman into silence. 'Thane fears and worries yet wherever he looks the sunlight sparkles ever brightly, thus on my counsel he has disbanded the battle crescents to spread eyes and ears throughout Elundium. We may be worrying over nothing and raise false fears.'

'But what would you counsel us to do as we huddle here, a tight ring of conspirators?' asked Fairday.

Nevian smiled and gathered a hand from each of them, one above the other, in a pledging knot. 'I would say you are wise to worry for Thane's safety and I would bind you, each of you, to watch with careful eyes.' Nevian hesitated, his forehead wrinkled in a thousand folds. Sharing secrets was never an easy task for one word led on to another and he must choose his words carefully. 'And I pledge you to watch over your Queen Elionbel, for a black shadow haunts her heart and I fear for her in the darker stretches of the night. Guard her closely, Breakmaster and Grey Goose, until the shadow passes, for you shall both be the closest to hand here in the Granite City.'

'The shadow she carries,' Eventine muttered, turning a smooth polished arrowshaft carefully between her fingers, 'it was there on the high plateau. Elionbel brought it out of the City of Night: it was there in Martbel's funeral pyre. There was a great tragedy that Elionbel would not speak about but the weight of which already bowed her shoulders. It is a burden too heavy for one person alone to carry.'

Nevian looked up sharply. 'What was that you saw in the flames? Tell me!' he urged.

Eventine thought back to the ghost tails of swirling mist on the high plateau, the tramp of armoured boots closing all around them and the quick hiss of Thane's spark as it burst into light and spread greedily through the dry kindling wood of the pyre. Frowning, she scratched absently at the polished shaft. 'Nothing. There was nothing save a shrivelled corpse tightly wrapped in a ragged cloak.'

'Think! Think!' cried Nevian, clasping at Eventine's hands. 'Go back to the high plateau in your mind. Stand as you did beside the pyre, remember everything, each crackle of the flames, each cry of sorrow, and then tell me what you saw that looked out of place.'

Eventine bit her lip and cried out. 'There! There!' she

193

shouted pointing down into the circle of stone benches between the feet of the others. 'There on the fire's edge are the bloody hems of Martbel's skirt.'

'And?' whispered Nevian gently. 'What else was there to see?'

Eventine shook her head and looked up, the memory fading away. 'That was all I saw, the bloody hems of Martbel's skirt, and Elionbel's terror. The hoofbeats sounded across the steep slopes of Mantern's Mountain and I looked up to see Tanglecrown and the two Border Runners leading Sprint and Stumble down on to the high plateau. All around us Marchers were emerging through the black fog. Tombel knelt at the pyre's edge, he had handfuls of hot ash trickling though his fingers.'

Nevian frowned and withdrew into the rainbow cloak: a dark figure, shrouded in thought, he paced beneath the low arches and strode from shadow to shadow. 'Did you scatter the pyre?' he asked, stopping before the circle of stone benches.

'No,' answered Kyot after a moment's thought. 'Tombel scattered a handful of Martbel's ashes to the four winds and then we left the high plateau to descend to the Causeway Field.'

Nevian turned and stared out across the sand school before gripping Breakmaster's hand. 'Keep special watch over your Queen,' he whispered.

Turning to Thunderstone he touched the hilt of the horsetail sword. 'Seek out the fastest of the Nighthorses and have them ready saddled.'

Turning to the Archers he crossed the bows of Orm and Clatterford. 'You are love-matched and these great bows will yet sing together in the service of your King. Be prepared with new-forged arrows in the quiver.'

Turning to Grey Goose he took the Captain Archer's hand and held it for a moment. 'Archer strikes,' he whispered, closing his eyes and trying to look far into the future, but sadly he saw only dim shapes retreating in wild disorder towards a mound or a hill that shone bright white above the shadows.

'I fear that darkness may lie ahead, Grey Goose, and your King will have great need of your steady hand and careful Archer's eye. Gather the Bowmen of the Granite City and form them into secret strikes. Do not alarm the people of the City but be ready lest the sunlight fails.'

'Lord,' cried Grey Goose, watching the magician melting away, 'how shall I marshal the bowmen?'

Nevian's voice laughed and echoed through the empty courtyards.'Be ready, all of you, in secret watchful wakefulness. Be ready . . . '

Thane waited, sitting easily upon Esteron's back. Beside him Elion was on Stumble in the shadow of the great gate. Kyot and Eventine were mounted ready for the journey home, waiting just beyond the gate and watching the long columns of Marchers, Gallopers and Archers assemble in the lower circles of the city.

'Todaylight,' Thane cried, standing in his stirrups and holding the Wayside Cup aloft, 'todaylight you shall journey home as men of peace. Equal men, each one casting his own shadow in honest labour. The nightmare, Krulshards, is dead and the battle against the darkness is over. But be watchful and ever ready as you plough and cut a deep furrow in the rich soil of Elundium. It is time to rest the sword and unstring the bow, to break the battle crescents and thank the brave Warhorses and the fearless Border Runners that fought beside us.' Thane paused and smiled, his rein-hand gently caressing Mulcade's shiny talons. 'It is time,' he said in a proud yet quiet voice, 'to thank the brave Battle Owls and the grey swans of doom, to thank each and every one who fought beneath our standard for they came freely and gave so much that we might have this sunlit freedom. Forget them not as you drink with me, Warriors of Elundium, for I pledge you

195

before you depart to drink a last battle cup at the Greenways' edge to a thousand daylights of peace.'

'Peace! Peace!' rose the chant throughout the lower circles of the city as the great press of warriors from Stumble Hill and Underfall surged towards the gates.

Ogion beat a clear path of white spray across Swanwater and spread his wings in graceful flight above Stumble Gate. Stoops of Battle Owls flew low across the morning sun, wheeling and turning beneath the high arched gate. Grannog, Lord of Dogs, broke cover from beneath the ancient trees and led the Border Runners in a huge pack into the shadows of the great wall, while beyond the first bend of the Greenway the ground trembled beneath the thunder of hooves as Equestrius, Lord of Horses, brought the Warhorses in a mighty crescent within a league of the Granite City.

Thane laughed with tears in his eyes and broke the binding cords on the summer scarf letting the standard of the sun spread out in the morning sunlight. 'I thank you all forever and ever,' he shouted, spurring Esteron forwards towards the crescent, and galloped out of the City.

Equestrius halted the Warhorses and waited for Thane, the dust settling around them in a drifting fog. Grannog barked once and led the Border Runners out of the shadows and away from the city, following closely on Esteron's heels.

Thane halted in the centre of the Warhorses and dismounted before Equestrius. Kneeling, he offered up the summer scarf. 'We should have many thousand daylights of peace but I fear new shadows are rising to threaten the sunlight of Elundium. Would you search for me in all the wild places and bring me word?'

Equestrius snorted, arched his neck and struck at the ground with his foreleg. Thane laughed, here among the Warhorses and the Border Runners there was little need for words and promises to hide the fears gnawing away inside him.

Grannog barked and lay down at Thane's feet. 'Come to

me often with every scrap of news,' Thane whispered, running his hand through the dog's thick sable coat.

Esteron brushed his soft muzzle on Thane's cheek and pulled at the bridle to follow Equestrius. 'You are a Lord of Horses,' Thane whispered, knowing he must allow Esteron to run with the Warhorses. He unbuckled the girths on Esteron's saddle and took it off, then untied the bridle knot and took the bit out of Esteron's mouth. 'I love you,' he cried, his arms tightly clasped around the horse's neck.

Esteron hesitated, snorted and pressed his head against Thane and began to kneel. 'No! No! It is just as King Holbian said, you are free, you belong to no man, not even a King,' cried Thane, stepping back quickly. 'My tears must not keep you. Remember that time we fought together in the sand school? You were a Lord of Horses then, who would have run free if the gates had been open. Remember?'

Thane stopped, trying to swallow the lump rising in his throat. 'Remember,' he whispered, as the picture of Esteron fighting his way across the hollow to rescue Elionbel formed clearly in his mind and he remembered the countless other times they had stood alone and together against the darkness.

'You must go,' he cried, gathering his failing courage and pushing the horse away. 'Go before I weaken and claim you as my own. Go and be free, run in all the wild and secret places, but if anything threatens the sunlight come back to me and we will fight it together.'

Equestrius neighed fiercely and moved between Thane and Esteron, nudging the horse into the crescent. Equestrius turned and snorted at Thane, holding his gaze with his soft eyes as if thanking him for keeping faith, for here in the final moment when Esteron sought his freedom Thane had kept nothing, no matter how precious, that was not his own.

Mulcade tightened his talons on Thane's shoulder and hooted softly. 'Fly, great Bird of War,' he whispered, turning his head and looking into Mulcade's unblinking eyes. 'Search for my sake over all Elundium and watch over Esteron, keep him safe.'

Mulcade bobbed his head backwards and forwards brushing his beak against Thane's cheek, hooting and quarrelling with soft gurgling sounds. Thane tried to laugh, blinking at his tears. 'Go, you foolish bird, you are free and belong to no man. Use your sharp eyes to keep the sunlight safe.'

Mulcade hooted and spread his wings. He rose slowly from Thane's shoulder, circled once and followed the fading hoofbeats. Thane stood on the dusty turf and wept. 'What say you now, Nevian?' he whispered. 'Have I spread my eyes and ears far enough across Elundium, chasing half-fears that hide in the shadows?'

For a moment a shadow crossed the sun, touching the place where Thane stood and he looked up, but the owl had gone and the sky was empty. There was nothing now but the tramp of warriors' feet and the dull measured beat of horses' hooves along the Greenway. The battle crescents were breaking up. The warriors were returning home.

The Rising

Willow held up his gnarled, blackened fingers, and the Tunnellers halted silently and crouched down as he passed between them.

'Wait!' he whispered, motioning to Oakapple to keep close to him as he parted the thick tangle of wild grass and weed-choked bushes bordering the edge of the overgrown Greenway. He caught his breath as he gazed out at the huge mound of dark earth towering above them. It was steep and in places it seemed to rise in sheer, narrow, flower-decked steps that swept up to an unknown summit beyond their sight. Along the base it looked as if there had once been a deep dyke now thick with low-branched tangle trees and hangman's creepers.

Oakapple shivered and turned away. 'What has brought us to this place?' she whispered.

'The trees,' answered Willow, pointing with a crooked finger. 'We have been following the magic trees, they have brought us here. Haven't you listened to their voices? For many daylights now this mound has been a beacon rising above the landscape and pulling us forwards. Look, look at it. There is something about it from the Elder's tales, I know it.'

Oakapple shook her head. 'No, it is a place of evil, of great tragedy. I can feel it in the air and almost taste it. Where are the sweeps of hills and secret lakes you spoke of? This place is wild and desolate, it makes my skin crawl.'

Willow laughed softly, satisfied that nobody evil was at the mound and stepped out on to the overgrown Greenway. 'If this is the place in the Elder's tales then time and wildness have merely spread a cloak across its beauty. Come, come let us climb to the summit. Let us see what lies beyond.'

Oakapple shook her head but followed reluctantly as Willow began to explore the base of the mound. 'Over here!' he cried. 'Look! There was once a gate and something that spanned the dyke.'

'There are the beginnings of another Greenway over here,' called a voice from amongst the Tunnellers.

'And here!' shouted another.

Darkness had long fallen before Willow and the Tunnellers had finished exploring the outer edges of the dyke and found a way across to the first sheer rise of the mound.

'By starlight we will follow that narrow ledge to the summit of the mound. Keep in single file,' he called carefully, moving forward. Twice he nearly slipped sending loose earth rattling down into the tangle trees below, and each time where the earth had been dislodged something bright white and smooth to the touch shone in the starlight.

'There are white rocks in this mound,' he whispered, turning his head to where Oakapple clung on to the sheer face of the rise just behind him.

She shuddered, curling the arches of her feet over the smooth stones lining the centre of the ledge. 'I feel as if I am walking on bones,' she hissed, digging her fingers into the soft earth of the sheer face of the mound, clutching at smooth tree roots or narrow spines of rock to keep her balance.

Willow laughed softly. This was the place the voices in the trees had whispered about, even in the darkness he could see for leagues and leagues across the countryside below. This was the place to build a fortress against the darkness. A fastness rising above the shadows. The ledge began to flatten, widening into a broad path as it reached the summit. Before them stretched a flat plateau crowded with the ruins of long low buildings. A single tower lay broken and creeper-tangled in the centre. Willow stopped on the edge and carefully searched each night shadow.

'Make camp on the plateau rim beneath the stars,' he called in a hushed whisper. 'Tomorrowlight we will explore this rising and begin the task of building a fortress against this new darkness.'

Oakapple sank wearily on to the hard earth beside Willow and drew her cloak around them both. 'We are here,' he whispered, shaking his head at the last bruised forest fruit she held out to him. 'You eat it. It will give you strength.' He smiled in the darkness. 'I must watch through the grey hours and see how the sun first touches this rising with the new morning light, and then I will know how to build, where to make the entrance, the walls, the . . .' Willow's head slumped as sleep overtook him.

Oakapple frowned with worry and drew him close to her. Ever since she had found him, crippled with terror in the tombs of Underfall, he had eaten little and driven himself without rest in this quest to find a fortress against the darkness. He had grown bone-thin and ragged with worry, refusing even the smallest offer of help, and he would let none carry him now that Starlight had departed to find her foal.

Willow mumbled something in his sleep and snuggled against Oakapple, who smiled softly, holding him close on the hard earth. 'One daylight,' she whispered, watching the grey hours light the sky, 'one daylight in better times we will sleep in a feather bed.'

Frowning, she thought back to the Elder's tales she had first heard in the darkness of the City of Night. She searched her memory but no matter how hard she looked there were no feather beds or easy times, just all the beauty of the sunlit world painted with loving care in brilliant detail.

Willow stirred beside her and opened his eyes. It was warm beneath the cloak and Oakapple's skin felt soft against him. He yawned and sat up, stretching cramped legs and crooked fingers as the sun breasted World's End. 'Look!' he whispered. 'Look how the first shaft of sunlight touched the rim of the summit. There! That must have been the entrance to the high place. Yes, look, there are the traces of a wide ramp, now little more than a dip in the ground, leading down to the shadows below.'

'It would be very steep,' answered Oakapple, peering cautiously across the sheer side of the rising to where the ramp vanished into the darkness below.

'Yes, yes,' answered Willow, an edge of impatience in his voice as he struggled to his feet, 'but there are countless suns of rubbish, trees and undergrowth blocking the ramp; it will be a gentler slope when it is cleared and dressed with new stone.'

All around them the Tunnellers were waking up, yawning and stretching in the warm sunlight and looking with curious eyes on the place far above the wild countryside Willow had brought them to in the darkness.

'The trees have settled on the edge of the Greenway!' laughed one of the Tunnellers. 'Look, Willow, they are standing in neat rows all around the crossroads below this mound.'

Willow smiled. 'The trees are a good omen for this place. Now we must search each blade of grass, each rock and stone to learn all we can before we build a fortress.'

'The narrow ledge we climbed in the night is the same height as we are,' shouted an excited voice from further down the rising. 'There are round stones as smooth as marble set in the path. They gleam white. There are ... they are ...' the voice trailed away as anxious faces peered down over the lip of the summit.

'What are they? What have you found?' called Willow, hurrying down the narrow ledge to where Fernleaf the Tunneller knelt with a trowel of soft earth in his shaking hand. 'What have you found?' Willow almost shouted as he shook Fernleaf by the shoulders.

'Eyes!' whispered the white-faced Tunneller, pointing with his trowel. 'Diamond-hard and as smooth as glass. They stare out across the wild countryside. Look for yourself!'

Willow took the trowel into his crippled hands. Locking his fingers around the smooth wooden handle, he carefully scraped away at the soft earth just below the narrow ledge, working his way downwards across the top of a smooth white stone. 'Eyes!' he cried, letting the trowel slip from his fingers and clatter its way into the tangle trees below. He knelt and brushed away the rest of the earth to reveal the forehead and cheekbones of an ancient skull.

Standing, Willow cleaned the earth from his fingers and looked closely at the sheer wall of the rising. 'There are others here,' he called to the anxious faces above. He turned, loosed his dagger and scraped at the wall, dislodging the soft earth and weed roots clinging between the smooth bleached bones. He moved a pace along the ledge and exposed another two staring diamond-bright eyes, set in hollow bones. Below the grinning jaw was a stark angular rib cage crushed flat into the wall of the rising.

Oakapple cried out in terror and fell on to her knees, burying her head in her hands. 'I could feel them through the soles of my feet,' she sobbed. 'We scrambled over a thousand bodies to reach the summit of this burial mound. Look! Look!' she shouted, pointing everywhere at once. 'Even here on the summit we are standing on the bones of . . . of . . .'

Willow resheathed his dagger and hurried back to the summit where he took Oakapple in his arms. '*No*! You judge too quickly. This place is more than just a burial mound. Be still and give me time to search amongst the ruins.'

'Willow, Willow,' a voice shouted from somewhere halfway down the sheer face of the rising. 'Come quickly!'

'Give me time,' Willow muttered to Oakapple as he rose and ran to the beginnings of the steep ramp. 'Where are you?'

he cried, pushing his way down through the waist-high bushes and sharp-thorned tangle trees.

'Here! Down here on the edge of the ramp.'

Willow scrambled down, cutting his crippled hands again and again as he lost his footing until Fernleaf caught him and pulled him on to the beginnings of a ledge.

'Chains!' he exclaimed, scratching his head and peering at the shackled skeleton Fernleaf had unearthed.

'They are all chained together,' added the Tunneller fearfully. 'In one unending circle they spiral up the sheer face of the rising. We are standing beside a solid wall of bones!'

'Thousands must have been slaughtered to raise this mound,' whispered Willow, looking up across the face of the rising.

'Many more than that,' answered Fernleaf. 'There are bodies behind those that we can see, they stand a solid crush of bones that goes deeper than I can reach with my searcher. But it is the eyes! Why haven't they rotted with the rest of the flesh? Why do they stare so brightly from the eye sockets?'

'Perhaps they watch for danger, or some other thing,' ventured Willow. 'Whatever these poor wretches were slaughtered for, to guard or to watch, I am sure this must have been a fortress once, long ago before the dust of ages settled between the bones and hid its purpose. But who were these helpless victims that now guard the rising, and who would have dared put so many of them to the sword?'

'Perhaps we are standing on a tomb,' called Oakapple, her voice shaking with fear, 'just like the tomb of the Granite Kings beneath the fortress of Underfall. It may be a sacred place best left undisturbed.'

'No!' said Willow. 'There is no place for chains in tombs. These people were set here for a purpose. Look how the white bones catch the light, see how they reflect the sunlight!'

'If we cleaned the earth away and polished the bones . . .' whispered Fernleaf, rubbing the tail of his cloak on the weathered cheekbone and high-domed forehead of the nearest skull.

'Yes!' Willow gasped, shading his eyes against the soft autumn sunlight reflected with burning brightness. 'And the eyes will reflect each station of the sunlight. The Rising will be a blaze of light!'

Willow nodded with excitement and ran back to the summit. He gathered the Tunnellers into a dense circle all around him. Pausing, he held up his twisted and blackened fingers then waited for silence. 'Tunnellers!' he cried. 'Whatever I have asked of you, you have done without question, even following the trees here to this rising of bones in the wilderness of Elundium. Keep faith with me now and labour as you have never done before. Scrape away the loose earth and polish bright the bones; clear the dykes and rebuild the fallen tower. Make this a strong fortress, a castle rising sheer against the new darkness. Make this a place where your King can retreat, beleaguered and battered by the new Nightmare, a place where he can rest and gather his strength. For I forewarn you that this rising, this brittle hill of bones, shall be the last place in all Elundium to stand against the sea of darkness.'

Oakapple bit her knuckles and shivered, the circle of Tunnellers tightened, white-lipped and frightened, pressing in around Willow.

'Make haste,' he whispered, the sound dry and crackling in his throat, 'lest our work is not finished before the darkness spreads.'

Darkness Takes the Fortress of Underfall

'Go before me, fool!' snapped Silverpurse prodding the Loremaster savagely in the back with the point of his sword.

Pinchface muttered under his breath, wishing the treacherous Chancellor's son had perished beside his foul father, Proudpurse, at the height of the Chancellor's treachery.

'What?' hissed Silverpurse. 'What did you say?'

'A warrior holds the Greenway against us,' mumbled the Loremaster, pointing ahead to a single Marcher who stood less than twenty paces before them.

Silverpurse halted and cast a nervous glance into the dense shadows on either side of the Greenway. 'Where are we?' he whispered, pulling the Loremaster closer to him. 'Is there a village or a Wayhouse nearby?'

Pinchface frowned and shook his head. 'No, Master, we have been wandering for so long, lost in Mantern's Forest that I am not sure where we are, but I think we are near to the fortress of Underfall. Yes, this must be the ancient road that leads from Notley Marsh to the very gates of the Palace of Kings. And over there is the stinking marsh where we hid from King Holbian.'

'Chancellor!' hissed Silverpurse fiercely and, raising his armoured fist against the Loremaster's face, continued: 'To honour my father you will call me Chancellor, for that will be my true title once I have enough strength to slay the Granite King and take Elundium as my own.'

'Yes, Chancellor, yes,' cried Pinchface, shrinking away.

Silverpurse glanced briefly at the cringing Loremaster and pushed him back roughly on to the crown of the road. 'Go to the black-clad warrior and find out what he wants. Ask him for news of King Holbian, search out some truth to our advantage.'

Pinchface hesitated, there was something fearful – no, terrifying – about the black-armoured warrior. The air around him seemed to be swallowed in darkness and his cloak and tunic moved without the slightest breath of air, rattling and swaying as it rippled up over the Marcher's shoulders.

'Go! Go now!' hissed Silverpurse impatiently, thrusting the point of his blade between the Loremaster's shoulders and making him stagger forwards to fall at Arbel's feet.

Arbel smiled, his armoured lips curling back into a welcoming whisper of laughter. 'Welcome! Welcome!' he cried, spreading the living cloak of shadow rats to embrace the Loremaster.

'No!' screamed Pinchface trying to stumble away from the horror. He could see the hard black glitter of a thousand rats' eyes, sharp claws were clutching at his clothing, plaited tails were thrashing in rising waves of darkness and teeth were tearing at his face and hands. Arbel had closed the cloak of shadow rats about the Loremaster's shoulders, and while the darkness swept through him in waves of terror he beckoned Silverpurse, pulling him forwards. A shadow rat jumped from his hand and bit the Chancellor's son, warming and tingling him, etching the shadows of night through his body, and showing him more power than ten Granite Kings could dare to hold in a world without light. Somewhere nearby a Nightbeast roared and Silverpurse saw the tall slender figure of Kruel standing before him, seeming to fill the crown of the Greenway with his power.

Silverpurse stretched out his hands to touch his new master. 'Lord of Darkness,' he murmured through tingling lips.

Kruel laughed and pushed Silverpurse down on to his knees, plucking the shadow rat from Silverpurse's shoulder and letting it drop to the ground where it scuttled away amongst the trees. 'False Chancellor!' he hissed, breaking the trance that had shown him all Silverpurse's secrets. 'You would have stolen the crown of Elundium from your father, taking for your own what he tried to steal treacherously from the last Granite King. I know each treacherous thought and every hidden secret in your head, but you are too late, fool. The crown of Elundium lays smashed into a thousand pieces in the tombs of Underfall, and Thanehand, the cursed Galloperspawn, has snatched the throne of Elundium while you crept away through the stinking marsh to hide in Mantern's Forest.'

'Thanehand, the candlebrat we chased out of the Learning Hall?' cried Silverpurse, his face black with rage. 'How could that ragged candlecur we hounded through the streets of the Granite City steal anything but the scraps from my table? How?'

Kruel snarled, his lips curling in hatred. He reached out and shook Silverpurse violently by the shoulders lifting him off his feet then threw him down beside the Loremaster. 'You let Thanehand escape too easily, you treacherous fool. You could have killed him with one arrow strike while he was nothing, before he stole the throne, before the Warhorses and the foul Battle Owls came to his aid.'

Silverpurse shook with terror, crouching close to the ground, hugging the coarse Greenway grasses. 'Master, Master, you know everything, you see each move we have made,' he sobbed, reaching out towards Kruel's feet.

'Shallow, treacherous fool!' Kruel hissed, his voice heavy with contempt as he trod on Silverpurse's fingers. 'I will swallow you now before I smother the daylight and destroy Thanehand and all those who flock to his bright standard. Everything will vanish beneath my shadows, it is my right as the Lord of Darkness to take Elundium as my own. But you, deceitful Chancellor's son, if you had the power you would take from your own blood what doesn't belong to you. You would use my darkness for your own ends.'

'Forgive me, Master, and let me serve you,' Silverpurse cried, licking at his sore fingers. 'Let me prove my loyalty.'

Kruel laughed and beckoned Arbel and the Nightbeasts to come to him. 'Shall we tread this treacherous Chancellor's son into the Greenway turf and leave him a black mark of our darkness, or . . .' Kruel paused with a hand on each Nightbeast's iron collar. 'Or shall we give him the Palace of Kings to govern and keep it as the first fortress of my darkness?'

'Kill him!' snarled Kerhunge, straining against Kruel's restraining hand.

'They are nothing but marsh creepers. Tread them both into the Greenway,' hissed Kerzolde, wiping at the trail of bubbling spittle that hung from his lips.

'No,' interrupted Arbel, stepping before the two Nightbeasts. 'This Chancellor's son will grow to hate Thanehand with such a passion it will overshadow his greed and treachery. He will make a good Chancellor of the Fortress of Underfall but the other . . .' Arbel turned and pointed at the quivering heap of rags and bones where the Loremaster huddled, crying with pain and terror on the crown of the road.

'He is mine,' cried Silverpurse. 'Let me prove my love and loyalty and tread the Loremaster into the turf.'

Kruel laughed and kicked both Silverpurse and Pinchface, sending them reeling into the mass of trees on the Greenways' edge. 'Nothing is yours, fool, only the will to serve me as your Master. I am Kruel the Shadowless, Lord of all Elundium!'

'Master, Master,' whispered Silverpurse, crawling back on to the Greenway and dragging the Loremaster by his cloak tail behind him. 'We will both serve you faithfully.'

Kruel smiled, his eyes boring into Silverpurse, and nodded.

'Yes, you will, and the shadow rats will watch you closely, spreading their darkness all around you.'

Pausing in a moment of doubt, Kruel stretched out his hand and lifted the Loremaster to his now-crippled feet. Frowning, he stared into his eyes, searching, probing, looking for the truth. 'Mindless fool!' he hissed, seeing nothing but a blank and muddled grey fog, before he let the wretched Loremaster topple on to his knees.

'Follow!' he commanded Silverpurse without another glance as he stepped on to the crown of the road and whistled the shadow rats all around them.

'Follow me to the gates of Underfall!' he laughed, sure of his power, blind and uncaring to the furtive sideways glance of hatred well hidden beneath the Loremaster's hooded eyes.

'Curse your darkness!' Pinchface muttered, biting his tongue against the burning pain that tore through his body as he stumbled forwards on his hands and knees, not daring to let his crippled feet touch the ground. All about him the shadow rats swarmed out over the road, their brittle spines rattling in the darkness as they forced him onwards.

'I must rest,' he wept, crumpling on to his side, beyond caring that the rats were gnawing at his torn and twisted toes, their sharp claws scratching at his bloody knees. Wearily he let his head sink to the ground. Without thinking he reached out and with numbing fingers he felt something that glowed white and soft in the nightmare darkness, something the rats would not go near. The petals folded in his fingers: warm and powdery they gave off a bittersweet scent that drove the shadow rats into a rage of high pitched shrieks.

The Loremaster lifted his head, a whisper of laughter on his tortured lips, and threw the Nightflower petals on to the grass around him, clearing back the shadow rats. 'Nightflowers!' he whispered, pulling himself closer to the tumbledown wall of broken stone and burying his hands among the bright white petals. Sighing, he began to sink down as the heavy scent filled his head. Deep deep down he heard old whispered chants and remembered the legends carved above the doorway of the ruined Wayhouse Hut of Thorns: *For any Man or Beast who loves the Light shall rest . . .*

'Loremaster! Loremaster!' Pinchface shook himself awake and sat up. Silverpurse was angrily shouting for him. A thousand black shadow rats crowded around his feet in hideous waves of darkness, waiting for the magic of the flowers to fade. 'Loremaster, where are you?' shouted Silverpurse. He was closer now to the ruined hut and Pinchface knew he must move quickly to keep his secret.

He bent forwards and stripped the Nightflower vines growing along the wall, snagging his fingers raw on their sharp barbed thorns until he had crammed full a deep leather pouch with their small white seeds. He pulled the drawstring tight and hid the pouch beneath his ragged jerkin then crawled back to the road leaving the safety of the flowers. 'Here, Chancellor,' he called. 'I fell into a black faint,' he mumbled, shuddering as the shadow rats swarmed over his hands and feet, their sharp claws scratching at his leathery skin.

Silverpurse snarled and grabbed the Loremaster by his cloak then pulled him roughly on to the crown of the road. 'Keep up, you fool,' he hissed, 'or those two Nightbeasts will eat you for their breakfast.'

Pinchface looked away and curled his lips in hatred of the Chancellor's son as he scrambled along as fast as he could.

Evening was falling; the shadows were long across the Greenway. Before them, sheer and terrible, granite-grey against the fading light, rose the walls of Underfall. Silverpurse laughed softly and pointed with an eager finger. 'That will be mine, Loremaster, all mine to guard for the Lord of Darkness. And you will be my Gatekeeper. Come, hurry, you miserable wretch, the Lord of Darkness grows impatient before the doors of Underfall.'

'Look, the doors are opening,' cried Pinchface, 'without a

single arrow loosed or a shout of defence. The Palace of Kings has surrendered!'

Silverpurse clapped his hands with delight and pushed the Loremaster out from beneath the ancient trees and on to the Causeway Field. 'Your first task, Gatekeeper will be to clear away these gnarled old trees that line the Greenways' edge. They look almost too rotten for burning but I'll wager a barrel of tallow wax they will make a blaze to celebrate our victory!'

Kruel and Arbel stood between the great doors of Underfall unsure of their victory and counting the warriors that knelt in a broad circle across the cobbles before them. A dozen guards, the Gatekeeper, and a handful of Watchmen were all Thunderstone had left to guard World's End while he and the warriors attended Thane's wedding ties in the Granite City.

'This is no victory,' muttered Kruel, silencing the kneeling warriors who held up their black-veined hands to greet him.

Shadow rats swarmed across the rough granite walk, spreading their terror through the long galleries overhead. Deep violet weed worms scuttled across the cobbles, their high-arched stings dripping with venom.

'Search every room' snarled Kruel. 'There must be more warriors hiding. Leave no stone unturned. Bring every warrior to kneel before me!'

'Tiethorm the Archer has retreated up to the Lamp gallery, Master,' cried one of the kneeling guards.

'And Merion the healer has fled into the corner courtyard. They are the only two who have defied the darkness,' called another traitor.

Kruel smiled, his anger calmed, and he searched the Gatekeeper's mind to see just where the Keeper of Underfall had escaped to, then stepped into the centre of the courtyard. 'Watch my power, brother,' he whispered and drew Arbel to his side as he drove the spearshaft holding the black malice deep into the cobbles. He let the shadowy fabric unfold and float out to cast darkness and despair across the rough granite walls. Searching the highest Lamp gallery with pitiless eyes, Kruel called to Tiethrom, mocking him. 'Who dares to stand against me, Kruel, the Master of Darkness and Lord of all Elundium?'

Above them on the highest gallery the Lamp of Underfall blazed out, bright white in the deepening shadows. 'I do!' shouted a desperate voice. 'I, Tiethorm, First Archer of this house. In Thunderstone's absence I guard the Light and trim the wick against all shadows and take no man but Thanehand as my rightful King!'

'Thanehand!' sneered Silverpurse entering the courtyard. 'He is nothing but a candlecur!'

'He is my King!' shouted Tiethorm angrily, nocking an arrow on to the bow string and loosing it into the shadows below.

Kruel laughed and pulled the Chancellor's son aside just before the arrow struck the cobbles sending up a shower of bright sparks. 'You shall wait beyond harm's way, Chancellor,' he hissed, thrusting Silverpurse beneath a low archway before he turned his pitiless eyes back towards the Lamp gallery.

'Your King is nothing, Archer,' he whispered, 'and you stand alone against the greatest power in all Elundium.'

'I love my King,' shouted Tiethorm, his hand trembling with terror as he fumbled for another arrow. He could feel Kruel's power filling the fortress, spreading over every stone, every wall, even pushing against the locked door of the highest gallery. Cowering against the Lamp, he nocked another arrow on to the string of his bow and waited. 'Where are you, Thunderstone?' he whispered in despair. 'Where are you, Lampmaster? For I have counted the daylights and you are long overdue. I cannot defend this fortress alone or escape to warn the King. These black rats watch my every move and none can leave while they guard the doors.'

Kruel laughed again, sending the pitiless sound echoing

through the empty galleries. He could hear the Archer's whispers and smell the fear that trickled through the pores of his skin. Slowly, he stretched his arm up, up, following the narrow winding stairway, past each darkened gallery, until his hand rested against the locked Lamp gallery door. 'There are none to help you!' he hissed, snapping the lock and bolts with one firm push of his hand and letting the door swing inwards, away from the darkened stairhead.

'I still have the Light,' shouted Tiethorm. In one last desperate move to defend the gallery he reached for the balance wheel and turned the wick to its full height. He filled the gallery with brilliant white light that sent the gathering shadows fleeing towards the darkened doorway.

'I am shadowless!' whispered Kruel. 'I do not fear your light. I am shadowless and all-powerful. Come to me, Archer, and be swallowed in my darkness. Your moment of defiance is over. Come to me.'

'By all that is good in the sunlight I will defend this place against your foul kind,' shouted Tiethorm, the bow drawn taut.

Two sets of rats' eyes gleamed on the threshold of the gallery. There were more behind: the Archer could hear them scuttling up the winding stairway.

'Shadow rats!' he hissed in terror, loosing the long-bladed dagger at his belt. He had seen them on the first daylight of their arrival in the fortress of Underfall and they had multiplied in the blink of an eye, then in one night of terror they had bitten all the guardians of Underfall, spreading a strange darkness amongst them. The shadows had grown and nightmare chants had filled the blackness. Gallery by gallery they had hunted him, driving him always upward away from the doors and now he was trapped, there was nowhere else to hide. Now, beside the Lamp, he would make one last desperate stand.

The first two rats blinked in the glare of the lamp and scuttled ahead. Tiethrom looked quickly from one rat to the

214

other, chose his target and loosed the arrow. 'By the sunlight!' he cried as the first rat arched its back, shrieking as the arrow pierced its flank, hurling it back through the doorway. Reaching behind him he snatched another arrow from the quiver and nocked it on to the bow. 'Where are you, Thunderstone?' he cried in despair, loosing the arrow wildly at the hideous shapes suddenly filling the doorway.

The shadow rats were everywhere, swarming across the gallery floor, alive now with their black squealing bodies. They attacked him, running up his legs, jumping at his arms, tearing the bow from his fingers. Their sharp teeth cut into his skin; they were on his chest, his neck. 'No! No!' he screamed, toppling forwards as the darkness took him, etching Kruel's black agony through his veins. Somewhere far off he could hear Kruel's voice laughing, mocking him as his bow-hand arched back, the blackened fingers twisting into hideous shapes. The hand that had broken the locks pulled him roughly to the stairhead and dragged him, bumping from step to step, down into the courtyard.

'Now you are mine!' laughed Kruel, lifting Tiethorm's head and staring deeply into his eyes, searching out the truth of this Archer who had dared to stand against him. Frowning, he blinked and looked again at the grey muddled fog filling Tiethorm's mind. 'Useless fool,' he muttered, letting the Archer fall forgotten on to the cobblestones as he turned his head towards the inner courtyard and shouted Merion's name, calling him out to kneel before the new Master of all Elundium.

'By Nevian's power I will never kneel before you, Nightmare, but I will stand against you,' answered a muffled but defiant voice.

Kruel laughed, cupped his hands to his mouth and shouted just once, a high-pitched shriek that burned the eardrums, splintered wood and shattered stone as it tore through the fortress of Underfall. Merion watched in terror as his stout timbered door splintered into a thousand jagged pieces and the stone archway surrounding it crumbled into dust. Stumbling backwards away from the ruined door, he snatched two bulrush torches from their wall brackets and lit them with his spark. Shadow rats swarmed over the rubble towards him, their piercing eyes shining in the torchlight.

'You shall not take me!' he cried, sweeping the torches down in a burning arch, setting fire to the black brittle fur of the closing circle of shadow rats.

Bitter smoke mixed with the acrid smell of burning flesh billowed, the shadow rats screamed with rage, trampling on each other to retreat as the bright flames scorched their skin. Merion shouted with victory and spread the burning circle wider. Each step he took brought him closer to the courtyard where Kruel waited silently, close-wrapped in black shadows. Arbel cursed the healer and lowered his long spear to charge at the circle of flames spreading through the brittle-black fur of the shadow rats faster than a new spark in dry kindling.

'Wait,' whispered Kruel, putting a stilling hand on Arbel's arm. 'Let the healer come to me, then all those that serve me here at Underfall will see him kneel.'

Merion's step faltered, his headlong rush shuffling to a halt. The figure that stood before him had grown, seeming now to fill the courtyard. Long shadows curled out towards him. A soft voice laughed and brought him forward. 'You would challenge me, the Lord of Night, the Master of all Elundium?'

'Thanehand is my King,' cried Merion, sweeping the burning torches aloft, 'and by the light in my hands I will answer to none other.'

Kruel smiled. 'You shall have light, healer, bright light that will fill this courtyard and then in blazing glory you will kneel before me.

'Never!' shouted Merion, lowering the flames towards Kruel.

Kruel stepped forwards and pursed his lips. He began to blow a hot wind at the healer's hands setting the flames twisting and dancing on the bulrush torches, fanning them into white-hot sheets of fire and turning them against Merion.

'NO! NO!' screamed Merion, trying to drop the torches as the flames swept over his hands. But it was too late, the heavy fabric of his sleeves was alight, the hem of his cloak was a blaze of greedy sparks; his beard, his eyebrows shrivelled. 'No!' he tried to shout as the fire engulfed him. Screaming he staggered forwards and fell, a blazing torch, at Kruel's feet, begging the Lord of all Elundium to put out the fire.

Kruel stood, silently watching the guardians of Underfall, waiting until each Warrior had seen his power, then he was going to turn and leave the Healer who had dared to stand against him to burn into nothing but brittle ash that would scatter in the morning wind. But something made him hesitate, something in Merion's tortured screams. He gathered a ball of spittle on his tongue and spit on the blazing healer to put out the fire. White smoke hissed and crackled, rising up to fog the courtyard and hide the shadow rats swarming across Merion's hands, biting through his blistered, blackened skin to bring him into the darkness.

Kruel had turned away and did not see the Healer's backbone twist as the darkness etched its way through his body. He was deaf to the terrible screams behind him as he strove to understand what had made him, the Master of Nightmares, put out the flames. 'Pity?' he whispered, forming the word with the tip of his tongue and searching deep in his mind to find where it had come from. He reached up and touched the hard ridge of skin on the top of his head. 'My father knew nothing of pity, he scorned it as a weakness born of men, he would have eaten the Healer and tossed the scraps to his Nightbeasts.' Frowning, he looked through the swirls of smoke to where Arbel stood with a sneer of delight on his armoured face as he watched the Healer trying to get to his feet.

'Martbel – the weakness must come through Martbel,' Kruel whispered, seeing clearly in Arbel's heart how she would have nursed the Healer and forgiven him for not entering the darkness. He searched Arbel's mind again and saw how he had put all pity and compassion aside in his love for the darkness.

Shrugging away the pity, afraid of it as a weakness, Kruel turned his back on the Healer and cried to the warriors of Underfall, 'Who is Master of all Elundium?'

The warriors of Underfall echoed Kruel's chant, moving in a slow circle around the smouldering Healer. Louder and louder grew their voices as the last shades of evening faded into the darkness.

Hoofbeats echoed on the Causeway Field but none heard them in the fortress of Underfall. Thunderstone, reaching the end of a long road home, sensed something was wrong in the fortress and lifted his battle-gloved hand and quietly dismounted between the ancient trees. 'Be easy,' he whispered to Rowantree who snorted and showed the whites of his eyes.

Thunderstone put a stilling hand upon the bridle before he motioned to the Warriors of Underfall to follow him out of the shadow of the trees and on to the Causeway Road. For a moment he paused and crouched down, listening to the hideous chant that spilled through the open doors, he cast an anxious look up to the feeble light shining out from the Lamp gallery.

'Evil has settled here in our absence,' he whispered, drawing the horsetail sword. 'Let every man be ready, Swordsmen to the centre, Archers on each flank, with the Spearmen in close order. Leave the horses here amongst the ancient trees until we have discovered who is within our fortress.'

'Who?' began one of the Spearmen as he took his place, but Thunderstone hushed him.

'I know not, but I fear those voices chanting. It reminds me of grim daylights when the Nighbeasts swarmed against the walls of Underfall. Now keep quiet and follow me.'

'Who is the Master of all Elundium?' shouted Kruel as the Warriors leapt and danced around him.

'None but the rightful King,' cried Thunderstone angrily from between the great doors, his feet planted firmly on the first line of cobblestone that edged the courtyard. The silver strands of the horsetail sword shone brightly in the early moonlight.

Kruel spun round with a snarl of hatred curling back his lips. The dancing warriors froze, their spears and swords turned towards the doorway. 'Thunderstone!' he hissed, spreading his arms to beckon the shadow rats. They were all around him in a swarming black tide. 'The Keeper of my fortress has returned to kneel at my feet!'

Thunderstone stared in horror at the figure before him, for he seemed both man and beast, both beautiful and hideous. 'Krulshards?' he half-whispered gripping the hilt of his sword tightly with both hands.

Kruel laughed and swept the black malice in a shadowy arc. 'I am more than my father, Krulshards. I am both daylight and darkness, shadowless and all-powerful, for I am Kruel, the new Master and Lord of all Elundium. Now, kneel, Keeper of the Light, and offer your sword to me.'

'By Nevian and all that is good in the sunlight, I will not!' cried Thunderstone, taking a step forward.

Kruel laughed and snapped his fingers. The guardians of Underfall who had already been bitten into the darkness rose and surged forwards, thrusting their bitter spears against Thunderstone. The black tide of shadow rats swarmed across the cobblestones towards Thunderstone's armoured boots.

'Kill the rats! Kill the rats! Escape and warn the King!' shouted Tiethorm desperately trying to close his twisted fingers around the long-bladed dagger he had earlier loosened in his belt.

Thunderstone heard his captain's warning and briefly saw him raise a cruelly twisted hand above the seething mass of shadows before the one-eyed Nightbeast clubbed him down.

'The rats! The rats!' shouted Thunderstone, using the flat of his sword against them and crushing a dozen beneath his armoured boots as he retreated out on to the Causeway Road. But it was too late. The cobblestones were lost beneath the foul shadows, they were swarming up his legs, biting at his battle-gloved hands, running up the hem of his cloak.

'Warn Thane!' he managed to shout as the tide of nightmare shadow rats reached the high collar of his jerkin, clawing for his throat. They weighed heavy on his arms making him stagger towards the doors.

Arbel snarled with rage as he saw the Keeper of World's End battling with the rats and pushed his way through the bitter black warriors raising his Marcher sword to strike down Thunderstone.

'By all that is good in the sunlight!' cried Thunderstone, using all his strength to lift his arms and swing the horsetail sword in a wide arc. The silver strands of Equion's tail flowed out in the chill night air as the blade struck once against Arbel's black armour. The sword shivered in his hands, the horsetail wrapped itself, clinging around his wrists as the blade shattered into a thousand splinters.

'By all . . .' he began, crashing to his knees. Rats' claws tore at his cloak collar, sharp teeth sank into his neck, he was falling into darkness, sinking beneath the black-armoured Warrior's shadow. Arbel sneered and opened his arms, embracing the last Lampmaster of Elundium spreading his living cloak of shadow rats about his shoulders.

Elionbel turned restlessly in her bed, her hands clenched tightly together. 'No!' she screamed, starting awake and sitting bolt upright. 'No! No!' she whispered in terror, clutching her head in her hands.

She dare not close her eyes again lest the nightmare she had seen swallow her up. Rising quickly she flung her cloak around her shoulders and hurried to the casement window that looked down into the deep cold of Swanwater. 'The bastard Kruel has entered Elundium,' she whispered, biting her knuckles, knowing now that he had not perished in the moment of Krulshards' death.

She had seen him in her dream standing in the darkened courtyard of Underfall. There had been cruel laughter on his pitiless face as he watched the horsetail sword shatter into a thousand bright splinters. 'I must seek him out and destroy him,' she muttered, her face drawn into grim lines of hatred and fear as she dressed hurriedly.

Thane mumbled and turned restlessly in his sleep. Moving noiselessly she knelt beside the bed. 'How I wish I could tell you and be rid of this burden,' she whispered with tears in her eyes as she kissed the first two fingers of his wedding-tied hand and gently placed them on Thane's forehead. Rising she felt for the black dagger Kerzolde had killed her mother with and which she had kept, and closed her fingers around the cold metal hilt.

Without a sound she descended the narrow winding stairway and felt her way down through the sleeping city until she stood before the door of Stumble's stable. 'Will you take me?' she whispered, blinking back her tears. 'And carry me through the darkest night to destroy the one born of my mother's torment? For I must kill the bastard Kruel before he treads darkness across all Elundium.'

Stumble snorted and stood quietly while Elionbel put a saddle upon his back and a silver-studded bit into his mouth, then he carefully knelt with his neck proudly arched for her to mount. Leaning forwards she gave Stumble the reins and whispered in his ear, 'The bastard Kruel is in the fortress of Underfall, I saw it in my dream. We must go there by the shortest route and seek his death.'

Stumble snorted and crouched low before he sprang forwards and cantered out into the starlit night beneath the high-arched gate that carried his name, following the silver road towards World's End.

'Wait! Wait!' shouted the guards running out on to the

beginning of the Greenway, but they were gone, their hoof-beats fading into the darkness.

Willow started awake on the rough earth of the Rising and fiercely shook Oakapple's shoulder, wakening her. 'It has begun,' he cried. 'I saw it in a dream. Thunderstone, the Keeper of Underfall, has fallen, his sword is shattered into a thousand pieces. There is not a moment to lose, we must finish this fortress before the darkness spreads!'

'Enough,' Kruel whispered, gripping Arbel's smooth armoured arm. 'We have all Elundium to swallow with the darkness. Give me the Lampmaster of Underfall, let him kneel before me and call me King.'

Arbel muttered black curses and pushed Thunderstone from beneath the swarming cloak of shadow rats.

'Kneel before me, Lampmaster!' Kruel gloated, pulling up Thunderstone by the roots of his flowing white hair. 'Call me King and Master of all Elundium.

Thunderstone shuddered and cried out as he fought against the terrible darkness flooding his body. Blinking his blood-filled eyes, he looked up into Kruel's gloating triumphant face and knew he had but moments before the darkness swallowed him up. 'Master,' he cried, reaching up black-etched, rat-bitten fingers to clasp Kruel's hand.

Kruel laughed, sure of his victory and gave his right hand to Thunderstone. The last Lampmaster, with what strength he had left, shouted Thanehand's name and savagely bit into Kruel's fingers, shearing through the strong knuckles, splintering the bones as he ground them between his teeth.

Kruel screamed and snatched back his bleeding hand then lifted Thunderstone clear off the cobblestones and hurled him against the furthest rough granite wall. 'Die! Die! You will die for this!' he shouted, the rage in his voice splitting the walls of the courtyard into crazy patterns and bringing down huge blocks of grey granite crashing into the courtyard.

Shaking with anger, Kruel strode across to where Thunderstone lay broken against the wall and stood towering over him. The blood was boiling through his veins, his muscles were swelling, rippling beneath the skin. The hard ridge on the top of his head had begun to burn, pulsing and throbbing beneath his winter-white dead locks of his hair. Reaching up, he touched the bony ridge with his hand and felt the skin begin to split. 'Now you will see beneath my gentle skin,' he snarled at the cowering warriors. 'Now you will see my real power as I grow to overshadow this courtyard.'

Laughing hideously he peeled the skin away from the crown of his head and crammed the glistening, blood-wet strips into his mouth. Arbel and the Nightbeasts danced around him, chanting and laughing as Kruel grew, but Pinchface watched in horror, forcing the knuckles of his left hand into his mouth to stifle his cries. The leather pouch of nightflower seed felt heavy as if it had swollen beneath his cloak. Secretly, he touched it and crept further into the darkness of the low archway leading into the second courtyard lest Kruel should see his fear.

Kruel stood staring down at Thunderstone, waiting for the new skin to form and harden in the chill dawn wind. The raw severed ends of the fingers on his right hand had grown new fingertips but they still burned and throbbed, though the new skin had been quick to cover the Lampmaster's teeth marks. Snarling with hatred, he lifted Thunderstone up above his head and carried him out on to the Causeway Road. He trod through the heaps of rat-bitten warriors that Thunderstone led against him when he had tried to storm the doors. 'Now you are a part of my darkness,' he shouted to the shadowy Warriors, stretching his arms upwards far above his head, ready to hurl Thunderstone down on to the Causeway Road, using his death to strike terror into any who might turn against him.

'Hang him, Master,' shouted a voice. 'Let him be a lesson to all who come to the fortress of Underfall!'

Kruel hesitated and turned his head to see Silverpurse hurrying down through the great doors, bowing and kneeling his way on to the Causeway Road. 'Hang him from those ancient trees, great Lord and Master of all Elundium. That would be just the place for the last Lampmaster to dance in the morning winds!'

Kruel smiled, drawing his lips back across his teeth. 'Yes, he would hang as a lesson to all who dared cross the true power, the real Master of all Elundium.'

Laughing, Kruel dropped Thunderstone and turned back towards the fortress calling his warriors. 'Come out on to the Causeway Road and bring me strong rope or binding cord and watch the last Lampmaster dance to the rising sun!'

Arbel ran to Kruel's side and pointed down amongst the trees. 'There are horses riding in the shadows of the trees. I can hear the jingle of their harness and smell them on the morning wind.'

Kruel knelt, whistling softly, and drew the black warriors and the swarms of shadow rats all about him until they covered the beginnings of the Causeway Road in deepest shadows. 'Take the horses,' he whispered. 'Kill them all and let none escape. If any break away from the trees follow them, hunt them without rest until they fall from weariness, then kill them.'

Arbel laughed softly and unsheathed a long black dagger. He led the warriors silently down towards the trees.

Thunderstone half-opened his eyes and gasped with pain. The Nightmare's darkness had flooded through his veins turning and twisting his neck until now he could only look over his right shoulder. 'Run! Scatter!' he tried to shout to the nighthorses but Kerzolde's claws were clamped firmly over his mouth before the first shout was out.

Frightened whinnies and neighs of terror filled the darkness. Hoofbeats scattered in every direction acros the Causeway Field. Cries of rage were everywhere, daggers rose and fell, spearblades were thrust at galloping flanks. 'How many escaped?' shouted Kruel, fitting the binding cord around Thunderstone's twisted neck and dragging him into the shadow of the ancient trees.

'Only two,' answered Arbel, running back breathlessly and licking at his blood-sticky blade. 'But the shadow rats and our fastest warriors are close on their heels.'

'You will never catch them!' whispered Thunderstone, desperately shaking Kerzolde's claw away from his mouth. 'For they are fleet of foot and were gathered on the dark side of morning. They will escape into the wild places. They will warn the King!'

Kruel laughed and threw the binding cord over the highest branch then began to hoist Thunderstone above his head. 'Dance for me, Lampmaster, and watch for your precious horses until the crows have plucked out your eyes!'

Arbel joined in the laughter and spun Thunderstone by his boots, shouting up into the branches overhead. 'Look in every direction. Look in all the wild places!'

Thunderstone jerked and kicked, his arms thrashing wildly in the grey morning light. The silver strands of horsetail from his broken sword clung tightly to his wrist catching the light from the new sunrise. Above his head the branches moved and the leaves rustled together in secret whisperings. Kruel had gone, leading the warriors of Underfall and the swarms of his black shadow rats to conquer Elundium. Underfall had fallen and stood wrapped in silent shadows.

Wise Counsel in Candlebane Hall

'Gone!' shouted Thane, crashing his fist heavily on the carved armrest of the high throne in Candlebane Hall. 'Where has she gone? Tell me that,' he asked in a quieter voice, looking down at the anxious faces crowded on the first step of the throne.

'My Lord,' Breakmaster began, pushing his way through the crowd and kneeling on the second step, his head bowed respectfully. 'Perhaps the Queen has ridden to Woodsedge, or the Tower at Stumble Hill. Perhaps she has ridden out to visit Eventine, the Lady of Clatterford.'

Thane muttered and snapped his fingers, bringing the horseman to an abrupt halt. 'Cantering out in the dead of night? Is that, Breakmaster, the way to start a visit? Where are the guards that sit by the Stumble Gate? Bring them to me!'

'Lord have mercy,' cried both the guards throwing themselves at Thane's feet. 'The Queen galloped out so fast none could stop her.'

Thane leaned forwards and pulled both guards up on to their knees. 'You must have heard her riding down through the city.'

'Lord, she burst upon us with a thunder of hooves and fountains of bright sparks scattering across the cobbles. We ran out on to the Greenway and followed as fast as we could but Stumble was galloping as if the Nightmare was upon him and we lost them in the darkness.'

Thane turned away and stared out blindly through the doors of Candlebane Hall, his knuckles whitening as he gripped the armrest of the throne. 'Where has Elionbel gone?' he whispered, half-lifting his hands towards his empty shoulder, wishing Mulcade was perching there ready to rise on silent wings and search the Greenway.

Turning back, he beckoned Breakmaster to come close to him as he rose to his feet. 'Saddle me the swiftest horse that stands in the breaking yards, I fear for Elionbel's life and will follow her before the noonday striker touches the bell.'

'Lord, you would risk the safety of all Elundium if you ride out alone beyond the walls of the Granite City without Esteron to keep you from danger or the sharp-eyed owls to watch the road.'

Thane turned on the horseman, his eyes blazing with anger and would have shouted, cursing him for daring to cross the King but he hesitated, remembering how Nevian had counselled him not to spread fear among the people. He saw past Breakmaster to the throng of anxious faces crowding the throne, waiting on his every word. 'Clear Candlebane Hall!' he ordered. 'Send each man about his duties so that we might walk awhile, Breakmaster, and talk on the Lady Elionbel's nightriding, for I am sure it is as you suggested and she merely canters out to visit her father, Tombel, at Woodsedge.'

A sigh of relief seemed to escape from the crowd and they turned to leave. Breakmaster had cleared the polished marble hall, slamming the tall doors securely, when he returned to the throne.

Thane had stripped off his royal cloak of blue velvet and soft kid slippers. Silver chains and gold seals lay scattered on the first two steps of the throne. 'Where are my riding clothes?' he asked in haste while he unbuckled his silk and silver woven jacket. 'I must hurry or Stumble's hoofprints will have faded as the sun thaws the morning frost.'

'Lord, it would be madness for you to ride alone!' cried Breakmaster, gathering up Thane's discarded clothes.

'Rumours of a new darkness are on every traveller's lips. Let me go in your place and ride after Elionbel.'

Thane laughed grimly and shook his head. 'As yet they are only rumours, none have brought me proof of the darkness. Do not forget that once I rode out in deepest winter with nothing but the Chancellor's shouts to comfort me on a bleak and dangerous road.'

'But, Lord, now you are the King and must remain secure within the city,' ventured Breakmaster without much hope, seeing Thane was clearly set on his purpose.

'And as your King I command you to saddle me the swiftest horse, Breakmaster. Enough time has trickled through the hourglass. I know there is more to Elion's ride than to visit her father. Now go and saddle me that horse!'

'Lord it will be done!' answered Breakmaster, knowing he dare not allow the King to ride alone. He retreated from the high throne, his hand shaking as he opened the doors, and he ran without stopping for breath across the bridge over Swanwater and down through the city.

'Be warned,' he gasped as he cautioned Grey Goose and caught his breath as he threw a saddle over Beacon Light's back. 'The King will have a black rage and call for my life, I know it, but I must prevent him leaving the safety of this city. Nevian forewarned us to guard the King and Queen and already we have failed, but I will follow Elionbel. You have my word and solemn pledge that I will bring her safely back into the city.'

Grey Goose moved close to Beacon Light's head and took the loose reins in his hand. 'How can I stop the King from following you? He will tread me down if I stand in his path and take the horse nearest the gate.'

Breakmaster laughed uneasily and looked along the neat line of stalls then cast a critical eye over the Errant horses who stood ready for the road. It was true that none of them could match Beacon Light for strength or pace but the truth in Grey Goose's words shouted clear across the cobbles.

Footsteps sounded in the entrance to the stables. Breakmaster and Grey Goose turned and made to kneel. 'Lord,' they whispered together.

Thane paused, his hands on his hips and looked steadily into Breakmaster's eyes. 'I have heard enough of your secret whispers to see you will risk my shouts of treason if it will keep me within the safety of the city.'

'Lord, I fear for you out there,' answered Breakmaster. 'If anything should happen to you Elundium would be without a King.'

Thane frowned and caught a glimpse of the wisdom in Breakmaster's words, knowing that as he was a shepherd to his people so he should let others ride out and search for Elionbel. 'Do you fear these rumours of the world beyond our gates, Breakmaster? Is that what prompts you to take my place?' he asked in a troubled voice. 'The Nightmare is dead, Elundium is free of his shadows. What are you afraid of?'

Breakmaster hesitated. 'Lord, Nevian told us a little of the shadows he fears and the darkness in the Lady Elionbel's heart and he pledged us to watch over her. He feared Elundium in all its peaceful beauty holds its breath against some terrible tragedy. He counselled us on the eve before you broke the battle crescents to be watchful and ready.'

Thane smiled, seeing how wide a net the Master of Magic had spread to keep him safe, and he handed the reins back to Breakmaster then slowly stepped away from Beacon Light. 'I would be a foolish King to close my ears or cast aside wise counsel, nor will I waste such loyalty. Go, Breakmaster, ride with the wind and find the Lady Elionbel. Bring her safely back.'

'Lord, I am pledged to it,' cried Breakmaster, springing up into the saddle and cantering Beacon Light towards the high arch of the Stumble Gate. Grey Goose hesitated. 'Lord, if new shadows threaten the daylight my Archers will defend the City.'

Thane laughed, saying, 'As yet, my brave Archer, you would only loose arrows at transparent rumours!'

229

A Chance Meeting in the Dark

Breakmaster eased the reins and brought Beacon Light to a walk before he bent to search the shadows beneath the eaves of the black forest for signs of Stumble's hoofprints. They had been easy to follow in the early winter frost that had spread across the Greenway but now, beneath the silent brooding trees, they had melted away to nothing.

'Which way did you go?' he muttered, turning first left and then right, riding in tight undecided circles beyond the dark sweep of the trees. He caught sight of a dirty streak of smoke rising in the cold morning air. 'Woodsedge!' he cried, urging Beacon Light forwards. 'Perhaps she did ride to her father's Wayhouse,' he whispered hopefully as he cantered towards the open doorway.

Tombel laughed and waved his hand; Thoron ran out shouting greetings and cast admiring eyes over Beacon Light before taking the reins from Breakmaster as he quickly dismounted.

'What news of the Granite City and of my beautiful daughter?' called Tombel, turning and clapping his hands for a server to bring meat and drink for the weary horseman.

'Lord, and dearest friend,' Breakmaster began, trying to disguise his fears but the tone of his voice brought Tombel back across the threshold, his face paling. 'Is the Lady Elionbel with you?' he asked, stamping his feet against the cold. 'Only she rode out from the city two nights ago.'

'There were hoofbeats on the Greenway just before the

230

grey hours gave way to the daylight,' interrupted Thoron, returning from the stables.

Breakmaster turned and looked out at the low winter sun. 'If it was the Lady Elionbel she is a good half a daylight ahead of me.'

'Where is she?' cried Tombel, not knowing which way to turn. 'Why did she leave the Granite City in the dead of night, and why did she pass my door without . . .?' Tombel sat down heavily, his head in his hands, feeling a great dread weighing down upon him. Thoron moved quietly past his friend to the deep recess by the fireside and picked up his cloak then threw it across his shoulders. He bent and pulled on his boots as Breakmaster answered.

'We know not, but a dark shadow seemed to trouble Elionbel. Nevian forewarned us to watch over her but she slipped through the Stumble Gate galloping so fast none could catch her.'

'I will search for her,' Thoron said quietly, his arm around Tombel's shoulder. 'No man in all Elundium knows the secret ways better than I do.'

'No! No!' Tombel cried, shaking off Thoron's arm and rising to his feet. 'I cannot sit here alone, fretting by the fireside. With all my family taken from me Elionbel was all I had left. Which way did the hoofbeats go? Why did you not wake me?'

Thoron lifted his arms in dismay. 'None would pass here in the night save the Warhorses moving to better grazing. I thought little of it and turned over in my sleep.'

Tombel muttered something about losing first Arbel and then Rubel before the foul Nightmare took Martbel. 'I will find her, mark my Marching blades!' he shouted angrily as he trampled on his boots and reached up for his two broad Marching swords hanging above the fireplace before running out on to the Greenway.

'Why did Thane not go after her?' he asked, halting and turning sharply towards Breakmaster. 'Is the black shadow

231

that haunts Elionbel of his doing? Did he drive her from the city?'

'Lord, Lord,' cried Breakmaster in dismay, knowing nothing of the bad blood that had once flowed between Thane and Tombel. 'It was all I could do to stop the King from riding out after her. She cried out in her sleep, waking him for a moment, but when he rose with the grey hours she had gone, taking Stumble with her. Riders have scoured the countryside around the Granite City but she is nowhere to be found. I had half-hoped she had ridden out to be with you at Woodsedge.'

Tombel frowned and mumbled an apology for his quick temper then turned back towards the Greenways' edge. Thoron ran to the stable yard and, pausing to choose one of the fastest relay horses for himself, he hastily resaddled Beacon Light then led them both, stirrups swinging, out on to the Greenway.

'We will keep pace,' he said, giving Breakmaster the reins of his horse, 'and we shall not rest or ease our stride until we find Elionbel.'

'But you cannot run, Tombel, nor match the horses' stride,' cried Breakmaster pirouetting the horse on the crown of the road, 'for we will not rest until we reach the Tower on Stumble Hill.'

Tombel laughed harshly as he tightened his belt. 'Nor do I, horseman, for I am Marcher-born and need drives me now as it has never done before.'

'We shall travel together,' called Thoron, 'and share one shadow just as we did long ago in battle against the Nightbeasts.'

'Need drives us forward!' cried Tombel as he took to the crown of the road flanked by the two horses. Then he fell silent and bent his back to run a little harder, hoping beyond hope that they could overtake Elionbel before she reached the wild lands.

* * *

Elionbel had forced herself to stay awake, losing count of the daylights, afraid that if she shut her eyes she would see the nightmare vision of Kruel that had filled her dreams and driven her out of the Granite City. She had driven Stumble relentlessly on past her father's house, past Gildersleeves, the fencing Master's house, until she was numb with exhaustion and lost on the wild road through the black forest. She let the reins slip through her fingers and slumped in the saddle, her eyelids closing as sleep finally took her. Stumble felt her slip and eased the pace to a walk, stretching his sweat-streaked neck against exhaustion. Snorting quietly he took mouthfuls of short grass from the Greenways' edge as he searched for a place for them to rest. The shadows were growing long and he knew night would soon fall.

Snap! Crack! Something moved ahead. Stumble whinnied in alarm, his ears flat back. Elionbel started awake and cried out in terror, the hood of her cloak falling forwards, just as a ragged warrior slipped out of the undergrowth, a hand's span from Stumble's head, and grabbed the reins. The warrior laughed, his dirty face split into a gloating leer as he pulled the reins tight, forcing Stumble's head down towards the ground. 'Where can you run to, Lady?' he mocked, reaching out to touch her fine embroidered gown and her rich velvet cloak.

Elionbel shuddered as the hand stretched towards her and she would have screamed as she reached for her dagger, yet there was something in the warrior's voice and the look of his eye. Something was there that she recognized and stopped her hand, something from a time when Woodsedge rang to a sound of laughter, to easier times before the Nightmare.

'Rubel?' she cried, recoiling and drawing as far back as the high cantle of the saddle would allow.

The warrior hesitated, his eyes narrowing, and he let the reins slip through his fingers. Nobody had called him that name for an age of daylights, not since he had cursed Thanehand and angered his father, Tombel, so much with his hatred that he had been forced out of the battle crescent and had had to live as a beggar travelling in secret and taking what he could.

Elionbel reached up and cast back the hood of her cloak to stare Rubel full in the face.

'Elionbel?' he whispered, blushing with shame beneath the dirt and rubbing his eyes as he stared at his sister. 'But the Nightmare took you. How can it be you?'

Elionbel laughed with joy and jumped to the ground. 'Rubel, oh Rubel,' she repeated over and over again, taking his rough calloused hands into hers and taking them to her lips. 'Father said you cursed Thane and vanished into the grasslands, but I always hoped, secretly hoped, that you would come back.'

Rubel frowned and drew away from her. 'I did curse Thanehand. I cursed him with every black word I could remember for bringing the Nightmare to Woodsedge, for losing you and Mother, and for turning Arbel against me. But you, you are safe! How did you escape?'

Elionbel shivered as she remembered those last moments in the high chamber of the City of Night with the Nightmare's life thread drawing tighter around her neck and choking the breath out of her. 'Without Thane I would be dead,' she whispered, trying to shut the terrible memories from her mind as she looked round at the deepening shadows.

'Did he rescue you?' Rubel asked.

'Yes. I thought all Elundium knew,' she answered simply. 'How is it that you, my brother, should have hidden for so long? Why did you not come to our wedding in the Granite City when he made me the Queen of all Elundium?'

Rubel laughed, his eyes round with surprise and whistled softly, looking up at the darkening sky in disbelief. 'My sister is now queen of all Elundium! So that is what the messengers were shouting about as they galloped along the Greenways. Father banished me and I keep well away from Marchers and warriors of all kinds. But you look half-starved. I will light a fire and roast you a royal supper and you will tell me how you became a Queen.'

'Supper? What supper? All you have is a tiny bundle over your shoulder,' said Elionbel, following Rubel into a small clearing beside the Greenway.

Rubel laughed and tossed her a long string of fat, grey-coated rats, each one neatly killed and tied to the rope by its tail. 'Thus, for my curses, am I fallen,' he answered, gathering an armful of kindling wood from beneath the trees. 'From Marcher's son to ratcatcher, that is how I live, keeping away from the villages, travelling in secret, living from hand to mouth.' Rubel paused and looked at Elionbel. 'Have you a spark?'

Elionbel stared in horror at the rats and fumbled, searching in her pockets. 'Keep it,' she whispered, pressing the spark into his hands and retreating away from him.

Rubel's face darkened as he skewered the rats and balanced them above the flames. 'Eat or go hungry but this is all I have. Thane took everything from me and filled me with hate when he came between us and sent Arbel back into Woodsedge to slay me. Why else would my own brother raise a blade against me?'

'No! No!' gasped Elion. 'Thane would never have done that. He loves us all, without him . . .'

Rubel shook his head fiercely and kicked the fire into a brighter blaze. 'Enough of yesterlights,' he snapped. 'I will settle that argument when I meet Thanehand blade with blade. Now tell me all that brought you out to ride alone upon the Greenway. Leave nothing out even if it takes all night, for I have had little company on the road save the ancient trees that line the Greenways' edge.'

'So Thane is a King,' sneered Rubel as the tale was told, stripping the fire-blackened skin from the choicest rat and passing it to Elion on a charred stick. 'Then I will have to seek an audience to settle our quarrel. But you say nothing of Mother or how things are at Woodsedge.'

Elion shivered, turning her head away from the rat and drew her cloak tightly about her shoulders as she reached beneath her skirts for Kerzolde's black-bladed dagger which she passed to her brother. 'I seek the death of the Nightbeast that once owned this blade for with it he cruelly took our mother's life.'

Tears froze in Rubel's eyes as he gripped the hilt of the dagger. Twice he opened his mouth to ask but dry sobs choked his throat.

'In the high chamber,' Elion whispered, putting her hand over Rubel's, 'moments before Thane drove his sword through Krulshards' foul heart, the one-eyed, one-clawed Nightbeast named Kerzolde stabbed Mother to death.'

Rubel started forwards and cried out. 'I know that monster! Arbel and I saw it on the lawns of Gildersleeves, it chased us and Arbel fell, caught in a black web of nightmesh, but how do you know this Nightbeast lives? Everywhere through the grasslands and wild forests I have come upon their rotting carcasses.'

Rubel stopped abruptly and looked down, blinking away his tears, his knuckles white with grief. 'What of Father?' he asked in a tight whisper without looking up.

'He grieves his loss and sits each daylight by the open doorway.'

'Does he talk of me or Arbel? Is his heart still darkened against me?'

Elionbel smiled softly and touched Rubel's chin making him look up. 'He is a proud man and warrior-born, but he loves you, Rubel, even though you cursed Thane and he says that if you are dead then somewhere in Elundium there is a wall of Nightbeast dead to mark the spot where you fell. Yet each daylight he watches by the Greenway Road and gathers his hope around him that you will return.'

Rubel stood up throwing the half-eaten supper angrily aside. 'I have wronged and cursed. I have shamed and hurt the very ones I love. Why, why did I do it?'

'We all do things in . . .' Elion began but Rubel cut her short, quickly smothering the fire with cold ashes and pulling her and Stumble in amongst the ancient trees that seemed to crowd around their little clearing.

'Hush!' he whispered between clenched teeth. 'A riderless horse is running on the Greenway, its battle harness jingling and something follows less than a league behind. Listen, listen!'

Elionbel caught her breath, her eyes widening in fear as the sound of fast-running hoofbeats passed the clearing. Crawling to the clearing's edge they watched and waited, catching their breath in horror as warriors filled the road. They were chanting and screaming and all around their feet the Greenway seethed and swarmed with black shadows.

Rubel pressed his finger on her lips and quickly pushed Elion out of sight. Once, twice his dagger rose and fell, then he was safely back amongst the trees in the clearing with two huge black rats dangling by their tails. Frowning he turned them gingerly, twisting them in his fingers, touching their brittle spines with the blade of his dagger.

'There is nothing in all Elundium . . .' he whispered, turning his head fearfuly and listening to the fading chants and screams of the shadowy warriors. 'Come, we must hurry for the safety of Stumble Hill, there are dark shadows and new terrors loose in Elundium and I fear for us out in the open.'

Beacon Light felt the hoofbeats through the ground and heard the horses' neighs of terror. Snorting, she arched her neck and crouched, ready to strike. Breakmaster drew his sword and called across to Thoron. 'A rider runs towards us. Listen, a horse's bit-rings are jingling in panic.'

'Clear the Greenway!' ordered Thoron in a whisper. 'Let the rider pass between us and then we will close the road.'

The hoofbeats drew closer, behind them, carried on the night wind, screams and chants of pursuit sounded through the darkness. 'Be ready!' Thoron whispered, whetting the edge of his long galloping blade. He had heard night sounds like these before and they sent cold fingers creeping along his spine.

The horse burst upon them, running fast on the crown of the road, his sides lathered white with sweat, his head hanging low with exhaustion, his eyes wide with terror. The riders let him pass silently between them then closed the road against the warriors who loomed out of the darkness. They were black-veined with shadows and ran with spearblades ready to strike.

'Now!' shouted Thoron, leaping out on to the Greenway with his long blade flashing in the starlight as he scythed his way through the shadows.

'Now!' answered Tombel, striding out beside the horses, both Marching swords swinging in glittering arcs. Together they cleared the crown of the road, and felled the shadowy warriors side by side. Breakmaster gave a mighty shout and galloped up on to the Greenway, his sword-arm rising and falling with each stride Beacon Light took.

'They are no match for us!' laughed Thoron, plunging his long galloping blade through the nearest towering shadow warrior.

Tombel began to laugh as he warmed to the battle but Thoron backed towards him shouting in panic. ''Ware the shadows! Look, they are alive with black rats.'

'There are swarms of them!' Tombel shouted in terror as the tide of darkness washed all around them. The shadow rats shrieked and screamed, their black spines rattling as they attacked and ran over Tombel's armoured boots. They jumped and clawed at Thoron's horse and climbed in black nightmare waves towards the saddle. They caught and held on to the hems of the cloaks.

'Use the flat of your sword,' Breakmaster cried as Beacon Light reared up, neighing in terror and thrashing at the black bodies jumping at her throat.

'We are lost!' shouted Tombel in despair, staggering forwards beneath the swarms of rats climbing up his tunic towards his throat. Thoron reeled backwards under the weight of the shadow rats and tried with one last desperate effort to spur his horse forwards, striking at the rats clinging to his jerkin. 'By all Nevian's power!' he cried out as he fell. Breakmaster clung on tightly to the saddle as Beacon Light began to topple sideways, his sword arm was raised as he snatched a last glimpse of the stars above.

'Hope is with us!' he cried. 'Look at the ancient trees!'

Thoron twisted his head and stared up into the night sky where he saw movement in the treetops. The branches were swaying backwards and forwards, the thick leathery leaves were rustling without a breath of wind touching them. Faster and faster the branches swayed, the trunks groaned and creaked, bending low over the Greenway. The tide of darkness seemed to hesitate and the rats began to scatter beneath the flailing branches, shrieking with rage as they were crushed or whipped high into the night sky.

Tombel trembled with fear as the branches closed about him but not one silver hair on his head did they harm as long twig-crooked fingers plucked off all the Nightmare's shadow rats from his arms, legs, hands and face to crush them as easily as stalks of new-harvested straw.

Both horses whinnied and snorted, their ears pricked forward as the branches checked their fall and set them down gently on the Greenway. Breakmaster looked nervously about him and slowly dismounted, shuddering as his feet touched the bodies of the shadow rats.

'Of all the wonders in Elundium!' Thoron whispered, looking up at the still silent trees.

'What magic did that?' asked Tombel, staring up at the branches.

'One moment we are defeated, overrun by those rats and the next . . .'

Breakmaster laughed quietly and resheathed his sword.

'Thane said the trees might be a blessing when they first appeared in Elundium. He is a great King who sees much more than mere men.'

Thoron shook his head. 'No, Breakmaster, he merely wanted no harm to come to something he did not understand. That is the real measure of our King.'

'Well, I for one am glad he forbade anyone to harm the trees,' contemplated Tombel, 'and I think we should thank them.'

Thoron smiled and knelt upon the Greenway turf beside Breakmaster and Tombel and together they offered up the hilts of their swords. 'No man shall raise a blade against you while we live!' shouted Thoron.

As if in answer the leaves above their heads rustled and a whisper ran far along the Greenway. Soft hoofbeats sounded on the road behind them. Thoron turned and saw the horse that had been running before the shadow Warriors, trotting towards them.

'I know that horse!' Breakmaster cried, catching the loose reins and putting calming hands on the horse's shoulder, whispering to it as he stroked its velvet-soft muzzle. 'It is Rowantree, the stallion Thunderstone rode on his return to Underfall.'

Thoron looked from the frightened horse down to the dead warriors that lay scattered amongst the heaps of black shadow rats. 'And I know that warrior, even though his face is etched with dark shadows,' he muttered, crossing the Greenway and turning over the shadowy pursuers with the toe of his armoured boot. 'He was once a Gatekeeper at Underfall.'

'But what was he doing chasing Thunderstone's horse and running with these foul vermin?' asked Tombel, spearing a shadow rat with the point of his sword and holding it up for closer inspection.

'Nothing like that has ever been seen in all Elundium, I'll wager a herd of wild horses against it. Not even in the foulest sewers of the meanest streets in the Granite City, never!' cried Breakmaster, shuddering and drawing away from the rat.

Thoron took Rowantree's broken reins and calmed him. Turning to the others he pointed along the darkened Greenway. 'I do not know what changes old friends into shadowy warriors but there are dark daylights ahead of us, I can feel it in my bones. There are changing times where none will know who is his friend or whom he can trust. Come, we must hurry to Stumble Hill and seek a safer bed than the open road.'

'Rowantree galloped from that direction, perhaps Stumble Hill has fallen!' said Tombel darkly, shouldering his two Marching swords.

Thoron pirouetted his horse drawing Rowantree close to his flank and looked down for a moment at the dead shadow-etched warriors. 'No, there is not an Archer among them,' he answered quietly. 'They were just a handful of the guardians of Underfall.'

'We must hurry,' Tombel cried fearfully. 'Elionbel is somewhere ahead of us!'

The Tower Falls

Thunderstone hung, dangling by his neck from the branches of the ancient trees that edged the Causeway Field, twisting and turning in the dismal winds blowing about the sheer walls of Underfall. Kruel had sneered up at Thunderstone, mocking the last Lampmaster, laughing at his weakness as he pushed his dangling boots aside impatiently. This first taste of victory had whetted his appetite and now he wanted to swallow all Elundium with his darkness.

Arbel urged him forwards. Kerzolde whispered of the road through Meremire Forest that led to the Tower on Stumble Hill where the Archer with the Bow of Orm forged his new arrowheads. Kruel smiled. Now was the moment. The shadow rats had proved their power, growing stronger, multiplying and biting everything into their darkness, swarming their webs of shadows far beyond the eaves of Mantern's Forest.

Silently they had passed through Meremire Forest, swallowing everything into their shadowlight. Kruel had knelt, watching the Warhorses and the Border Runners grazing in the grasslands and whispered his shadow rats in amongst them, telling them not to kill, hoping that some of the dogs and horses would love his darkness enough to serve him, but they had fought savagely, rearing and plunging, growling and snarling, falling, hopelessly crippled by the shadows. Now they waited, crouching in the shadows of Stumble Hill.

Kruel licked his lips, tasting the drying Warhorse blood as

he looked back at the spreading shadows. 'Just before night falls,' he whispered to Arbel, pointing a bloody finger at the single tower crowding the summit of the hill. 'Then we will let the shadow rats pour through the closing doors and strike terror into the Archers in the half light.'

Arbel laughed and gnawed at a still-warm hoof. 'There is nothing that can stop us now, brother. I knew the Warhorses and the Border Runners would turn and fight but once bitten by the shadow rats they were crippled and fell at the slightest push.'

'Easy meat,' growled Kerzolde, tearing off long strips of Warhorse flesh from the carcass he had dragged through the grasslands and hanging the pieces from his belt.

'Few escaped us,' laughed Kerhunge, rubbing a full belly.

Kruel frowned and glared the Nightbeasts into silence. 'It would have been better if some of them had served the darkness, then we would have had shadowy gallopers to set against Thanehand. It would have been much better if none had survived to tell of our conquest. We shadow the light in secret, spreading our darkness further across Elundium with each daylight and with each warrior bitten our army grows. Soon we will be ready to ring the Granite City with my father's malice, then everything Thanehand sees will be in shadowlight.'

'Rest easy,' Arbel answered. 'Those crippled dogs and horses won't travel far walking on their fetlocks.'

'Or their knees,' gloated Kerzolde. 'I could have easily killed a dozen more!'

'Quiet! Lay still!' snapped Kruel, watching two Archers standing on a platform at the top of the high Tower.

'Night has gathered too early,' Eventine muttered, arching her hands against her forehead and staring out at the waves of darkness that seemed to be flowing towards the tower through the grasslands.

'Night cannot gather before the sun slips below World's

End. That is the way of things,' answered Kyot, sweeping the Glass of Orm slowly across the trees below.

'Listen!' hissed Eventine, putting her bow hand on his arm.

'What? What is it?' Kyot asked in a hushed whisper, his hand upon the soft grey goose feathers of the first arrow in his quiver.

'No! Listen and tell me what you hear,' she whispered back, her head tilted to one side.

Kyot stood perfectly still, his fingertips closed around the feathered flight of the arrow. He rose on tiptoe, turning his head from left to right. Frowning, he turned his head again, only this time more slowly. 'Nothing! I hear nothing, there is only silence as far as the horizon's edge.'

'That is what is wrong – the early darkness and the silence,' Eventine whispered, the skin prickling at the nape of her neck. 'There is too much silence. Where is the birdsong and the evening sounds that herald the darkness?'

Kyot looked out at the waves of darkness sweeping towards them through the grasslands, moving faster now than the winter wind. 'Yes, something is badly wrong,' he shouted, nocking an arrow on to his bow. 'Those waves of darkness that wash about us, they are almost at our very doors.'

'Ring the warning bell. Bolt the doors,' he cried to Eventine who leapt forwards at his shout, slashing the bell rope with one sweep of her dagger and rushing as fast as she could to the stairhead.

Kyot was a pace behind her, his face white with terror, the glass of Orm had slipped from his hand and bounced its way past them both, shattering as it fell down the winding stairway.

'The darkness is full of rats,' he stuttered, 'thousand upon thousand of rats!'

Below them the courtyard was filled with panic and the black shadows were everywhere. Archers screamed and shouted, arrows whined and shrieked high into the air.

Eventine knelt on the first step of the tower and reached for an arrow. 'No time,' cried Kyot, pulling her to her feet and shouting above the Archers' screams for Sprint and Tanglecrown to come to them.

'Use your dagger. Stamp on the foul creatures with your boots and make for the open doors, we must shut them.'

'I cannot!' Eventine shouted and retreated, shuddering, as the first wave of shadows reached the foot of the tower.

Tanglecrown heard Kyot's cry of panic and roared out in answer, and with his lowered crown of glittering antlers he cleared a path from the stable yard through the swarming rats and charged for the tower. Sprint followed, keeping close to his shoulder, rearing and plunging his way through the darkness.

'Defend the doors!' shouted Kyot, loosing his arrow at a dark shape that filled the entrance. He vaulted into the saddle as he pulled Eventine on to Tanglecrown's back before Sprint reared beneath him with a mass of shadow rats clinging to his fetlocks.

Kyot turned towards the entrance, the figure between the doors laughed and stretched out its hand to take the arrow mid-flight, melting the steel blade between its fingertips in a shower of sparks.

Kyot's blood froze, his hand hovered over the quiver, his fingers lightly touching the soft grey goose-feather flights. 'Look, in the doorway surely – no, no, it cannot be Krulshards! No, the Nightmare is dead!'

Kyot searched through the arrow flights with his fingertips, feeling for the last spine from Clatterford. 'The Nightmare has arisen, use your father's arrows if you have any left!' he shouted to Eventine as he nocked his last arrow from Clatterford on to his bow and loosed it, shrieking, low across the courtyard.

Kruel laughed again and pushed Arbel through the doors into the courtyard. 'Take the woman,' he snarled, reaching

245

out and smashing Kyot's glass arrowblade with his fist, filling the courtyard of Stumble Hill with a searing white light that black-etched his shadowy warriors and swarms of shadow rats in hideous shadows against the tower wall.

'Krulshards!' Kyot cried, grabbing for another arrow yet knowing in despair there was nothing in his quiver to fell the Nightmare. Turning the spur, he urged Sprint towards the open doors, willing Eventine with all his heart to follow him.

Searching the quiver, she had found only new-forged steel arrowblades and nocked one quickly on to the Bow of Clatterford to loose it at the black–armoured beast rushing towards her. It seemed to fill the courtyard, laughing and shouting as it drew closer, spreading a hideous writhing cloak of black shadows to engulf her. The arrow struck the black armour and bounced, skidding harmlessly away in a shower of bright sparks. Tanglecrown lowered his antlers and struck Arbel hard below the knees, lifting him up on his sword-sharp crown and tossing him high against the tower wall. 'Gallop, gallop!' she shouted, urging the Lord of Stags to follow Sprint for the lighter patch of sky between the doors where starlight still shone in the darkness.

Kruel cried out in rage and snatched at Eventine's cloak as she fled, hooking his fingers on to the smooth handle of her bow. 'Let the bow go!' shouted Kyot twisting in his saddle and loosing another arrow.

As Kyot looked back through the doors something that shone purple black landed on his shoulder falling from the dark archway above the entrance. Eventine screamed and snatched at something that had fallen on her neck also, and let the bow slip from her fingers. Kyot cried out as a needle-sharp pain struck him behind his ear and he fell forwards in the saddle. Sprint and Tanglecrown began to slow up, overwhelmed by the shadow rats swarming about their hooves. Neighing in terror, Sprint fell to his knees as sharp teeth sank into his tendons. He was falling through the Nightmare's darkness: it was flooding through his veins: his forelegs were twisting and buckling beneath him. Tangle-crown roared once and fell beside him, impaling his flank with his own glittering stand of antlers as the darkness twisted through him.

Kyot rose to his knees, reached up and plucked the armoured weed worm from his neck. He shuddered in horror and cried out as he hurled it aside; he was sinking, falling into the darkness, his head was turning, twisting on his shoulders. Behind him, less than half a league away, he could see the Nightmare figure silhouetted between the doors, laughing, gloating with victory. Beside him, the black-armoured warrior pointed out into the grasslands and whispered something urgently. The Nightmare figure took a giant step towards the place where Kyot and Eventine lay, then hesitated, turned and vanished into the tower. Without a sound the shadow rats melted away leaving the Greenway empty beneath the cold night sky. Stormclouds had shrouded the stars and large raindrops began to fall. Kyot tried to move, crying out as darkness etched its way into his fingers.

'Hold the bow,' cried Eventine from where she lay beside him. 'Whatever you do, hold on to the Bow of Orm!'

'There is the Tower,' Rubel called out, pointing to the slender shape that stood out on the summit of Stumble Hill against the heavy stormclouds. 'We will be safe and dry once we are within the doors.'

Elionbel lifted her hood against the rain and pressed Stumble forwards, going over and over in her mind what she should have told her brother. 'Why did you pledge me, Mother?' she whispered, bending forwards against the driving rain and hating herself more with each lie and half-truth she had to tell to keep that pledge. 'Soon all Elundium will know your nightmare secret if I cannot kill the bastard,' she muttered miserably.

Rubel paused between the open doors blinking the rain-water out of his eyes as he searched the shadows. 'Something is wrong,' he whispered, taking a half–backward step and bumping into Stumble's shoulder.

'What is it?' Elion asked in a hushed whisper, casting back her hood and looking into the empty rain-glistening courtyard.

It was too quiet. There were always Archers in the casement slits at each twist of the stairway in the Tower. They should have been challenged long before they reached the doors.

'Perhaps the rain ... look, there is a light in the inner courtyard, and another one beneath that doorway.'

Rubel wrinkled his nose, still sensing that something was wrong, and reluctantly passed under the high archway, leading Stumble into the Tower. The horse flattened his ears, snorting in alarm as they passed beneath the archway and fought against Rubel's hand upon his bridle but Elionbel soothed him and coaxed him forwards step by step.

'There, there,' she began to say as they reached the centre of the courtyard when a voice in the darkness laughed cruelly and whispered her name.

'Rubel!' she cried in panic, snatching the reins from his hand and pirouetting Stumble in a shower of wet sparks, but shadowy warriors, their faces hideously etched with veins of darkness, leapt out of the shadows beneath the Tower walls and slammed the doors cutting off her escape. Again the voice laughed and whispered in the darkness. 'Welcome, Elionbel, my sister!'

Elionbel's face drained of colour, her heart pounded wildly, the blood thundered in her ears. It was the voice and the laugh from her nightmare dream, she knew it as soon as she heard it.

'Welcome, sisterspawn!' called another voice from behind them in the shadow of the doors.

Rubel backed a step until his shoulders were against Stumble's saddle. 'What is it, sister?' he whispered, his eyes narrowing, his eyebrows drawing together in a frown as he

248

searched the shadows beneath the archway. That second voice, he knew it, or would have sworn in better dayligths that it belonged to his brother Arbel, but how could he be here? The Nightbeasts had taken and killed him long ago.

'Arbel?' he called in a voice shaking with uncertainty as he felt in his dirty pockets for the spark Elionbel had given him. Something was moving in the darkness; he could sense rather than see it. His fingers found the spark and closed about it. Quickly he held it aloft and squeezed it alight.

'Arbel!' he cried in horror as the spark blazed in his hand sending long shadows leaping up the Tower walls from the black-armoured warrior who loomed towards them.

Arbel sneered at him in the sparklight and curled his armoured lips back across his teeth then lunged forwards with a long spear. 'I should have killed you in the Wayhouse at Woodsedge when I first loved the darkness!' he hissed.

Stumble snorted in terror and reared up away from a dark figure approaching on his other flank then plunged sideways, knocking Rubel off his feet and sending him sprawling across the cobbles. Arbel screamed with rage as the long spear ploughed a harmless groove of sparks across the courtyard. Elionbel heard Kruel's footsteps and twisted in the saddle. She saw him in that split-seecond as the spark blazed in Rubel's hand.

'Bastard!' she shouted as the horse crashed sideways, flinging her on to the cobbles. 'Bastard! Bastard!' she shouted again and again as she rolled across the courtyard, fumbling beneath her skirts for the black-bladed dagger.

Kruel stared at her as she rolled helplessly, splashing through the puddles, and he felt his hatred weaken. Pity welled up in his heart as he watched her rise to face him.

'Enough! There will be no killing,' he snapped, pointing a long finger at Arbel and making him drop the long spear on the wet cobbles without taking his eye off Elionbel. 'If there is blood between you and this beggar then he must also be my brother.'

'That is Elionbel,' snarled Kerzolde running out from the inner courtyard and pointing with his one good claw. 'The one that swore to kill you, the one whose foul name was linked on the silver cup with the Galloperspawn, Thanehand!'

Kruel smiled and wet his lips with the tip of his tongue. 'Brother and sister,' he whispered, motioning Arbel to bring both Elion and Rubel before him.

Elionbel found the dagger moments before Arbel pulled her to her feet and firmly closed her fingers around the hilt as he pushed her roughly forwards to kneel upon the wet cobblestones at Kruel's feet.

'Gently, gently, there is blood between us,' Kruel cried.

Rubel fell beside her, grazing his dirty knuckles in an effort to keep his balance. 'Brothers?' he cried, looking in bewilderment from Elion to Arbel and then up into Kruel's face. 'How are you my brother?'

Kruel frowned, searching their faces and seeing something of himself in each of them. Slowly he reached out his hand and touched Elionbel's chin. 'Ask your sisterspawn, or is she so proud of the mixing of our bloods that she keeps it a secret all to herself?' he whispered, seeing the hatred in her eyes.

He gripped her jaw in his strong fingers, forcing her mouth open. 'Tell him! Tell your brother how my father, Krulshards, the Master of Nightmares, spawned me on the high wall of the Granite City in the moment of his victory. Tell him how he took the Marcherwoman, Martbel, and how she laughed and sang with joy to be so honoured!'

'No! No! No!' screamed Elionbel tearing her face free from Kruel's iron grip, and knocking Rubel out of Arbel's slippery armoured hold with the force of her struggle.

The great doors creaked unnoticed and swung inwards a hand's span.

Elionbel raised the dagger high above her head and brought it down at Kruel's heart double-handed. 'You lie!' she screamed, releasing all the pent up anger, the half-lies and untruths, tearing aside the deceits that her mother had unwittingly pledged her to in order to keep the truth well hidden. 'The Nightmare took my mother and cruelly raped her,' she shouted, almost choking on the words. 'In his moment of defeat he dragged my mother screaming inside the malice on the high walls of the Granite City. I tried to help her, to stop the foul . . .'

Kruel stared at her, seeing all her blind hatred, and he caught her wrist in his strong fingers then tore the dagger out of her hands and threw it harmlessly across the cobbles. Pushing her downwards he forced her back on to her knees on the wet ground. 'Martbel was honoured to bear the new Lord of Darkness,' he hissed. 'I was going to share my darkness with you – you are my sister by blood, but now you shall die here on the cobbles for your hatred and your treachery, for twice now you have raised a blade against me.'

'I curse you! I curse you!' shouted Elionbel, struggling to rise. 'And while there is breath in my body I shall seek your death, you–you–you foul bastard of the darkness!'

Kruel curled his lips in mirthless laughter. Elionbel's hatred had smothered his pity and reaching down, he pulled a long blade from his belt. 'For you there shall be no breath, nor will you share my darkness, sisterspawn, but you will die alone, unaided and without friends, here in the courtyard of Stumble Hill.'

Rubel had crawled away as far as he could and now hid in the shadows beneath the Tower wall where he balled his fist in anger. At first he had knelt, smothered in confusion, looking from Arbel to Kruel trying to understand but now Elionbel had told him all he needed to know about the foul Nightmare holding her life at daggerpoint. Desperately he searched the cobbles for a weapon, a discarded arrowshaft, a spear, anything with which to fight. Elion's dagger glinted, the raindrops splashed on the black metal and they caught his eye. Crouching, he bent forwards and stretched his hand towards the hilt then began to open his mouth to shout a challenge at Kruel when, with the crash of splintered wood, the great doors were flung open.

'She is not alone!' a strong voice shouted angrily as sparklight blazed across the rain-soaked courtyard.

Kruel turned, dagger posed above his head, ready for the killing stroke, his mouth half-open with surprise. Elion twisted in his grip and cried out. Horseshoes scattered bright sparks across the cobbles. Thoron and Breakmaster were amongst the shadowy warriors that thronged the cobbles but Tombel ran before them both. Marching swords swinging in rhythm as he charged at Kruel. Arbel snarled and sprang at his father, thrusting the long spear hard at his throat.

With one stroke Tombel smashed the spearshaft and turned both swords against his son. 'You are a curse on all of us, a black Nightmare curse,' he snarled, putting all his strength behind the blades as they swept down against Arbel's arms.

Arbel laughed and staggered backwards, the living cloak of shadow rats shrieking with rage as the Marching blades cut through them. Kruel whistled once for the shadow rats to attack and threw Elion down amongst their tide of darkness as it flooded the courtyard. Lunging forwards, he plunged the long dagger hilt-deep through Tombel's armoured shirt just above his heart, driving him down on to his knees on the cobbles. The tattoo of the owl in blue and gold on Tombel's arm blazed with pure white light as his blood gushed over the handle of the dagger. The shadow rats squealed and shrieked, fighting each other as the light burned their eyes and cleared a broad circle around him. Breakmaster slipped from the saddle, bitten by the darkness just as Beacon Light stumbled to his knees and fell, the shadow rats swarming all over him.

Thoron saw Kruel laughing at the light as Breakmaster and Beacon Light fell, and spurred his horse.

Rowantree neighed and reared up with terror, breaking free from Thoron's hand as the shadow rats swarmed towards him and he turned and fled, galloping out through the open doors. Rubel jumped out of the shadows and clung to Rowantree's swinging stirrups, taking giant strides beside the horse as it vanished from sight.

Thoron rode forwards and ploughed his way across the courtyard through the shadow warriors until he faced Kruel and lowered his sword, his face set in grim lines of defiance. 'By all that is good in the sunlight you shall not leave this Tower alive!'

Kruel laughed from where he towered over Tombel and snapped his fingers, sending the shadow rats swarming against Thoron. 'You are nothing but an ancient galloper,' he mocked, 'you cannot harm me, for I am Kruel, the new Master of Nightmares, and I am Lord of Elundium! Take him!' he shouted, snapping his fingers again.

Thoron twice raised his sword arm and tried to shout something against the Nightmare but the swarm of shadows was too great and his horse fell backwards, toppling beneath the weight of the foul black rats. Thoron's head twisted backwards to touch his spine as the nightmare blackness etched through his veins.

Kruel licked his lips and shook Tombel roughly. 'Watch!' he hissed, forcing Tombel's eyes open. 'Watch your daughter, Elionbel, and your son, Rubel, become a part of my darkness.'

Arbel gripped his sister's wrist and cruelly twisted it up behind her back then held her over her father's body. 'Watch her, Father!' Arbel whispered, letting the living cloak of shadow rats fall across her shoulders.

Tombel tried to rise, the blood bubbling in his throat, but the shadow rats clawed at Elionbel's soft skin. 'I love you, Father,' she shouted as sharp teeth cut into her neck. 'Mother loved you and pledged me to kill . . .'

Elion sank forwards, her mouth choking on the darkness, her head spinning as the blackness swallowed her up. Etchings of spider-fine shadows appeared across her skin, twisting her fingers, crippling them into tight balls of agony.

Tears were flooding down Tombel's cheeks, hopeless tears

253

of pain and rage as he fought to stand, but with each haunted breath he was growing weaker and sinking further back on to the cobbles.

'Everything that was once yours will be mine,' gloated Kruel impatiently, motioning Arbel to bring Rubel forwards. 'Gone?' shouted Kruel, half-rising, his face black with anger. 'How has he gone? Who let him escape?'

Tombel gathered the last of his strength and laughed into Kruel's face then stared blindly into his eyes as he whispered, 'You shall keep nothing of mine or of the sunlight, you will keep nothing while one of us is free, mark my words on that!'

'No!' shouted Kruel, gripping Tombel by his metal shirt and shaking him violently. Black rage swept through his body and he lifted the Marcher high above his head, but it was useless, the moment of victory had been lost. Tombel hung dead from his fingertips. Rubel had escaped and now Elionbel was a part of the darkness. For a moment he stared at her and saw something of himself in her face as their eyes met. He raised the dagger but he could not kill her. He frowned and tried again to lift the blade but hastily turned away. Elionbel caught her breath. For a moment, she thought she had seen something in his eyes, a shadow of her mother.

'A curse on all Marchers,' he cried, throwing the body down and turning towards the open doors.

'Bind them all in chains and take them to Underfall,' he snapped, pointing a quivering finger at Breakmaster, Thoron and Elionbel where they lay amongst the shadow rats. 'They shall hang in chains beside the Galloperspawn, Thanehand, in the City of Night. They will suffer for this night.'

'What of Rubel and the two Archers who escaped?' asked Arbel, fearing to come too close to Kruel's black rage and marshalling the shadowy Warriors and night-bitten Archers on the far side of the courtyard.

Kruel stood for a moment, licking at the blood on his dagger. 'Let the shadow rats follow Rubel and bring him back to us, for there is blood between us!'

He turned towards the wild grasslands and smiled cruelly then whistled a huge swarm of black shadow rats about his feet. Crouching, he spoke to them in a soft voice. 'Spread my darkness across the grasslands. Take Clatterford and destroy it, leave nothing for the Archers to escape to, nothing but destruction.'

Rising, he laughed and called Arbel to his side then linked arms with him. 'Come, brother, let us move forwards and take all Elundium as our own.'

A Dark Road Through the Grasslands

Kyot shuddered and fought against the darkness. He was being moved, rolled over. Something sharp was digging, pushing at his side; there was a gentle sound, a clicking as if dry bones were rattling against each other. Wet tongues licked his face, warm breath moistened his cheeks and a damp nose was sniffing at his eyelids. He was being lifted off the ground. The Bow of Orm felt heavy, still locked within his paralysed fingers it snagged on an unseen branch or rock and twisted until, with a final jerk, it broke free. Soft whinnies and deep-throated calls were all around him: he was moving, swaying amongst soft branches in a summer wind. Muffled hoofbeats were everywhere, a dog growled and another answered it nearby. Kyot's fingertips began to burn and tingle, the darkness was fading, the noises all about him were growing suddenly louder, now he could hear the raindrops beating on the branches overhead and feel the cold water splashing on to his forehead.

'No!' he whispered in panic, trying to push himself up with his free hand. 'My face, my head – I cannot feel the rain, I am lying face down,' he cried. Then the terror of it all flooded back, the hopeless battle in the Tower, the new Nightmare, the one without a shadow who had so easily smashed the last glass arrowhead and laughed at the light, and now their desperate flight out on to the Greenway had come to nothing. 'Eventine,' he half-whispered, half-sobbed, the word strangling in his twisted throat as he finally managed to sit up, balancing on the velvet-soft branches, clinging on with his free hand.

Blinking, he forced his eyelids open and cried out. All about him as far as his twisted neck would let him see were antlers, huge crowns of glittering bone that clicked and rattled as they touched. Beyond the antlers amber eyes filled the rain-soaked darkness.

'Be quiet!' hissed Eventine's voice out of the darkness beside him. 'Lie still and let Orgas, the stag, carry you to safety.'

'Safety?' whispered Kyot, trying to turn towrds Eventine's voice and making Orgas stumble as he moved his weight within the crown of his antlers.

'Lie still or Orgas will fall,' answered Eventine in a hushed whisper. 'Quiet, we are only two leagues from the Tower on Stumble Hill.'

'How did the stags find us?' Kyot asked. 'And where did those Border Runners come from?'

Eventine looked across with tears in her eyes and smiled sadly to see the greatest Archer in all Elundium hunched and crippled within the crown of Orgas' antlers. 'We were escaping from the Tower when Sprint and Tanglecrown fell. Tanglecrown called for the stags as he went. In those last few moments before the black rats swarmed over us he lifted his great head and called to all his kind; the Border Runners must have heard his cry and come to our aid.' Eventine fell silent and watched the road where the stags were turning, picking their way between the ancient trees that lined the Greenways' edge. Their way took them out into the wild grasslands where they vanished from the Greenway as silently as they had come.

Suddenly there were hoofbeats on the road, galloping hoofbeats that rushed past them on the Greenway and quickly faded into nothing. 'The stags will take us to Clatterford,' she whispered, 'and there my father will rearm us with new glass arrowblades to use against that foul Nightmare.' Eventine paused for a moment, forcing back the shadows of despair, knowing deep down in her heart that she could never hold a bow again or that Kyot could ever look down a smooth arrowshaft. 'We must warn Thane that Krulshards has arisen from the dead!' she cried, near to tears.

Kyot tried to nod his head and almost tumbled out of the antlers as both his shoulders swayed backwards and forwards. 'Yes,' he muttered angrily, remembering how easily the Nightmare had smashed the last glass arrowblade in the courtyard and realizing that with such power he could destroy the Granite City. Kyot thought back: it had all happened so quickly but when the arrowblade shattered and the sunlight from Clatterford blazed across the courtyard the new Nightmare did not have a shadow. There had been nothing to trap him with.

'Shadowless!' gasped Eventine, listening to Kyot's fears. 'You mean he was so powerful he could defy the light!'

Kyot blinked his eyelids despairingly, not daring to try and nod his head again. 'Yes, nothing can stop him and even if your father can forge an arrowblade against him we cannot use it. Your bow is broken and lost in the Tower on Stumble Hill and I, with the Bow of Orm locked within my fingers, could never loose the arrow. I am worse than a blind man with my head twisted back behind my shoulder. Even if we could gallop to the Granite City we are useless to Thane.'

Eventine reached out and brushed her own injured hand against his arm. 'My father has great power – he may know a cure; he may have an antidote to those armoured weed worms that dropped from the Tower archway on to our necks.'

Kyot laughed bitterly. 'There will be no cure,' he hissed fiercely. 'Whoever stormed the Tower will swallow all Elundium beneath his darkness. There is nothing strong enough to stop him, nothing but weak Wayhouses and unguarded villages all the way to the Granite City.'

'Yes there is,' answered Eventine. 'There are the War-horses and the Border Runners, and the Battle Owls; they will not let him pass, they will fight for every league, every blade of grass, every . . .' Her voice faded away. They were skirting a large area of trampled grassland. Border Runners and Warhorses lay scattered everywhere. The stench of death drifted out to meet them on the wet night air and it choked in her throat making her cry out.

'What is it?' Kyot asked, trying to turn.

Orgas moved forwards and swung his body, letting Kyot see the full horror of the slaughtered animals spread in a great crescent throughout the grassland. A league beyond, Meremire Forest stood wrapped in blackest shadows as if mourning them in silence.

Tears welled up, blurring Kyot's eyes, and his mouth thinned into a grim line of hatred. 'I will hunt that Nightmare even if I have to follow him like a blind man tapping my bow to find the way,' he hissed.

'They are not all dead – look,' whispered Eventine pointing a crooked finger at the misshapen bodies, twisted fetlocks and distorted legs cruelly taken by the darkness. 'Some of them are so badly crippled that they cannot rise.'

A horse whinnied within the circle of stags and Kyot urged Orgas to turn for him. He laughed with joy as he saw Sprint's head and neck resting in Tanglecrown's twisted crown of antlers. Looking more closely he saw how Tanglecrown's head had been bent sideways until his crown of antlers had pierced his own flank making him unable to see in front of him. Sprint's forelegs had buckled and twisted out of shape but half-mounted on the Lord of Stags they together could still find a path through the grasslands.

Kyot stared at Tanglecrown and Sprint for a moment, the seed of an idea growing in his mind. 'Let me down, Orgas,' he whispered, stepping out of the crown of antlers and stumbling blindly backwards in the wet grass clutching at winter-spent seed heads to keep his balance. Kneeling beside the nearest Warhorse that showed signs of life he felt along its twisted legs. The horse could not rise on its own, but he tried to get Orgas and the other stags to push their antlers beneath its flanks and shoulder.

Eventine laughed softly, seeing clearly what Kyot was trying to do and carefully climbed to the ground. She called to the stags and led them forwards amongst the crippled Warhorses. Bending, whispering, pointing, she helped to smooth and guide the huge antler crowns beneath the fallen animals. They were lifted one by one with neighs, shouts, grunts and groans of pain, until all the Warhorses that had survived Kruel's attack were back on their feet.

Kyot watched in sorrow as the once-proud crescent of Warhorses hobbled and stumbled towards him. 'Where are you now, great beasts of war?' he whispered. 'Where now is your strength to rear and plunge or measure the winter wind in your flowing manes?'

The closest horse whinnied softly and brushed its muzzle on Kyot's arm; his proud neck was arched, his ears pricked forward. Kyot smiled sadly, blinking away the tears of defeat and ran his hand through the Warhorse's silky mane. 'Come with us to Clatterford and there we will find a way to fight this Nightmare,' he whispered.

Looking down, he recognized the lame Border Runner licking at his bow hand. Crouching, he hugged the dog, feeling its soft wet fur against his neck and remembering all the hardships they had shared.

Eventine was shaking his shoulder, breaking into his thoughts and whispering and pointing into the long grass. 'Black rats!' she hissed. 'They are spreading through the grasslands all around us. Quick, we must hurry.'

Kyot made to follow, took one stride and fell, cursing his blindness. 'Clatterford will be a ruin if we keep to my pace,' he muttered crossly, climbing back on to his feet.

'Orgas will carry you – quickly, climb up on to his back,' Eventine urged.

Kyot gripped the smooth fingers of antler and sprang awkwardly on to the stag's back. 'Well, seeing only backwards can be quite useful. Look, those trees are following us into the grasslands.'

Eventine turned her head and gasped with delight. There was a lot of magic in those trees: she could have sworn that just beyond the doors of Stumble Hill as Sprint and Tanglecrown were overpowered on the Greenway the trees had attacked the shadow rats, snaking down and beating them away.

Kyot smiled and remembered how Errant had told the Archers not to fear the trees. 'We must warn Thane,' he urged again, remembering how he was alone in the City with only the horseman Breakmaster and Grey Goose and his strike of Archers. 'We must go to him, warn him, but how can we when we move forwards more slowly than the slowest funeral?'

'The owls!' whispered Eventine. 'He would heed their warning.'

Kyot lifted his free hand and motioned helplessly across the dark rainswept grassland. 'The owls are free and fly far beyond our sight. How are we ever going to find them?'

The Border Runner limping beside Orgas suddenly barked and began careering in wild circles amongst the other dogs, bringing forward the sound ones not bitten by the darkness. 'Oh yes, there is a way,' laughed Eventine, leaning down to run her twisted fingers through their thick sable coats. 'The Border Runners will find the Owls, they will carry the word of this new Nightmare through all Elundium.'

Siege-Locked

'How many more daylights? How many?' muttered Thane, pacing endlessly backwards and forwards the length and breadth of Candlebane Hall. Each time he reached the great doors he would pause and stare out, searching the Greenway, looking along the broad sweep of the horizon. 'What news is there?' he would call to the man beside the daylight bell.

And the answer was always the same. 'None my great Lord, and King, the road is empty.'

Thane turned away and slowly paced the broad aisle to the high throne, treading carefully in each measured footprint on the polished marble floor. Now he knew how King Holbian had worn these footprints, dragging the weights and the worries of a kingdom backwards and forwards in a cage without locks or bars. Now he knew why the last Granite King had worn so brittle with the rub of time, fretting each daylight to set his foot in the stirrup, to hear the music of hoofbeats on the road, and feel the wind tugging.

'Lord, Great King.' Grey Goose was between the doors, calling, pointing urgently with a new-forged arrowblade out beyond the city.

Thane turned, throwing off his cloak and ran.

'There, my Lord, something is there; a horse, yes a horse is coming fast along the Greenway.'

Thane snatched up the long slender glass that stood beside the doors of Candlebane Hall and searched the empty road. Backwards and forwards he looked with the glass shaking in

262

his hand. There was a dust cloud. Slowly he followed it, twisting the brass cylinder and holding his breath as first the tail, the quarters and then the saddle came into view.

'It is not Stumble!' he cried in despair, thrusting the glass at Grey Goose and turning sharply on his heel.

'No, Lord,' answered the Archer, carefully watching the riderless horse galloping towrds them. 'It is the horse Rowan-tree that Thunderstone rode on his return to Underfall. He is riderless and hard pressed with exhaustion. He . . .'

Thane snatched back the glass and searched the road behind the weary horse. 'Gather your Archers, Grey Goose,' he shouted, casting the glass aside and running out through the doors. 'Follow me on to the Greenway. That horse must run before something, its eyes are wide with terror and its flanks are white with sweat.'

'Lord!' shouted Grey Goose, following Thane as fast as he could. 'You should stay here and let me go out. There may be danger . . .'

'No!' shouted Thane, letting his standard of the sun flow out behind him as he ran across the Swanwater bridge, down the winding steps and sprang into the next level of the city. 'My place is out there upon the crown of the Greenway, for a King should always be the first where there is danger. I have sat far too long in idleness upon the throne.'

Thane tossed aside the crown and every seal of office then ran down through each level of the city. His lungs were burning as he gulped in mouthfuls of air, his legs ached as he forced them onwards.

'Lord, Great King,' the crowds of startled city folk cried out in surprise, and fell back out of his way, kneeling in the winding gutters and bowing and curtseying in confusion.

'I need warriors to line the Greenways' edge with sharp swords and Marchers' long spears against an unknown enemy, not kneeling, pomp and ceremony!' he shouted. He was red-faced and blowing hard as he descended into the first circle of the city and tried to force a passage through the milling throng that blocked the gates.

Grey Goose caught up with Thane and moved in beside him, the Archers following were closing around the King in a protective hollow column, their arrows ready-nocked upon the strings. 'Make way for the King!' shouted Grey Goose above the thunder of his Archers' armoured boots. 'Clear a path for the greatest Lord of Elundium,' he cried, overturning carts and upsetting humble criers' booths in his haste to reach the gates before the King.

'No! No!' shouted Thane above the rising panic, putting a firm hand on the Archer's shoulder. 'Move quietly through the people. I shall go first and then you shall follow.' Thane pressed the Archer into silence and slipped out between the last two carts that blocked the road. Pausing, he searched the Greenway.

'There he is, less than half a league, my Lord,' cried Grey Goose, running to Thane's side. 'Beyond that line of ancient trees.

Thane lifted the summer scarf above his head and ran forwards out of the shadows of the great wall, calling Rowantree's name. The galloping hoofbeats slowed, the wild jangle of battle harness grew softer. Rowantree stretched his blackened, sweat-streaked neck and whinnied. He could hear Thane's voice and see the bright sparkling standard of the sunlight. He halted beneath the ancient trees and stared back along the empty Greenway; he pricked his ears and turned them to lisen to the spreading silence.

'Be easy! Be easy!' Thane whispered, slowing as he passed beneath the shadows of the trees and quietly putting his hand upon the frightened horse's bridle. Bringing the reins over Rowantree's head, he ran his hand across the sweat-soaked skin and felt the horse's pounding heartbeat with his finger-tips. Rowantree snorted, struck out at the Greenway and turned his head towards the empty road. There was fear in the whites of his eyes, and terror seemed to haunt each shallow breath. Thane frowned and knelt. There was blood on the horse's hooves, foul black blood that had splattered up over his fetlocks and on to his legs and along the underside of his belly. Thane reached out and touched the speckled marks, bringing a soiled finger to his nose.

The colour faded from Thane's cheeks, as he quickly cleaned the blood from his hand in the coarse grasses that grew along the Greenways' edge. Shuddering, he stood up. 'There is death on the road, Grey Goose,' he muttered, turning towards the silent horizon. 'Nevian feared new shadows were moving beyond our sight: dark desperate shadows that have the smell and reek of nightmares wrapped about them. This is our warning. Nevian gave me wise counsel to spread our eyes and ears far across Elundium. Thunderstone must be hard pressed and desperate to send us such a messenger. But where is Elionbel? Where in all Elundium is Elionbel?'

'Lord, the trees, the trees!' Grey Goose cried and sprang backwards, an arrow drawn taut upon the string. 'Look up above your head.'

Thane looked up and stepped quickly away from the Greenways' edge. 'Put down your bows,' he shouted, watching the gnarled and twisted branches swaying backwards and forwards. It was as if they were pointing first out towards the horizon and then back towards the Granite City to tell him something.

'Perhaps the trees are urging us to retreat into the City. Perhaps this exhausted horse runs before a storm of new shadows,' Thane muttered, frowning.

Grey Goose laughed harshly and pointed back towards the City with his bow. 'If new shadows are rising against us we could never defend the Granite City, my Lord. Willow built a honeycomb of open archways and windows on each level. Only on the summit where there is the wall that holds Swanwater is it sheer enough to keep danger away. That is the only place that the Nightbeasts or any new shadows could not overrun, the one that surrounds Candlebane Hall.'

Thane turned sharply on his Captain Archer, his eyes blazing with anger. 'Willow and his people laboured freely to give us back what Krulshards had destroyed. Never, never speak ill of the Tunnellers, but look to what we must do to block each arch and barricade each empty window space. Come quickly and prepare the city in whatever time this great horse has bought for us.'

Rowantree neighed and reared up, thrashing at the empty air with his forelegs and pulling at the bridle to be gone.

'Run, hurry,' shouted Thane, sending the Archers before him, but he paused a moment beneath the ancient trees. A frown creased his forehead as he looked up into the moving branches. Nevian had feared they lived on the edge of troubled times and he shivered as he sniffed the winter wind. There was something in the air, he could smell it.

The branches swayed faster and the leaves rustled louder as Thane turned and began to run towards Stumble Gate. 'I shall prepare the City for a siege,' he shouted over his shoulder to the ancient trees as the great gate swallowed him up.

Torchlights blazed against the dark night air, men shouted and cursed their rising and falling hammers as they demolished the second circle of the city, and they choked on the blinding stone dust that billowed up to fill their throats. 'Bring that cart closer!' shouted Arrachatt the stonemason, cursing the carters as the collapsing wall fell two paces short of their cart.

'We feared . . .' began one of the carters, falling back as Arrachatt strode towards him.

'I have brought a granite tower sliding down on its own foundations, built bridges in the dark for Granite Kings to walk upon and you thought that toppling mound of stones would fall on you! Get it cleared up now! We must fill every window and archway in the outer wall with the stone choke. Hurry!'

'Be easy on them,' whispered a firm voice at Arrachatt's elbow. 'We must all work together against ...' Thane hesitated looking out into the darkness. 'Against whatever grows to threaten the sunlight.'

'Lord!' the mason cried, trying to fall on to his knees but Thane held him up.

'There is no time for ceremony, mason, you serve me better on your feet!'

Arrachatt smiled in the darkness knowing that when the danger came this new King of Elundium would stand just as proud as the last Granite King. 'Lord,' he said quietly, 'every archway and window space on the ground level in the great wall will be filled with rubble and sealed before the new sun rises, but it will take us many daylights to block the upper walkways.'

Thane nodded and smiled in the darkness. Elionbel's flight, Nevian's fears and a frightened horse had made him perhaps a little overquick to prepare for a siege. What if Nevian was questing at shadows and jumping at half-truths? What if nothing threatened the sunlight and Elionbel was safe at Woodsedge? If only she had not galloped out in a rush of hoofbeats, taking Fate into her own hands.

Grey Goose touched his arm and pointed up to where the striker waited by the daylight bell with his hammer poised to herald the new morning and to the criers who ringed the great wall, turning their hourglasses in anxious hope of the new daylight, but still the grey hours had not given way to the rising sun.

Thane frowned and stared out into the darkness, straining his ears against the growing silence and wishing Mulcade was on his shoulder perch. He sighed and drew his cloak more tightly about his shoulders then looked up towards the cold winter stars. 'I am the King,' he whispered to himself. 'I must lead without a shadow of doubt treading on my heels. I must not show my fears or hesitate. I must not show how Elionbel's absence fills me with dread.'

Gathering his courage, he laughed as he turned and gripped the Archer's arm. 'We can do nothing but wait for the new morning, why even the sun has held its breath and given the stonemason precious moments to secure the Granite City.'

'Lord, the City is not secure,' whispered Grey Goose, trying to edge the King away from the mason. 'There are a thousand culverts and gutterings that pass through the great wall, surely they should be filled with stone choke?'

Thane laughed again. 'Nevian spoke of rumours and a horse runs to us with blood on its fetlocks and you tremble with fear that something may crawl through the sewers to cover us with shadows. No, we wall up our defences against . . .' Thane paused and spread his hands helplessly. 'Night-beasts? Shadowy nightmares large enough to swing a sword against? Now go down amongst the people and if it calms your fears break open the armoury and arm them, let every man and woman, young or old, be ready for whatever the new daylight brings.'

Thane looked up at the stars seeing how pale they were against the lightening sky and knew that the grey hours would soon be upon them, but as he arched his hand against his forehead he watched the horizon and saw a darkness that would spoil the daylight. He ordered every candleman and lamplighter up on to the great wall and warned them to be ready with sharp sparks in their hands, telling them they must wait for the King's signal. No matter where he stood, they must look for the banner of the sun, follow it with their eyes and be ready.

'Lord,' Grey Goose pleaded, returning to the King, 'I beg you to retire within the sheer wall that encircles Swanwater and Candlebane Hall. There you will be safe and my archer strike can defend you.'

Thane smiled at his Captain and turned him, sweeping his

outstretched hand across the frantic crowds preparing for a siege in the first circle of the city. 'Where should a King stand, my brave Archer, but first before the storm, for that is the purpose of a King: to spread his cloak of courage as far as the cloth will stretch to keep the people from harm. Go now amongst the people and marshal them, calm them, just in case the new daylight threatens to do no more than cast cool shadows through the Stumble Gate and a safe road winds out past those ancient trees towards the horizon's edge.'

'Lord,' cried Grey Goose, his voice now fully edged with despair. 'King Holbian pledged me to guard you with my life. I beg you, if you will not seek safety at least let the armourers clothe you in the strongest steel. Let . . .'

'No!' laughed Thane, putting an end to the Archer's pleas by casting his cloak aside to show the fine steel-ringed battle shirt he wore. 'This is armour enough. More would only burden my sword-arm and make me leaden-footed in the shock of battle. Go quietly now and gather the candlemen.'

'Lord, there are black shadows closing in about the City,' shouted a watchman above the Stumble Gate.

Thane frowned. How could shadows have closed in all about them, there had been no Nightbeasts' screams, nothing but an unnatural silence to herald the dawn. Twisting the long slender glass he had brought down from Candlebane Hall, he swept it backwards and forwards along the edge of the advancing shadows and watched them eat away at the bleak winter fields and hedgerows, swallowing the grey morning light in their darkness. Slowly he moved the glass to the crown of the Greenway and stopped. There were War-horses, Border Runners and a great crowd of wild animals pressed together on the crown of the road, racing the shadows towards the Granite City.

Thane blinked, rubbed his eyes and stared again. 'By all the wonders of Elundium,' he cried.

Steadying the glass and twisting the slender cylinder

between his fingertips he brought the fleeing animals clearly into focus and then he saw them, desperate figures, running, limping, stumbling along amongst the close–pressed War-horses. 'Keep the gates open! All Nature runs before this unnatural darkness!' he shouted, thrusting the glass into the nearest Archer's hand before he turned towards the long ramp that led down into the first circle of the city.

'Lord, the gates are closed,' cried Grey Goose, running to keep pace with Thane. 'They were closed and sealed before night fell. We cannot . . .'

'Open them!' demanded Thane. 'Elionbel may be amongst those on the Greenway, I know not who nor how many run before that dark storm but I saw flashes of light, sparks or swordblades shining in this shadowlight. It could be the warriors of Underfall, or Stumble Hill, or . . .' His voice faltered, his knuckles whitened on the hilt of his sword. '. . . or Elion.'

'Open the gates,' shouted Arrachatt the mason, tearing at the jumble of carts and baskets of rubble piled high against the gates.

Rumbling and grinding across the broken cobbles, pushing the litter and stone choke aside, the great gates slowly creaked open just wide enough to let Thane through.

'We are with you, Lord,' cried a throng of city folk, spilling through the widening door crack, their spears and swords held awkwardly in their hands.

Thane laughed with pride to see them follow him so bravely and brought them to a halt with an outstretched hand. 'You are a great people,' he shouted, 'and I will make you into even greater Warriors.'

Thane called to the Archers and sent them up on to the high ground beyond the dyke. 'Grey Goose and his Archer strike will watch over us and cover our retreat back to the city.'

Taking the nearest long spear, Thane showed the city folk how to dig the shaft butt deep into the frosty turf and kneel with the spearblade pointing out towards the advancing shadows. 'The swordsmen must stay between the spearmen,' he instructed, 'shoulder to shoulder, on each side of the Greenway. Let whoever runs before those foul shadows pass between you and then retreat inwards through the hollow column you have formed. Remember, everyone of you must keep his place or the hollow column will crumble to nothing. The Archers have the high ground and will keep you safe.'

Silently, the grim-faced city folk nodded and formed a tight hollow column that bristled with sharp-bladed spears and stretched out until it reached the first grove of the ancient trees. Thane knelt beneath the trees and pressed his ear to the ground. 'They are drawing closer,' he muttered, turning his head and putting the other ear to the frost-cold turf.

As he knelt he frowned at the muddle of noise he could hear. There were hoofbeats, slow irregular hoofbeats that were without a rhythm, and the patter of lighter feet. Now he could hear wild growling, barking and the screaming of Warhorses. Jumping to his feet he drew his sword.

'Be ready!' he shouted, unfurling the standard of the sun to catch what little light there was. He strode out upon the crown of the Greenway.

The candlemen on the high wall of the city saw the banner and each one struck his spark. Bright lights blazed out against the advancing shadowlight and for a moment turned the gathering darkness back into day. The ancient trees rustled and swayed backwards and forwards and seemed in that brief flash of light to gather closer around their King. The dark line of shadows hesitated and swayed on the crown of the road. Thane cried out and froze mid-stride as the ground about his feet suddenly seemed alive with fleeing panic-stricken animals. Long-eared hares, forest deer and silver foxes fought and scrambled with sharp-spined hedgehogs and savage night boars for the crown of the road.

'Let them pass between you,' he shouted to the city folk in the hollow column. 'Let all Nature's creatures pass beneath

271

your spearblades into the city for they run as chaff before this nightmare darkness.'

Now there were shouts and the thunder of hoofbeats. Thane spun around, the bright banner of the sun fanning out behind him, and saw the Greenway crowded with Warhorses and Border Runners. Pressed in amongst them were desperate warriors running on the crown of the road. Thane swept his sword aloft and made to leap forwards but the shout of joy died on his lips and his sword-arm fell helplessly to his side. The Warhorses and the Border Runners were hideously crippled, limping and crawling, pressing together for safety, running on bloody fetlocks and shattered knees. Their once-proud heads and necks cast strange shadows, twisted and out of shape, and their white eyes rolled in terror. Neighing shouts of panic filled the air.

'Lord, retreat back into the City,' shouted Errant from amongst the crowd, with his broken bloody sword still locked between his crippled fingers. 'You cannot stand and fight. Run before the black rats bite you!'

'Run for your life!' he cried again from between two Warhorses on the crown of the road.'

'Elionbel! Is Elion with you?' cried Thane, forcing his way forwards through the retreating warriors and seeing Duclos the deaf swordsman fighting for his life on the edge of the Greenway as the Border Runners and Warhorses swept all around him.

'She is not on the road, Lord,' cried Errant, stumbling to his knees at Thane's feet.

'She must be with you,' cried Thane desperately, catching the falling horseman and gathering him up in his arms as he searched frantically amongst the figures fleeing towards the City.

Panicstricken, Errant thrust his gnarled hands up into the air and swept them across the crowded road. 'These are all I could gather as I fled from the new darkness. I was on the road near Stumble Hill searching for Willow when the black

272

rats struck. They carry a darkness that etches and burns its way through you and there are shadowy warriors following behind them that will kill anyone they catch. We had no time to stop or rest. You must run, my King. Everything they bite is filled with nightmare shadows. Run before it is too late!'

'What of Woodsedge? Was Tombel or Thoron there? Have they seen Elionbel?' Thane cried, pulling Errant to his feet and staring at the advancing shadows. Now he could see the black rats' brittle spines and hear their shrieks of rage as they swarmed against the last retreating Warhorses, biting at their fetlocks and trying to pull them down.

'Woodsedge was empty, my Lord. The door hung open swinging on its hinges,' Errant answered against the fierce neighing and wild barking that suddenly broke out beneath the very edge of the shadows where the Warhorses and the Border Runners were rearing and plunging as best they could to drive the shadow rats back.

'Esteron! Equestrius!' shouted Thane, recognizing the two great battle-weary Warhorses holding back the rats.

'The Warhorses came to us in the grasslands,' Errant shouted. 'They have fought against the black rats without rest, crushing them beneath their hooves, but you must escape while there is still time.'

'No!' shouted Thane as the swarming shadows began to engulf them. 'I will not abandon the ones I love. I will not leave the Greenway while the Warhorses or the Border Runners fight.'

Esteron heard Thane's voice and, lifting his head, he roared out the Warhorse challenge. Thane let the standard of the sun flow out from his sword arm and called across the Greenway. 'I am with you, Esteron, though all the darkness swarms before us. I will never leave your side again.'

Crushing the foul black rats beneath his armoured boots Thane fought his way to Esteron's side. 'If only we had warriors now,' he shouted above the screaming of the shadow rats and the neighing of the Warhorses as he lifted his blade with both hands firmly on the hilt.

Esteron snorted and brushed his bloody muzzle on Thane's cheek. Thane smiled and looked up past Esteron's head. 'Look! the trees have come to our aid. Look!'

Esteron whinnied and Thane laughed as the branches twisted downwards all around them, crushing the shadow rats, lifting and hurling them high into the air.

'There are metal helms, sharp swords and spears in the branches,' cried Errant, falling on to his knees in terror. 'Look, up there at the trees! They are changing into warriors!'

Thane laughed again and shook his head. The ground about their feet was clear of the nightmare rats, the ancient trees had driven them back to the edge of the Greenway. 'There is no need to fear them, their magic is of great help to us.'

Thane turned towards the city, pointing with his bloody sword to where the last of the Warhorses had safely passed through the hollow column. 'Now we must retreat as fast as we can,' he shouted as Esteron and Equestrius closed in on either side of him. He turned and gave a great shout of joy as he saw Grannog, the Lord of Dogs, limping to his heels. They had won a great battle and had rescued all those that fled before the shadow rats but he knew they would need more than magic trees to reach the safety of the City before the rats overran them. He bent and rubbed his hand across Grannog's battle-weary head.

'Lord, the sky is growing darker,' cried Errant, turning in despair towards the city only to see the last of the hollow column shrink beneath the Stumble Gate. 'We stand all alone, abandoned. Now the blackest night will swallow us up.'

Thane looked from the dark shapes crossing the weak morning sunlight to the closing gates and made his decision. 'Where better, Errant, to make a stand than here upon the crown of the road?' he laughed, the grim light of battle in his eyes. 'And who better to have at your shoulder than the Lord of Horses and the fiercest Border Runners who ever roamed Elundium? Come, brave horseman, and stand beside me. Help me build a wall of dead that will climb higher than the evening stars!'

Esteron neighed and roared, Equestrius arched his neck and turned proudly while Grannog bared his fangs and crouched between Thane's feet. 'We shall have light,' cried Thane, letting the standard of the sun float freely from his arm and the summer scarf rippled and began to float across the Greenway as if tugged by secret winds. Thane felt a cold breeze touch his forehead and caught the scent of a clean bright winter's dawn from far far away. The shadow rats were closing in a tight circle, huge swarms of them were scuttling between the trees, overpowering the flailing branches, gnawing at the roots and toppling the trees one by one. Thane tensed his muscles and turned his sword to use the flat of the blade and stole a glance up into the darkening sky.

'By all Elundium! We are saved!' he shouted, stamping on the first shadow rats to attack.

Then Errant looked up and laughed and cried with joy as the air about his head filled with stooping Battle Owls. Sharp beaks and razor talons ripped and tore at the rats and carried them high into the lightening sky before letting them hurtle to their deaths on the hard frosty earth below.

'I missed you, Mulcade!' Thane wept as the great bird of war settled lightly on his shoulder.

'Run, Lord, the road behind you is clear,' shouted Grey Goose from the high ground beyond the dyke. 'The owls have cleared you a path. Escape while you can!'

Thane laughed and caressed the owl's soft chest feathers. Mulcade hooted and stooped to Thane's feet, hooking a huge black shadow rat in his talons. 'Keep the doors open just a crack,' shouted Thane as they ran.

Trotting and stumbling, they covered the last few strides and squeezed through the closing doors. Arrows and spearshafts thrown from the walls above fell behind them as thick as winter rain on to the rats that were close on their heels. Thane turned, his sword in his hand, and looked out between the closing gates of the city where he caught a glimpse, a frozen picture of a tall nightmare figure that seemed to rise above the shadows. Dead locks of hair streaming out from the bony crown of his head, he had a black shadowy flag floating at his side that seemed to swallow the daylight.

'Krulshards!' he whispered, sinking down in despair on the cold cobbles. 'The Master of Nightmares is once again loose in Elundium!'

Kruel halted amongst the ancient trees that now lay shattered and broken beside the road and gloated with triumph as he watched Thanehand marshal into the city the last of the wretched warriors, Warhorses and dogs. Everywhere behind him his shadowlight fogged the Greenway; all Elundium, right to the very gate of the Granite City, had fallen so easily beneath his darkness. He would starve the city level by level, spreading his darkness street by street, forcing Thanehand to retreat ever upwards towards Candlebane Hall. Laughing, he cast his warriors in a tightening ring of terror around the great wall so that none would escape him and sent forward his black tide of shadow rats into the culverts and sewers to do their work. Soon Thanehand's warriors would be fighting each other as the darkness spread, soon everything would fall beneath the shadows.

Rubel Finds his Purpose

Rubel had caught hold of Rowantree's empty stirrup as the horse galloped free of the Tower of Stumble Hill and clung on to him until his fingers had burned themselves raw with numbness. Looking back he saw dark shadows spread out far across the grasslands behind them. 'We cannot escape together,' he shouted against the rushing wind. 'Without my weight burdening the saddle you can gallop to the Granite City and warn the . . .'

Rubel fell silent, biting his lips. There were tears in his eyes: tears of anger and cold hatred, tears of despair and shame at having abandoned Elionbel and his father so easily in that dark courtyard. 'I will find a way to destroy that bastard half-brother,' he shouted through his tears. 'Tell the King.'

As he let the stirrup slip through his fingers he fell and sprawled headlong across the crown of the road. Climbing painfully to his knees he watched the galloping horse until its hoofbeats faded into nothing. 'For all Elundium's sake, warn the King!' he whispered desperately before turning back towards the advancing shadows.

Crouching, he quickly looked left and right across the Greenway. Circumstance had reduced him to a hunter of vermin and he knew all their foul ways and dirty secrets. 'Shadow rats!' he hissed through clenched teeth, knowing he could not outrun them, knowing they would scent him no matter where he hid. He caught on the hem of an idea as he moved to the side of the road and lay flat. He slipped noiselessly beneath a low branched tangle tree and waited, his hands outstretched, his thumbs and first two fingers almost touching.

He smelt them and heard the sharp rattle of their claws long before they reached the place where he hid. Blinking, he held his breath. They were almost upon him now, spread out in a ragged line of darkness. Flattening his hands, he let the first dozen rats run, unaware of him, across his fingers. They were slowing, squealing and sniffing, running in circles, searching for his scent. Rubel had waited as long as he dared. Flexing the muscles in his arms he snapped his fingers shut on two long rats' tails; a quick flick of his wrist and both their backs were broken as neatly as stalks of straw. The shrieks of surprise were cut short in their throats. Rubel quietly drew the black rats into his hiding place beneath the tangle trees, and with the blade he had snatched up from the courtyard on Stumble Hill he slit open their bellies with one stroke of the knife then rubbed their foul black blood all over his hands, arms and face. Holding each rat by its tail he stripped back the skin and wrapped it around his hands. Reaching forwards from beneath the branches he plucked another two shadow rats from the Greenway, killed and skinned them; again and again his hands slipped silently out between the close-grown branches until he was clothed from head to foot in the brittle-spined rats' skins.

Laughing silently, his teeth showing stark white against the streaks of black blood, he crawled out on to the Greenway and passed unnoticed through the swarms of shadow rats and night-bitten warriors. He did not stop until he was far away from the Greenway. He found a dark tree-ringed hollow beside a stagnant pool and there he sank down, covered his head with his hands, and wept.

For several shadowy daylights he sank deeper and deeper into despair beside the stagnant water and lay deaf to the tramp of Kruel's growing nightmare army as it passed all

278

around him, closing and tightening its grip on the Granite City. Shadow rats swarmed down through the hollow in black droves, drank their fill from the fetid waters in the pool and quickly moved on, leaving their muddy clawprints in grey crisscross patterns on the brittle skins he had spread across his back.

'Rubel, Rubel,' whispered a voice form beneath the overhanging trees, 'your King has great need of you.'

Rubel shook his head, putting his hands over his ears and tried to crawl deeper into the mud but the voice cut through the shadowy light, forcing him to look up.

'Rubel, the King stands siege-locked in the Granite City. None can enter or leave, not even I with all my magic can pass through the shadow rats. The King has nothing but a strike of Archers to defend the sunlight.'

Rubel opened his blood-streaked eyelids and stared at the muted colours in the rainbow cloak, each one shrouded so that it was no stronger than the flickering of a candle flame. 'Nevian!' he hissed, not daring to do more than whisper. 'The shadow rats or the Nightmare Warriors will see you on the rim of this hollow, get down and out of sight.'

Nevian laughed quietly and wrapped the colours of the rainbow cloak into even tighter folds to hide their beautiful colours, then descended to the bottom of the hollow and sat down beside Rubel. 'Tell me all,' he whispered, taking Rubel's hands and running his aged fingers across the brittle spines of fur on the shadow rats' skins.

'Lord, you must know more than a simple ratcatcher for you are Nevian, the Master of Magic who has a hand on every man's destiny.'

Nevian laughed softly and held Rubel's eye. 'And you, Rubel, can catch and kill the very beasts that are laying waste to all Elundium. That would seem a mighty task for a simple ratcatcher. Now, tell me quickly all you know, for in truth I am stumbling blindly in this darkness with only a few threads at my fingertips and know not where next to tread.'

Rubel drew closer to the Master of Magic and spread a dozen ratskins across his back to hide him from the shadow rats before telling him all that had happened since he met Elionbel upon the road.

'Now I begin to see why the rainbow cloak has not faded,' whispered Nevian, rubbing his hand across his forehead. 'This beast that calls himself your half-brother must be a part of Krulshards and the mixing of his blood with Martbel's has made him so powerful he can deny the sun a shadow. Now I see the shadow that burdened Elionbel's heart. Martbel must have pledged her to keep the rape a secret.'

Rubel nodded silently and shrunk down into the stinking ratskins he had laced about his body. 'Nothing can harm him. Nothing!' he whispered miserably, looking out of the hollow at the shadowy half light and frowning. The wind had changed and there was a smell of snow in the air.

Nevian touched his arm, bringing his mind back into the hollow. 'You are wrong, Rubel,' he whispered, 'everything has a weakness, a flaw or a hairline crack just below the surface. Nothing is all good or all bad.'

'But I saw him smash spearblades and shatter swords, melting the forged steel between his fingertips. Nothing in all Elundium is as strong as that! Nothing save Krulshards, the Master of Nightmares.'

Nevian smiled and gripped Rubel's arm. 'Yet Thanehand trod on Krulshards' shadow and slew him. Think, Marcher Rubel, think, there must be a weakness. You have stood close to him, you must have seen it.'

Rubel threw up his hands in despair. 'There is nothing. All I see is his foul shadowless shape filling the courtyard of the Tower of the Stumble Hill, sneering and gloating as he tortured poor Elionbel.'

'Enough of your weakness!' snapped Nevian, shaking Rubel firmly by both his shoulders. 'Your sister is a prisoner of this new Nightmare, your King fights a hopeless battle trapped on the Granite City while you lie here, weeping with self-pity in the mud of this hollow because you shrank away into the darkness rather than stand and fight.'

Rubel slowly looked up into the magician's ancient face. 'What, Lord, could I have done against Kruel's power?'

Nevian smiled, his eyes softening as he gripped Rubel's hand. 'Your thread of Fate is closely woven with the King's through Elionbel. You have cursed him and now seen the wrong in those hateful words. You hesitate to ask his forgiveness yet you have the power to pass secretly through the Nightmare's shadows and fetch the sword forged by Durondel.'

'Sword?' cried Rubel, forgetting for a moment the swarms of shadow rats beyond the lip of the hollow.

'Hush!' whispered Nevian, putting a finger on his lips and pulling the Marcher to the ground. 'Your King fights without the blade of Durondel hot-forged to pierce Krulshards' rotten heart. If there is no other weakness in this Nightmare's spawn perhaps that blade might in some way cut through his strength.'

'Where is it?' hissed Rubel, the whites of his eyes flashing in the darkness.

Nevian lifted his arm and pointed out beyond the wild grassland towards World's End. 'One mighty thrust drove that sword through Krulshards' heart, pinning him to a column of rock in the high chamber of the City of Night. Go quickly, my brave Marcher, for each daylight grows darker and more desperate.'

'But you say that none can enter the Granite City – what good will the sword do if I cannot put it into the King's hand?' asked Rubel, half-rising and crouching, ready to slip out of the hollow.

Nevian frowned and tilted his aged head to one side searching into his foresight through the webs of shadows Kruel had woven across Elundium. 'Everything will be swallowed by this shadowlight,' he whispered, turning to Rubel. 'The sunlight will fade to nothing and the Granite City will fall beneath Kruel's darkness, but Thane will escape from the City. I can see him in the last ray of sunlight. You will find him there by following the ancient trees that now line the Greenways' edge.'

'Trees! What trees? Elundium is full of trees!' hissed Rubel. 'What trees do I follow?'

Nevian smiled and pointed up to where the row of twisted ancient stands of timber lined the hollow's edge. 'Those trees were my last great act of magic at Thane's crowning. Have faith, Rubel, for they will lead you to the last ray of sunlight to shine in all Elundium. Follow them and they will bring you to your King.'

'Nevian, I am so afraid, so alone, stay with me and guide me through the darkness,' Rubel implored the magician, gripping his cloak with his trembling fingers. 'Help me!'

Nevian smiled sadly at the frightened Marcher and carefully drew a glowing thread from the rainbow cloak which he bound around Rubel's wrist. 'Hide this magic thread beneath those foul ratskins and use it in the darkness in the City of Night; it will guide you in the dark and give you courage to carry the sword. Now I must find a secret way into the Granite City and warn Thanehand before this Nightmare darkness swallows up everything.'

'Nevian – the ratskins, use them to hide your scent. I can collect more as I travel,' urged Rubel.

Nevian laughed and took the foul brittle strips of fur the Marcher offered and fashioned a cloak of shadows that hid his purpose and would allow him to pass unseen and unnoticed through Kruel's army of darkness. 'Remember,' he whispered, as Rubel rose to leave the hollow, 'once you have the sword follow the ancient trees and they will lead you to the King.'

The Loremaster Finds his Courage

Silverpurse's eyes were greedy with desire as he crept towards Elionbel.

'Master, leave her be!' cried Pinchface the Loremaster. From the moment that Elionbel was thrown into the dungeons of Underfall he had tried to stop Silverpurse from taking her. 'She is bound by ties of blood to our Lord Kruel. He would kill you for . . .'

Silverpurse turned savagely on the Loremaster and knocked him off his crippled feet, sending him with one sweeping blow hard against the dungeon wall. Turning back, the Chancellor's son bared his teeth and reached out for the hem of Elionbel's cloak and, gripping the fabric, he began to pull her towards him. 'I shall take you, Queen of Elundium; the cursed candlecur's wife shall be mine!' he gloated, a fine trickle of saliva escaping from his bleak and bloodless lips.

'No!' shouted Breakmaster, straining against the chains that bound him to the sheer granite walls of Underfall.

Thoron cursed Silverpurse as the iron shackles bit into his bleeding wrists, but they were both powerless.

Twisting against the rusty iron links that held him Breakmaster glared across the dirty chamber to where the huddle of rags and bones that had once been the Loremaster of the Granite City lay, nursing his cuts and bruises. 'How many times will you betray your true King?' he shouted angrily.

Pinchface huddled closer to the wall, scratching his fingernails across the rough granite to shut out the horseman's words.

'Twice King Holbian forgave your treachery and twice you trod on his mercy and turned against him. Now you lie there cowering while that base treacherous Chancellor's son defiles your Queen!'

Silverpurse laughed at the horseman, a howling savage sound that had about it the cry of wolves, blood-hungry for an easy kill, and he drove his dagger deep into Breakmaster's neck. 'Bite on my blade and shout about that!' he snarled, thrusting the dagger to the hilt and wiping his bloody hands on Elionbel's skirts. His eyes half-closed with delight as he hovered over her. 'You shall crawl in the dust beside that wretched Loremaster and do all my bidding.' Elionbel shrank against the wall, paralysed with terror and disgust.

'Now is your moment, loremaster,' urged Thoron, pulling desperately against his shackles. 'Thane will pardon every treachery if you . . .'

Silverpurse cackled with triumph and cut across Thoron's words as with one hand clamped across her mouth to drown her screams he tore at Elionbel's skirts. 'Loremaster can do nothing, Thoronhand. His life is mine to treat and tread on as I please. Mine to crush and crumble.'

Pinchface huddled against the rough granite wall pressing his hands hard into his ears but Thoron's words echoed and thundered in his head. He saw shafts of sunlight in the Learning Hall and a boy who once dared to stand against him. Bright shining colours in a rainbow cloak and a strong voice that had once made him tell the truth. 'Nevian, give me courage!' he whispered, flexing his fingers and twisting them together. Slowly he rose, pressing himself flat against the wall.

Elionbel bit at the hand clamped across her mouth and cried out, fighting with all her strength. Pinchface blinked and bit his lip at each screaming cry and hobbled as fast as his feet would allow to where Breakmaster hung limply in his chains. Reaching up he grasped the hilt of the bloody dagger and pulled it from the horseman's throat.

'Fear drove me to treachery,' he whispered, leaning heavily against Breakmaster while he carefully turned his damaged feet towards the Chancellor's son. Balancing as best he could he raised the dagger above his head and threw himself on Silverpurse's back, plunging the dagger into his back. 'I am no man's slave!' he shouted as all the hidden anger and hatred of the Chancellors boiled to the surface.

Silverpurse screamed as the blade cut into him and he sprawled forwards across the dirty stone floor. Rolling over he reached with his hand and searched with his fingertips for the hilt of the dagger. 'Curse you, you foul nothing, you worm!' he snarled, choking on the hot sticky blood that filled his mouth. Rising to his knees he stumbled; anger and surprise crossed his hateful face as he began to topple forwards and he clutched the Loremaster's ragged claok. 'You serve no man – no man but me, Loremas . . .'

Pinchface prised Silverpurse's fingers from his cloak as he wriggled away from the dead Chancellor's son. He shuddered and searched through Silverpurse's pockets for the dungeon keys.

'Are there others held prisoner?' Thoron whispered as he helped Elionbel hold Breakmaster while the Loremaster steadied his shaking hands and unlocked the chains.

'Only two,' answered Pinchface, nodding towards a small door set on the far side of the chamber. 'A crippled Archer and a charred healer who dared to stand against this foul new Master of Nightmares. He set the Healer alight and laughed as he burned.'

'Merion the Healer? Quick, set him free before Breakmaster bleeds to death,' Thoron cried, snatching the bunch of keys from the Loremaster's hands and searching for the one that would turn the lock.

'Oiled cottons, use oiled cottons,' whispered a voice from a pile of burnt rags that huddled on the floor, pointing with his blackened fingers to a bag half-hidden beneath his bed of straw.

Tiethorm bent and hooked the bag of oiled cottons on his injured fingers and passed them to Elionbel. She shuddered, her throat tightening, as she watched Tiethorm carefully lift Merion and carry him over to where Breakmaster lay. Bending, she put her ear against his cracked lips and searched through the oiled cottons for the one he whispered would heal a knife wound.

'We must escape,' Thoron muttered, opening the chamber door by the merest crack and peering down a long dark tunnel. Footsteps and the sharp scrape of rats' claws echoed in the courtyard somewhere above.

'How many shadowy warriors are there?' he asked, closing the door and turning towards Pinchface. 'How many?'

Pinchface threw up his hands. 'Ten? Twenty? I have never counted them. But there are thousands of those foul black rats, far too many to count. They come and go,' he answered. 'Sometimes there are only a dozen shadowy warriors, but the rats . . .'

'No,' whispered Tiethorm shaking his head, 'the rats will not harm us. They have already bitten each one of us into the darkness, they cannot harm us again, but we must be wary of the shadowy warriors for unlike us they have become a real part of the new darkness.'

'Why?' asked Elionbel looking up from Breakmaster's wound. 'What makes us different from the shadowy warriors? How do you tell us apart?'

Tiethorm laughed bitterly and held up his bow-hand. 'It is clear to see, my Lady. Those that love the darkness are etched with veins of night, while those who love the sunlight are crippled by the rats' bite.'

'Thus we shall know our enemies,' choked a voice at Elionbel's side.

'Hush!' she scolded, turning on Breakmaster. 'You will see less if you do not rest until the wound closes.'

286

Breakmaster smiled and took her twisted hands into his and whispered. 'I pledged the King I would find you and bring you safe home.'

'Home will be a black ruin,' answered Thoron, stumbling blindly against Silverpurse's body as he crossed the chamber, cursing the shadows for his twisted neck.

Tiethorm laughed harshly. 'If you stood there, Thoron, without a flaw I would surely have to kill you!'

Thoron laughed in return and nodded painfully. 'Come, we must hurry and escape to warn Thane of . . .' he paused and looked at Elionbel.

'Of Kruel,' she answered tearfully, unable to hold his gaze. 'That bastard beast that crawled out of my mother's belly to cause all this pain, all this . . .'

Thoron reached out and turned her head, holding her gaze and for long moments looked into her heart. 'I know, child,' he whispered softly. 'We heard it all through the doorcrack of Stumble Hill. Martbel pledged you to hide her shame, making you cover the truth with a web of lies when there was no shame to hide. None would have mocked her or cursed her. What happened on the high wall of the Granite City was beyond her power.'

'But I hid the truth,' Elionbel sobbed. 'I knew it was wrong, but I loved Mother so. If only I had had the strength to break the pledge none of this darkness would have happened, Father would not have died, or Rubel . . .'

'Be easy, be easy,' Thoron whispered, feeling her tear-stained cheek against his aged chin. 'The pledge is now broken, Elionbel, and we must fight our way to Thane's side and warn him of this new Nightmare.'

There were footsteps and coarse laughing voices just beyond the doorway. Tiethorm reached down and pulled the dagger with both hands from Silverpurse's back then forced it between his twisted fingers. Thoron gathered up a length of chain from the floor, locked one end around his wrist and gave the other to Elionel. 'Around their throats,' he whispered. 'As I raise my arm, run around behind them and pull the chain tight.'

The footsteps halted, the heavy doorhandle began to turn; Thoron held his breath and raised the chain. Tiethorm crouched beside him, the dagger ready.

'Yes, Master, yes, Master, I will tell then,' Pinchface suddenly burst out, pushing Thoron away out of sight and pulling the doorway open a hand's span. 'My Master says you make too much noise and spoil his pleasure. Go! Go before he flogs you both.'

Elionbel gave a scream and both shadowy Warriors laughed. 'We bring news for Silverpurse, the Keeper of the Underfall. There are more of those old trees at the edge of the Causeway.'

'I will go and look at these ancient trees, Master,' Pinchface called across his shoulder and he slipped through the doorway, pulling it firmly shut behind him.

'King Holbian saw that grain of courage in the Loremaster where the rest of us saw only treachery,' whispered Breakmaster, slowly rising to his feet, an oiled cotton pressed against his throat.

Thoron drew a deep breath and let the chain fall to his side. He nodded and slowly opened the door.

'Yes,' muttered Tiethorm, gathering Merion up in his arms, 'that is, if he doesn't sell our hides to the highest bidder in the courtyard.'

'No, he will not sell us across the cobbles,' answered Merion in a cracked whisper. 'I have watched the Loremaster and seen his hatred of the Chancellor's son grow and blossom in this shadowlight. He was once a good man destroyed by his own weakness, now through this one act he has found those strengths the Chancellors stole so long ago. He will empty the courtyard of shadowy warriors and give us a clear path on to the Greenway.'

'Follow me quickly,' urged Thoron, 'before the chance to escape is lost.'

Tiethorm stood for a moment in the shadow of the great doors of Underfall and felt Merion shiver in his arms at the cold winter wind against his blackened blistered cheeks. 'There is snow in the air, pure white driven snow,' he whispered, covering the healer's face with the tail of his cloak.

Breakmaster and Elionbel crept silently forwards through the doors. Suddenly a figure climbed out of the dyke waving and beckoning to them. 'Hurry, hurry,' hissed the Loremaster, 'I have sent the shadow warriors to change the guard and sharpen their axes. You have but moments to reach the safety of the ancient trees.'

'What of the horses?' asked Breakmaster fearfully. 'Have the shadow warriors killed them?'

'Down there. Down there beyond where Thunderstone hangs, there between the first line of trees,' Pinchface answered, pushing them out frantically on to the Causeway. 'I took them secretly from the stables, binding their feet with rags to dull the clatter of their hooves and sent them out the moment the guards' backs were turned. Now go, hurry, run as fast as you can.'

'Come with us,' Elionbel urged, turning and grasping the Loremaster's sleeve. 'Thane will forgive you everything and shower you with honours for this daylight's work. Come.'

Pinchface took a step and hesitated. There were angry voices and the thunder of armoured boots across the cobbles in the courtyard behind them. 'No, my Queen,' he whispered, reaching beneath his cloak for the secret bag of nightflower seeds. He pulled it out and wove the age-stained string of the pouch between her crippled fingers saying, 'This pouch has a great power against the darkness, Elionbel. Give it to Thane and beg him to forgive me for all those harsh daylights in the Learning Hall. Tell him that the Loremaster is once more strong and ready to defend the sunlight – tell him!' Turning back, Pinchface began hobbling towards the doors. 'Tell him to plant the seeds against the darkness,' he shouted, proudly blocking the Causeway as the first shadowy warrior lowered his spear and charged.

Beacon Light and Stumble neighed and cantered out towards them. Beacon Light's head was twisted along her flank and Stumble hobbled on twisted fetlocks. The shadow warriors were almost upon them, the safety of the trees lay less than a dozen paces away, arrows and spearblades were striking sparks from the rough stone of the Causeway all about them.

'Put me down and run without me,' gasped Merion, trying to free himself from the Archer's arms.'

'No, you shall ride!' shouted Tiethorm as Beacon Light drew level with him, slowing so that he could lay the Healer across her back. The ancient trees seemed to sway and drift apart as if pushed aside by a strong wind as they passed between them. The branches began to writhe and weave together above their heads creaking and groaning as they dropped across the Greenway in gnarled impenetrable loops and twists.

Thoron stopped, the breath rattling in his twisted throat and turned, drawing the chain tight between his hands. He could run no further but he would stand and fight and sing of the sunlight. A voice laughed quietly in the branches above his head. Thoron spun around, tripped and fell as he tried to look up. A tall figure jumped stiffly to the ground and turned to face the company.

'Thunderstone!' Elionbel cried with joy.

Thunderstone laughed again and hushed them into silence then led them deeper amongst the ancient trees, telling them how the ancient trees had saved his life, showing them the white rope marks that had burned into his throat before the trees had caught and held his head and shoulders in a net of finely woven twigs until the shadowmaker, Kruel, had turned away.

'But that body hanging from the tree?' interrupted Tiethorm. 'Who is that?'

Thunderstone laughed and drew a long black-bladed dagger, pointing towards the shadow warriors on the Causeway Road as he whispered how he had killed one of them and hung him in his place.

'Look!' Elionbel cried, pointing back between two tree-trunks towards the sheer grey walls of Underfall. 'They have overrun the Loremaster and are charging towards us with long-handled axes in their shadowy hands.'

Thunderstone stood and watched the advancing shadows for a moment. A slight shiver trembled his hands as he tilted his head to one side and listened to the leaves whispering overhead.

Turning back, he took Elionbel's hands into his own and looked deeply into her eyes. 'These trees are a part of Nevian's magic and carry news far across Elundium. They saw you face Kruel and heard you shout your mother's secret in the courtyard of Stumble Hill. Few would have had the courage to keep such a pledge but now it is broken and we must warn Thane before it is too late.'

'We are too late,' whispered Merion, turning his burned ears towards the trees and listening to the tale of Thane's great battle before the gates of the Granite City.

Elionbel looked up at the rustling leathery leaves that had somehow defied the autumn and still clung on to the twisted age-scarred branches. She frowned. 'I hear nothing but the wind amongst those leaves,' she answered, brushing the tears from her cheeks.

'There is little enough wind to bend the winter grasses but still they talk, Elionbel,' he replied in a hushed whisper. 'They told me of your brother Rubel's escape from the Tower at Stumble Hill and how he wallows in self-pity beside a stagnant pool, and there are whisperings that Willow Leaf has built a fortress on a Rising that stands alone high above the shadows.' Thunderstone paused and looked up, his eyebrows creased together. 'Come, we must hurry,' he urged, 'the Granite City is falling beneath the shadows.'

'The Greenway is the quickest road,' called Breakmaster, dabbing at the wound on his throat as Thunderstone led them deeper into the trees.

'The warriors with axes!' cried Elionbel, gathering Stumble's reins and helping him along. 'They will harm the trees!'

Thunderstone laughed harshly and pointed back with his dagger blade to where the first shadowy warrior had been plucked off the Causeway Road and thrown high in the air. 'Fear not, Elionbel, the trees are like great warriors, they will not be harmed.'

'Where are you taking us?' called Thoron, keeping pace with the last Lampmaster of Elundium. 'This is not the road to the Granite City.'

'I know not,' answered Thunderstone, 'but the trees will lead us to Thane and to the last ray of sunlight to shine in Elundium. Listen, it is in their whispering.'

Merion looked up from where Breakmaster had sat him astride Beacon Light and tried to smile. The first snowflakes were falling, brightening the shadowlight and cooling his blistered cheeks, sizzling and melting as they touched his face.

The City Falls

Kruel tightened his grip, blackening the daylight around the Granite City. There was snow in the air, he could smell it blizzarding its way across Elundium, weakening his shadow-light beneath its thick white blanket.

'We cannot hold the outer wall, my Lord,' shouted Grey Goose above the roar of the shadowy warriors and the shrieking black rats that suddenly stormed against the city, swarming in through every drain and gutter hole the masons had not filled with stone choke. Crying with terror the warriors stamped their armoured boots and swung their swords at the black waves of shadow rats sweeping all around them. Owls hooted and stooped out of the shadowy dark sky, Border Runners growled and snarled, hurling the foul brittle-spined creatures high into the air, and again and again Esteron and Equestrius led the crippled Warhorses through the lower circles of the city, crushing and killing every shadow on their path. But the tide of darkness was slowly rising, forcing them backwards step by step, up through the inner circles of the city towards the high walls that protected Swanwater and Candlebane Hall.

Behind them in every alleyway and street the city folk were screaming with terror. The black shadow rats had overrun the great wall and they were amongst the people, biting their heels and ankles, pulling them down on to the cold winter cobbles, taking them into Kruel's growing darkness. Their shouts against the shadowlight ceased as they became etched with veins of darkness and swept up through the city beside the shadow warriors. Gradually, silence spread through the lower circle of the city, smoke billowed out unchecked from fire-burned houses and bright flames crackled in the darkness, lighting up the shadowy shapes advancing through the ruins.

'The city folk, what has happened to the city folk?' Thane asked, straining his ears against the silence and wiping a dirty blood-soaked battle glove across his forehead.

'You cannot help them, my Lord,' answered Errant, trying to find a better grip for his fingers on the hilt of his sword. 'Those rats carry the bite of darkness in their jaws and only those that show a blemish still love the sunlight.'

Thane turned sharply on the horseman and grasped one of his twisted hands. 'So this is the sign of the darkness – this crippled hand, the lame Warhorses and limping Border Runners?'

'No, Lord,' cried Errant, proudly lifting up his hand. 'This is the sign of those that are true to you and of their love of the sunlight. It shows that the darkness holds no power over them; it is as bright a mark upon us as the tattooed owl in blue and gold that Nevian traced upon the warriors' arms for King Holbian.'

Thane laughed softly and embraced Errant. 'Then I shall know you all and count you on the fingers of one hand. Look about you, brave warrior, and see how many have been bitten and survived.'

'The Warhorses and the Border Runners are with us. They came unasked to help me reach the city and without them I would have fallen beneath the shadows many leagues from here.'

'Yes,' answered Thane, smiling gently at his friends. 'They are bitten and cruelly crippled, and I weep to watch them limp and make such easy targets in battle.'

'Lord, me must retreat into Candlebane Hall,' urged Grey Goose. 'The shadows are closing in all about us.'

Thane held on to Errant's hand for a moment and looked straight into his eyes. 'I love each and every one of you that has suffered the darkness and survived.'

'We stand together, men and horses, dogs and owls, together to fight against these shadows. Now hurry to the top of the ramp and help marshal the Warhorses and the Border Runners across the bridge into Candlebane Hall.'

Turning, Thane summoned Arrachatt to his side. 'This ramp,' he asked, placing his armoured boot on the base, 'can you remove it once we are safe on the wall above?'

Arrachatt frowned, rubbing his stone-pitted fingers across his chin and bent down to examine Willow's handiwork. 'The Tunnellers are Mastermasons, Lord, but even they leave hairline flaws for the sharp-eyed to see. Give me half a daylight and the ramp will be a pile of rubble scattered through the lower circles of the city.'

'Too long, mason,' Thane snapped, his eye upon the advancing shadows swallowing up the city. 'But the owls will buy what time they can.'

Turning his head he called to Mulcade. 'I need time, great Bird of War, time to get all those who love the sunlight into Candlebane Hall.'

Mulcade flexed his talons, hooted and spread his wings. He lifted up into the dark winter air and called to his stoops of Battle Owls, drawing them into a dense cloud above Candlebane Hall. The tightening circle of shadows slowed and stopped as the shadow rats fought amongst themselves to find shelter from the owls.

'Find Kyot and Eventine,' Thane whispered as Rockspray stooped to him. 'Tell them the City has fallen, and we are hard pressed and desperate, siege-locked in Candlebane Hall.'

Rockspray spread his wings and lifted high into the cold winter sky, circled the city once then vanished in the gathering snow clouds.

Kruel had reached the second circle of the city. Everywhere victory looked complete but above, silhouetted against the fading daylight he saw the stonemason destroying the ramp that led up to the Swanwater bridge. With a terrible shout he drove the shadow rats on and the cry echoed in the lower circles of the city, shattering stone and splintering wood as it spread through the ruins towards Candlebane Hall. Fine stone dust billowed out of the cracks Arrachatt had opened in the ramp and his stone-searcher trembled in his hand.

'Lord, I am ready,' he shouted breathlessly as the last Warhorse breasted the top of the ramp and made its way across the bridge into Candlebane Hall.

Thane brushed his hand through Esteron's mane and ordered the Archers to retreat up the ramp on either side of him. Keeping pace with Esteron he ran to the top of the ramp, turned and looked down. The shadow rats had grown bold, driven on by the nightmare shout, and swarmed now at the base of the ramp.

Arrachatt spat on his hands and drove the stone-searcher point-deep into a broad crack he had fashioned between the ramp and the sheer wall encircling Candlebane Hall. 'Now, Lord?' he asked with an edge of uncertainty in his voice.

Thane stepped back and raised his hand. 'No, wait!' he cried, bending forwards and catching a glimpse of a dark fleeing figure running through the swarm of rats, treading on them in his haste to reach the ramp. With one last bound he leapt on to the ramp. He turned as he landed and used the flat of his sword to sweep the nightmare shadows from the rising cobbles, forcing them back into the city below. Turning again in a flurry of cloak tails the figure raced up the ramp, casting off his foul ratskins as he ran, letting the colours of his cloak stream out in the shadowlight. Nevian ran up the steep cobblestones without a backward glance, glad to be rid of the ratskin cloak yet thankful it had hidden him so well as he slipped under the Stumble Gate and ran from alleyway to alleyway in his race through the City. None had noticed him but he had heard much and learned many secrets with each hurried footstep.

'Nevian!' Thane shouted with delight, grasping the magician's hands and pulling him clear of the swaying, crumbling ramp.

Arrachatt put his weight behind the stone-searcher and jumped clear of the ramp just as it drifted away from the wall. Slowly at first, puffs of stone dust hissed from the widening crack, a moment's pause and the ramp began to settle, roaring and rumbling as it collapsed in an avalanche of stones on the swarms of shadow rats below.

Thane began to laugh but Nevian turned him with a firm hand and pointed out into the shadowlight, making him look at the black flags hanging and fluttering from every hill and mound, every fence and field for as far as he could see.

Nevian shivered and pulled the rainbow cloak tightly about his shoulders, wrinkling his nose against the foul smell of the ratskins that had filtered into the fabric of the cloth. 'I guessed at new shadows, fearing that something threatened the sunlight, but it is far far worse than ever I thought.'

'Lord, Lord,' cried Grey Goose, cutting across Nevian's words and pulling desperately at Thane's sleeve. 'The black rats are swarming up the other side of the wall. Even with the owls' help we cannot drive them back.'

Thane looked from his Captain Archer to the Master of Magic and threw his hands up helplessly. 'What can I do but wear my sword-arm numb against these shadows?' he shouted, the flat of his bloody blade sweeping against the shadowlight as he turned to run to where the Archers fought amongst the rats.

'Retreat,' answered Nevian in a firm voice, calling him back. 'Retreat across the bridge that spans the deep waters of Swanwater and seek refuge in Candlebane Hall. Here upon the high rim of the City you have but a moment before the darkness overwhelms you but within the strong walls of

Candlebane Hall with the deep water between you and this new Nightmare you will be safe.'

Thane ran across the bridge and entered the Candle Hall, pausing to wait for the Master of Magic. Nevian hurried to Thane's side and linked arms with him as they walked slowly to the high throne, telling him with each step they took all that had come to pass and been kept a secret since he had entered the City of Night and driven his sword through Krulshards' black heart.

Thane sank heavily on to the first step of the dais and reached out for the armrest of the throne to steady himself, his knuckles turning white as he gripped the smooth stone. He saw how little Elion had trusted him and how she had carried that dark secret all on her own. 'But where is she now? What has that creature done with her?' he cried desperately, burying his head in his arms.

Nevian could have wept with him but he shook his arm. 'Tears must come later. Now we must find a way to fight against this new Nightmare, Kruel.'

'Soon there will be nothing left of the sunlight,' Thane shouted as he strode through the doors of Candlebane Hall and turned to watch helplessly as Arrachatt broke the span of the bridge and raced back towards them across the falling masonry.

'Now we are an island in this sea of darkness,' he said quietly.

Turning away from the dark rippling waters that had swallowed up the broken bridge he stared at the empty throne set on the high dais at the far end of the Candle Hall, and slowly lifted his head, seeing clearly now why Martbel had looked so shrivelled and wasted in the City of Night, why there had been a shadow between him and Elionbel. Rising, he drew his sword. 'How can I fight against him? How can I destroy this Kruel? His darkness has crippled and distorted everything that loves the light, why even the trees that you filled with magic lie broken beside the Greenways' edge. Has all Elundium fallen beneath his shadowlight? What of Kyot? What of Thunderstone? What of the Warriors from the battle crescents I sent home?' Thane's voice trailed into silence as he remembered the Lampmaster's horse galloping to them on the Greenway.

Nevian nodded his head slowly. 'Everything as far as the eye can see is covered by shadowlight. This Kruel is both man and beast and thus is a mightier Nightmare than Krulshards, the one who spawned him. He is so powerful, Rubel says, that he can deny the sun a shadow.'

'Shadowless!' muttered Thane. 'Then what hope do you bring us? What light or wise counsel have you to help us against this new Nightmare? I have crippled horses, lame Border Runners and just enough Warriors to count on both hands.'

'Lord, come quickly,' cried Errant in terror, stumbling backwards away from the Candle doors as a chilling voice called out Thane's name, laughing, mocking and cracking the tall slender crystal candle-stems as it flooded into Candlebane Hall.

'Thanehand! Galloperspawn! I have come for you!' it mocked from scant wind-driven whispers to bone-shattering shouts that drove the Warhorses into panic, sending them rearing and plunging against each other in the crowded hall. Border Runners growled and snarled, their fangs bared bright white in the shadowlight and stoops of owls rose up to scatter amongst the tallow-blackened rafters. Thane jumped to his feet and fought his way through the rising panic to the brink of the broad steps leading down into the deep water.

'I know your name, Kruel, the Master of Nothing, the one who hides in the dark,' he shouted, searching the rim of the wall.

'Take care, Thane,' Nevian whispered from the shadow of the Candle door at his elbow. 'Do not show yourself as too easy a target.'

The pitiless voice laughed again yet Thane could not see

where it came from as it sent broken ripples across the deep, still waters that ringed the Candle Hall.

'Yes, I am Kruel,' it soothed, letting the words flow up over the broad steps and swirl around Thane's feet. 'Kruel, the Master of all this darkness that has swallowed the light and I am the rightful Lord of all Elundium!'

Thane took a deep breath, gathered what little courage he had left and bravely faced the empty rim of the wall saying, 'You are only a robber, a stealer of what belongs to others, who has crept like a thief through this darkness, taking by force what does not belong to you.'

Kruel snarled with rage and rose above the rim of the wall to hurl a dagger across Swanwater, driving the blade a hand's span deep into the Candle door beside Thane's head.

'I come as I please,' he hissed, 'and I claim what Krulshards, my father, took as he swept across Elundium. Now it is all mine, mine do you hear? And you, foul Galloperspawn, shall pay for that sword-thrust you pierced through my father's heart, for you shall hang beside him in the City of Night and curse the day that Kruel crawled from the Marcherwoman's belly to avenge his death!'

Thane held his breath and stared at the tall figure that had arisen above the rim of the wall, seeing Krulshards in the dead locks of frost-white hair streaming out and seeming to glow in the shadowlight, and the pale pitiless eyes that bore into him probing and searching for all his weaknesses. But in the shape of the mouth and the smooth perfect teeth there was a little of Martbel – he was just as Nevian had described him, both man and beast.

'I could take you now,' Kruel mocked, stretching out his hand across the water, 'for there is no power strong enough in all Elundium to stop me; no, not even you, Thanehand, can lift a finger against me!'

Laughing, Kruel closed his hand on the sharp edge of Thane's sword and melted the blade between his fingertips. 'Nothing can stop my darkness,' he laughed, sneering as he

300

dropped the severed length of steel in a bubbling froth of steam into the icy depths of Swanwater.

Thane cried out as the hilt glowed dull red in his hand and he hurled it with all his strength across the water only to see it fall well short of the wall and drop hissing into the deep lake. 'Why do you wait and taunt me with words if you can take me so easily?' Thane shouted, shaking his blistered fingers in hopeless anger at Kruel.

'Hush!' whispered Nevian, pulling at the King's sleeve. 'Do not goad the Nightmare or show him all our weaknesses.'

'Use some magic! Strike him down with a bolt of fire, a ray of sunlight, anything!' hissed Thane, stepping back into the shadows of the doorway.

'What magic strengths I have belonged to the time of the Granite Kings. you are now the greatest strength in Elundium, the first man-King and champion of the sunlight.'

'But I have no strength against Kruel,' hissed Thane in despair, turning back to stare at the Nightmare figure on the wall.

Kruel laughed and shouted in triumph, splintering the doorposts of Candlebane Hall and pulled up beside him on to the rim of the wall a black armoured warrior with a heavy sack across his shoulder. Lifting a hand, Kruel pointed a long slender finger at Arbel and pushed him forwards to the edge of the wall. 'Look carefully, Thanehand, at my Marcher Captain and first warrior, for he is my blood brother Arbel!' Sneering with delight he tapped the smooth black polished armour that followed every groove and swelling ridge of muscle on Arbel's body and laughed again. 'Once you could have matched him blade for blade, but now Arbel is clothed in Nightshards' armour taken from the City of Night and nothing can harm him.'

Arbel sneered across the dark waters at Thane, his black shiny cheeks crackling as the armour rippled. He lifted the sack off his shoulder high above his head. 'I followed you, Thanehand,' he shouted. 'After you had left our Wayhouse I stabbed Rubel and followed you, but the Nightbeasts caught me before I could plunge the dagger through your rotten heart!'

'Why?' cried Thane in dismay and disbelief. 'I was running on Krulshards' heels to try and rescue your sister Elionbel.'

Arbel snarled savagely and hurled the sack, spinning it high across Swanwater. 'Because I love the darkness, and I hate your sunlight!" he spat out as the bundle crushed against the Candle doors and came to rest at Thane's feet.

Thane stared for a moment at Arbel in dumb silence and then slowly knelt to unwind the edges of the damp rough hemp sacking. 'Take care, my Lord,' cried Errant as Thane lifted and tipped the sack.

Kruel shrieked with delight as twisted hands and feet roughly severed at the wrists and ankles tumbled out across the broad stone steps. Thane cried in horror and staggered backwards, tripping and falling heavily against the Candle doors.

'You had one strength, Thanehand,' sneered Arbel, tossing a severed hand to Kerzolde who had climbed up on to the wall and now squatted beside him. 'One little thing that my brother Kruel had missed on our triumphant sweep across Elundium.'

Thane stared open-mouthed from Arbel to Kruel. What had been a strength? They had been defeated and chased up through the ruins of the City, they had been driven before the darkness as dust before a broom.

'It was only a little thing, Thanehand,' whispered Kruel, pointing at the heap of severed hands and feet, 'but now I know by the crippled warriors and Warhorses that fight at your side that any who are left are blemished after my shadow rats have bitten them and they hate my darkness. When all the city folk who show a blemish are dead and piled high along this wall then, Thanehand, I will come for you. Then I will walk across the water and my darkness will be complete.'

'No!' shouted Thane, taking a step forwards. 'Leave the

city folk unharmed. There are people amongst them who were blemished with misfortune long before you spread your darkness through Elundium. Let them be and I will come to you. I will surrender.'

But Kruel and Arbel had gone, vanishing in an echo of laughter, only Kerzolde sat leering on the high rim of the wall, gnawing on the severed hand.

'Grey Goose, your best arrow,' whispered Thane through clenched teeth, beckoning to his Captain Archer. Grey Goose ran down the broad steps passing his fingertips over his quiver and he chose the finest new-forged steel-bladed arrow. Whetting the blade he nocked it on to the bow.

'Shall I aim at his heart or put the arrow through his throat?' he asked in a hushed whisper.

'No!' hissed Nevian, touching the Archer's arm. 'Save every spine and do nothing to anger or enrage this Kruel. Come, retreat into the Candle Hall where the Nightbeast cannot see us.'

Kerzolde cackled with delight and danced along the rim of the wall as he watched Thane retreat into Candlebane Hall.

'What now? What can I do against this Nightmare?' he shouted, turning desperately on the magician and clutching on to the coloured folds of the rainbow cloak. 'How can I fight against this Kruel?'

The Candle Hall fell silent and every breath was held, all eyes turned towards the Master of Magic. Nevian looked up and smiled, gathering his cloak tightly about his shoulders.

'For the moment we are safe here in Candlebane Hall. The shadow rats cannot get to us, their spines are too brittle to keep them afloat and Kruel will not attack until he has searched every warrior and all the city folk he can find. Now we must find a way to escape from this City before he returns.'

'Lord, we are not trapped,' ventured Arrachatt the Mason, steppng hesitantly into the clear space before the King.

'There are no secret ways, mason. You forget the Granite

King is dead,' Thane muttered, turning his back towards the Candle doors and raising his hand to dismiss the stonemason.

Nevian smiled and checked Thane then pushed the mason before him saying, 'Every man may have some wisdom to offer to his King for it is not only magicians who pull on the strings of fate. Listen to what the mason has to tell us.'

And silence spread across the Candle Hall as Arrachatt told them of the two key stones, one set upon the other well below the waterline that acted as a fountain, sending a steady flow of water down through the City to the Stumble Gate. Willow Leaf had set these two stones back to front and only the mortar held them in place. If they could be loosened then the whole wall would collapse and the great lake would flood down, smashing its way through the City, killing the shadow warriors and drowning the shadow rats.

'We could ride the water!' shouted Nevian, grasping the Mason's calloused hands and dancing him in a tight circle.

Thane laughed and slapped the mason firmly on his back.

'But . . .' Arrachatt cried, breaking free, 'but the key stones are well below the water and I am not quite sure how to reach them with my stone-searcher.'

Nevian frowned and came to a stumbling halt, releasing his hold on the mason's hands. Thane felt the laughter die on his lips and he slowly turned to follow in Nevian's footsteps out on to the broad steps that edged Swanwater. Shivering and drawing his cloak about his shoulders as the first snowflakes brushed against his cheeks he said, 'Where would I go, Nevian? If there was a way to escape from the Candle Hall, where would I go?'

Nevian laughed quietly and drew Thane to him. 'Fate chose you well, Thanehand: you are a good guardian of the sunlight. If there is a way to flood the city and escape beyond these high walls we must follow the ancient trees for they are pledged to help you and they know of the road leading to a place that rises far above the shadows.'

'If we escape, Kruel will follow us, I know it, but how can I fight against him?'

Nevian smiled and placed his lips close to Thane's ear then told him of Rubel's great race to the City of Night to fetch the sword that pierced Krulshards' heart.

'Rubel!' cried Thane in dismay. 'But he cursed me before vanishing into the grasslands. Was there none other . . .'

'Hush!' hissed Nevian, clamping his hand to the King's mouth. 'Need drove me hard and there were no others to send. Rubel has much to hate this Nightmare for and, remember, through Elionbel his thread is woven closely into yours. Now think no more of it lest Kruel sees it in your mind; think only of escape and the road ahead.'

Thane nodded and stared out into the black shadows cast by the fallen tower that rose as a jumble of dressed stone in the centre of the lake. Nevian followed his gaze and saw ghost-white shapes riding on the water close beneath the largest overhanging blocks of stone. 'The swans!' he whispered. 'I thought they had fled the city as the darkness closed about us.'

Thane smiled and called gently across the waters, stretching out his hands to the grey swans of doom. Ogion spread his wings and beat the water into a white foam then settled quietly to listen as Thane knelt between them and whispered of their need to escape from the Granite City.

Thane rose and took the magician's arm. 'It is settled. Arrachatt can ride upon the Lord of Swans to the place where the key stones are set into the wall. Now all you have to do, Master of Magic, is dangle him in the cold dark waters and let him chip away at the binding mortar without drowning him and freezing him to death!'

Nevian thought for a moment, his heavy eyebrows creased into a thousand frowns. 'Yes . . .' he began when a cry of terror cut through the shadowlight. It rose in thin echoes from the lower circles of the City.

'We must hurry!' shouted Nevian vanishing into the

Candle Hall in a flurry of cloak tails. The slaughter of the city folk had begun.

Running backwards and forwards across the smooth polished floor Nevian marshalled the Warhorses. He shouted for Angishand, Thane's mother, to use her weaver's fingers and knot them a slender rope, then he gathered the Archers into a tall tottering pyramid to join the slender candle-stems with hot tallow from the wax channels around the throne, while with a strong hand, now sure of its purpose, he stripped the mason bare and dipped him three times into a vat of cooling candle wax.

'Shout as much as you like, Mastermason, but you cannot drown out the screams of slaughter from the City below,' grumbled Nevian as the warm wax splashed up across the hem of the rainbow cloak.

Errant laughed and lifted the drying mason then set him gently astride Ogion's feathery back. 'Sit still, you will not freeze to death beneath this coat of wax.'

'Nor drown,' marvelled Grey Goose, slipping the end of the hollow candle-stem into the mason's open mouth and cutting short his stuttering protest as he sealed Arrachatt's lips on to the fine crystal with a layer of cooling wax.

Nevian placed the mason's stone-searcher into his hands and pressed his stiffening fingers around the handle then knelt down beside Ogion on the lowest stone step, the cold water lapping against his fingertips. 'Take care,' he whispered, knotting the slender woven rope around Arrachatt's waist and looking up into the snow-driven wind to where a stoop of Battle Owls fought to keep the candle–stems Arrachatt would use to breathe from crashing against the wall of Candlebane Hall. 'Find the hollow grooves Willow used to haul the blocks of stone up through the city and thread the rope between them; the Warhorses have the other end of the rope tied between them. Once the key stones give the slightest sign of moving drop the searcher and kick for the surface.

Ogion and Ousious will be waiting to bring you back to these steps.'

Thane knelt beside the magician and closed his hand around the cold stiff layer of wax coating the mason's fingers. 'All Elundium will hold its breath for you, Arrachatt, and shout your praises in the sunlight when this daylight's work is over.'

Arrachatt tried to turn and answer the King but the layers of wax had hardened in the bitter wind and Ogion had moved away from the steps and was taking him into the darkest shadows beneath the sheer wall that encircled Candlebane Hall. They were moving silently through the ranks of grey swans. His teeth chattered against the crystal candle-stems and his hands shook on the handle of the stone-searcher. Soon his legs bumped against rough hard stone and he knew he had reached the wall. Ogion flapped his wings, half-stood in the water and Arrachatt slipped backwards in a splash of bubbles then sank beneath the cold black waters. Down, down, he sank, taking the knotted rope with him, the crystal candle–stem twisted and tried to turn in his mouth but he clamped it between his teeth. The stone-searcher grated against the wall, slipping in his fingers. His feet touched the slippery weed-covered cobblestones; he had reached the bottom of the lake and began fumbling blindly along the wall. Two paces to the left, two paces to the right, he scratched his fingernails across the rough stone, searching, feeling for those tell-tale grooves he knew must be there. His fingers caught on something, a hard edge, the beginnings of a groove. Carefully he dug with the point of his searcher, clearing the silt and weeds from the groove, and threading the rope little by little between the stones. The layers of wax were crazing into thousands of spider-fine cracks, the water was seeping in, chilling his bones, his hands were numb and burning with the cold. He knotted the rope, drew a deep breath through the candle-stem and struck with all his strenght at the mortar around the key stones, twisting as the searcher struck. He slipped off the cobbles and fell, breaking the seal that held the candle-stem between his teeth. Icy waters flooded into his mouth, he choked, flung his weight against the metal spike and kicked for the surface. The owls hooted and let the broken candle-stems fall into the black water then they flew back to the Candle Hall.

Arrachatt broke the surface, spluttering and coughing. 'I have not finished yet,' he gasped, shaking off the swans and treading water while he took deep breaths. Five times he dived and five times he found the stone-searcher and drove it into the mortar between the key stones. Exhausted and numb with cold his feet touched the cold slippery cobbles for the sixth time and he felt for the stone-searcher where he had left it wedged in the groove of the key stone. But it had gone, fallen out of the widening crack between the stones. Arrachatt put his hand against the key stones and felt the escaping water suck against it. Kicking frantically, he reached the surface and let the swan carry him to the brink of the broad steps.

'It is done, my Lord,' he gasped as Grey Goose bundled him in warm clohting and took him into the warmth of Candlebane Hall.

Warhorse hooves skidded and clattered across the stone floor sending up bright fountains of sparks as they fought to hold the key stones on the knotted rope.

'We have but moments,' cried Nevian.

'How will we stay together and ride the flood down through the city?' asked Thane, jumping high into the air to avoid the knotted rope as it drew as tight as a bow string between the Warhorses and the two key stones now loosened in the wall.

'Wind this thread between us,' called Angishand, holding up a bundle of glittering thread in her hands.

Nevian laughed and swept Thane's mother off her feet saying, 'You are a blessing to us all.'

'It is nothing, Lord,' she answered, blushing. 'Nothing but the rag-end threads that were left over after I had finished weaving the summer scarf.'

'That is more than enough, great lady, for it will light our way through the shadowlight. Thread each animal together,' cried Nevian, running through the Candle Hall, and joining each Warhorse and Border Runner to the knotted rope.

'Errant, Grey Goose – quickly, settle the Archers and the warriors on the soundest Warhorses, tie yourselves as tightly as possible on to them. Duclos, Duclos – where is the deaf swordsman, Morolda?'

'We are here, Nevian,' Morolda shouted back, 'and Angishand is with us.'

Thane ran out through the Candle doors and on to the broad steps. Swanwater was swirling angrily, twisting and turning in dark eddies, pushing itself against the key stones. 'Fly, fly,' he urged, kneeling between Ogion and Ousious on the lowest step.

Ousious brushed her beak against Thane's cheek and descended into the swirling waters. Ogion followed her and together they led the grey swans of doom to beat a path across Swanwater and rise up into the darkening shadowlight.

'We will meet again!' called Thane, raising his hand.

The knotted rope sang and shrieked, the fibres twisting together, spraying fine beads of cold water across the steps. It was shredding, only moments from breaking. Thane turned, raced up the steps and leapt on to Esteron's back. Nevian leaned across from Equestrius and wound the end of the glittering thread around Thane's waist and tied it firmly.

'Now, my Lord, we are truly in the hands of Fate,' he cried as the knotted rope snapped.

Thane quickly glanced behind him in the moment of silence that followed the breaking of the rope. The Border Runners were tied, crouching on the Warhorse's haunches, the Archers were sitting straight-backed with arrows readynocked upon their bow strings, the warriors were ready with spears and swords; everyone in the crowded gathering was drawn rigid together as if holding their breaths.

'Run, gallop,' shouted Nevian, urging Equestrius forwards. 'We must ride on the first surge of water.'

Thane turned to shout something as they descended the broad steps and swam out in Swanwater but his voice was lost in the thunder of falling masonry and the roar of the water as the wall burst apart and swept them down into the City below on a high crest of foam.

High above the ruined roofs and broken windows, they rode the crest of white-plumed water. Border Runners snarled and snapped at the black shadow rats washed up against them, and Grey Goose and his Archers loosed their arrows out of the water, felling startled shadow warriors as they surged past. Then they were gone, swept on downwards faster and faster in the thundering wave of water towards the Stumble Gate.

'The gates are open!' shouted Thane, letting the standard of the sun ripple out taut behind them, but none heard his shout nor cared as they crowded together, clinging on to one another as they were swept beneath the high-arched gate, out on to the beginnings of the Greenway.

'The trees! Run for the trees!' urged Nevian as Equestrius' feet touched firm ground and he stumbled forwards.

Behind them a screaming shout of rage filled the Granite City spiralling slowly up through every level until it burst out through the roof of Candlebane Hall. Thane turned his head and watched sadly as the weather-bleached tiles and tallow-blackened rafters of the hall collapsed on to the smooth-polished marble floor below in a thundering shower of brittle splinters.

'The trees! Make for the trees!' Nevian shouted again, pulling hard at Thane's sleeve. 'There is no time to stand and watch the destruction! Kruel will be hard on our heels before the waters have drained away.'

The Shadowlight Deepens

The darkness had spread far across the grasslands tightening its grip as the winter took hold. It smothered the daylights with its silent terror. Shivering with cold, Eventine knelt in the long grass on the edges of Clatterford and watched a tall column of black smoke curl up to vanish into the shadowlight. Faintly she could hear shouts and the ring of steel.

'We come too late,' Kyot muttered, clumsily kneeling down beside her, trying to turn the Bow of Orm between his twisted fingers and keep it from snagging or getting wet in the coarse winter grasses.

'There is fighting. Listen to the peacocks scream. Quickly, the House of Clatterford has not fallen yet,' she cried, leaping to her feet, but her voice trailed miserably into silence as she swept her eyes across the Warhorses and lame Border Runners in the long grass behind her.

'Father, oh Father,' she wept, clenching her crippled hand in frustration.

Tanglecrown roared out and Sprint neighed fiercely, and the little relay horse with his twisted forelegs held securely in Tanglecrown's huge stand of antlers moved through the long grass to where Eventine stood. Kyot stared at the Lord of Stags and saw the beginnings of an idea. Quickly he climbed to his feet and caressed Sprint's muzzle then whispered to Tanglecrown, putting his hand boldly in amongst the razor-sharp antlers.

Tanglecrown roared and carefully bent his forelegs. Kyot

turned to Eventine and pulled at her sleeve. 'There is a way that we can ride to Clatterford and let the Bow of Orm sing out against these foul shadows – if I sit upon Sprint and hold the Bow of Orm, and you sit upon Tanglecrown and link your arms through mine. You take each arrow from the quiver and nock it on to the bow . . .'

Eventine looked closely at the Lord of Stags and laughed. Yes, it was a brilliant idea, they would fight against the darkness, it might just work. 'Would you carry us?' she asked quickly. Tanglecrown roared in answer and Sprint snorted, the light of battle in his eyes.

Eventine sprang up on to Tanglecrown's back and reached across to unclip Kyot's quiver then hung it beside her own. 'You must hold the bow rock-steady,' she whispered, linking her arms tenderly through his.

Tanglecrown and Sprint, as one, sprang forwards into the dark shadows of the tall yew trees growing beside the ford. White water foamed and splashed about their feet; they were quickly across and on to the steep banks of the lawns. Orgas led the stags with the Warhorses and Border Runners a pace behind in a rush of hoofbeats on to the lawns of Clatterford.

Twice the Bow of Orm sang out felling two shadowy warriors crouching over a body closely wrapped in a cloak of sky-washed blue that lay sprawled upon the steps of the house. 'Father, Father,' Eventine cried, letting the third steel-tipped bladed arrowshaft slip from her fingers as she jumped to the ground and ran to where he lay.

'Eventine, beware, there are more shadow warriors,' Kyot shouted in warning as he struggled to dismount but Orgas had heard his cry and charged, antlers lowered, across the battle-strewn lawn. He reached the crystal steps and leapt high over Eventine in the shadowlight as she knelt and gathered her father's body up into her arms.

'Father, oh Father,' she whispered, rocking him slowly backwards and forwards, deaf to the thunder of hoofbeats that closed protectively all around her and the crash of antler

312

horns as Orgas cleared the house of Clatterford of Kruel's shadow warriors.

Slowly Fairday blinked then opened his eyes and smiled up at her, calling her name falteringly. 'My ray of sunlight, my joy and treasure, I knew you would come to me, daughter, I knew.'

'Rest, Father,' she answered, bending close to his blood-wet lips to catch each word and letting her unchecked tears splash in a silver rain of grief on to the collar of his cloak, turning the colour to deep indigo.

'There is only one arrowblade they did not find, my child. Use it well against the darkness,' he whispered. His words were getting slower, his head was sinking in her arms. 'One arrowblade, beneath my cloak . . .'

'Father!' she cried, her voice full of despair as she gathered him closer, but with one last gentle sigh he was gone, his cloak of sky-washed blue billowed open and there, clutched tightly in his fingers, kept safe from the darkness was the last glass arrowblade of Clatterford, sparkling bright with all the glories of the summer sun.

'No! Do not touch it,' Eventine cried, pushing Kyot's hand away from the glass blade as he reached forwards to take it from her father's hand. 'You are the Bow and I am the striker, the Arrowmaiden. I did not see it until the moment Father died.'

Eventine fell silent, her body shaking with grief as she carefully unclasped Fairday's fingers from the arrowshaft and slipped it into her quiver.

'See what?' asked Kyot gently.

Eventine smiled at him through her tears and took his hand. 'I thought the legends about the great Bows of Clatterford and Orm were over when mine was destroyed in the courtyard of Stumble Hill. I thought we were helpless – no, powerless – to fight against this new darkness, but mounted together with the last glass arrowblade on my hand and the great Bow of Orm in yours we can hunt that foul

Nightmare and drive an arrow strike through his black heart. But first I must ring my father's body with crystal-tipped spears then we ...' She stopped and stared out across the desolate ruined lawns, straining her eyes, watching something moving towards them. 'Kyot, look!' she hissed, making him spin around.

Kyot blinked and raised the Bow of Orm, a shout of joy on his lips, for flying low across the wild grassland was Rock-spray, the Battle Owl. 'He will be our eyes and lead us through this shadowlight, he will find us a path!' Kyot shouted as the owl stooped to his shoulder.

Rubel passed silently through the shadowlight, following all the secret roads and long forgotten paths that he had found on his wanderings. Climbing without rest amongst the ancient trees that had spread themselves up the towering shoulders of Mantern's Mountain he reached the summit. Now he paused for breath, crouching and searching the barren shale-strewn slopes before he slipped down, unheard and unseen, through the broken dome of the high chamber in the City of Night. Landing quietly on the balls of his feet he carefully searched the shadows. He shivered as he rubbed his numb fingers together, cursing the ratskins' brittle spines as they snagged and tore his forearms. A dozen shadow rats scavenged amongst the Nightshards' carcasses and weed worms, curled against the cold, hung in small clusters from the lower edges of the rough dome ceiling. There were no shadow warriors or black carrion crows to shout a warning; the chamber was bleak and seemed empty but for the refuse of battle.

'I must find the sword,' he muttered, forcing himself to creep towards the tall column of rock that stood alone in the centre of the chamber. The closer he came the more the darkness seemed to close about him. Now he could see the outline of Krulshards, the Master of Darkness, the ragged strips of hanging flesh, the bone-black fingers locked around the blade of Thane's sword. Something moved, billowing, reaching out. Rubel cried out in terror, strangling the shout in his throat as the ragged strip of the black malice settled back across the spark-scarred blade piercing Krulshards' heart. Rubel looked fearfully around him; nothing had heard his cry, the shadow rats were still busy, undisturbed, burrowing through the Nightshards' armour.

'I must take the sword,' he hissed, clenching his teeth and crawling forwards again.

He saw the hilt with its smooth bright metal catching and reflecting what little light shone down into the high chamber through the broken roof. Rubel felt blindly for the hilt, knowing that he dare not look up into Krulshards' nightmare face lest it drive him out. His fingers touched the hilt, he breathed a sigh of relief and closed his hands about it.

'Nevian give me strength!' he gasped, leaning backwards, pulling with all his strength, knotting his muscles with the effort, cramping his fingers as they locked on to the hilt. The blood pounded in his ears, he felt dizzy and light-headed, his fingers were slipping off the smooth metal. He staggered and overbalanced, falling heavily on to the chamber floor. Cursing, he knelt and waited for the roaring in his ears to fade. He turned his head and listened to the sharp scraping of the shadow rats amongst the Nightshards. The sword had not moved, it was stuck fast, fused into the column of rock. Slowly he rose and closed his hand on the hilt for a second time and thought about his mother and how she had suffered at Krulshards' hands. He could feel those cruel blind eyes boring down into him and could almost see that skinless snarling mouth. Shuddering, he locked his hands on the hilt and snapped back his head then stared full into Krulshards' face.

'Curse you! Curse you!' he shouted, throwing stealth and caution to the winds, letting the hatred and the anger boil up and feed him with new strength as he fought to pull the sword upwards.

He put his shoulder beneath the hilt, sideways, downwards,

315

twisting and turning, but nothing he tried would ease the blade. Lashing out in blind anger Rubel kicked at Krulshards' legs, smashing his shin, trampling on his toes and tearing his bone-black fingers away from the blade of the sword, but all his anger did was warn the shadow rats and send them swarming across the chamber floor.

Rubel cursed silently and stood rigid, letting the foul rats crawl up his legs and over his hands and face, sniffing and scenting. The weed worms twisted and turned, rattling their armoured bodies together and then hung silently from the rough dome. The rats ran briefly in circles and returned to feasting inside the Nightshards' carcasses. Rubel breathed a sigh of relief and placed his hands back on the hilt. Muttering, he closed his fingers, if only the metal were rougher, if only he could get a better purchase.

'The black cloth! If I bound that carefully around the hilt, yes, the malice!' he whispered, tearing away the strip of malice Kruel had left.

He wound it tightly around the blade and the hilt. 'Now!' he whispered, setting his feet apart and grasping the hilt with both hands. He took a deep breath, screwed his eyes tightly shut and pulled. The fabric of the malice felt icy cold and hid his hands in blackest shadows but the sword moved a fraction, grating in the rock. The malice unwound in folds of darkness along the blade and slipped between his fingers. Cursing, Rubel fell backwards and lay for long moments on the chamber floor gathering his strength. The sword had moved, he had felt it, if only the black malice had stayed wound on to the blade, if . . . Rubel sat up and thought, searching in every corner of his mind, and then he remembered the thread: the magician had said to use the thread from the rainbow cloak that was tied around his wrist. In the darkness he bent forwards and peeled back the rat skin that hid Nevian's gift then unwound the rainbow thread. Binding the strip of malice about the hilt and winding it firmly along the blade for as long as it would reach, Rubel wound the rainbow

316

thread around the shadow cloth about a hand's span from the hilt and tied it tightly. The thread sparkled and shone with soft light in the darkness, the shadow rats stopped their scavenging and left the Nightshards' carcasses and began moving uneasily towards him across the chamber floor.

Rubel steadied himself, flexed his arms, and gripped the hilt once more, burying his hands deep in the shadows of the malice. Now was the moment, now or never. He licked his lips and pulled, his shoulders bulged, the muscles knotting, his back arched with the effort. 'By all your power, Nevian,' he shouted as the rainbow thread blazed with colour, fizzing and sparkling, lighting the high-domed chamber with pure white fire.

The sword was moving, he had pulled it free! The shadow rats were shrieking and screaming, their hideous shadows leaping and soaring up across the lighted dome. Rubel turned and fled, crossing the chamber in three giant strides, running for the lowest edge of the broken roof. The sword felt heavy in his hands, bumping and dragging on the chamber floor.

'Escape, I must escape!' The words echoed and shouted in his head, the rats were on his heels, weed worms were droppng on to the ground uncoiling their venomous stings and scuttling towards him.

Something was hanging down through the broken roof, long tendrils that waved and swayed, whispering, beckoning him forwards. Rubel laughed, remembering the wizard's words, and threw himself into the waiting branches then felt them curl tightly around his arms and legs. He found himself being lifted, carried upwards out of the darkness; below in the chamber the floor was alive, boiling with shadows. He sank back, weak with terror, and closed his eyes, laughing helplessly. He cried out his thanks to Nevian for the magic tree and felt the ice-cold snowflakes stinging his cheeks. The trees were descending, taking him down the mountainside and carrying him away from the City of Night.

'Nevian's magic will bring me to you, Thane,' he

whispered, strengthening his grip on the sword and patting the branch that held him.

Willow had used every moment of the failing daylight to finish the defences of the Rising. He straightened his back and stared out into the gathering shadows. There were figures, horses, Border Runners and a whole company of animals he had never seen before filling the wild overgrown road running towards him.

'Oakapple,' he called, dropping the small trowel he had been using to clean between the brittle white bones that crowned the summit of the Rising. Oakapple came quickly and stood beside him, arching her hand against the low dying sunlight and followed his crippled finger.

'There, look between the rows of ancient trees, it's . . .' Willow paused raising himself on tiptoe. 'It's Star!' he shouted, running forwards down the steep ramp of polished bones. 'Star has come with her foal and all those that she could gather . . .'

Willow's voice died away as he passed between the gates and stopped on the lip of the narrow causeway spanning the deep water-filled dyke. He had caught sight of the beautiful young stallion trotting beside Starlight and it took his breath away. He was as white as the driven snow yet ghosted with the dapples of summer shadows, he strode across the open space before the narrow causeway, moving with elastic ease and as he halted he tossed his head proudly in the air and scraped at the thin powdery covering of snow that covered the ground with his front hoof.

Star whinnied a greeting and brushed her velvet muzzle against Willow's chest. 'Now you must name him,' she snorted, passing the words clearly into Willow's head, 'for he is yours to ride into battle against the new darkness. Remember Equestrius, the Lord of Horses, promised him to you before the Gates of Underfall.'

Willow took a step and hesitated. 'But . . . but . . .'

Star pushed him forwards. 'He will not hurt you, for now he has come of age and knows how in the moment of his birth you stood all alone with just one blade to keep him safe from the Nightbeasts.'

The beautiful horse snorted, arched his neck and brushed his muzzle against Willow's arm. For all his strength and power he was soft and gentle with his touch.

'Naming is not easy,' Willow answered, stepping back a pace. 'Names are something we carry all our life. They speak our purpose and tell others who we are. Names are for our Elders, or for Kings to give. No, I could not name him.'

Starlight snorted angrily, flattening her ears against the side of her head. 'The gift was given and cannot be taken away. You must name him, just as Thane named Esteron – you must.'

'But Thane is a King and I am only Willow Leaf, the Tunnel slave,' cried Willow, 'and I can think of nothing beautiful or proud enough.'

Star whinnied softly, calling to her foal, making him bend his forelegs and kneel before Willow. 'He is yours to set against the darkness.'

Willow reached out a hand and ran his twisted fingers through the horse's silken mane, felt the soft warmth of his coat and looked for long moments into his large liquid eyes that hid the sparkle of secret fire.

'Only Kings and Elders,' he smiled, running his gnarled fingers across the horse's shoulders and thinking back to a time of despair in the City of Night when the Elder had taken him to a long-forgotten chamber, whispering him into silence and making him kneel and touch a smooth round stone stuck fast in the rough rock wall. 'Eryus,' he had whispered, tapping the stone's hard outer shell. 'It is a great power against the darkness, for if you split it open it shines and glows pure white. Milkstone is its common name but you must never call it that or even whisper its real name, Eryus, here in the City

319

of Night because the Nightmare does not know that I have found it.'

Willow had opened his mouth to speak, to beg the Elder to split the stone but the Elder had firmly shaken his head and pressed him into silence. 'It is enough, child, that you know of the milkstone. Perhaps one daylight you will use the light trapped within the stone, perhaps then you will shout its name as you help to banish the Nightmare's darkness, perhaps . . .'

The memory was fading, fresh snowflakes were beginning to fall. Willow looked up, the Elder's voice was becoming a faint echo. That would be a good name, a proud name. Smiling, he stepped close to the horse. 'Eryus. I name you Eryus, the secret light that had its beginnings in the darkness, the light that is waiting to shine.' Laughing with relief, Willow carefully put his leg over Eryus' back and held tightly on to the mane. He sat very still as the horse rose beneath him.

'Trot steady,' he whispered, but Eryus snorted and arched his neck, he cantered in a broad circle, turned and strode up across the narrow causeway bridge and did not stop until he had reached the summit of the Rising.

'Be easy, be easy,' whispered Willow, trying not to show his fear. Riding Starlight had been almost natural but Eryus was part Warhorse, his muscles rippled, he moved with the speed of a summer shadow. 'Easy,' Willow whispered again, straightening his back and looking out through the falling snow at the darkening horizon.

It had grown blacker with new shadows rising on the edge of the wind. He leaned forwards as Fernleaf ran to his side and, frowning, Willow followed his urgent pointing hand to the very edge of sight on the wild road that had once led to the Granite City. 'The shadows are darkest in that direction and they seem almost to blend land and sky together.'

Willow nodded, arching his hand to shade his eyes against the falling snow. He had thought it was black snowclouds on the horizon but now he was sure it was more than that.

Fernleaf was pulling at his sleeve, pointing to a great company, turning him in the direction of the wild grasslands. Mighty stags, Warhorses and a huge pack of Border Runners were coming towards them through the deepening snowstorm.

'There are travellers on the road from Underfall,' called Oakapple, arriving breathlessly on the summit of the Rising, 'they are following the road lined with the ancient trees.'

Willow turned Eryus and cantered slowly around the high summit of the Rising. Yes, there was the flash of light reflected from crystal-tipped antlers in the grasslands and a small company of warriors on the road from Underfall, but who was it running before that darkness on the horizon's edge, who?

Willow dismounted quickly and called all the Tunnellers to the summit of the Rising. 'There is more than blizzards in that darkness and it is spreading and flowing as a black tide towards us. Sharpen your senses and have a keen edge on your shovels. Go quickly and bring in the travellers from the grasslands and Underfall for they run hard pressed before gathering shadows.'

Breakmaster stumbled wearily forwards through the deepening snow. He had lost count of the daylights as he trudged along beside Beacon Light with one hand pressed against the oiled cotton and the other wound in the horse's stirrup leather to keep him from falling. Thoron half-ran, half-staggered at the other stirrup leather, his hand on Merion's leg to keep him steady in the saddle. Thunderstone and Tiethorm followed a dozen paces behind the company, constantly twisting and turning, daggers ready in case the rats or the shadow warriors should overtake them.

'There! Look just ahead,' cried Elionbel, shaking the snowflakes out of her hair. 'That must be the place.'

Merion blinked his sore eyelids and laughed, the noise rising in dry crackles from his blistered throat as he caught sight of the Rising looming out of the gloomy snowstorm. Willow's Tunnellers were suddenly crowding all around them with sharp axes and spades honed for battle in their hands or slung across their shoulders. 'Beautiful, beautiful,' he sighed, slumping forwards as strong hands took him gently from the saddle and carried him across the narrow causeway.

Willow cantered out of the rising and halted in a spray of wind-driven snow a pace from where Thunderstone had stopped and stood, staring at the Rising. 'Are there more on the road behind you?' he shouted against the creaking and groaning of the trees standing in neat rows beside the road.

'No,' answered the last Lampmaster, staring past Willow, his eyes round, his mouth hanging open with wonder. He raised his hand and pointed at the Rising, unable to form any question.

Willow laughed and turned Eryus towards the wild grass-land road. 'It is the Rising, a fortress built against the darkness. Hurry, climb to the summit, there is hot food and shelter in the Tower.'

'Did you build this?' Thunderstone shouted as Eryus broke into a canter.

'No, oh no,' called Willow across his shoulder. 'We will talk of it later. There are others running before this dark storm; I must hurry.'

Thunderstone smiled and rubbed his chin with difficulty. There had always been something different about Willow, something that went beyond those large round eyes and shell-shaped ears.

'Master, we must hurry.' Tiethorm was tugging impatiently at the hem of his cloak as if he was afraid to cross the narrow causeway and climb the steep ramp to tread on the thousands of glittering eyes.

'Sometimes,' laughed Thunderstone, 'it is a distinct advantage to have your head twisted the wrong way around for then you cannot see what you are afraid of!'

322

Elionbel looked up the ramp and caught her breath, pointing to the stone crown.

'It is the crown of Elundium,' answered Oakapple shyly, hurrying out to meet them. 'Kruel smashed it into a thousand pieces in the tombs of Underfall. I gathered up the pieces and brought them with us; it seemed only right that the crown should be here in the last ray of sunlight.'

Thunderstone turned and looked up at King Holbian's crown where it hung, the smooth polished stone reflecting the dull winter light that still shone above the shadows. He opened his mouth to answer when a shout and the noise of thundering hoofbeats made him turn and jump quickly aside. Huge stags, Warhorses and Border Runners were everywhere, ploughing through the snow and cantering up the steep ramp, rearing and plunging all around him.

A Battle Owl stooped to Thunderstone's shoulder and he laughed then began searching the dense fog of snow dust the animals had churned up. 'Kyot, Eventine! Where are you?' he shouted.

A dark monstrous shape loomed before him, sending him tumbling backwards with fright. Crying out, he reached for his dagger but a soft voice laughed and a strong hand pulled him to his feet. 'Kyot?' he whispered, searching two faces that now seemed to grow from the same body, two heads, four arms. 'Kyot? ... Eventine? What has Kruel done to you?' he asked, brushing snow from his knees and staring at Tanglecrown and Sprint, seeing only a nightmare shape with six legs.

Kyot looked past Thunderstone as he was about to answer and instead whispered quickly to Eventine who loosed an arrow in amongst the trees. A shadow warrior screamed and fell forwards into a clear patch of snow.

'As one we can still fight the darkness,' answered Eventine grimly, nocking another arrow shaft on to Kyot's bow and sweeping her careful Archer's eyes across the trees.

'Beware! You must not harm the trees!' cried Willow as she drew the feathered flight against her cheek.

A shadow rat shrieked, its back snapped in two as it was flung by a fast-moving branch high above the whispering leaves. 'We will not harm them, the trees are great warriors,' she answered. 'Without their help we would never have reached the Rising.'

'Is Thane here?' asked Elionbel, turning breathlessly to Willow. 'Only, Thunderstone – the trees tell of the fall of the Granite City.' Her words spilt out in a nervous torrent as she searched desperately across the summit of the Rising. 'The Granite City has fallen and they said that we should meet him here in the last ray of sunlight.'

Willow shrugged his shoulders helplessly and threw up his hands in despair. 'He came too late, my Lady. All Elundium is covered beneath a blanket of snow. We are surrounded by a sea of darkest shadows.'

Elionbel turned away in despair, burying her head in her hands. All this darkness was her fault, it had only happened because she could not find the courage to tell the truth. The killing and the cruel maiming, the ruin and the terror that cried out beneath the crush of shadowlight spreading across Elundium, it was all her fault. A gentle hand touched her forehead, a strong arm closed about her shoulders drawing her towards the Tower and shelter from the storm. Eventine smiled, softly brushing snowflakes from her face and whispered, 'We shall shoulder Martbel's tragedy between us and all Elundium will fight beside us to win back the sunlight. Come, come into the warm amongst those who love you.'

The Last Ray of Sunlight

Thane barely had time to turn and look back through the swirling snowstorm at the chaos of Kruel's shadowy army flooding through the Stumble Gate. Nevian had pulled him forwards, pressing him to flee, to follow the ancient trees and vanish before Kruel could summon more shadow rats and warriors to overrun them. The trees had heard the magician's shout and closed tightly around Thane and those who had escaped with him from Candlebane Hall. They began gently but firmly to shepherd them through the snowstorm towards the Rising.

'Is there no end to this shadowlight?' shouted Thane. 'Will it ever stop snowing?' he cried angrily against the biting, stinging wind.

'It snows to our advantage,' cried Nevian through the folds of the rainbow cloak he had tied across his face against the blinding snow.

Thane laughed harshly, putting his tired aching shoulder against the flanks of a faltering Warhorse and helping the exhausted Archers push him forwards through the snow. 'How does it help when it wearies our weak and pulls them down? There is a litter of those who loved the light and who I could not save spread clear across Elundium because of this cursed snow!'

'It burdens us, yes,' answered the magician, bumping clumsily into Thane as he breasted a deep drift of snow, 'but it has slowed down the shadows that tread on our heels and the trees will not let them attack us. It gives us time to find the sunlight.'

'Lord, I can go no further,' cried a voice of despair close to the ancient trees. Thane stopped and turned his aching feet to search the gloomy snow-fogged space between the last straggling Warhorses and the close ring of ancient trees shielding them from Kruel's Nightmare warriors.

Running back, he bent, hooking his numb fingers into Errant's ice-ringed cloak collar and pulled the horseman to his feet. 'Go forwards, Errant,' he shouted against the creaking, grinding movement of the trees, shaking him, beating him awake. 'Go amongst the Warhorses before you freeze to death. Ride awhile on Dawnrise – hurry before the ancient trees tread on you.'

Errant smiled foolishly, his eyes dark-ringed with tiredness and blinked his frozen eyelashes. 'I cannot, my Lord. My legs . . . I cannot move.'

Thane smiled and lifted the frozen horseman up across his shoulders. 'You will not leave me so easily, Errant, nor fall beneath the ancient trees,' he muttered fiercely, forcing his way forwards through the weary frozen warriors who stumbled beside the Warhorses, their blackened, frostbitten fingers woven through the horses' wet tangled manes.

'No, Lord,' Errant mumbled through chattering teeth, 'the trees are our shepherds, they will not harm us. Look how the ice-rimmed branches reach down to push us forwards.'

Thane nodded without looking back. He had seen the branches scoop up staggering Warhorses and Border Runners and help them forwards and he had also seen them gently check amongst the frozen dead before silently parting to leave them untouched in the deep untrampled snow. 'Yes, Errant,' he answered with a voice heavy with tiredness, 'they are good shepherds and a great blessing in these desperate shadowlights, but I wish I could stand and fight against Kruel and that army of shadows that follow in our footsteps. With each daylight, each hour in this half light more of us die.

How long, Errant, how many daylights must I run? If only I had . . .'

'No, Lord,' shouted Nevian, clutching at Thane's arm and cracking the thin layer of ice with his fingers, 'do not say it. Do not even think of it, for now is not the moment. The Archers' quivers are empty and there are less than a dozen fire-forged blades between us now. It is not the time to stop, to turn or even to hesitate. Let the trees lead us forward to the last ray of sunlight. There you may ask for all that you desire.'

'Forwards! Always forwards,' muttered Thane, pausing beside Errant's horse. Dawnrise whinnied and staggered as he bravely tried to arch his neck and take the rider's weight. 'No,' whispered Thane, moving slowly away between the crowded horses and searching until he found Esteron. He lifted the horseman carefully from his shoulders and laid him across Esteron's back. 'Dawnrise has worn his great heart to a shadow and I fear for him. Will you carry Errant until the strength flows through his legs again?' Thane asked, stroking Esteron's strong shoulder.

Esteron snorted, brushing his ice-cold muzzle on Thane's cheek.

'Cover his legs with the scarf, Thane. The sun I wove into the cloth will thaw them.'

'Mother!' Thane cried, spinning around at the familiar voice. 'Why do you walk?' he asked angrily, breaking the frozen leather thongs that bound the scarf on to his arm and folding it tightly around Errant's legs.

'To save Mulberry's strength,' she replied proudly, 'and I will not ride while others walk.'

Thane smiled at her and gathered her up in his strong arms to set her firmly on Mulberry's back. 'You will serve me better, Mother, if you ride beside Errant and watch over him. When his strength returns go with the standard of the sun and use it to warm and help those who are frozen, and give them comfort in this darkness.'

327

Nevian pulled at Thane's arm shouting against the storm and pointing ahead out of the narrow funnel of slow-moving treetrunks. 'There is something ahead, I saw it. I saw something shining brightly.'

Thane let go of Mulberry's bridle and ran forwards as fast as he could through the deep snow. Nevian ran on his heels treading easily into Thane's footprints, the rainbow cloak gathered in both arms.

'What did you see?' shouted Thane as he stopped, his eyes squeezed into tight slits against the stinging snow.

'Wait! Wait until the wind drops and then you will see it.'

Both of them stood rock-still, bent forwards against the wind. On either side of them the close-ranked trees marched steadily onwards.

'There it is! A ray of light!' shouted Thane, pointing to what looked like a bright beacon that rose in the swirling snowstorm crystal white, against the shadow-dark sky.

Thane laughed and shouted to the Battle Owls sheltering in the branches of the ancient trees, sending them up to search the snow ahead, then his voice faded into silence: he hesitated. 'What place is this that the ancient trees have brought us to?' he asked, gripping Nevian's cloak as he stared at the Rising.

Nevian brushed the snow from his eyebrows and took a cautious step forwards and stopped. 'By all my magic, it is the greatest wonder in Elundium. It is the Rising, the place that Willow Leaf sought. Look how it shines even in this shadowlight. Look how it sparkles!'

'The snowstorm is weakening. Look, there are more ancient trees gathered in dense groves around the base of that frost-glittering hill and they are moving slowly across the snow towards us in neat columns,' cried Grey Goose, running to Thane's side.

Thane swept his gaze from the trees to the Rising. He saw a horse the colour of hammered silver galloping towards them down a steep ramp brushed free of snow. It seemed to stare at him with thousands of eyes.

'There are Warriors.' Nevian paused, his frozen eyebrows cracking into a frown. 'Willow's people have armed themselves,' he whispered, clapping his numb fingers together as the frown softened into his broadest smile.

The Warhorses and the Border Runners had caught up with Thane and Nevian and shuffled to a halt. Grey Goose hurried in amongst them and brought out his half-frozen Archers. 'Draw your swords and be ready,' he commanded before running back to Thane's side.

'Lord, the Archers . . .' he began but Thane put his hand on Grey Goose's arm, pushing his half-drawn sword firmly back into the scabboard and turned him towards the galloping horseman.

Grey Goose laughed and threw his arms high into the air. Thane strode forwards through the deep snow, shouting Willow's name against the shadowlight and Nevian smiled up at the ancient trees drawn all around him and whispered. 'You have waited almost long enough, be ready, for your King will have great need of you!'

'Elionbel?' Thane whispered, reaching the top of the steep ramp. 'Oh, Elion,' he shouted, running forwards across the summit of the Rising and catching her up in his arms. 'Through all the darkness and each cry of terror I never dared to hope. Oh, Elion, I love you, I love you.'

Thane wept, closing his arms and lifting her off the ground.

'No! No!' she cried, twisting in his arms. 'I am worse than a traitor, to have lied, to have kept Kruel's bastard birth a secret. If only I had broken the pledge and told you none of this darkness, none of the cruel crippling, the killing . . . forgive me, please forgive me!'

Thane pressed his lips on hers, calming her into silence. 'We have so little time,' he whispered. 'Of course I forgive you, I forgive you every single silent moment. Fate gave you the hardest road, Elion, for you could not break such a pledge and there are none in all Elundium who would have asked you to.'

'But the darkness!' she cried, breaking free. 'If I had followed the one-eyed Nightbeast, if I had killed the bastard before he had the power to do all this . . .'

Thane smiled and pulled her to him. 'When Kruel is dead then we will talk on it.'

'How! How will you kill him? He has grown into the most powerful nightmare in all Elundium.' She wept, burying her head in her hands. 'How? How will you do it?'

Thane smiled and put his hand under her chin. He lifted her face until he could look into her eyes. 'I know not how, my love, but Kruel had victory at his fingertips as he stood on the high wall of the Granite City yet we defeated him, drowning his warriors and shadow rats. We have outrun him across the length of Elundium to stand here upon the summit of this, the strongest fortress in Elundium. We will find a way to defeat him. I know it.' Thane paused, searching her eyes carefully. 'I know that today I am stronger and more sure of my purpose because the shadow that once haunted you and drove a wedge between us has gone. Now there is sunlight once more in your eyes.'

'Lord, come quickly. Kruel's shadow army is a league beyond the ancient trees!' shouted Errant, making Thane spin around and let go of Elion's hand.

Running to the edge of the summit he looked out at the advancing shadows, his lips thinning into a line of bitter determination as he watched the shadows close all about them.

'Thanehand! Galloperspawn! I have come to take you and all the people of Elundium into my darkness!' cried Kruel's voice from the edge of the advancing shadows.

Thane looked out quickly to where the trees had drawn together on the furthest side of the Rising and then down into the deep dyke. 'How long will that narrow causeway

330

hold? How strong are the gates? These steep slopes, what makes them glow?' he asked without turning.

'Lord, the Rising is made of bones, polished bright to catch each tiny ray of light that still shines in Elundium.'

Thane turned quickly and smiled at Willow then took his hand. 'Once more, Willow Leaf, once more you come and save us from defeat as the darkness is about to swallow us. Once more, great warrior, your people have worked with pick and shovel to raise a fortress.'

Willow smiled and knelt before Thane. 'Lord, there were voices in the ancient trees that led us here to prepare this Rising as the last fortress against the darkness. We found bones, whole skeletons chained together that rise up in an unending spiral to this summit. All we did was to clear away the earth that shrouded them and polish them to catch the light.'

Thane frowned, remembering clearly and hearing the echo of Nevian's words in Candlebane Hall. *A proud people born to torment and bound in chains.*

'Willow,' he whispered, searching quickly with his eyes for the magician, 'in all your wanderings have you found the place to call your own? Have you discovered your beginnings?'

Willow hesitated, almost saying 'yes' but the word stuck in his throat. Nevian caught Thane's eye and smiled secretly, nodding his head. Thane laughed softly and pulled Willow to his feet. 'Of all the places in the whole wide world, this Rising that the trees brought you to, this ring of bones with all its history is your home. You could feel it in the earth beneath your feet, you could smell it in the very air, yet you hesitated and would not have taken it, would you?'

Willow looked down at his feet. 'No, Lord, we could not claim the last ray of sunlight. It belongs to the people of Elundium.'

'It is yours, Willow Leaf, this Rising and all the lands that surround it as far as the eye can see are yours, by the toil and suffering of your forefathers.'

Calling in a loud voice he pledged to break the chains that bound the Tunnel slaves. Now they would be truly free to be the masters of their own destiny.

'Oakapple, we are free!' Willow began to shout but Nevian held up his hand and in the shadowy silence they heard the snapping and rattle of countless chains breaking, echoing down through the heart of the Rising, making the very bones of the earth tremble.

Kruel heard Thane's pledge and screamed with rage throwing his hatred against the strong gates of the Rising and shouting. 'They are mine! Mine! They are my father's slaves that you stole from the City of Night.'

Willow laughed and shook his blackened, crippled fist at Kruel. 'I was born to Krulshards' nightmare darkness, yes, but I fought and led my people to their freedom and none shall take it away. No one, do you hear!'

'Take care,' whispered Nevian, easing Willow back away from the edge of the summit. 'We do not yet have the strength to fight against this Kruel or know of his weakness.'

'I can hear your whisperings and I know all your weaknesses, magician,' Kruel laughed, but the sound of his laugh was hollow as it shrieked pitilessly through the shadowlight across the Rising, shattering the ivory-smooth skulls that ringed the summit and muffling into dull echoes as it faded away across the snow-covered causeway back into the gloomy shadowlight.

Arbel strode to his side, the black malice fluttering from his hands. Kerzolde and Kerhunge followed in his footprints and squatted on either side of Kruel, cursing and shouting, calling on Thanehand to come out and do battle with their master.

'Which Nightbeast shall I silence?' whispered Eventine, reaching back into her quiver.

Elionbel started and half-turned at Eventine's voice. 'The

hideous one-eyed hairy beast,' she answered hatefully. 'The one that took the bastard from within the malice.'

Eventine narrowed her eyes, wet the cold steel blade of the arrow with her tongue and nocked it on to Kyot's bow. 'Hold very steady,' she whispered into his ear, locking her fingers on the bow string and drawing the feathered flight back against her cheek. She slowly searched the shadowlight below. Tanglecrown moved beneath her, seeking a better footing on the slippery smooth summit of bones. Sprint followed, sparks dancing from his hind shoes. 'Be still,' Eventine barely whispered, squeezing her knees into Tangle-crown's flanks. Kruel was moving away from the narrow causeway taking the Nightbeasts with him; they seemed to merge, to blend together in the shadows. Eventine blinked and widened her eyes. There he was, the Nightbeast, a dark hideous shape against the snow.

'No!' cried Nevian, turning in panic as he heard the Bow of Orm groan as it tightened but it was too late, Eventine had loosed her arrow and the empty bow string sang out with sweet music in the darkness. 'You move too quickly, now Kruel will attack!' he hissed, jumping and turning back as Kerhunge's scream shattered the uneasy silence. Eventine's arrow had flown wide of Kerzolde and struck Kerhunge in the chest tearing through his armoured hide and lifting him high into the air, tumbling him over and over and spilling his black blood across the trampled snow.

'Strengthen the gates!' shouted Thane, rushing to the brink of the steep ramp as the shadows surged forwards.

'There are arrows and spears and swords for any strong enough to use them,' shouted Willow against the roaring tide of darkness that now swept at breakneck speed across the snow towards them.

'Take Grey Goose and the Archer strike down the outer spiral of the Rising. We must defend the gates for as long as possible,' cried Thane.

'Fly for your King, defend the Rising,' shouted Nevian, sending up the Battle Owls.

Grannog growled and snarled, his teeth gleaming in the shadowlight, his hackles were razor-sharp along his back and he led the Border Runners beside the Warhorses to the very brink of the narrow causeway.

Esteron roared out a challenge and cantered to Thane's side, rearing and plunging amongst Kruel's nightmare warriors as he fought to hold the gates, crushing the rats beneath his steel-rimmed feet as they swarmed on to the narrow causeway in black waves of terror. Arbel ran screaming on to the causeway, the black shadowy malice spreading darkness and despair as it flowed out behind him; the shadow warriors cheered and surged with new strength across the causeway.

'It is hopeless, my Lord,' shouted Errant, driven to his knees beneath the fury of Arbel's attack, seeing the gates falling beneath the weight of the shadow rats. Soon they will be swarming on to the Rising. Nothing can stop them.'

'Go to Thane, take him the standard of the sun,' cried Angishand, running across the summit of the Rising with the summer scarf streaming from her hands as she searched for the owls. Mulcade and Rockspray heard her cry above the roar of battle. Rockspray came first, hooking his blood-wet talons on to the scarf and took it spiralling high above the Rising to catch what little light there was. Mulcade hooted proudly and closed his talons on the scarf. Together they stooped across the Rising bringing light into the darkness below.

'Sow them against the darkness.' The words suddenly shouted in Elionbel's head drowning out the noise of the battle and making her feel beneath her cloak for the leather pouch that Pinchface had thrust into her hands as they escaped from Underfall. Now she remembered the Loremaster's words. They were seeds, nightflower seeds and he had said that Thane must use them against the darkness. Running recklessly down the ramp, heedless to the warning shouts of those around her she passed in amongst the Warhorses, scattering the small round seeds across the brittle bones beneath their feet. Kneeling, blind and deaf to the terror that swarmed about her, she pushed the seeds in between the skulls. Jostled and trampled she climbed across the steep sides of the Rising, sowing a precious seed between each broken link in the chains that had for suns beyond counting bound Willow's people into slavery.

Step by step Thane was being driven back into the Rising. Mulcade and Rockspray brought him the standard of the sun but even that could not stem the tide of darkness. Arbel was but a dozen strides away, smashing all that stood before him with a huge black battle mace. Thane raised a hand and shouted to Grey Goose to cover their retreat. He called the Warhorses and the Border Runners to go back into the Rising. Reaching down, he gripped Errant by the shoulder and pulled him backwards only a moment before Arbel's black mace shattered the ground where he had been.

Grey Goose dropped his hand and the Archers' arrows sang through the air, clearing the narrow causeway and sending the hoards of shadowy warriors screaming into the deep dyke below. Thane turned and fled, running as fast as he could up the steep ramp. Grannog was at his heels and Esteron cantered beside him. Halfway up Thane stopped and turned, the sound of battle had melted to an eerie silence, the black shadows had halted on the brink of the causeway, the shadow rats crowded statue-still along the edge of the dyke, keeping well clear of the close-ranked trees that had moved slowly forwards on either side of the Rising. Arbel stood alone in the centre of the causeway, his armoured lips curled in a sneer as he faced Grey Goose's strike of Archers.

'Nothing can harm me!' he gloated, striding forwards.

Grey Goose dropped his hand again and every Archer on his strike loosed an arrow at the black-armoured warrior. Arbel laughed as the arrows shattered and splintered against the Nightshards' armour and he strode through the broken

335

gates up into the Rising. 'Nothing can harm me!' he shouted, raining savage blows with his mace at the countless eyes staring up at him from the skulls set on the ramp.

Thane took a step towards him. Esteron turned and crouched, his hocks close to the ground, his ears flat against the side of his head; he was ready to spring. Arbel sneered, taunting Thane, trying to draw him on. Thane raised his notched and bloody sword and took a step forward.

'No!' cried Elionbel. 'Do not go to him, he will kill you.'

Arbel looked up at his sister, his lips curling with hatred as he pointed an armoured finger at her. 'You shall hang beside him in the City of Night.'

Thane stopped mid-stride and sniffed at the cold winter air and laughed. There was a scent, a beautiful heavy scent. Smiling, he beckoned to Arbel with his sword, goading him to follow, welcoming him into the Rising, and with each backward stride that drew the black-armoured warrior up the ramp bright flowers sprang up tangling about his legs, sharp thorns scratched and tore at his armour and bitter fumes blinded him, choking him. Screaming with rage Arbel broke loose from the nightflower vines that clung to his ankles and ran back through the broken gates across the causeway, shouting as he ran for the shadow rats to attack, driving his shadow warriors on up the ramp. But none could touch or cross the nightflowers, and with each assault the barrier of white petals grew deeper and thicker until the dyke was buried beneath them in dazzling brightness, and the brittle hill of bones shone out, blazing in the darkness.

Kruel watched his army falter in the banks of brilliant flowers and called them back sending them out of the Archers' range. 'I know the legends!' he shouted, striding between the gates and treading to the very edge of the first flowers. 'I know the nightflowers will protect you only for the passage of one night. With the dawn my darkness will be amongst you and I shall destroy you all.'

Nevian thought for a moment then spread his rainbow

cloak in glowing colours and laughed at Kruel. 'If real daylight comes, foul demon of the darkness, then it will be you who loses everything, for we shall have destroyed the shadows and have the power of the sunlight.'

'What power?' whispered Thane, desperately trying to hone the notches from the blade of his sword.

Nevian laughed quietly. He knew Kruel did not fear the sunlight but it would weaken his shadow warriors and those black rats. If the sun did shine with the breaking of the new daylight all would change, he was sure of it.

'But I cannot even fight against Arbel, how will I fight Kruel?' Thane asked.

Nevian pressed his finger on to Thane's lips and whispered. 'Look beyond the shadow warriors far out along the wild road that once led to the Palace of Kings.'

Thane frowned. 'To Underfall?' he muttered, taking Elionbel's hand into his own and leading her to the edge of the summit. But he could see nothing in the snowy darkness, nothing save the tops of the ancient trees that had drawn in close to the banks of sweet-smelling nightflowers.

'Be ready to ride out, my King,' whispered Nevian. 'When the first ray of sunlight touches the summit of the Rising and the blackbirds sing upon the Greenway's edge, then you must trust in the threads of Fate, for they will bring the sword that Durondel hot-forged to strike at Krulshards' heart.'

'Rubel? Has Rubel brought the sword?' Thane hissed, turning on the magician and gripping the rainbow cloak so tightly he drained the colours between his fingertips.

'Rubel?' Elionbel whispered, stepping quickly forwards. 'Have you seen my brother? Where is he?'

Nevian smiled and drew them both into the folds of the rainbow cloak. 'He is out there, yes. I saw him racing the road towards us in a grove of ancient trees.'

'Did he carry the sword? Are you sure?' pressed Thane. 'Was the bright metal hilt in his hands?'

Nevian shook his head. 'No! No, it was but a moment's

glimpse as Rockspray took your banner of the sun high above the Rising. It was but a curtain briefly parting the darkness.'

Thane shivered and looked up into the night-dark sky and saw far above his head bright stars sewn across the darkness. 'It will be as you have foretold,' he whispered, holding Nevian's gaze. 'The dawn will be bright and the sun will cast long shadows on the snow.'

'The wind was changing as Kruel spoke, that is why the sun will shine. The storms are over, the weather turns to our advantage. Yes, the sun will cast shadows,' muttered Nevian, rubbing his chin and turning away slowly to pace round and round the high rim of the Rising. Whispering, he called by rote as he wore away the night hours until with a final step and a shout of laughter he stopped and clapped his hands. 'Yes, yes, of course, Kruel is so powerful that he can deny the sun a shadow. That must also be his weakness, his weakness must lie somewhere in that strength. Thane! Thane!'

Turning to left and right Nevian called and searched the summit. He saw Thane and Elionbel's huddle of cloaks and began to cross over to them. 'No, tomorrow will be soon enough,' he whispered to himself smiling, seeing them so closely entwined in each other's arms. He silently unclasped the rainbow cloak and carefully spread it across them covering them both with warm colours from a summer's day.

'We must do all we can,' whispered Nevian, drawing Thane, Errant, Breakmaster, Thoron, Kyot, Eventine and Willow and all his people into a tight Battle Council on the lip of the steep ramp beneath the glittering stars. Equestrius snorted, marshalling the Warhorses into the Council and Grannog led the Border Runnrs to sit at the magician's feet. Mulcade hooted softly and the Battle Owls stooped silently to perch, unblinking, at the last Battle Council before the grey hours touched the sky.

'Lord, you must take it,' begged Breakmaster, kneeling

and offering up the steelsilver battle coat King Holbian had given to him before the gates of Underfall.

Thane smiled in the cold grey light of the new dawn and took the gift of Kings, feeling the smooth touch of watered silk between his fingers as he carefully spread the battle coat across Esteron's back. 'It is a great gift and Esteron thanks you,' he cried, gripping the horseman's hand.

Breakmaster blinked, forcing back his tears as he held the stirrup for Thane to mount. 'Let me ride with you, Lord,' he whispered.

'No,' answered Thane, pirouetting Esteron firmly to face the crowded summit. 'None of you will follow me. I must ride out alone to face this Kruel.'

Nevian stepped forwards, buckling the clasp of the rainbow cloak at his throat. 'The Warhorses and the Border Runners take no man as their master, Thane. They will lead you down into the swarming shadows and match you stride for stride, no matter what you say.'

Willow laughed and squeezed through the press of warriors and Warhorses. 'You gave us our freedom, my Lord, so we shall use it and run at your stirrup.'

'Tanglecrown and Sprint shall gallop beside you,' shouted Kyot, holding up the great Bow of Orm.

Elionbel reached up and caught Thane's hand, holding on to it tightly before saying, 'There is just one handful of nightflower seeds left in the Loremaster's pouch and I shall ride beside you on Stumble and scatter them against the darkness.'

'But,' cried Thane, 'I am the King and I must go out alone.'

'There is no time for debate, my Lord. The sun is rising and the nightflowers are fading,' shouted Nevian, running to Esteron's side and gripping the bridle. 'Every one of us here upon the Rising loves you, Thane, and would rather die beside you, fighting for the daylight, than wait here in terror of the darkness that will surely come if you fail.'

339

Thane laughed and swept the summer scarf high above his head to catch all the first rays of sunlight. 'Then ride and run and sing and shout and follow your destiny, stride for stride beside me, into the blackest shadows, for I love you all!'

'Lord, Lord,' shouted Nevian, keeping a hold on Esteron's bridle and striding the smooth summit of bones as the horse surged forwards, 'when you cross the causeway shout to the ancient trees, tell them that now you have great need of them.'

'Trees?' laughed Thane across his shoulder. 'They are brave shepherds that brought us safely to the Rising, but how can they help me now?'

'Call on them, Lord,' shouted Nevian as Esteron broke free and began to canter down the ramp, 'and all those Warriors who did not pledge themselves upon the Causeway Field will come to you, for they have watched and listened and seen that you are truly worthy of the Kingship of Elundium.'

The roar of hoofbeats and fierce growling echoed and thundered down the ramp as the Warhorses and Border Runners trampled a path through the withering nightflowers.

'Wait!' cried Nevian, catching hold of Willow's sleeve as he reached the lip of the ramp. Turning him, Nevian pointed out across the top of Kruel's advancing shadow army towards the grove of trees and a lone figure struggling through the snow. 'Rubel will come too late. Look, the sword is too heavy for him to carry alone. Go to him, Willow. Gallop out on Eryus for he is a Lord of Horses and he could carry the sword.'

Willow ran to the tower and took the reins of the bridle he had fitted on to the beautiful horse then sprang up on to his back, calling to the magician as he cantered towards the ramp. 'The Elder was right when he showed me the milk-stone, Eryus – it is the secret light that I can use against the darkness.'

Thane halted on the brink of the narrow causeway.

340

Elionbel pressed Stumble close to Esteron's flank, the night-flower seeds held tightly in her hand. 'Warriors! I have great need of all the warriors of Elundium who love the daylight!' he shouted, standing in the stirrups and turning towards the trees.

The ancient trees groaned and creaked and were suddenly still. Their whispering leaves fell into silence.

'Warriors! Brave men who love the sunlight,' he shouted desperately, seeing Kruel's swarming shadow army rising up to tower over him and seeing just how much darkness he had to cross to reach the ancient grove of trees where Rubel carried the sword of Durondel.

'Warriors!' he shouted, the word turning to a cry of laughter as the trees began to sway and crumble into hollow strips of bark. They broke and shattered into a fog of splinters and in their place a glittering forest of spearblades were lowered against the shadows and with a roaring shout for Thane as King the grim-faced warriors who had once doubted his worthiness surged forward, clearing a broad path through the shadow warriors and closing in about their King.

Kruel screamed with rage and drove his shadow army onwards. Arbel waded with giant strides towards Esteron, crushing everything in his path. Willow crouched, holding tightly on to Eryus' back, his hands wound into the flowing mane as the horse raced quicker than a silver shadow through the darkness.

'Give me your hand, your hand,' Willow shouted breathlessly, leaning out and locking his fingers around Rubel's wrist and pulling him up on to Eryus' back. 'Run, Eryus. Run as you never have before,' he shouted and urged the horse to gallop back through the shadows.

Arbel reached out with armoured fingers for Thane. Esteron reared, crashing his forelegs helplessly against Arbel's armour and fell, sending Thane sprawling in the snow.

'No! No! You foul monster,' shouted Elionbel, hurling the

handful of nightflower seeds in Arbel's face and cursing him as he drove Stumble on to his knees with one blow from his armoured hand.

'Now, sister, I shall kill you,' he snarled, brushing the stoops of Battle Owls away from his face as if they were harmless sparrows while he pulled Elionbel roughly to her feet.

Thane struggled to rise. Galloping hoofbeats sounded close by. A blood-freezing cry of triumph made him look up and stagger to his knees. Kruel had run forwards as Thane fell and now he towered over him, a black-bladed dagger in his hands. Darkness was spreading, boiling across the trampled snow, black shadows were drifting across the sun.

'Thane! The sword! Catch the sword!' cried Rubel, throwing it with all his strength to where Thane knelt as Eryus galloped past Kruel's shadowless figure.

Thane lunged forwards, his hand outstretched and caught the hilt of the sword, crying out as he closed his fingers around the strip of ice-cold shadow malice still bound around the blade. Turning, he struggled to rise, the strip of malice unwinding from the weapon and billowing out against him as he fought to thrust the sword.

But there was nothing; no sword. The blade had been sheared through by the rainbow thread Rubel had bound about the strip of black malice. There was nothing but a hand's span of broken blade wrapped in the cloth. Kruel laughed. This was his moment of victory. He swept his dagger high above his head to make the killing stroke Arbel sneered and closed his fingers about Elionbel's throat to choke the life out of her.

'Steady, steady,' whispered Eventine. The Bow of Orm was drawn tight, the last glass arrowblade aimed at Kruel, ready on the string.

Kruel rose, towering, the dagger raised above Thane's head. Arbel was crushing his fingers about Elionbel's throat. 'No!' Eventine shouted as Tanglecrown moved, bumping against Sprint. She released her fingers, sending the glass arrowblade spinning past its target, shrieking its way across the battlefield. Arbel screamed, dropping Elionbel as the glass arrowblade smashed into his armour, shattering in a blaze of light, etching black shadows across the snow and sending him high into the air.

Thane threw himself sideways digging the broken blade of the sword and the strip of black shadowy malice deep into Kruel's footprints in the snow as he dodged the dagger blade. Kruel toppled forwards his foot stuck fast to the shadowy cloth.

'The shadow! That is his weakness, give him a shadow!' cried Nevian from the high summit of the Rising. 'Use the Sword. Use the strip of malice. Dig! Dig!'

Thane rolled over with a shout of laughter on his lips as Kruel's dagger cut into the snow beside his head and he began to drive the malice into Kruel's footprints with the short broken blade of the sword.

'No! No!' screamed Kruel, the dagger slipping from his weakening fingers. He stumbled backwards away from Thane, tearing at the dead locks of hair on the top of his head and trying to shed the skin and escape from the shadow, digging his nails into the hard bony ridge of his brow. But with each footprint he left on the snow the shadow grew stronger and darker. He was shrinking, crying out as he crawled away from Thane and hid in Kerzolde's arms.

Kerzolde snarled, baring his ragged teeth as Thane advanced but the noise rattled dry in his throat. The darkness was melting away, the sunlight was growing stronger, his rotten Nightbeast heart was fading. 'Galloperspawn!' he hissed weakly, trying to raise the broken claw to protect his master.

The roar of battle faltered, the shadowy warriors hesitated and silence slowly spread in rippling, widening circles from where Thane stood. One by one the dark-etched shadow warriors dropped their spears and swords and crumpled,

343

falling helpless and blind in the strengthening sunlight, crying out for mercy.

Merion saw the shadow grow at Kruel's feet and snatched up a lighted bulrush torch in his charred and blackened fingers then ran headlong amongst the shadow rats that had assaulted the Rising, setting fire to their foul brittle-spined skins, setting a blaze that spread far across Elundium to rid the sunlit world of their black shadows. Thane advanced on Kerzolde pushing his carcass aside and picked up Kruel. He held him at arm's length, turning him and twisting him in the sunlight, frowning as he looked at his shrunken body. Raising the broken blade he prepared to make the killing stroke and rid Elundium of the shadowlight.

'No, no!' cried Elionbel, running to his side and grabbing his sleeve. Reaching out she took the hilt of the sword from his hands. 'Do not kill him, Thane. Remember Nevian's words, remember that nothing can be all bad. Look, he has shrunk to less than a man, a boy, a mere child, his power is gone, the darkness is over. Look, look at my fingers, they are healing, the Warhorses and the Border Runners are not lame. Sprint's legs are whole again and Kyot can see which way he is walking. Look, our hurts are vanishing in the sunlight, we are all healed.'

'You would spare his life?' asked Thane, his jaw already set in judgement as he stared down at the weeping child-like figure struggling in his arms. 'You would spare Krulshards' black seed and let it grow strong to bring the terror of his Nightmare darkness once more across Elundium? You would give in to some foolish weakness and show mercy?'

Elionbel spread her hands, struggling for the words. 'He is not all darkness, Thane. He is a part of Martbel, I saw it the moment you sewed the shadow into his footprints. It is in his eyes, his face. You have destroyed the Nightmare, what lies before you is . . .' Elionbel faltered, grasping at the words. 'He is my brother!'

'Kill him! Kill the bastard Kruel, and curse the daylight he ever called himself our brother!' shouted Rubel, forcing a passage through the kneeling shadow warriors and pushing them roughly aside as he rushed at Kruel, a dagger in his hand.

Thane acted quickly and leapt on Rubel, knocking him to the ground. Mulcade stooped from a cloudless sky and hooked his talons on the dagger, taking it up out of Rubel's reach.

'Be still, Rubel,' ordered Thane. 'You have done enough this daylight to gain the shouts and praise of all Elundium by carrying the sword out of the City of Night. It is I, and I alone, who must hold Kruel's life in the palm of my hand, for through my judgements, my strengths and my weaknesses will Elundium grow and flourish in the sunlight.'

Turning slowly to Elionbel he took her hand and pressed into it the tiny silver finger bowl he had carried through the darkness and shadowlight of Kruel's reign of terror. Kneeling, he gazed down at Kruel, searching for the slightest hint of darkness. Esteron snorted and looked over his shoulder, sniffing and blowing gently at the baby's soft form that now lay helpless in the snow. Mulcade stooped swiftly and hooked his talons on to Kerzolde's iron collar and stared unblinking past the Nightbeast into the child's eyes.

'Yes,' whispered Thane, touching the owl's blood-sticky talons, 'there is a likeness to Martbel, a straight look of innocence in those pale blue eyes, perhaps . . .'

Mulcade hooted and rose to perch on Thane's shoulder. Thane sighed and looked up at the shadow warriors who waited with baited breath for his judgement. Beyond them he saw Kruel's black standards shredding into nothing but forgotten rags in the sunlight and made his decision.

Reaching forwards he carefully gathered up the helpless child into his arms and rose to face Elionbel. 'I am a warrior who sweeps all before him, yet my judgement shall show mercy and my strengths will be forgiveness and compassion. You have shown me that, Elion, and I love you for it. Take the baby Kruel, for as you say he is our brother and we will bring him up to love our sunlight.'

Elionbel smiled. Her eyes met Thane's with joy as she took his hand and together they held the baby up for all to see. A roaring shout echoed across the battlefield. Spear butts clashed on shields and the thunder of it flowed up over the Rising.

'You shall be a great King!' called a voice above the neighing of the Warhorses and the barking of the Border Runners.

Thane smiled and laughed, tears of joy running down his face as he turned towards the Rising, but Nevian had gone, the last colours of the rainbow cloak were melting in the sunlight. The age of the Granite Kings had truly passed forever.

Glitterspike Hall
Mike Jefferies

Book One of *The Heirs to Gnarlsmyre*

From his ancient palace high above the twisting narrow streets of the City of Glor and the treacherous frozen marshes of Gnarlsmyre, Miresnare, Lord of the Glitterspike, rules with an iron hand. But his days are numbered and he has no son – only countless daughters in a world where women are worthless . . .

It is the Eve of the Allbeast Feast, and Marrimian, first-born of the daughters of the hall, directs the final preparations for the annual joust, when the barbarous marshlords compete for her hand, and the lands that are her dowry. But this year the magic mumbling men foretell the marshlords' victory and the end of Miresnare's power . . . unless he changes the rules. The new joust will leave his daughters in poverty; it will bring misery and chaos to Gnarlsmyre . . . but Lord Miresnare will sacrifice *anything* to keep his throne.

Outraged by her life of oppression, wounded by her father's treachery, Marrimian is determined to compete for his throne, to win her rightful inheritance and to free the hate-bound land. But to defeat her many enemies she will need all the courage and strength that is woman's – and the help of a stranger who will come from beyond the rolling mists of Rainbows' End . . .

FONTANA PAPERBACKS

Stephen Donaldson

MORDANT'S NEED

1: The Mirror of her Dreams

King Joyse and the kingdom of Mordant are in dire need; threatened by the evil Arch-Imager Vagel and the hordes of Cadwal from without, betrayed by unknown enemies within. Terisa Morgan is Mordant's unlikely champion, plucked from a life of wealthy dreariness in New York by the accidental magic of the apprentice Imager Geraden. The kingdom is directed by the power of images, of visions and of mirrors and Terisa and Geraden must master this power if Mordant is to survive. But the traps laid for them are many and treacherous . . .

2: A Man Rides Through

Terisa Morgan desperately needs to escape. Gilbur is trying to kill her, Castellan Lebbick wants to torture her and she needs to find Geraden. The forces of Cadwal, led by the Arch-Imager Vagel, are poised to strike; the traitor Eremis is preparing the ground for the hated enemies; and King Joyse's actions are more baffling than ever. Everything Geraden and Terisa love in the land of Mordant is about to be destroyed – unless they can find a way to prevent it using their new-found talent for mirrors and Imagery. But Terisa knows Eremis will resort to every evil power at his disposal to ensure the success of his terrible master plan.

FONTANA PAPERBACKS

The Lemurian Stone
Stephen F. Hickman

These are the tidings of Pharazar's doom . . .

An enemy force crossing the sea, led by a demon no mortal weapon can slay.

Pharazar's best archers flying into battle on their glorious winged horses, but falling helplessly from the skies.

Magnificent palaces of jade and ivory, sundered by war and stained with blood . . .

Such are the prophecies of the Lemurian Stone. Haunted by its visions of destruction, the Empress of Pharazar must send her most trusted allies on a search for three unearthly weapons. Weapons which exist far beyond the palace walls – in alternate worlds of magic and danger – deep within the very heart of . . .

THE LEMURIAN STONE

FONTANA PAPERBACKS

Reindeer Moon
Elizabeth Marshall Thomas

Yanan was born over twenty thousand years ago, in a
lodge on the ice-swept tundra, in a land where death
was always near. Her people were hunters, living in
kinship with the tigers, and the wolves, struggling
through the long winters when meat and wood were
scarce . . . rejoicing in the brief, glorious summers.

In this land of great and terrible beauty, Yanan
survived to womanhood – passionate and brave, richly
sensuous and dangerously proud. From the perils of
the hunt to the timeless wonders of love and marriage,
birth and death, Yanan's life was a grand and thrilling
adventure in a harsh, magnificent world . . .

'I lived and breathed this book . . . Yanan is fascinating,
completely real . . . magnificent.'
Washington Post Book World

'Wonderful . . . a tour de force.'
John Updike *The New Yorker*

FONTANA PAPERBACKS

Fontana Fiction

Fontana is a leading paperback publisher of fiction. Below are some recent titles.

- ☐ KRYSALIS John Trenhaile £3.99
- ☐ PRINCES OF SANDASTRE Antony Swithin £2.99
- ☐ NIGHT WATCH Alastair MacNeill £3.50
- ☐ THE MINOTAUR Stephen Coonts £4.50
- ☐ THE QUEEN'S SECRET Jean Plaidy £3.99
- ☐ THE LEMON TREE Helen Forrester £3.99
- ☐ THE THIRTEEN-GUN SALUTE Patrick O'Brian £3.50
- ☐ STONE CITY Mitchell Smith £4.50
- ☐ ONLY YESTERDAY Syrell Leahy £2.99
- ☐ SHARPE'S WATERLOO Bernard Cornwell £3.50
- ☐ BLOOD BROTHER Brian Morrison £3.50
- ☐ THE BROW OF THE GALLOWGATE Doris Davidson £3.50

You can buy Fontana paperbacks at your local bookshop or newsagent. Or you can order them from Fontana, Cash Sales Department, Box 29, Douglas, Isle of Man. Please send a cheque, postal or money order (not currency) worth the purchase price plus 22p per book for postage (maximum postage required is £3.00 for orders within the UK).

NAME (Block letters)_____

ADDRESS_____

_____